# TRAFFICK DEADLOCK

A SMITHSON EVERMORE NOVEL BOOK 3

# TRAFFICK DEADLOCK

By

## Vance Arnett

**ARNETT PUBLISHING**
2025 Greenville, SC

Traffick Deadlock
A Smithson Evermore Novel Book 3
Copyright © May 2025 by Vance Arnett | All Rights Reserved.


Paperback Edition
ISBN 13: 979-8-9925527-0-6
Self Published by Vance Arnett Publishing
224 Glenbrooke Way
Greenville, South Carolina 29615
www.authorvancearnett.com


Cover Design by Meaghan and Shawn Scalise
Tada Traditional and Digital Arts
Greenville, South Carolina
www.traditionalanddigitalarts.com

The proceeds of this book after costs will be donated to support non-profit organizations that serve the needs of the survivors of human trafficking and sexual exploitation. You support to the author's rights is greatly appreciated.

For Jane, forever.

# Other Works

**Works by Vance Arnett**

**Fiction:**

Tampa Traffick:
A Smithson Evermore Novel Book One

The Rooster and the Faded Rose:
A Smithson Evermore Novel Book Two

**Non-Fiction:**

Not Done Yet: Retirement as an Encore Not and Ending

# PROLOGUE

It was 02:00 when FBI Agent Phelps Wheeler, the agent in charge of the Southeast Regional Anti-Human Trafficking Task Force realized the agency jet was beginning its descent into Joint Base Andrews near Washington. It had been over a month since he had been home with his family in Tampa. He had been headed there when he got the call, so spending time with his wife Charley and his daughters would have to wait, AGAIN. He had led the task force for four years along with his partner Mary Close who was seated across from him lost in her own thoughts of home. They had worked together so long that the silence between them wasn't bothersome. They had also become too accustomed to this type of unexpected order. Mary spoke as she tightened her seat belt for landing.

"When was the last time you were able to spend more than three days with Charley and your girls?"

"I can't remember. Too long for sure. How are things going with Greg? Is his name Greg?"

Mary laughed. "I can't remember, so it must not be going well. It's hard to start a relationship let alone keep it going when you do it three hours at a time. But Greg is no longer interested."

They both sighed as the jet set down and taxied to a dark corner of the air base toward a blacked-out hangar.

Mary looked out the window as the jet was towed inside. "CIA or Homeland Security, no doubt."

The hangar was heavily guarded by personnel all in black tactical gear. Mary commented, "This is a bit different, isn't it?"

Phelps answered as he continued to look out the window. "Very, very different."

They deplaned and were escorted by U.S. Marshals into a briefing room where they were greeted by an old friend Marshal Luke Ludlow. Phelps smiled as Mary hugged Luke then spoke.

"It's really good to see you. The last time you were hooked up to a half dozen medical devices and had at least four paramedics working on you. It looks like you made a full recovery. You look stronger than ever." She smiled as she released him." You feel stronger than ever too. Seems like the gym was part of the therapy. It's so good to see you. The bad guys just about got you, didn't they?"

Ludlow smiled as he stepped back. "If it hadn't been for Lily Michaels, they would have."

They found their seats along with about 15 other ranking justice officers as the lights dimmed and the Attorney General for the United States, Gwen Vespers, appeared at the podium. The doors behind them were shut and locked. There was a slight hum in the air as the electronic jamming system began to make sure only those in the room would hear what was about to be said. All three officers had always been impressed by Gwen Vespers and they weren't disappointed this time.

"As of this moment, you are all assigned to a special task force with the mission of bringing down the Nightshade Trafficking Enterprise. Each of you has been selected for your experience and demonstrated skill in dealing with the problem. FBI agents Wheeler and Close will be assigned as lead investigators. Marshal Ludlow will be the operational leader. The remainder of the operational team are all Marshals picked by Ludlow. This group will be joined by four specialists from the Smithson Institute. Most of you know their survivor specialists Lily Michaels and Alex Pellegrino. They will be joined in the field by a new member, Dr. Henry Leonard, a specialist in aerial surveillance. All logistics will be coordinated through Charles Jenkins, the lead intelligence and operations coordinator for Smithson. The Institute will also be adding their fleet of fixed and rotary wing aircraft to our capabilities." She paused and let that settle in then continued.

"For the past six months, with the aid of a highly advanced data processing and artificial intelligence system, we have been analyzing every business transaction, large or small, that even remotely indicated involvement with Nightshade. That analysis has identified key players and at least the basics of how they launder the billions of dollars they make from trafficking people, arms, drugs, and exotic animals. Unfortunately, some of our own people have been identified as having aided the Nightshade Group in their activities. The next phase is to actively pursue and arrest the people calling the shots and those conspiring to allow them to operate. That will be your sole assignment and you will be given any resource necessary to accomplish that mission. Because of the treachery from within I mentioned, this operation will be conducted on a need-to-know basis even within your respective agencies. We will be operating on a dedicated Smithson secured satellite communications systems with their newest surveillance technology to protect the level of secrecy we need.

For now, we must wait for the traffickers to make a mistake large enough to give us traction to move forward. I doubt we will have to wait long. Your capabilities combined with the specialized training and equipment offered by the Smithson Institute will be something that Nightshade has never encountered. It has been my experience that when the members of a criminal enterprise feel they have protection from the inside and access to information provided by conspirators, they get overconfident and make mistakes. That is why staying off the law enforcement airways and trusting only in the other members of this task force is so important. Go home, be with those you love and wait for our call. Good night."

As they rose to leave, Phelps spoke.

"Good news is we all get to spend some time at home. Bad news is we don't know how long that will be."

# CHAPTER 1

Interstate 20 at 1:00 am is desolate, particularly in the stretch between Augusta and Atlanta. Tiffany sat behind the driver and stared out at the south side of the road as they headed west. Beth on the other end of the backseat, did the same to the north side of the road. The third woman in the car, Jillian, sat all the way back in the third seat watching every mile marker and exit they passed. She was keeping track of where they were. She leaned forward and tapped Tiffany lightly on the shoulder.

Tiffany risked breaking the mandatory silence for the "passengers" on these late-night trips. "Dex, I really have to pee. Can we please pull over?"

Dexter Holder, the driver, sneered. "Fuck no we can't pull over. I don't need to be attracting any attention out here and the only people out this time of night are cops and truckers. I don't like either. Shut up and hold it and don't you piss in my Cadillac."

On the opposite side, Beth didn't even turn her head from the window. "I have to go too. And I'm pretty sure I just started my period so if you don't want to be cleaning that up, you better figure something out Dexter. Your precious leather back here is about to pay the price."

That was the one situation that made him powerless over the women he oversaw.

"There is a rest stop about two miles up. I'll pull over there but I don't want any crap from either of you. Jillian, go with them and watch them."

"I will Dex, don't worry." She threw in a chuckle for effect.

"You two better behave. I mean it. You run and we'll find you. Just keep in mind what happened to Lucy and Crystal. Everybody understand?" He looked in the review mirror and saw two heads nod. Jillian just smiled.

Holder sped up just a bit as he pulled into the rest area to blur the video image just in case there was a camera. He parked as close to the women's restroom as he could but as far from the security office as possible. He noted where the surveillance cameras were mounted on the buildings. He could see the flickering of a computer screen in the security office and the head of the officer sitting in front of it.

He turned. "You two get in there and get your business done. Keep your heads pointed at the ground and stay off the sidewalk. Get your asses back out here quickly. Jillian, you go to watch them and if you have to go, do it. We aren't supposed to stop."

The three women walked through the grass, heads down, paying attention to the angle of the two video cameras and entered the restroom. As planned, Tiffany was the first one out and walked up to Holder who was smoking nervously as he leaned against the far side of the car. She smiled and held out her hand for his cigarette. He smirked and offered her one from his pack along with his lighter. She took it, lit her cigarette and looked around.

"Thanks Dex. I really needed to go."

Holder looked toward the restroom. "What's keeping them?"

Tiffany laughed and stepped closer to him. " It's a long ride from Charleston. We've been holding it for miles. It takes a girl a bit of time to get rid of that much and Beth is dealing with her monthly. Relax, we aren't about to try anything."

Holder was unconvinced. "Like shit you won't. I've been working with you two long enough I've learned all your tricks." He went over to the restroom door. "Hurry up you two. If I have to come in there, you'll pay." He walked back to Tiffany, who struck just the right pose for him. He looked her up and down. "Damn girl. I may need a little soothing after this as payment for being so patient." He reached over and stroked her hip. "You sit up front with me."

Tiffany dropped her cigarette and stepped on it. "I'll go hurry them up then." She turned with a provocative smile and headed to the restroom.

Once inside, Tiffany spoke. "He's getting suspicious and it's already going to cost me a blow job. Everything set?"

Beth laughed. "What an opportunity. I would bite it off and shove it down the bastard's throat."

Jillian didn't laugh. "Did you get his lighter?"

Tiffany carefully handed it to her. Jillian put it in her shirt pocket and nodded toward the door. They all stepped out and headed toward the car. Tiffany got in the front passenger seat and Jillian took the seat behind the driver. Holder didn't get in the car. Instead, he walked into the restroom and checked every stall. He found nothing and returned to the car. Once inside, he started to buckle up and then remembered. He turned to Tiffany. "Cute, where's my lighter?"

She dug through her pockets and came up empty handed. "I must have dropped it. I'll go look for it. It's got to be either in the restroom or between there and where we were smoking."

Holder glared at her. 'You fucking stay right where you are. Jillian, you go find my lighter and be quick. We've already been here too long."

Jillian got out of the car and checked the ground as she walked toward the restroom. Once inside she pulled the note written with Beth's lipstick out of her pocket and set it on top of the tissue holder in the last stall. She pulled out her own lipstick and added her message at the bottom. She smiled and wrote, "Please help. I turned 15 three weeks ago." She propped the note up with the lighter. She pulled another identical lighter out of her pocket and headed back outside. Three steps outside the door she bent down and pretended to pick up the new lighter. She held it up as she headed back to the car.

She got in and passed it to Holder in the front seat. He examined it carefully and decided it was his lighter, cheap and disposable, but always notched on the bottom like a clock face, at 11 and 3. The notches were there. He turned and smiled at Jillian then turned back, and as he did the smile disappeared replaced by a frown. He swung hard and backhanded Tiffany sitting across from him.

"Don't you ever lose my shit, Tiffany or I'll lose my shit with you and you won't want that."

She wiped the blood from her lip as he laughed and pulled the large SUV back onto I-20 and headed west. He didn't realize what he was leaving. The note and the lighter were sitting on the tissue dispenser right under a Georgia Stop Human Trafficking Poster that was attached to the wall in each of the stalls in all rest rooms. It had a clear message.

"Stop Human Trafficking. See Something, Say Something."

The note below was brief but just as clear and to the point.

"We are being trafficked for sex. This lighter belongs to our transporter. We are headed west in a black Escalade." At the bottom was the important message and date Jillian had added. "Help us, please!"

Minutes later the earpiece in Dexter's right ear buzzed just as Tiffany finished "soothing" him. She zipped up his jeans and pulled her hand back with the tissue she had used to keep things neat. She had downgraded his session. She wasn't about to do anything with a busted lip that put her more in contact with this asshole. Plus, she now had the crumpled tissue with additional evidence which she palmed and pretended to put in the litter bag he always had in his car. Holder pushed the button on his earpiece and answered.

"Got it. We will be there in 15 minutes." He hung up. "Looks like we have a change in plans. I'm going to hand you off to Stokes." He looked over at Tiffany and smiled. "Looks like you finished just in time."

Tiffany and Beth were used to this type of thing. They were always moved at night and often transferred into other vehicles and driven in different directions. Jillian was not used to this but knew better than to question Holder. She didn't think he would ever hurt her because she was Frank and Vivian's daughter. But things had changed in the last year. Up until recently, she only traveled with her parents, Vivian and Frank Bartram. It was different now. This was her third trip where she traveled like the others. She watched everything that was happening closely.

In 15 minutes, they pulled off the Interstate at an exit in the middle of nowhere. A white transit van waited off to the side of an all-night gas station. It was parked next to a semi rig which blocked the view from the gas station.

Holder got out and looked at the other driver, Lester Stokes, with a sarcastic glance as he nodded slightly at the idling truck parked next to the van. The look clearly sent the message: "Too close, too risky, dumbass".

He told the women to get out and wait by the rear of the transit van while they transferred their bags. The van was spartan compared to Holder's SUV. The entire operation took less than five minutes. Without saying a word, Holder got back in his Cadillac and pulled back onto I-20 headed back the way they had come.

Stokes got in the driver's seat without saying a word. He hardly ever spoke and never touched the girls. He didn't care much about the humans he moved or what they did. For that matter he didn't care about much of anything except money. To him these women were just property that needed to be relocated. He knew to take care of Jillian differently. She was family. He pulled out and headed north on the road that crossed the Interstate into the darker world of rural north Georgia.

Neither driver noticed that Tiffany had dropped the tissue near the curb and that Jillian had dropped her lipstick on the grass next to it. Neither transporter had noticed the man watching the entire episode from behind the curtain of the sleeping compartment on his truck. From the time the van pulled in he knew something was amiss. That van driver stayed by the van and left the motor running. He took a whizz in the grass behind it. If he needed a bathroom or wake up break, he would have gone inside.

Most truckers are independent folks that know how to take care of themselves whether they are a man or a woman. They train themselves to be vigilant. Ted Morris was the epitome of that clan. From the time he was awakened by the van pulling up, he watched through the crack in his curtains. He reached under his pillow for his Glock Model 30 and paid close attention to what was happening. Ted surmised this guy was waiting so he wasn't surprised when the other vehicle showed up. This one was fancy, the opposite of the utility van. Then both drivers got out and hustled three women out of the fancy SUV and into the back of the van. One of them didn't look any older than his granddaughter. Ted saw one of the women drop something near the rear of the van. He reached for his phone but didn't get it ready in time to take a video. He did manage a couple of pictures before the van was loaded and they pulled out. Once both of them were gone, he got up and pulled on his cowboy boots. He grabbed his T-Shirt and swung down into the cab of his rig as his phone rang and scared the daylights out of him. It was the night clerk in the station, Samir.

"Ted, what's up with those cars out there behind you?"

Ted answered. "Nothing good Samir. Call the State Police. I'm going to take a look around."

"Be careful Ted. I don't like that kind of stuff. I'm calling now."

Ted grabbed his big rig lantern and tucked the Glock in its holster that was always strung on his belt under his shirt. He searched the area where the van had been parked and where the SUV had idled during the transfer. He was about to shut the light off when the four big LEDs reflected off something near the curb and he remembered the women dropping something. He walked over and found the lipstick which had landed perfectly upright in the grass. Next to it was a crumpled tissue.

For a trucker, lights and cones mean safety and security. He walked back to his rig and pulled out his emergency cones. He placed the cones around where the suspicious vehicles had been parked setting one carefully next to the tissue and lipstick that he had found. He walked back to the truck, turned on its trailer lights, retrieved his wallet from the dash of the rig with his driver's license and concealed weapons permit and waited for a trooper to arrive. It didn't take long. Apparently something was up out on I-20 because the trooper showed up in less than 10 minutes.

The Georgia State Trooper listened to Ted's story, looked at the litter the girls had left behind, then asked for a copy of the video from the property which Samir had already made for him. Both Ted and Samir suspected they had observed human trafficking. Their company training had been worth it. The Trooper left Ted's cones in place to secure the scene and updated his post. The dispatcher at his headquarters advised his shift commander was on the way. They had received a call about similar suspicious activity that might be connected. He was ordered to standby at the scene until the supervisor and help arrived. Samir brought the trooper and Ted each a large fresh coffee while they waited. They watched two more state troopers fly by east bound with their rotating lights casting blue shadows in all directions.

Trooper Elaine West had arrived at the rest stop at mile marker 182 near Harlem, Georgia at 02:15 am. She looked at the note found by another long-haul truck driver. That driver too had been to a class on human trafficking required by her company and she knew enough to alert the authorities immediately. She had even stopped the guard from touching the note.

Trooper West updated her post in Grovetown and carefully secured the note and lighter, then closed off a large perimeter around the restroom.

Cigarette butts were found where they shouldn't be. The post immediately notified the Georgia Bureau of Investigation who dispatched a forensic team to the rest area and gas station within the hour. Deputies from the County Sheriff's Office with assistance from two other responding troopers closed the rest area. A BOLO notice was issued for a black Cadillac Escalade and the transit van. Requests were issued for copies of the relevant CCTV reels monitoring the Interstate and exits both east and west. The security guard's log indicated that he had last checked the rest rooms at midnight. They had left the note sometime between midnight and 01:45 when the note was found. That was added to the search parameter.

When Trooper West was notified by her dispatcher that there had been a similar suspicious incident reported west of her location, she smiled and thought to herself as she looked at the poster in the stall. "Sometimes the magic works."

Per their anti-trafficking protocol, the GBI immediately notified the FBI regional field office in Atlanta who in turn notified the Office of the U.S. Marshal's Human Trafficking Task Force.

Somewhere in a small communications office in Washington D.C. deep within the Justice Department, a dedicated phone rang and was answered by a special duty officer. Ten minutes later, Attorney General Gwen Vespers received a call at home. She called three people. Phelps Wheeler in Tampa, Luke Ludlow in Atlanta, and Slade Smithson at Smithson Evermore's Institute also in Tampa.

Three women left a note in a restroom in Georgia in the middle of the night. Their cry for help had been heard and reverberated in Washington, Tampa, and Atlanta.

# CHAPTER 2

It had been three weeks since the meeting at Joint Base Andrews. For once the call hadn't come in the middle of the night. All of the people who had been at the secret briefing received the notice to report at their designated muster points.

Phelps Wheeler and Mary Close waited in the FBI command center in Atlanta for their other federal counterparts to arrive. They each had years of experience dealing with human trafficking mostly with local law enforcement and state. Their work with the Marshals was more recent.

The U.S. Marshal's initiative was the latest addition to the federal response. They hunted people down, kicked in doors, arrested and transported arrestees and protected witnesses. Their skills at finding fugitives and managing witness protection were a natural fit for dealing with trafficking syndicates that were well financed, highly mobile, and extremely careful about leaving the type of evidence that was necessary for trafficking convictions. Ten Marshals assigned to the task force joined the FBI agents in the briefing room led by Marshal Luke Ludlow.

The two FBI agents and Ludlow had worked with the specialists from Smithson before and several others on the team at least knew about Smithson. The specialists were flying in on one of their company jets from their Tampa headquarters and would join the federal officers for a meeting at the Smithson Atlanta command center which would be the official HQ for the mission. That raised some questions with one of the Marshals.

Marshal Tim Collins was newly assigned and curious. "Boss, how come we are going to have these civilians helping us and how does that work anyway? Ludlow turned to Collins mildly annoyed, which was rare. He was known for not showing emotion.

"Slade Smithson, the founder of the Smithson Evermore anti-trafficking initiative started this program fifteen years ago to help the FBI recover kidnap victims. His Tactical Research and Development lab has developed all of the anti-ballistic gear you've been issued. Each of the people assigned for this operation focus their efforts on rescuing and stabilizing survivors of human trafficking so we can focus in on the bad guys. You'll learn more about that once we join them at their command center which is where we all will be working from."

Collins interrupted. "You mean like the government contractors we saw when deployed overseas? They had better gear than we were issued and way better communications." There was a mixture of disdain and envy in his tone.

Agent Wheeler stepped in to give Ludlow a break. "Good you mentioned that. The intelligence and communications system we will be using on this operation is part of their communications satellite system. It is more sophisticated, advanced, and more secure than our current equipment."

Ludlow glared at Collins and continued. "And before you ask, each of them will be armed and have been deputized by the Attorney General to function just like we do. They are particularly well equipped for the type of surveillance and intelligence gathering we will need to secure arrest warrants. They are assigning two women specialists who are both seasoned and decorated former military who will be in the field with us." He looked at Phelps who continued.

"Alex Pellegrino and Lily Michaels, who you are about to meet, have rescued and helped more trafficking survivors than any of us. They have special training in how to deal with fragile victims and survivors. And in case you have any doubts about these women in a tactical situation, both qualified as experts at the U.S. Marine sniper school at 1,000 yards and have demonstrated their abilities to protect themselves, their teammates, and the people they will be tasked with recovering. Don't doubt they will have your back if it gets heated."

Ludlow finished as he looked at Hal Story, the one other Marshal that had been there the day he almost died. "On a very personal note, Lily Michaels won our Medal of Valor for saving my life in the San Diego shootout two years ago. I wouldn't be standing here if it weren't for her."

Agent Close stepped forward. "Four years ago, Agent Wheeler and I were involved in a major international case along with the Smithson team. Alex Pelligrino directed the interdiction of five traffickers on the Canadian border that resulted in over 120 recovered survivors and twenty arrests and convictions all the way from Washington D.C. to China and Viet Nam. She did that using high-definition video and audio equipment perched in a tree 50 feet above the transfer point on the U.S. Canadian border in the dead of winter. As if that weren't enough, she personally disarmed and handcuffed the largest and deadliest of the bunch. Alex stands just under five feet and weighs 97 pounds. She benches three hundred. She speaks multiple languages and she and Lily Michaels both serve as instructors at our academy in Quantico and your training facility in Waycross." She looked directly at Collins. "I hope that answers all your questions at least about Lily and Alex."

Collins didn't seem to hear and piped up again as he thumbed through his orders. "Why are we not working out of our command center?"

Ludlow eyed Collins again.

"We are working from their command center because no one knows it's there. We suspect that both the FBI and our offices are under continuous surveillance by the group we believe is behind this effort. We also suspect that someone, maybe more than one, in both our organizations is supplying information to the Nightshade syndicate."

There was dead silence in the room. Even Collins couldn't find the wind to blurt out the "holy shit" each one of them was thinking. For most of them, Nightshade had been the topic of classes throughout their careers. Almost once a month, there was an additional training memo or alert about the activities of this syndicate which included interstate money laundering, the sale of illegal weapons, gambling, prostitution, and human trafficking. Hundreds of arrests had been made and a handful of prosecutions had been successful, but Nightshade survived and thrived.

Ludlow gave each of the team a new cell phone to be used only for this operation. "Don't program any number into these phones. They have all the numbers you need already and scramble the conversation automatically, another Smithson invention. Pack your bags and gear and be ready to respond in two hours. When you leave this meeting room, all communication will be restricted to those of us on this operational team."

As they left, Hal Story, the most senior Marshal after Luke stopped Collins in the hallway. He put his massive arm around Collins as he spoke.

"Welcome to the team little brother. Since you are such a vocal rookie, let me give you some advice. We work together, no matter who we are assigned to work with. They wouldn't be here if people above our paygrade didn't think that they would function as a force multiplier for us." He tightened his grip, pinching Collins' neck. "Stop interrupting the Boss and stop asking so many fucking questions. Listen more. Speak less. Understand?" Collins nodded.

Approximately 25,000 feet above Macon the Smithson Citation jet was on a flight path that would skirt Hartsfield International and head for the DeKalb Peachtree Airport carrying four of the Smithson Evermore team that would take part in this special operation. Lily Michaels sat next to Alex Pellegrino who was sitting across from her fiancé, Claymore Jenkins. Claymore would be the technical support coordinator connecting everyone to resources no matter what they needed.

The newest member of the team, Henry Leonard alias Birdman, was thumbing through a popular magazine that specialized in stories from the southeast. Lily looked across at him.

"What are you doing browsing through that?"

Leonard looked up. "I have a photographic article featured in it on the raptors of the southeast."

Lily laughed. "I keep forgetting. Your first love is birds, Dr. Leonard."

Leonard blinked. "I prefer the nickname you people gave me."

"You have two PhDs and you prefer Birdman." Leonard nodded but put the magazine away and pulled out his laptop to watch their flight trajectory as they began to make their approach.

Claymore spoke. "Time to get ready people. We will touch down in about 10 minutes. Our Atlanta team will transport the equipment to our building where we will meet with our federal partners. Birdman and I will go with the equipment. You two go in the helicopter and sync the communications." Everyone nodded.

Claymore Jenkins reached down and unclipped his wheelchair from its fittings and relocated to similar fittings adjacent to the door of the jet. They landed and taxied to a stop next to a Smithson helicopter. As the door opened and the steps unfolded, a special track would carry Claymore and his wheelchair down to the tarmac. He was always the first out of their aircraft to supervise the transfer of all the equipment. Lily and Alex got off the plane and into the nearby Smithson helicopter which would take them to the rooftop of their regional command center in Dunwoody. While they flew, they would test the satellite connections. After depositing them on the roof, the helicopter would patrol the area and blanket the building with jamming signals that would not allow covert listening.

# CHAPTER 3

Dunwoody Georgia is a bustling suburb full of tall buildings, malls, beautiful homes and businesses. From the outside the Smithson headquarters looked like all the other office buildings in the area. Very few people knew or cared about the company that was located there. But just in case there were people who had a special interest in the work that Smithson did, it was heavily secured and fortified. Smithson people were trained to always be aware of any threat.

All over the metropolitan Atlanta area, the special phones Ludlow had issued to his team began going off in a sequence so that his people would arrive in small groups. To the public in the area of the Smithson building, it would look like normal daily business traffic. The vehicles they would use for the operation were already stored in the building's garage and really didn't look that tactical as long as you didn't see them all together. Each vehicle was armored, with secure on-board GPS and advanced secure communications. And unlike most federal vehicles, only a few were equipped with lights and sirens. There were three additional specially designed vehicles located in the garage. One was a fortified transport vehicle for arrestees. It could hold up to 12 people, each secured in their own enclosure separated by sight and sound. The second was designed to transport up to 10 rescued survivors. It was designed and staffed with people with special training like Lily and Alex. The survivors rescued were treated with care from the time Smithson had them to the time they were turned over to shelters or housed in protective settings.

Along with the new phones, each federal team member was supplied with a small digital tablet, protected by advanced facial recognition and back up three finger scan access. These devices came with ear pieces and wireless capability to connect to tactical glasses that broadcast video information onto a heads-up display in the left lens if needed. There were also assault helmets issued with the same capability, all developed and supplied by

Smithson Evermore, all tested in combat theaters around the world.

The federal team members arrived and assembled in the command briefing room. Three walls were like giant computer screens capable of displaying maps, photos, data, and live feeds. It was like nothing most of the federal officers had ever seen before.

Claymore Jenkins wheeled himself into the room and up to the master control desk at the front of the room.

"Good morning. For those of you who I haven't worked with before, my name is Charles Jenkins. I would prefer you call me Claymore. I will be your information control, supply and intelligence officer for the entire operation. Either I or my assistant will be here 24-hours a day. If you need anything, you push the green button on either of your new communication devices. It is my job to make sure you are all connected, coordinated, and supplied with what you need."

Lily Michaels and Alex Pelligrino came in and took seats with the Marshalls. They both turned and smiled at the others.

Phelps Wheeler, Mary Close, and Luke Ludlow came in and took seats facing the team. Smithson technical staff were busy fitting the Marshals with their ear pieces and programming their command tablets, showing them how the displays worked. Each of the Marshals also received a special anti-ballistic vest which had the extra compartments needed for the new equipment. The vests were lighter but stronger than their normal equipment. It took them awhile to take it all in. Collins looked like he was going to ask a question. Hal Story stopped him by putting a finger to his lips then pointing to his ear.

Claymore explained their new equipment and the expanded tactical capability available for field operations. They had secure satellite communication for both video and audio communication. There would be no law enforcement radio communication. They likewise had Smithson aircraft both fixed wing and rotary available. For once, they could communicate and move in real time as quickly if not more so than the traffickers.

Alex stood and climbed up on her chair so everyone could see her.

"The screen on the left displays the five remote broadcast transmitters we have as well as the trackers that can be attached to any solid surface. We have aerial and fixed specialized surveillance equipment we can deploy if and when the proper warrants are secured. I can answer any of your questions and if you see an opportunity we miss, no matter how farfetched it seems, say something to me or one of the other Smithson team members. We have eyes and ears you wouldn't believe."

As Alex hopped down, Lily stood up. At six feet she didn't need to stand on a chair.

"Both Alex and I are trained and experienced in handling survivors of human trafficking. We are also trained in intelligence gathering and rescue and protection techniques. Once a rescue is accomplished, Alex and I will coordinate with the survivors. From the time we breach the door until the time we walk in for trial it will be our job to stabilize and protect the survivors along with the U.S. Marshals Service." She smiled and sat down.

Henry "Birdman" Leonard's face was broadcast on one of the screens. He was on the roof of the building flying two drones. The first one was aloft above the building and sending pictures of the surrounding area. He demonstrated the optics and zoom capabilities as well as the ability of the drone to receive sounds and broadcast to their handsets from one of the listening devices Alex had described. The second drone was broadcasting from inside the room. It was the size of a quarter, and aptly called Quarterback. It had been flying in the room unnoticed since they assembled. It was now attached to the bottom of Collins' chair. Those who had just been exposed to this type of equipment sat in disbelief.

The room went dark. The main screen filled with the image of U.S. Attorney General Gwen Vespers.

"Good morning, ladies and gentlemen."

As those on the team recognized the face on the wall the room went silent.

"Now that you've met your Smithson partners and been given new equipment, its time to talk about mission. Marshal Ludlow under my authority, has been conducting an investigation for eight months related to the identification of individuals within our own government that aid and facilitate the success of the Nightshade traffickers. We've been waiting for them to make an error. We think that happened at around 1:00 am this morning. Three women, one of them underage, left a note at a rest stop on I-20. That note is the mistake we have been waiting for and offers us the opportunity we need."

The Attorney General let that settle in. A screen on the side lit up.

"I want to introduce you to one other team member that will be helping us with advanced analytical capabilities. She will not be joining us in person but operating from her own secure facility. This is Dr. Jeanine Morozov. She is a specialist in advanced analytical modeling, artificial intelligence, and analysis generated simulations. She will be helping us link all the tiny bits of information we develop about Nightshade, it's possible components and, in this particular situation, where we need to look and who we need to look for to recover these women. The work she has already accomplished has given us additional information."

A picture of an attractive woman in outdoor gear with a massive Russian Wolf Hound sitting next to her appeared on the side screen. She had a warm smile but a down-to-business face.

"It is a pleasure to be able to see the people I work with for a change. This is Rasputin. He is a Russian but a friendly one. The material gathered by the Georgia law enforcement agencies has been fed into my system. I have named the system SYBIL after the Greek oracle. The information you gather will be entered as it becomes available. I will be working from my laboratory here to keep analyzing and reanalyzing the information you discover as you move forward with the operation." She smiled again as Rasputin lay down next to her chair.

Mary Close stood up and waited until she had eye contact with everyone in the room.

"Using DNA and fingerprint evidence we have been able to identify three of the four people who we know were the rest stop on westbound I-20. One set of DNA and fingerprints recovered at the rest stop belongs to a known felon named Dexter Holder. Holder has several prior arrests related to pandering, pimping, armed assault, and has confirmed links to several suspected members of the Nightshade Group. He has an outstanding warrant in Georgia that will give us grounds for surveillance if necessary. Any questions?

No one raised a brow, let alone a hand.

"The second individual identified is Tiffany Holmes originally from Richland, South Carolina. Tiffany has a minimal juvenile record and was reported by her family as a runaway when she was 17. She is now 23. The third person identified is Elizabeth Ellers from Belton, South Carolina. She goes by Beth and has a notation on her record from Atlanta PD where her information was collected as part of a club sweep for underage drinkers four years ago in the Buckhead area of Atlanta. She was working as a server.

A final set of fingerprints and DNA associated with the note are not on file anywhere. Whoever she is, she is smart enough to know that adding her age is why we are all here. The main body of the note we believe was written by Beth. The last part was definitely added by this third unknown woman at the scene."

Collins had to interrupt. "Any evidence of prior prostitution?"

There was a giggle from behind. It was Alex.

She whispered. "Didn't they teach you anything when you worked for the Secret Service?"

Collins shocked, turned to respond but Hal Story kicked his chair to shut him up.

Mary waited for the interruption to die down before she continued. She did sneak a quick smile at Alex at the same time Ludlow fixed his gaze on Collins.

"There is a second related scene at a gas station further westbound. Investigators found a lipstick, a tissue with semen, and a DNA sample collected as urine. The semen comes back to Holder. The urine comes back to Lester Stokes another suspected associate of Nightshade. The lipstick at the gas station belongs to the unknown person who added the age statement."

Collins raised his hand. He hadn't learned yet. "How do we know that?"

Lily laughed. "Different handwriting, different brand of lipstick and definitely different shade made them look for the different DNA."

Everyone laughed. Collins turned around and looked at Hal who gave him the look that there would be further discussion about interrupting a briefing.

Phelps took over from Mary.

"We are lucky to have had two truckers who paid attention to anti-trafficking awareness training. The vehicles involved are a 2023 Cadillac Escalade and a full-sized Dodge transit van. The Cadillac is a luxury model, fully loaded. We're still working on a good image of the plates. The transit van is a different story. The van has no windows other than the front and rear and fits the profile of a transport vehicle often used by traffickers. Same situation with the plates. The video and witness testimony from the gas station supports all of the above. The entrance pole camera also caught one of the females. Enhanced facial recognition indicates it is most likely

Tiffany dropping the tissue. The only other person that is seen on the video is a man facing away from the camera at the back of the van, relieving himself. We are sure that was Stokes. He did a three-year federal prison stretch for trafficking. DNA confirms that.

In your intelligence notes supplied by SYBIL, Stokes is a suspected associate of Dexter Holder and a flashy panderer named Charles Tobin. Tobin has been documented as a known associate of Vivian and Frank Bartram of the Nightshade Group."

Ludlow took over.

"Now we have some idea who we might be dealing with, the next question is where to look. The video clearly shows the SUV leaving the gas station heading back toward the Interstate. The exchange camera shows that it turned back east instead of continuing west. It is picked up at the next exit, turning south in the direction of Augusta. The Transit van heads north out of the gas station and is not seen later on the Interstate. It traveled on back county roads. No video." He paused and checked his notes. Then continued.

"Dr. Morozov's forecasting gives us three probable alternatives. First is Atlanta. Dr. Morozov has given us five addresses the analysis suggests might be associated with Nightshade. Some of you will be assigned to check these locations along with Agent Wheeler, Close and Alex Pellegrino.

Given the reversal of the Escalade it could have been headed back to a North Charleston motel where the stationery the note is written on is from. The motel has a history with Charleston Vice. The analysis indicates a link to the property list mentioned earlier.

The third possibility is, I think, the strongest. Lester Stokes was stopped by the Greenville, South Carolina Police Department for a noise ordinance violation last month. Stokes has a passion for loud muscle cars when he is not driving people around in vans. Greenville authorities we trust have been alerted and we will be assisting if necessary. I will accompany

Lily to meet them. Each of you has your assignments."

Thinking the meeting was over, Collins stood up, grabbed his gear and started to leave without another question. Everyone else remained seated understanding the briefing wasn't over. Luke continued.

"I see our newbie is ready to go. Alex, would you mind taking Collins with you to check out Midtown and Buckhead? I'm afraid you're the only one in the room that might not kill him before we even get started."

Alex stood up and saluted. "I got this, Marshal."

# CHAPTER 4

Dexter didn't like changing plans and he didn't like being told what to do. Both had happened last night and he was in a foul mood. He sipped his coffee as he waited in the cafe in Augusta where he had been told to go. Vivian Bartram was rarely late. He saw her get out of her car with one of their security guys. Something wasn't right. She rarely went anywhere with them. He stood up as the two approached.

"Relax, Dex. He's not staying. Give me the keys to your car." It wasn't a request. It was an instruction and he knew better than to cross Vivian. Crossing her meant crossing her husband Frank, who was one deadly bastard. He faked a smile.

"Vivian, I love my Caddy. I just got it. Why do you need my keys?"

The man with Viv stepped toward him but Vivian stopped him with a touch on his arm. "Dexter, first, it's not your car, it's our car. Second, there is a black Caddy all over the police scanners we've been monitoring. They find the car, they find you. They find you they start looking for us. Those are just the hard facts. Another fact is it appears someone left a note saying they were being trafficked at a rest stop near Harlem, Georgia. Did you stop there with the girls, Dex?"

Holder's face fell. "Fuck. I knew they were up to something. I even checked the restroom after they had been in there. Is that the reason for the change in plans?" Vivian nodded.

He handed her his keys and Vivian handed them to the security man who turned and left immediately with the Cadillac. She directed Dexter to sit down as she motioned the waitress over.

She ordered coffee and smiled at him as she sat down. "Even though he sent me to get you, it's really Frank's fault. He's always trusted you too much which is something we both know he shouldn't do. She let her shoe slip off and rubbed the inside of his right calf with her bare foot seductively as she pushed the keys to her Mercedes across the table. "We are going on a little trip to the upstate of South Carolina on the back roads. My car is much nicer with much more room. I want to take our time getting there."

Dexter's mood took a huge swing to the brighter side. He had enjoyed time with Vivian before. She was very experienced and very enthusiastic when it was her idea. So far, it certainly seemed like it was her idea. She looked down at the menu. "I'm starving, Dexter. First you feed me, then you fuck me. I know you hate people ordering you around but I have an idea that may not apply to me. Does that sound like a good plan?" It was Dexter's turn to motion the waitress over.

Dexter always marveled at how much Vivian Bartram could eat. Perhaps it was her addictions both chemical and physical. She was elegant and beautiful but something lurked beneath her skin that made him uneasy. It wasn't that her husband would find out. They had an arrangement. That was the one thing that didn't seem to piss Frank off lately. There was just something different, even sinister, within Vivian. She ate breakfast, he sipped his coffee. When she was done, he paid cash and left a normal tip. No need to be remembered by a waitress.

They drove north to the town of Greenwood. Vivian directed him to a house a mile off U.S. 25 on the north side of the city. Who would suspect that a major international crime syndicate would be in a town like this. The house itself was hidden and private, set well off the road. She pushed the button on the mirror and the garage door raised automatically. He pulled into the garage. She was naked before she got out of the car. An order of French toast, a short stack of pancakes, two eggs and a biscuit had done nothing to her Georgia peach ass, and he followed her into the house, picking up her clothes as he went.

Vivian went straight to the master bedroom which was huge. As she pulled him down, she whispered, "I know just where to hide that face of yours for a couple of days until everything quiets down."

The Nightshade Group owned interests in property all over Georgia and South Carolina. Ownership was scattered across several holding companies to hide and manage. Some of these had big, elegant homes used for fancy expensive sex parties. The plainer ones were used to provide prostitution service to a lower class of client for a cheaper fee. To avoid the suspicion that comes with such a predictable and habitual use pattern, the group would renovate them and sell them regularly. That kept the houses and the money moving enough that no one bothered to check what was going on. It was the perfect scheme for laundering money and hiding illicit activity.

It had taken Stokes several hours changing direction and doubling back using the back roads of Georgia to get to Interstate 85. He wasn't on it long before he exited and headed to a property. He turned onto the driveway of a brick ranch just miles from the Georgia/South Carolina border, took out his phone and made the call. The driveway was equipped with sensors to alert those inside. He was given the all clear to proceed. The company called these places service stations. He backed into the covered parking pad with the van pointed toward the gravel road at the rear of the property. If they needed to leave quickly, he didn't want to waste time backing up. He looked across at Tobin's RV on its pad hooked up. To Stokes it looked as flashy and impractical as Tobin did. Then he looked at his Dodge Charger under its cover. He smiled thinking about the new headers this trip would pay for. He opened the van door and directed the women inside the house.

They had remained silent for the whole trip. They assumed their plan with the note had failed and just hoped that the transfer wasn't because of their attempt. Beth and Tiffany had been to this service station before. They were surprised to find Charles Tobin already there. He was overdressed and smarmy as usual. He only worked the fancy high-end parties in the big mansions with the rich clients. Even so, you looked at him and just thought "pimp". He smiled and spoke.

"Ladies, you know the drill. For tonight it is one to a room and no, you won't be busy with guests. We are in a holding pattern for the time being." Jillian was the last through the door and Tobin seemed surprised. "Jillian, I had no idea you were in this group. This is a surprise. How are your parents?"

Jillian smiled. She had learned to smile in such situations. "Frank is fine. I haven't seen Vivian in about a week. I guess she's on one of her adventures. Have you seen my brother, Jessie, lately?" Tobin kept the smile, shook his head, but ended the conversation by showing her to a room. "Get some rest. You've all had a long and confusing journey."

She paused outside the room. "Charles, nothing has happened, has it? Should I be worried?"

Charles put his hand on her shoulder. "Sweetheart, in Frank and Vivian's eyes, you can do no wrong. They're your parents. Everything is fine."

Jillian thought to herself. Some parents. Sleep with your own children, teach them how to please adult women and men, use them in videos with each other. Yeah, they are just the perfect model for parenthood.

After the women including Jillian were locked in their rooms, Tobin went into the kitchen where Stokes was pouring himself two fingers of Jack Daniels. "Why is Jillian with these two?"

Stokes shook his head. "I just haul them. I have no idea and it's none of my business. I was supposed to pick them up in Athens then head here, but something happened and I was told to get them early at an exit on 20. I've been driving all night on back roads. I'm going to bed. Wake me if you need me." Stokes was talking as he was walking to the couch. He always slept in his own sleeping bag on the couch when he was in a service station. He knew what happened in the beds.

When preparing for an event, Tobin normally slept in his recreational vehicle. This service station had a full hook up designed for just that purpose. He lived in the RV most of the time when on the road. It was luxurious, it was mobile, and it suited his needs as he moved about the south finding clients that needed the type of female or male attention that he and his partners sold. He belonged to a host of private clubs in various cities. When he wasn't traveling, he had use of apartments and homes in Atlanta, Charleston, Charlotte, and Raleigh. He didn't consider himself a pimp. He felt he was more of a party organizer. He hated the word panderer, the legal word for what he was. He never attended the parties. Once he knew their money had transferred into the company accounts, he left his "guests" and would be miles away before the first act of lust. The money was never in the same place as the entertainment. He was well paid, part of the management team along with Frank and Vivian Bartram, and never slept with the help. He had special tastes which he kept to himself. In this business, a special appetite quickly became a weakness and a liability. He found too many willing clients with special appetites and had no wish to mix with them.

This event was planned for a 12-bedroom estate in the South Carolina foothills of the Blue Ridge. He still had a few arrangements to make. But for now, he had to stay here. It was company rules. If there was help in a service station, one person had to be awake and monitoring for possible escapes. Stokes was dead tired and needed rest. The girls were worn out and he didn't want to be the one on watch if something happened especially with Jillian in residence. He would have to make some final arrangements for food and liquor on the phone.

He finished his calls and made one more to the owner of a small apartment he rented three months at a time in downtown Greenville. When Stokes woke up, Tobin would take his BMW sport coupe to town. He had been stuck out here for two days. He wanted a night of fun before the party. The piano bar in the hotel would be a nice start then down the street for a small steak and a fine bottle of red. It may just be a bit over an hour away from this dismal squat but downtown Greenville was a league away in sophistication and style.

They had slept briefly. Vivian had been almost insatiable. Around 1:00 pm she bounced into the room, naked with a cup of coffee for Holder. He pulled himself up in bed. She smiled.

"I'm making you a toasted cheese sandwich. You'll need to keep your strength up. We have another whole day here." She put the coffee down and kissed him deeply. Holder couldn't believe she already tasted like whisky. She turned to leave and as she did so she asked the question. "How many girls were you transporting?"

He sipped his coffee. "Three."

"That's odd. Just three?"

"Yeah, I picked up Beth and Tiffany at the Tide Times Motel."

Vivian turned in the doorway. "Who was the third?"

Holder didn't even think twice. "It was Jillian. Frank had me pick her up at the Charleston mansion before I picked up the other two."

Vivian paused for a brief second then walked to the nightstand on her side of the bed. Holder really wasn't paying any attention to her although he started to smell something burning. Vivian pulled her Beretta Tomcat 32 caliber pistol from the drawer, reached under the sheets and pushed the barrel hard against the base of Dexter's male member.

"Viv, what the hell?"

Vivian smiled. "Dex, if you want to keep the only part of you that I have any use for at all, you will tell me why my daughter is travelling with the help?"

"I don't know Vivian. I honestly don't" He tried to pull back but she pushed the gun even harder into his pubic bone. "Frank called me and gave me the instructions. I picked them up and was on my way to handing them off to Stokes in Athens. That's all I know."

Vivian pulled the small pistol back just a touch and pushed it against the base of his scrotum.

"Exactly how many times has Frank ordered you to take Jillian anywhere with the help? Don't take too long to think, Dexter. That will make me suspicious you are making up the answer."

"Three times but this is the first that far away."

"You do know she's just turned 15, right?" She pushed the pistol against him harder. "Think hard Dexter, when did this start?"

Holder thought quickly then answered.

"It was after Frank made you move Jessie in with Stella."

Vivian pulled the pistol out from under the covers. Viv, is it OK if I go to the bathroom? I'm about to pee myself."

"Go ahead, then get dressed. We need to get moving. I have to get my little girl before Frank and that foppish pimp Tobin rent her out or sell her to God knows who at this party that's in the works. I'll clean up the mess in the kitchen. You throw these sheets in the washer. We are leaving as soon as they come out of the dryer and the bed is made. I'll wipe down the rest. We leave in an hour."

Dexter came back from the bathroom. "Do we have time for a shower?"

Vivian looked down at the small deadly little weapon in her hand. "Dexter, this is loaded with high impact hollow points. If I had pulled the trigger, it would have blown your dick off and everything that makes you a boy with it. I'm not very happy with the males in my life right now. What do you think?"

Dexter reached for his clothes. "I'm on it, Viv. Just put that thing away, please."

# CHAPTER 5

Back in Atlanta, members of the team were heading out to check the addresses managed by a holding company called Mid-Atlantic. It was a shell company the intelligence associated with the Nightshade Group. Phelps and Mary were headed to check the addresses in the historic districts. Alex and Marshal Collins, along with a Smithson driver, began checking the luxury apartments located in Buckhead and Midtown.

Phelps spoke as Mary drove.

"I can never get quite used to Atlanta. It's so big and crazy."

Mary laughed. "You grew up in DC, you went to school in Boston, your first post was in Chicago, and you think Atlanta is big and crazy?"

"It's like it can't decide what it wants to be other than big. Every time I come back here, they've torn whole blocks and built new and better to replace them but it just never seems to catch up. I guess you have to be here or from here to love it."

Mary laughed. "I like Atlanta. It's got a certain charm but it is too big for me. I've been thinking that Tampa is too big for me. How were the three weeks we had off for you and your family?"

"I'm never sure if it helps or makes leaving again almost impossible. I just feel like I'm missing so much of my girl's life. Charley is so understanding but between her ER schedule and managing the household alone, it's starting to take its toll. I've got to figure something out and soon. What about you? When we talked that night on the way to Andrews, I got the impressions that you were thinking of a transfer.

"I wasn't thinking of a transfer. I have been considering leaving the Bureau."

They had arrived at the first mansion. As Phelps got out of the car he spoke.

"This conversation is not over, not by a long shot."

The house was old, beautiful, and had been well-maintained on a large lot with plantings around it that insured privacy. There was a landscape maintenance crew there working. Mary struck up a conversation with the crew chief and discovered they maintained both of the properties on the list. The company, Helping Hand Landscaping, cut and trimmed the properties weekly. The crew chief said they never had contact with the occupants. The company was paid by the management firm.

They got back in the car and drove to the second address. This house was even grander than the first. Phelps knocked on the door. No one answered so he attempted to interview the neighbors on either side with no luck. Across the street, Mary rang the bell and a maid answered and showed her into the living room of the well-maintained home. The owner, a widow in her eighties, was seated in her chair which faced the mansion in question. She looked at Mary's credentials.

"My oh my. An FBI agent and a woman. How refreshing and progressive and you are lovely as well. Please sit down. My name is Marian Ackerman. What can this little old lady help you with? We don't have many visits from the police out here you know, even if you call them."

Mary smiled, surprised. "Someone has called the police in this beautiful, quiet neighborhood?"

"Yes, I have called them every time those 'people' across the way have thrown one of their parties. I can't believe I'm the only one but it appears that I am."

Mary pulled out her notebook. "Do you mind if I make notes and summon my partner?"

"Miss, or is it Agent Close, I've been trying to get someone to pay attention to this for quite some time now. Of course. Shall we wait?" Mary nodded.

Once Phelps had introduced himself and received a sizeable once over from the sweet old woman, she continued.

"I did get a visit from an Atlanta police investigator who told me basically 'to mind my own business'. That was disheartening. I've just let it go."

Mary continued. "Tell me about these parties. Were they loud and raucous?"

" No, it was the opposite. They were quiet and it looked to me like a great deal of effort was being made to keep the gathering a secret. Lots of men located on the edge of the property, patrolling more than walking. Also, there was an unusual amount of help that would arrive just minutes before the guests. My late husband and I used to throw the most wonderful parties but we never needed that many well-dressed young females. If I had to guess I'd say they weren't being used in the kitchen or passing drinks in the parlor."

"When was the last time you noticed one of these happening?"

"Oh, it's been months now. I think the place is for sale. We don't allow those nasty yard signs in our community. There is a slick overdressed real estate agent that I've seen showing it to the same couple several times."

Mary opened her tablet. "Do you think you would recognize these people if I showed you a couple of pictures?"

"Well, my eyes are old and I don't want you to think that I sit here spying on my neighbors but I'll look at your pictures if you want me to."

They both knew this woman missed nothing that went on in her neighborhood. Mary thought about the reference to couple. She took a leap of faith and pulled up a picture of Frank and Vivian Bartram on her tablet, locked it in place, and turned it around to show the woman.

"Look at you. Got it in one. That would be the couple I've seen. You can't miss the woman. She's beautiful."

Mary smiled at her as she took the tablet back. She pulled up a picture of Charles Tobin, locked it in place and handed it to the woman. The widow paused, called her maid into the front room. "Tess, is this that little banty rooster we've seen showing the house across the street?"

The maid studied the picture. "Yes Ma'am. He's always looked familiar to me although I can't think where I would have seen him before. I've seen him around those parties as well. Mostly earlier in the day, you know, when the caterers and the real help arrive."

Mary took down their information and Phelps handed the older woman their business cards. "Thank you so much. This has been very helpful. If you think of anything else, please give us a call."

The older woman handed the cards to her maid. "Tess if you see anything you call theses FBI agents. You don't need my permission to help these people."

Tess smiled. "Yes Ma'am. There is one more thing. Most of those young girls were foreign, Spanish speakers and some Asians. I heard them talking as I was taking out the trash."

The older woman laughed. "Tess, I know you go out back to smoke your cigarettes. That's fine." She then turned her attention to Mary. "So why is the FBI looking into these little house parties?" Then she answered her own question. "It's not the parties, it's the guests and the girls I would bet. We will call if we see anything out of the ordinary. And, you can stop wasting time at the other neighbors. Everyone is at their mountain home or the lake house this time of the year."

Alex and Collins had a Smithson agent driving for them as they began checking the mid-town addresses. Alex thought about Atlanta. It is so large, so spread out, so diverse, that everyone seems to live in their own little patch. Want terrific Asian, head to Beaufort Highway. Need a good fix of old Atlanta, jump on the Beltline that weaves its way through several of the older historic neighborhoods. Once abandoned, rat-infested, and mostly destroyed industrial buildings got turned into upscale boutique malls. She was fascinated with it.

All of the neighborhoods that had addresses for Nightshade holdings were in upscale areas. She and Collins were checking the ones in Buckhead and Midtown. They had checked the midtown locations without much success and were headed to the last one in Buckhead. Collins couldn't hold his questions inside any longer. He turned and looked at Alex.

"So, what's your story?"

Alex laughed. "You lasted longer than we thought you would. Why are you so curious?"

Collins tried another tactic. "Look, I just thought if we were going to be partners, then we should get to know each other. Aren't you curious about me?"

"We are teammates not partners. I'm not trying to be rude but at Smithson we've learned to keep private lives, private."

If Tim Collins was anything he was persistent. "How did you know that I worked for the Secret Service before joining the Marshals Office? "Have you seen my confidential personnel file?"

"Easy, your hair. You're the only one on the team that doesn't have a 'high and tight' military cut. That means you're new, and in your previous job, you kept your hair neat but well-managed in case your assignment put you on camera. I'll guess one more thing, the person you were assigned to keep safe didn't get re-elected or appointed and they didn't select you to continue their reduced detail."

Collins was unnerved. "I can't believe you got all that from my haircut."

Alex smiled and softened her tone. "Marshal, I was picked, just like Lily, because I have a natural ability to do two skills, observe things others might miss and talk to people in a way that calms them down. Look, I'm not making fun of you or your career. But, on a job like this, any piece of personal information shared is a possible risk factor. We only work with high-profile dangerous cases. We assume they know as much about us as we do about them. Do you want someone poking around your apartment asking questions about you? Worse yet, do you want the bad guys to actually find someone you care about and 'make' them talk? Do you want to put your girlfriend at risk?"

"I don't have a girlfriend right now. My schedule is not very conducive to building a relationship. How about you?"

Alex laughed. "I don't have a girlfriend if that's what you're asking. I do have a fiancé. You've met him. Charles Jenkins."

Collins was shocked. "Claymore Jenkins, the guy in the wheelchair?"

Now Alex did change her tone. "See how easy it is to get under someone's skin about personal stuff. That guy in the wheelchair left his legs in Afghanistan keeping a kid from running after a soccer ball in a minefield. He was hit by a surplus U.S. claymore mine. Thus, the nickname. Don't let the wheelchair fool you."

Collins apologized immediately. "Look, I didn't mean to offend you or Claymore."

She turned toward the window but quickly had the Smithson driver pull the car over to the curb. They were across and down the street from the last address on their list. Alex got out of the car and walked toward a stand of trees on the embankment under an overpass.

Collins was bewildered and looked at the driver. "Did I piss her off? The driver smiled and turned toward him.

"You can't piss her off. But she is good at ignoring things that she doesn't find relevant. Her reaction isn't about you. She spotted signs of a homeless camp. See the cardboard and trash? They are invisible to everyday residents which makes them great intelligence sources. To survive on the street, they develop a high level of observation and awareness. Alex is good at gaining trust and talking with them, one of those special talents she mentioned. And, in case you're thinking of joining her, don't until she takes you. No offense, they'd correctly read you as cop and wouldn't say a thing. Sit tight. She won't be long."

Alex returned and walked to the rear of the car. She nodded and the driver released the trunk lid. She pulled three small packages out of the trunk and returned to the overgrowth.

The driver continued. "Sit tight. She has developed sources and is giving them burner phones. A cell phone is a huge asset for living on the street. It means she found information and they have agreed to watch for us."

"Can we trust that type of intelligence? They're bums and addicts for God's sake."

The driver had tired of his attitude. "They don't dress as well as we do but not all of them are addicts or mentally ill. They know how to manipulate us more prosperous folks to survive. Alex has obviously found three that are willing to help. Before you get too worried about it, it won't be intelligence until we vet it. If I know Alex, you're both about to walk into that condo, talk to management, and find out the homeless know just what's inside. My guess is we've found an active site to watch and they will help."

Alex spoke as she got back in the car.

"I will introduce you to our new friends after we find out if they are correct. If they are, the property manager's office is in the lobby. I think we need a plan to talk to her. We should be a couple looking to rent. We need to see some apartments maybe even the ones on our address from the analysis."

"How do you know it's a she?"

"My new friends were really clear about that. She's run them off the dumpsters several times. Her name is Helena and she works for the company called Kidder Properties." The driver began typing into his tablet as she spoke. Collins looked flabbergasted.

"You got all that from the people in the cardboard huts."

"Everyone throws out trash. These people go through it. They think she's at least 35, big rock on her right hand, and overly friendly with several of the residents after hours. Make a note of how many floors you count as we walk up."

Collins looked up at the building as he spoke. I count 15. How do you want to handle this?"

"Let's go shopping for a new place. Should I call you Tim since we are going to make this woman believe we are looking for a place together?"

Collins smiled. "You can call me anything but Tim. My cover credentials say David."

Alex smiled. I'll call you Davey"

The driver moved the car up and they got out to cross the street.

Alex took his arm and laughed. "I'm Ashley."

The first thing they noticed when they entered the lobby was the imposing, obviously armed security guard standing behind the reception desk. Most of these condos have concierge staff to welcome guests, accept packages etc. This guy projected a different demeanor than welcome.

"Can I help you?" No smile. Heavy foreign accent that Alex recognized as Slavic in origin.

Collins took the lead with a smile. "We're looking for an apartment. We've had our eyes on this building for awhile so we'd like to speak to someone about leasing one."

The guard didn't even look up. He dialed a number and spoke in Russian. He hung up the phone and pointed down the hall where a sign read Kidder. "Go there." Again, no smile.

They were greeted at the office door by a well-dressed woman in her late thirties to early forties. Alex nudged Collins.

"I'm Helena Reagan, the manager and agent here. I understand you're looking for an apartment. We only have two that I can show you at the moment. They're both on the 5th floor looking south. It's a beautiful view."

"I'm Dave, this is Ashley. We've had our eye on this building for a long time now. We live in mid-town and it's just getting too crowded. We were hoping for something higher up, like the top."

Helena gave a cutesy frowny face. "There is nothing available on the 10th floor. It is very exclusive with just two apartments where there are normally six. They are privately owned and not available." She replaced the frowny face with one that was clearly sizing Dave up. "But, let me show you what we have on the 5th floor. They're lovely places with almost the same view." She pulled open her desk drawer, bent over exposing a well-engineered cleavage for Dave and got her keys.

The apartments were unremarkable with builder-grade finishes and nothing worth anywhere near the asking price. Alex took note that an elevator key was required for all floors above five. The number of buttons didn't match the floor count. Some of them must be two story places. There were armed security personnel everywhere, even one sitting at a desk on the 5th floor. Most property security guards aren't armed. They cost too much for the average condo association and all have standing orders to call the police in case of trouble. Alex knew these guys had standing orders to not call the police. As they were walking back into the lobby, Alex spoke.

"I love these Davey." She turned to Helena. "You certainly have great security here. Should we be worried that this is a high-risk area?"

Helena didn't miss a beat with her rehearsed response. "Our owners and renters are very private people. Some are movie stars and film producers. We cater to the exclusive client. We go out of our way to make sure that they feel safe. Unfortunately, not so far away there are other less exclusive residents. She nodded toward the trees under the overpass across the street. I've even had to run those people away from the trash receptacles out back. So, we make sure they are never a problem."

Collins stuck out his hand. "Thanks so much for showing us the units. We need to do some calculating and talking. We appreciate your time."

Helena ignored Alex and focused on Collins. "Any time, Davey. I look forward to seeing you again." She turned on her Jimmy Choo stilettos and headed toward her office.

As they exited the building, Alex looked over at Collins as she kept her arm within his until they got back to the car. She knew they were being watched.

"Well done. Other than the fact that you just had the eye fucking of a lifetime, what did observe?"

Collins didn't hesitate. "This is the place, isn't it."

"What makes you say that?"

"Those weren't normal security guards. They were all armed and they were all foreign. Did you catch what language they were speaking?"

"Russian, and that includes your new girlfriend, Helena. And you're right. They are not security guards. They are not there to protect that building. They are there to make sure whoever is on the 9th floor and above doesn't leave. This is, indeed, the place. Now it's time for you to meet our new friends. It seems they had the right information."

Alex was on the phone with Phelps as soon as they pulled away from the curb and down the street out of sight of the building. Phelps in turn was on the phone with Ludlow.

"Alex and Collins caught a break. We have a location that appears to currently be occupied, as indicated by the number of armed security people onsite. I'd like to suggest that we set surveillance on the building, stir up the hornet's nest and see what comes out."

Ludlow loved working with these people. "Sounds like a plan. How are you going to stir them up?"

"I thought we'd send the locals in pretending to respond to a call for a welfare check. They probably won't want to give us access. That's OK. We just need to fire them up enough that they want to clear out what's on the limited access floors."

"Good plan. Sounds like one Alex came up with. Do we arrest them when they come out?"

"That's only funny because it was her idea. No. We follow them. See where they take us. Mary and I found other witnesses at one of the locations in the historic district mansions that identified the Bartrams and Tobin. Seems like someone has been throwing parties there. Maybe we could watch that as well."

Ludlow spoke. "I don't want the locals involved. If we're right, it sounds too big to have gone unnoticed by the cops. Use my people to go stir the pot. I don't want to risk a leak and have the whole show vanish before we get there."

"Let's have Mary be one of them. Alex says she heard Russian being spoken by the guards. Mary speaks Russian."

"Mary is full of surprises. How soon can you put someone on the building?"

"Alex and Collins are already there. She has Collins watching the building with some street people she recruited with burgers, fries and phones. They will get closer and set up some of her equipment as it gets darker. "

"Alex has managed to get Collins working with homeless people. That I've got to see. "

# CHAPTER 6

In Atlanta, Claymore was busy tracking everyone and keeping each of the teams up-to-date on their findings. He was tracking Smithson Air One as it landed with Ludlow and Lily at the downtown Greenville airport to meet with trusted members of the anti-human trafficking effort active in upstate South Carolina. If there was a lead stronger than a noise ordinance for Stokes, these two officers would know. Ludlow spoke as they looked out over the lakes and foothills they were flying over.

"The officers we're meeting work intelligence for the area anti-trafficking task force. Officer Roseanne Smith of Greenville Police Department, in particular, does a lot with the community. We know Stokes has been here but it will be good to find out if they have any idea about the others."

Lily smiled. "Since we are playing this operation close to the vest, can we trust them?"

Ludlow smiled back. "Yes. I've tried to recruit both of them but they like being close to the community they work in."

Lily nodded her head. "Phelps and Mary are like that. They love getting out there and talking to the people. I'm looking forward to meeting these two. Who is the second?"

"Deputy Rex Wormer. He's just a good old-fashioned country boy."

The Smithson helicopter landed at the downtown airport where the two locals led them to an empty hanger. Officer Smith gathered intelligence on labor and sex trafficking. Her coffee-colored skin and southern accent let everyone know she was from the South. She looked at each picture but didn't recognize any of the people. Deputy Wormer did the same but paused at Tobin's picture.

"I know I've seen this guy but I can't remember where. It's not so much his face. It's something else. Is that the only picture you have of him?" Lily sent a message to Claymore.

In five minutes, several pictures arrived and Wormer recognized the person in the third picture.

"I was working security for a golf tournament a month ago. This guy was with a bunch of high rollers from the River Club. I remember his watch more than him. See, it's in the picture and has to be worth $15,000. He couldn't seem to follow instructions and we had to intervene when he got nasty with one of the course officials. Shit head yes, human trafficker doubtful."

Officer Smith laughed out loud. "What would a good old Seneca boy know about a $15,000 watch?" Wormer smiled back and blushed as well. "I guess I remembered the watch because it was on a loudmouthed loser."

Smith looked at the new pics. "Who can I share these with?"

Lily shook her head. "These have to stay with us."

"Do you have some time to take a ride with me downtown? I have two sources that might prove helpful."

Lily looked at Ludlow who nodded. "I'll stay here and go over some things with Deputy Wormer."

Roseanne started the conversation as she drove.

"Your accent says low-country."

Lily smiled. "Good catch. Beaufort County."

Roseanne laughed and spoke the Geechee equivalent of "homegirl."

Lily smiled and answered her using Gullah dialect.

"The people that adopted me are Gullah, Lydia and Sam Michaels, from St Helena Island. They raised me on those salt marshes. Sam is dead but Lydia, who has always insisted I call her Aunt Lydia, still calls me everyday. It's nice to hear the sea island language.

Roseanne got serious. "A tall blond Gullah. Now I have seen everything. You've been a lot of places and done a lot of shit since you left those marshes. It must be something to be working with the Smithson people."

"You know much about Smithson?"

"Only that if you and Marshal Ludlow are here, it's serious shit. How serious are we talking?

"Nightshade serious."

"Fuck, I was afraid of that." It took a moment for her to process that notion.

"The two people I have in mind have been solid sources for spotting trafficking behavior before. The first is a barber named CeeKay Miller. She works at an exclusive barber shop downtown. Something about the watch and seeing the other pictures of that guy you called Tobin reminded me of something she brought to my attention not too long ago. We laughed about it at the time but it may be something."

"A barber?"

"CeeKay, and she spells it C E E K A Y, was one of the first to step up when the shelters put out the word, they needed someone to volunteer their services for survivors. She also organized a drive for donated clothes to start up a lending closet with some other barbers and hair stylists. The bulk of this community is really behind our efforts and supportive. They help style and dress our survivors for court. Looking presentable and serious helps them be strong in their testimony."

Lily caught the hitch in the statement. "You said 'the bulk' of the community. Are there people you think support trafficking here?"

"Traffickers offer services and they have customers whether it is a cheap cleaning service, under the table laborers, nannies, or your wildest sexual fantasy. These assholes always need other assholes to buy what they peddle. I love this community but I'm not naive. Having said that, when we need help from the community, we normally get it."

Lily nodded. "You said you had second source?"

"Paul Romo. He's the piano player in the lobby bar of the Central Hotel. The elite and those who feed off them often begin or end their evenings there. He's great at spotting girls being managed and any pair of eyes in a hotel is good for us watching the turnover in staff."

Roseanne parked her car in a space reserved for police vehicles. Lily noticed a significant police presence. "Your department believes in visibility. That's different."

Roseanne laughed. "They have their not-so-visible side as well. We have a lot of tourists as you can see. They don't have to go far to find help. CeeKay is right in here."

They entered an older building that had been restored so that it had all the modern necessities but kept the historic vibe. Roseanne introduced her to an attractive well-dressed woman who had a huge smile. She gave them both a hug as she spoke.

"Lord Roseanne, I haven't seen you in seems like forever." She turned to Lily. "You in the same business this fabulous woman is?" Lily nodded as Roseanne posed the question.

"CeeKay, do you remember the guy you talked to me about with the big watch that had the weird picture on his phone a month or so ago?"

"Mr. Dupont. Hard to forget him even when you try hard. Believe me, all of us in this shop try hard. I only agree to cut his hair. He always wants more services but he has made too many off color remarks about my body and what he'd like to watch me do with it that I limit my exposure to him. He gets a haircut, that's it. The word freak is apt."

Lily asked. "Tell me how freaky?"

"Well, I've had guys try to reach under my dress in the shampoo room or try to cop a feel sitting in the chair. But Dupont has something nastier about him. The way he looks me up and down makes me feel creepy and then there was the picture."

Roseanne prompted her to continue. "I had finished cutting his hair and he got huffy when I wouldn't meet him for a drink. He stormed out screaming there were plenty of women who would love to have his attention. We all laughed but after he stormed out, I realized his phone was sitting on the counter at my station. I picked it up to try to catch him and the screen activated. The home screen image was of an older woman, totally naked and smiling. It was raw and I'm not that much of a prude. I saw him coming back into the shop so I put it back face down on the counter just as he entered. I don't think he thought I had seen the picture."

Lily thought a moment. "When you say 'older', how old?"

CeeKay looked Lily in the eye. "Like my mother or grandmother old."

"Did the woman in the picture look scared or like she was threatened?" Lily was serious.

"No, she was smiling and posing. There wasn't much left to the imagination and like I said, I'm not easily shocked."

Lily pulled out her tablet.

"I'm going to show you a picture of someone. Just say the word yes if it's him."

CeeKay looked down at the screen. "Yes"

They hugged again and Lily and Roseanne moved on to the hotel. Roseanne explained that the hotel had been a Greenville hotspot for decades.

Like most downtown icons, it had risen from the ashes of a downtown exodus to become great again. It seemed to be a thing with downtown Greenville. It had preserved the best parts of what had been great before.

Paul Romo didn't go on until 5:00 pm but he had texted that he was at the bar having a late lunch. Roseanne greeted Paul warmly as he stopped eating.

"Paul. How are you?"

He stood and smiled at both of them as he put up his hands. "I swear officers, I didn't do it. Well, maybe I did, but only once. Okay, maybe more than once but I'm sorry. Alright, I'm only sorry that you caught me. I confess. Take me away." He hugged Roseanne and shook Lily's hand.

Roseanne prompted Lily to pull out a picture of Tobin.

Lily showed it to him. "Can you look at this and see if you recognize the person? If you do, just say yes."

He looked at the picture. "Ronald Dupont. Oops, sorry. Yes."

Lily took a risk. She scrolled to the picture of Vivian and Frank Bartram.'

"And how about these people?"

He smiled. "Yes. They were here about six weeks ago and spent the evening in the lobby. Gruff guy but big, big tipper. I didn't see them with Dupont but I remember her. She's so beautiful she's hard to forget. Knows how to have a good time in a very quiet way. Just looked like she was enjoying herself. They had a young girl with them that they said was their daughter. They said they were celebrating her 15th birthday. She was as beautiful as her mother. They ordered dinner and the girl had a full grown-up dinner. She didn't drink a drop but was very mature. She readily conversed with adults, knew how to behave. None of this cell phone babysitting crap you see so much of today. I remember because she was very unlike most of the teenaged girls we get in here. Much more adult than teen."

Lily then showed pictures of Holder and Stokes.

"Nope, neither one."

Roseanne stuck out her hand. Thanks Paul. We appreciate it as always and as always, not a word to anyone."

He smiled and hugged her. "My lips are sealed."

Outside Lilly got on her phone. Ludlow answered in one ring.

"Tobin comes to Greenville regularly under the name of Ronald Dupont. The Bartrams were here six weeks ago with a young teen woman. It may be our unknown woman from the rest stop."

Ludlow was direct. "Get back to the airport. We will standby here until we hear from the other teams."

West of Greenville, Stokes was awake by 2:00 pm. He could hear the girls moving around in their rooms. He went and unlocked each one. Beth and Tiffany came out of their rooms and headed straight for the bathroom then the refrigerator. Jillian opened the door but stayed in her room. There was a strict no-smoking policy in the houses. Tiffany put two fingers to her lips and looked at Stokes. He ushered her outside and handed her a pack of cigarettes and lighter. She finished and he stripped the cigarette of tobacco and disposed of the filter and any part she had touched. She turned and went back in.

Charles Tobin emerged from his RV and locked it. He looked at Stokes. "I've got business in town making arrangements. I may not be back this evening. Can you handle these three or do I need to call in some help?"

Stokes laughed. "If you mean the guys Frank calls his soldiers, no. They are worse than useless and way too tempted by the girls, these two in particular. And you know as well as I do, security is not to be left alone with

Jillian under any circumstances."

Tobin seemed troubled. "Why do you think Frank moved her here? Jillian and Jessie never travel with us and I don't think they've ever worked with the others. Their clients have always been arranged by Frank and Vivian."

"Maybe they have made an arrangement we don't know about. I haven't seen Jessie in months. Do you know where he is?""

Tobin shuddered. "They sent him to that witch of a lawyer, Stella St. John. He was probably payment for some legal service that probably wasn't that legal anyway. That poor boy. Just looking at that St. John woman scares me."

Stokes laughed out loud. "Just looking at you scares me. Anyway, I don't give a shit about any of them. I move them when I'm told to where I'm told. When do I move these?"

"Frank texted. There's another group of women being brought in just before the party tomorrow. They will be taken directly to the event. We just need to get these three delivered there by 6:30. The location is about an hour and fifteen minutes all on back roads. I will text you with instructions. I should be back tomorrow morning to help."

"Like you're any help."

Tobin pretended not to hear him and headed toward his car.

On the way to the location, Tobin called the caterers and the liquor provider. He arranged for the deliveries to happen just before the party the following day. The cleaners would be arriving to tidy within the hour. All they needed to do was dust and vacuum. When they were done, he would lock up the house. There weren't that many neighbors, but stringing out the activity was the best way to keep the curious away. Frank arranged security for the party which would be a one-night with no sleepovers. Right after the party everyone would leave and the place would be thoroughly cleaned afterwards by their people. Two hours after the last guest was loaded into a limo, the place would be forensically clean, dark, and locked up. The property would be back on the six-month lease market the following day.

He got to the house, turned off the alarms and sensors along the driveway, and finished making the limo arrangements. It was the normal drill. One 10-passenger luxury van would pick him up at the house. He would ride with the driver to pick up the guests and drop them off at the party. He would leave them at that point to trade the BMW for the RV and be on his way to Raleigh. It was a sedate affair. They would start with cocktails at the bar, a short ride to the mountains, some expensive hors d'oeuvres, the guests would screw their brains out according to whatever weird request they'd made, and back to the hotel for a nightcap. Just your average $12,000 per guest for the evening. Tobin thought to himself as he saw the cleaning people coming up the drive on the monitors, "Where would we all be without the rich and perverted?"

# CHAPTER 7

Phelps and Mary were back in the Atlanta command center going over the new information Lily and Ludlow had discovered in Greenville when his phone rang twice.

"Agent Phelps, this is Tess. I met you with Mrs. Ackerman earlier. The man, the one that was part of the couple arrived alone across the street a few minutes ago."

Phelps gave Mary an astonished look then turned back to the phone.

"Do you think Mrs. Ackerman would mind if I came back and sat in the living room and just watched the house?"

"Agent Phelps, she's way ahead of you. She has me making biscuits and I've already thawed out some ham. She had me set up the upstairs bedroom which will give you a better view. Should we expect Agent Close as well?"

"It will just be me. Agent Close will be busy elsewhere. Thank you. I will see you in about 30 minutes."

Mary sent out updates on the situation for both sites in Atlanta to the AG and the people in Greenville. Then she advised Hal Story that she would meet him in uniform at a mobile command center Smithson was setting up near the Buckhead site. Since the FBI normally wear suits, she only had her tactical uniform. That would work just fine.

Meanwhile, Phelps arrived at the Ackerman house with a pair of night vision binoculars and the small drone Birdman called Kestrel. It was the size of the actual bird, had a communication range of 15 miles and a flying range of 20. It could stay aloft for five hours and was night vision equipped. Phelps parked on an adjacent street, pulled the drone out of the case and set it on the trunk lid. He called Birdman who activated the drone and Phelps watched it rise off the lid and silently ascend into the sky. He pulled out his tablet and saw that it was quietly moving over the neighborhood. Its size made it impossible to see.

Tess answered the door. "Hello again Agent Wheeler. Please come in."

Mrs. Ackerman sat in her chair with her eyes glued to the house.

"He hasn't moved since he got here. I wish Arthur was still alive. He'd love this. What's our plan?"

Phelps smiled. "How about I watch from upstairs and you watch from down here?"

The old woman smiled. "What do we do if he takes it on the lam?"

Phelps almost laughed out loud at the old detective story reference.

"You stay here. I will follow him. We have to make sure it's the right guy."

Mrs. Ackerman huffed. "You get all the action while I sit here on my fanny like I do every day."

Phelps was ready. "Someone needs to stay here in case I lose him."

She nodded and was happy with that answer. "Tess will show you the way."

Tess led him upstairs and when they got to the room, there was already a basket of ham biscuits and a pitcher of sweet tea. She smiled. "I can bring you water as well if sweet tea is not your drink. Mrs. Ackerman suggested I check if you want something stronger, but I figured you're on duty."

Phelps took a seat and spoke to her. "Sweet tea is fine. You and Mrs.

Ackerman have been great."

The maid started to leave then turned. "She is having more fun than you can imagine. She has been ignored so often. That happens a lot to older people. Thank you for taking her seriously."

"Of course, Tess. You've both been a great help. How long have you worked for Mrs. Ackerman?"

She smiled. "I've been in this house 36 years. She and her husband have been wonderful to my girls and me. They put my two daughters through college and helped them get a start. Please do me one favor. Don't lose him. I'm not sure what she'd do if you did and he came back."

"We won't. And, you know, it's not just me, right?"

She nodded.

Just as Dexter and Vivian crossed the Greenville County line, Vivian dialed Frank. He answered almost immediately.

"Viv, my love. Did you take care of our Dexter problem?"

In her sweetly southern voice that scared the living shit out of Dexter no matter where or when he heard it, she spoke. "Oh, don't you worry about Mr. Holder. I got him."

Frank laughed. "Thank God. Where are you?"

Viv's smile disappeared. "Well, I will be happy to answer that question as soon as you explain to me where my daughter is and why she is traveling with the help."

There as a long pause on the other end of the line. "Viv, Foster and I decided it was time to make some other arrangements concerning the twins. I thought you understood that when we moved Jessie in with Stella."

"Stella's not a stranger and I knew she would care for Jessie like I would. Since when do you and Foster make decisions about my daughter without talking to me? You left me out of the loop Frank, and doing so makes me think I will hate the plan you two have for her."

Frank was scrambling not so much because he was scared of what Vivian would do to him but what she could do to the organization. He measured his words.

"Viv, sweetheart, you know Foster calls the shots for our operation. He has supported us over the years. Hell, he's made us rich. We knew we would have to make some concessions once the twins got older. We just felt it was time to address Jillian's future. You handled Jessie's relocation so well."

There was silence. Vivian was thinking. Dexter was sweating and driving. She motioned for him to pull into a parking lot on the south side of the city. He did so but gripped the wheel so hard his knuckles were turning white. Vivian continued to think. The silence continued.

"Viv, are you still there?" Frank was now sweating.

Another five minutes passed. Vivian took a long slow breath in as she measured every word.

"Hollins Foster hasn't made us rich. A bunch of sick bastards that can't get laid without paying for it is what has made us rich. You and fucking Foster are planning on making us richer by selling Jillian to one of those sick bastards." She paused to let that sink in. She continued.

"You were going to deliver her to him without my knowledge, weren't you?"

It was now Frank's turn to be silent but it wasn't because he was thinking. Now he was scared.

"Vivian. It is really important you don't do anything rash. We can talk about it after this next event. You just come join me here in Atlanta."

Vivian didn't hesitate this time. "I don't think I like that idea. I think I'm going to get Jillian and then maybe we'll talk. Until then you tell Foster to go fuck himself. Oh, and Frank, you can join him."

"Goddammit, Vivian. You don't tell a man like Foster to go fuck himself. You're lucky he has put up with you this long. He's made sure you've had adequate supply of your pills and I've tolerated the little sexual adventures you love. All of those expose the entire organization, Vivian. You better watch your mouth."

There was another five-minute silence. Dexter stared straight ahead. Frank threw his tumbler full of whisky against the wall and screeched into the phone. The small drone hovering about the house picked up Frank's growing rage.

"Vivian, tell me where you fucking are! He got up and threw his chair through the window into the back yard.

Vivian had played him for the anger. When Frank was angry you had to be careful if he was anywhere near you. He wasn't and she had him right where she wanted him.

"I'm going to remind you of a bit of history. Let's start with the oldest, almost ancient episodes. You've slept with and had sex with your own daughter. You've forced her to act like she was having sex with her brother. You've forced me to have sex with all of you. Some of that was on film. Oh, I take that back, almost all of that was on film, wasn't it? Now the more recent. You traded your own son to a lawyer with a thing for young boys in exchange for some legal mumbo jumbo on several property transfers that enabled you to launder hundreds of thousands of dollars for Nightshade."

She could hear things breaking. When Frank got this angry, he broke things near him. If there were people around, he broke them too. Badly. The one thing Frank didn't do when he was angry, was think. He came back on the line and hissed into the phone. "Tell me where you are or you're fucking dead."

She laughed. She knew it would drive him over the edge. "Oh Frank, the opposite is true. If you could get to me right now, I'm sure I would be dead. I think I will just find my own way for a bit." She hung up.

Dexter sat perfectly still, with his eyes fixed straight ahead. Vivian matter-of-factly turned to him and quietly spoke.

"Well, Dex, Frank wants us both dead. I need you to tell me where Jillian is going to end up. We will go there but not just yet."

"Why would Frank want me dead?"

Vivian laughed as she reached over and gently rubbed his crotch. "Because you fucked up. The girls got a message out, and now his plan to give Jillian to the boss has been exposed. See, I told you. It was Frank's fault from the start. I suggest we hide in plain sight. Where is Jillian being taken, Dex?" She tightened her grip.

"A place in the mountains just north of Greenville. There's a party tomorrow night. But, she's not there yet. Tobin is coordinating everything." That made her smile.

"Let's go check into my favorite hotel in Greenville. We'll be safe there. How far away are they holding her now?"

"The service station in Oconee County a little over an hour away."

"See that wasn't so hard, was it? We can have some fun before all this 'killing' that Frank is raving about starts. We can make love while he is busy breaking up our beautiful Atlanta mansion and figuring out what to do next." She lightened her grip and gave him a soft stroke.

Holder liked where her hand was. "Vivian, aren't you worried that the cops will be looking for me? I could lead them right to you."

"Ah well. If that happens it happens. Besides, they're busy elsewhere. How would they know where to look?"

On the video the drone was broadcasting, Phelps saw the chair fly out into the backyard of the mansion. He pressed his ear piece to ping Birdman. "What the hell was that?" He could hear Birdman laughing.

"It was a chair. He's so pissed that if he stays there much longer, he'll tear the whole place apart. What do you think about planting a tracker on the Audi outside?"

Phelps responded. "Let me check our legal status. If we plant it, can you control it enough to disengage it if we get denied?"

"Of course. It's just the push of a button. But if we are going to plant it, we need to do it soon. He just threatened to kill someone. Right now, he's talking on the phone but I'm not sure how long he is going stay there."

Phelps didn't take two seconds. "Plant the tracker. We can always make it drop off if we get denied."

"You do know those things are expensive, right?"

Phelps laughed. "I do, but I think the AG will get us the warrants for here and the Buckhead site."

Phelps pushed the green button on his phone and Claymore answered.

"Phelps, what do you need?"

"Time to contact the AG for warrants for both sites."

"I'm on it." Claymore was gone.

Phelps took a sip of sweet tea and a bite of ham biscuit and said aloud: "Go ahead Frank, lose your shit. We need you to take us there."

In Greenville, Lily was watching the updates and getting antsy. It was not her nature to wait while everyone else was engaged. She looked over at Ludlow who was watching messages being exchanged on his command tablet. "How do you manage to stay so focused and calm all the time?"

He smiled, a rare occurrence. "You do know they are not the same thing, right? The calm part is part of my nature. The focus part, I've had to teach myself since I became a supervisor. It's not just me out there when the shit hits the fan. I have to focus to keep everyone safe because if you let the adrenalin take over people get hurt. I know that from experience as you well know. I lost my focus and you saved my ass."

"I just followed the training. Anyone out there would have done the same."

"Be that as it may, during my recovery I worked on my focus and on thinking like the bad guys as much as anything. It helps me prepare."

"And what does that exercise teach you about all this stuff? I am not good at waiting."

"Actually, I think they are about to make a mistake and you're waiting will be over." He smiled again. Lily looked across at him.

"Ludlow, you have a very nice smile. You should do more of it."

"I'll try to focus on that and improve."

Phelps interrupted the conversation and Ludlow put it on speaker.

"Go ahead Phelps, you're on speaker with Lily.

"We are getting warrants for surveillance and tracking in Atlanta. The simulation model says what's in Atlanta is going to move your way. I think we will all be joining you shortly. Lily, do you have a dress with you?"

"Of course, I have a dress with me. Why?"

"What do you think about going on a date with Ludlow? That airport is too far away from the action. I'm having Claymore get rooms at this hotel you mentioned. I think it would be a great idea for you two to spend some time in the lobby, blending in. If they are coming your way, their advance man may show up."

Ludlow chimed in. "That is a good idea. We may need back up. OK to let the local officers we trust in on this for support? " Get your local friends to get you some cars and additional help."

Ludlow nodded. "I'll make that happen. See you soon."

Lily got on her phone and looked up five minutes later. "The cars will be here in 15 minutes. Roseanne says SLED is lending them to us and they are right around the corner. Where do you need the officers?"

"In plain clothes, posted outside the hotel with some trackers. They should be enough for now. If what happens at the Buckhead location plays out like I think it will, we will have plenty of our people following right along with the parade headed this way. By this time tomorrow this hanger will be very crowded." He looked up and smiled.

Lily laughed. "Wow, you are improving. I have a dress. Do you have any civilian clothes at all? I've never seen you in anything but tactical gear."

"I always travel with something for non-duty hours."

Lily smiled at that. "I don't think I've ever seen you when you weren't on duty."

"Then we're both in for a new experience." And, another smile.

The cars arrived right on time. They packed up and let the Atlanta command post know they were relocating to the Central Hotel in downtown Greenville.

# CHAPTER 8

In Buckhead, Alex read that Lily and Ludlow were repositioning to sit in the lounge of a good hotel. She was perched on the wall behind the dumpsters where the building's CCTV couldn't see her. She had already attached a transmitter to the camera and it was sending the video feed to their command center six miles away. If a car pulled into the garage, they would know it. She spoke into her headset.

"Lily gets to have all the fun. I'm watching a dumpster."

Claymore answered her. "Then you'll be happy to learn that our warrants are signed and active. We need to figure out a way to get a device inside the building."

Birdman interrupted. "I have one. Quarterback, the drone we used in the briefing would do nicely if we can figure a way to get it inside the front door."

Collins who was hidden across the street with the homeless people Alex had introduced him to broke in. "Davey could send a bottle of champagne to Helena. That would get it inside the building."

Alex laughed. "That is a brilliant idea. Once inside the building Quarterback needs to get to the elevator. If the bees decide to leave the nest, that is where we are going to want to hear the conversations."

Claymore's spoke. "I'll make that happen. What kind of champagne?"

Collins said "cheap" about the same time Alex said "French and expensive."

An expensive French bottle was delivered by a Marshal in plain clothes 30 minutes later. The guard accepted it at the front desk. Annoyed, he called Helena to come and get it. She had some not-so-nice things to say to him in perfect Russian when she picked it up and read the card.

"Aww, it's from Davey." She took the package back towards her office. She didn't even notice when Quarterback disengaged from the bottom of the bag and flew silently to a place just above the elevator door.

Mary met Marshal Story at the command center to visit and stir the bee's nest at 5:30 pm. They used their own badges because they believed that no one would even look. They didn't need to be granted access. They just needed to make them nervous.

They pulled up in an unmarked police vehicle and walked into the lobby. The guard stood up immediately and pressed a button on the desk. Helena appeared from her office. It was obvious she had already enjoyed some of the gift that had arrived earlier.

"Good evening, officers. Can I help you?"

Mary did the talking. "We've received a request to conduct a welfare check. The caller said someone on the 10th floor needed assistance."

Helena took that news in stride. "Well, I don't know how that could be. There is no one on the 10th floor. I will be happy to take you up there so you can check. The owners of both apartments are in Europe."

Neither of the officers let their surprise show.

Mary answered. "We would really appreciate that ma'am."

Helena headed to the elevators and motioned for them to follow. They did and just after Helena entered the elevator, Birdman moved Quarterback to Story's shoulder then into the elevator attached it to the ceiling before the doors closed.

They got off on the 10th floor and inspected both apartments. They were vacant and looked like no one had spent very much time in them. They followed Helena back into the elevator and returned to the lobby. Quarterback stayed in the elevator.

Mary began. "We're sorry to have bothered you. But we have to check when someone calls it in."

Helena answered warmly. "Of course. You're just doing your job. Have a good night."

They left and she turned and walked back to the desk. She gave the guard an instruction in Russian and he got on the phone. As soon as she was sure they were gone she got in the elevator and spoke into her phone. "We need to move our 'working' residents out of here. These cops were just here and weren't from our local friends. I think we may be compromised and need to clear this site of everyone. I will call for transport and get them all ready to move."

Everyone on the team heard that in their earpieces as clear as if she was standing next to them. Alex silently crossed the street and rounded up her homeless friends out of sight. They had hidden across and down the street on the edge of their encampment watching since Alex had given them phones. Alex spoke.

"Thank you so much for your help. You need to stay here. We don't want them to know you helped us. Otherwise, it won't be safe for you to stay here after we leave."

They understood what she was saying. Penny, the first one Alex had recruited stepped up. "Can we keep the phones?"

Alex went over and hugged her. It was the first hug Penny had enjoyed in a long time.

"Stop, you'll get yourself all dirty." Penny smiled as she pulled back. "No offense, Alex, but you kind of smell like a dumpster."

Alex laughed and hugged her again just before they disappeared into the fabric of the Buckhead undergrowth. Collins was shaking Willy the Shopping Cart King's hand and high fiving the other men. He walked with them back to their camp. After he was sure they were well hidden he said something to Willy, and as he was crossing back, he heard the general notice as he got close to Alex.

"Clear the area. We have a passenger van approaching from the west."

At 6:00 pm Lily and Ludlow met in the lobby bar. Ludlow had arrived first and made sure he had a seat facing the bar and piano. He stood up when Lily walked out of the elevator toward him. She was stunning. She had on a summer weight strapless dress, Espadrilles, and had taken her long blond hair down and pulled it back out of her face using two barrettes. Not many had seen that hair down. Ludlow was dressed in a tailored light blue suit with a custom-made linen shirt and beautiful hand made bespoke Italian loafers, with no socks. Both of them looked at each other and said simultaneously, "Wow."

Lily smiled and said quietly, "You need to be off duty more often. You're not wearing anything off the rack, are you?""

He smiled and motioned to the waitress. "I'm not built for off the rack. What will you have?"

"Chardonnay, I like more oak than fruit." Ludlow ordered.

Paul Romo was at the piano. He had spotted Lily the moment she walked in and smiled to himself.

The waitress brought the drinks. As she stepped away, Lily looked over at the piano. Paul was nodding toward the stairs that led up from the lower lobby. There, in all his glory, stood Ronald Dupont AKA Charles Tobin. He smiled at Paul as he walked toward the bar and shook hands with several older gentlemen.

Lily and Ludlow were stunned. She looked at Ludlow. "You knew he would show up."

"Not exactly but I hoped." He whispered into his lapel. "Tobin just arrived. See if the valet parked the car. We need to get a tracker on it."

Deputy Wormer checked with the valet and found they had not parked Tobin's car. He advised and was told to stay outside and follow Tobin if he left. He took up a seat at an out-door table in front of the bookstore next door. He had just settled in and texted Ludlow.

"I'm sitting at an outdoor table outside of Sweet Reads. You won't believe who just pulled up in a Mercedes."

Ludlow answered. "Who?"

"Vivian Bertram and Dexter Holder. It looks like they are checking in. The valet has the Mercedes. Do you need me to adjust?"

"No, enjoy your Sweet Reads. Stay there and stay on Tobin. Send us the description of the Mercedes. And, we need to put a tag on it."

Ludlow had just finished texting instructions when Tobin walked over to their table and nodded to Ludlow as he spoke.

"Please don't be offended. I just had to come over and tell this woman how absolutely stunning she is." He turned to Lily. " My darling, you are a vision." With that he turned and walked back toward the bar.

Ludlow laughed. "You're about to get another surprise. Watch the desk."

She looked toward the front desk and almost burst out laughing. She turned back to Ludlow. "Is that who I think it is?"

He nodded. "It is and it seems like Phelps was right again. This is turning into a Nightshade Group convention."

The two watched as Tobin caught sight of Holder and Vivian. Tobin dropped his drink, which drew way more attention than Tobin wanted. He rushed over to the desk and the three had a brief conversation. Then Tobin returned to the bar paid for his drinks and rushed to the exit. The other two took their luggage and waited by the elevator, got in and went up to their rooms.

Lily looked at Ludlow. "Are we going to arrest Holder? He has an outstanding warrant."

Ludlow shook his head. "No. We need to see where this takes us. We know where he is and will know where he's going."

Ludlow called the officers downstairs. "Stand by with those trackers I gave you. Get a tracker on Tobin's car and on the one Holder and Bartram arrived in."

Deputy Wormer got up and headed to the rear door of the hotel that led into the garage. Officer Smith had been waiting in the lower lobby and moved into the garage.

Tobin almost ran from the lobby. He left the hotel through the rear exit directly into the parking garage elevator. Wormer was completely ignored by the agitated Tobin. Smith was waiting on the third floor of the parking garage. Tobin didn't even notice that Wormer passed him as they got off the elevator and had walked ahead of him. Just as he got to his car, Smith called out to him. "Mr. Dupont!"

Tobin turned completely around to see who had called him by that name. He saw no one so he unlocked his car, got in and backed out and headed toward the exit.

Roseanne stood back in the shadows and watched him go. Deputy Wormer walked up and she spoke. "We good?"

He smiled. "We're good." She nodded.

"Now let's find that Mercedes that Vivian Bartram and Dexter Holder arrived in and get this tracker placed."

Charles Tobin cleared the garage, headed southwest out of the downtown toward Easley returning to the service station further west. U.S. 123 starts out as a narrow four-lane city street flanked with a mixture of new and old houses as gentrification moves like waves, the new displacing the old. The new are really nice. The old are shuttered and shattered. It turns into a six-lane any road USA by the time it emerges across the Saluda River into Pickens County.

Tobin's mind was racing frantically. He had to keep reminding himself to slow down the speed of the car. Vivian left no question and no room for argument. She wanted her daughter by tomorrow at a time she would designate or he was going to pay the price. Friction and disagreement between Frank and Vivian meant someone was going to pay. He didn't want it to be him. He was starving, but there was no time for a steak and a relaxing dinner now. He pulled into a place to buy a burger. He got it for the road in Easley and had to pull over 20 minutes later and throw it up. Being in the middle of an argument between two very dangerous people made him sick. He wanted hard not to die or go to prison because these two crazy people put personal issues before company profits.

Stokes was surprised when he called to have the sensors turned off. Charles burst into the house in a cold sweat. It was obvious something had happened. The girls were already locked in their rooms. Stokes poured himself and Tobin a whisky and motioned for them to have their chat outside. Tobin took his drink and led the way to the RV.

Stokes had no use for Tobin but if he was that upset, something had happened that might affect everything.

"Catch your breath and start talking. What's happened?"

"Vivian and Holder are in Greenville. I bumped into them in the hotel. She demanded that I deliver Jillian to her tomorrow. It was obvious she had not been told that Jillian was here. Holder wouldn't have moved her without Frank telling him to. I'm in the middle of two of the most dangerous people in the organization."

"Wait a minute. You're not in the middle. You didn't tell Holder to pick up Jillian. Frank did. They need to work out this family squabble before it causes the business serious damage."

"Dammit Stokes, Frank obviously had plans for Jillian he didn't want Vivian or Jillian to know about. Vivian knows now and is here. Stokes, she's fucking an hour away from where we are having an event tomorrow night. You know neither of them is ever at the parties. They are never anywhere that connect them with the clients. This kind of shit always rolls downhill and I'm at the bottom."

Stokes thought a moment while he took another sip. "Vivian is a businesswoman. She won't want to screw up the event. Call her back. Tell her Jillian is fine but bringing her too early will jeopardize the party. I will deliver the other two to you at the site and meet her with Jillian anywhere she wants after they are there. Once she has Jillian she can deal with Frank."

Tobin thought a moment then picked up his phone and made the call. He was shocked when Vivian agreed to the suggestion but added the caveat that she wanted all the girls at the party house by midafternoon. He hung up and looked at Stokes.

"She agreed. She wants all of them by 3:00 pm. That's a couple of hours early but we can watch them. This might work. Frank won't be anywhere near this party."

# CHAPTER 9

Even in the middle of the night, it is never dark in Buckhead. The van was parked on the 6th floor waiting to be loaded. Collins was hidden and filming everything for the team to see.

Birdman's tiny drone was perched in the main elevator listening and transmitting everything it heard. The conversations from the guards were automatically being translated from Russian to English. From the conversations between Helena and the guards, they learned there were two different groups being moved. In addition to the van on the sixth floor, they were talking about moving SUVs to the ninth floor to take a second group away.

Alex was on the ninth floor of the garage near the doorway between the building and the garage. She had installed a device on the video camera above the door. She walked to the edge of the building and looked over. She could not see any of the Marshals that were hidden in case they needed help. She crouched down and sent a message to Birdman and in two minutes a drone landed in front of her with a small packet of trackers and a device he called the Spring Board. She took it and the drone left to assume its position to follow whichever vehicle it was assigned. There were two others just like it, hovering silently above the building. Alex then slipped over the side and using the tether and climbing rope she had installed descended to the sixth floor where Collins was waiting. She spoke quietly.

"You stay here. I need to set a few trackers." Collins looked panicked. He shook his head side-to-side and pointed to the guard and made a gun sign with his hand.

Alex smiled and patted his arm. There were several large SUVs parked on this floor all backed in. They were each capable of carrying seven people including the driver. Alex used them as cover and attached trackers to each of them. She maneuvered as close to the waiting van as she could safely and pulled out Spring Board and attached a tracker to the front of the device. She aimed carefully but held her fire as people began exiting and being loaded into the van.

Collins didn't even see her disappear over the side again.

They were all listening to the feed from the drone in the elevator. They all heard Helena's voice.

"These 12 go in the van. The driver knows where to take them. The others will be split four to a car with security and head east. The second group will leave in 10 minutes. Bring the cars up to nine. Hurry, we are behind schedule."

A group of men and women emerged from the doorway and were directed by the driver and three security guards into the van. It started to pull away as soon as it was loaded. Alex directed Collins to rappel to the ground where she would meet him.

She was impressed that Collins had remembered his military training as she watched him rappel down six floors. She shared her plan then repositioned in the bushes near the exit lane with a tracker and Spring Board.

As the passenger van pulled up to check for oncoming traffic, a homeless man with a shopping cart stopped right in front of the van. The driver pounded on the horn and leaned out the window screaming. The man with the shopping cart just acted like he didn't hear him and started looking through the pile of belongings he had crammed in the cart. It took about a minute and a half. The homeless man moved on and the driver cussed at him as he pulled out and headed toward the Interstate. The homeless man who had distracted the driver just enough for Alex to fire Spring Board and plant a new tracker, continued across the driveway.

He crossed the street where Willy was waiting for Collins to get his gear back. Collins pulled off Willy's coat and hat and handed him his cart back.

"Thanks, Willy."

Willy laughed. "You gonna get that cleaned now that you've worn it."

Collins helped him put his coat back on and gave him his hat. "I will make sure you have a new coat tomorrow."

Willy shook his head. "I just got this one broken in just right. I was just kidding bout the cleanin'." Now go help Alex."

Three of the SUV's pulled onto the ninth-floor parking deck. Alex had locked herself into a climbing loop she had secured on the outside of the building. She hung there recording everything with the camera attached to her helmet. They brought four out at a time. They were all young foreign-looking women. At least three of them were Asian for sure. Within five minutes the first car was loaded, and away. The second car pulled up immediately, was loaded and left. Helena was in the doorway and watched it leave. The last car was loaded with security men.

Two minutes later she was heard on the phone. "We're all clear here. I'm the only one left in the building aside from two of the guards. I need a drink."

Birdman smiled from the command center. It was time to get his tiny drone out of the elevator. They all listened as Helena rode the elevator all the way to the lobby. The coin-sized drone disengaged from the ceiling and hovered behind Helena right between her shoulder blades. She paused and turned around once sensing that someone might be following her. The drone worked perfectly. It had been programed with body movement recognition. Helena could have danced around the lobby and never seen the device. She stopped at the security desk. This time she spoke in English. "Check outside. We need to be sure we are clear."

Helena turned and walked back toward her office. The guard nodded, got up and walked outside. As the glass doors opened automatically, the device flew out into the night above his head and headed right into Alex's hands.

In the command center, the team were tracking the vehicles. The passenger van had headed south toward Macon. The three SUVs pulled onto I-85 and headed east toward Greenville. Resources were redeployed to follow all three of the vehicles. All the trackers were transmitting. Two teams of Marshals departed the Smithson command center and positioned themselves to follow the vehicles headed toward Greenville. One team followed the van heading south. Once the Marshalls confirmed they had visual and a signal. Ludlow sent a message for Birdman to land the Buckhead drones and check on Phelps.

Phelps was totally focused on the house across the street. He could hear updates about what was going on in Buckhead through his earpiece. He couldn't believe one of the major targets of the investigation was across the street. Downstairs, Mrs. Ackerman dozed as Tess put a light blanket over her and pulled up a chair to watch from the ground floor.

The audio inside the house had been horrendous since the chair had been thrown through the window. It sounded like Frank was systematically taking the place apart piece by piece. He had been so absorbed he didn't notice that Birdman had used the small drone to attach a small surveillance pod inside the house. It was now sending video and audio.

For almost an hour nothing but furniture destruction happened. Then, the sound of Frank's phone ringing brought everyone listening to attention. He answered the phone.

"I don't know how that could have happened. No, I know. I'll get right on it. Helena can handle that. Alright, alright. I will see it gets done and then head east. Yes, I understand. I promise. I will take care of it."

There was silence for about two minutes, then Franks voice could almost be heard without the listening devices. "FUCK, FUCK, FUCK! That crazy bitch is going to land us all either in jail or buried in a construction site."

The back door slammed open so hard that it came off its hinges. Frank was heading to the car as he was talking on the phone. Birdman repositioned the drone silently above the car.

"Helena, stop the cleaning service people in Macon. If nothing happens at the building tonight bring them back. We have commitments. I need you to get a crew over to fix a window and a door at the mansion. There are some holes in the wall that will need some repair. I will leave it to your judgement to replace the pieces of furniture that are broken. I'm headed to Athens and make sure everything goes smoothly there. Oh, and Helena, Foster is pleased you cleared the building. That's about the only thing, he's happy about right now." Helena listened and thought to herself what an idiot Frank was. He had no idea who he was talking to.

He hung up, started the car and pulled quietly out of the driveway. Phelps watched and when he was out of sight continued to watch on his command tablet. The tracker was working. He picked up his phone and called Mary.

"Frank has left the building. I'm not sure how much of it is left after his meltdown but he got a call that spooked him back into thinking clearly. You heard he was talking with Helena, correct?"

Mary answered as she watched the tracker come up on the master map in the command center. All of the Smithson trackers were locked onto their satellite system and working perfectly. "I think we're all on our way to Greenville. Frank may be making a stop in Athens, but my money is he is headed to find his wife who we know is in Greenville. Birdman will land the drone when you return to your car. I'll brief the team in Greenville. You headed back here? You must be hungry."

Phelps laughed. "I'm headed back there but I'm not hungry." He looked at the empty basket where the ham biscuits had been. He quietly gathered his things and went downstairs. Tess was waiting for him at the bottom.

She spoke quietly. "She fell asleep a couple of hours ago. Can you give her call in the morning and tell her how important it was that you were here?"

Phelps smiled. "I can do that easily. Thank you again."

Tess smiled as she opened the back door for him. "Just follow that path, turn right when you get to the alley and it will put you out on the street where you parked. You be careful. That man is crazy. We will call if he shows back up."

Phelps thanked her again. "I don't think he will be coming back here but when someone shows up to fix the damage, I think he caused, could you give me a call? Tell Mrs. Ackerman it's the next important step."

Tess smiled. "That is exactly what I'll tell her. Good night, Agent Phelps and be careful."

Just as Phelps arrived back at his car, the small drone landed on the hood. He packed it away and headed to the Smithson Command Center.

In both Atlanta and Greenville, team members were gathered around watching the blinking moving lights on big and little screens. All the trackers were working fine. The one on the vehicle Vivian and Holder had arrived in was flashing away in the garage. Tobin's tracker was stationary somewhere to the west of Westminster, SC. Ludlow sent the two local officers to get some sleep. After they left, Lily looked at Ludlow.

"Do you think they're really coming here?"

"Yes. I don't have a doubt about it. I'm just not sure Vivian and Holder are supposed to be here. I sent that information to Dr. Morozov to put in the mix while you were changing. There has never been a documented instance where either she or her husband were at an event. Likewise, showing up here with Holder is strange. Maybe there is no event, but Tobin being so chatty in the bar tells me otherwise. Morozov is conducting some property record inquiries. We should have them in the morning."

"You think something is not going as expected. That means they are vulnerable to making a mistake. You want me in tactical gear tomorrow?"

Ludlow smiled. "I don't know. You were quite tactical in that dress tonight."

Lily punched him in the upper arm but hurt her fist. "Look who is talking, Mr. Custom-Made Suit and Shoes. We aren't going to say anything else about that dress. Why is it that everybody gets so crazy when I look like a woman?"

"Crazy isn't the right word. Lily, stop worrying about when you show your feminine side. Own it. Aside from being great at your job, the fact that you are pretty is just one more positive attribute. Don't let anyone turn that into a vulnerability. Don't indulge that as a distraction. You even kept your cool when Tobin approached you."

Lily laughed. "Tobin is not interested in me. I'm too young for him. He has 'granny' issues. You think he is here because they have a party planned."

Ludlow nodded. "When Charles Tobin is in town, the party can't be far behind. I'll say one thing for him. Like all pimps, he dresses the part, just a higher and more costly level."

"He certainly doesn't deny himself anything but you can't hide tacky. We got lucky with the watch."

Ludlow smiled. "All of this has been lucky for us. A few hours ago, we got a message that a few years ago most people would have ignored. But, lucky for us, a truck driver who gives a shit found that message. Also lucky for us, another truck driver paid close attention to behavior that he felt matched what he knew about trafficking. And let's not forget, again lucky for us, we have an Attorney General who takes human trafficking seriously and called us all in."

Lily smiled. "I like both her and Dr. Morozov. They're direct, don't suffer nonsense, and listen. She reminds me of Aunt Lydia. Always thinking, and rarely out of control."

Both of their command tablets buzzed.

Phelps came on the screen. "We are all headed your way. We will know where more clearly in the morning but I'm sending additional team members tonight just in case. Frank's heading east to Athens may mean he's headed to Greenville. We have the cars with the women who left the building stopped at a house in Athens. It looks like they will be staying over. The rest of us will be flying the jet in and landing early at the downtown airport tomorrow. I think we should stage from there. If they turn back west from Athens tomorrow, we can shift resources but since Vivian and Holder are there and we've had Tobin active, my gut tells me Greenville is where action is going to happen."

Lily cut Phelps off as she leaned in. "We'll be ready."

# CHAPTER 10

Tobin was in his RV drinking. Stokes had let the girls out of their rooms. Beth, Tiffany and Jillian were all gathered in Jillian's room. Stokes walked in and sat down with the girls. That was unusual.

"We are going to be headed to the final destination earlier than usual tomorrow." He nodded at Beth and Tiffany. "You two make sure you have what's needed for the party. You two can room together tonight if you want. "

He turned to Jillian. "I am going to be taking you to your mother. Before you ask, I don't know why or where yet. She's close by with Holder. I'll leave you three to it but it's lights out and doors locked in 30 minutes."

He turned and left. The three looked at each other. Beth was the first to speak.

"That's never happened before. You think this is some kind of setup?"

Tiffany looked just as shocked. "Stokes actually seemed like he was being nice. What do you think is up with that?"

Jillian was still looking at the space where he had been sitting. "He's not being nice. He's scared. Something has happened and it has to do with my mother and why I'm here."

Tiffany nodded her head. "You're right. He's scared shitless and so is fancy pants out there. Why are you here?"

"Everything changed when my brother was sent to live with Aunt Stella."

Beth looked shocked. "Stella St. John, the lawyer that is always getting us released from jail and the one that defended Holder last year? That Stella?"

Jillian nodded. "Jessie and I have never been separated before. We were never allowed to mix with other kids or any of you. We were the only company we had other than adults who most of the time were poking us or stroking us or doing worse."

Beth laughed. "You mean you were never allowed around us sluts?"

Jillian shook her head. "No, I don't think of you like prostitutes."

It was Tiffany's turn. "Sweetheart. We're not whores. There's a difference. Even hookers get to say no. We can't do that. I have to do everything they tell me or they'll kill me. Same with Beth. That's not whoring. That's slavery and it's gone on too long for me and Beth. We're both fed up. What we learned from the death of our two friends, Lucy and Crystal is to never come back. They did, they're dead. Being forced to listen to them being slaughtered in the film at first made us afraid. Later it just pissed us off. That's why we jumped at your revision of our plan when we did. Why did you decide to haul ass?"

Jillian looked them both straight in the eye. "My brother and I are slaves, too. He was sold and moved to another stable. My guess is this trip means that I'm next."

Beth stood up, walked over and used her toe to shut the door. She then hugged Jillian. "You don't know that, baby girl. But thanks for trying to help get us out, too."

Jillian hugged her then pulled back. "Something is wrong. Real wrong. My mother shouldn't be here and definitely not with Dex. What if our plan worked? What if help is on the way?"

Tiffany got up and hugged her. "Sweetheart, help has never been on the way."

They could hear someone walking down the hallway. Beth instinctively broke away and pulled the door ajar as she opened it. It was Tobin.

"Ladies, our gruff friend says its time to turn in." He looked at Beth and Tiffany. "I understand you two get to sleep together tonight. Don't do anything I wouldn't do. You'll need all your energy for tomorrow."

He turned to Jillian and hugged her. She didn't shrink back. She wanted him to continue to think of her as he always had.

"And you, my little darling, you will be reunited with your sweet mother. She is very anxious to see you. Stokes has assured both your mother and me that he will guard you with his life until you're back in her arms." He put his arm around her and guided her back to her room and once again, locked it as he left.

Jillian whispered to herself as she heard the lock turn. "Prick, fancily-dressed, but still a prick."

The following morning Frank woke Tobin at 7:00 am.

"Charley, go to the site early and make sure everything is set. If you find anything unusual call me. You did a good job putting the guest list together. Most of them have already transferred their fees. Have Stokes get the girls to the party at 6:30 pm. I have the party kicking off at 7:00 pm. The Atlanta entertainment will be arriving with security at 6:45 pm. Once you are sure the other guests have transferred the money, you can head off to your next destination. Raleigh is in a week. Any questions?"

Tobin hated being called Charley. Only Mommy could use that name for him, but it was Frank so he answered politely.

"I'll leave as soon as I talk to Stokes. Don't worry. It will be perfect. If you think of anything else, I'll be at the house in an hour and forty-five minutes."

Tobin wasn't even sure Frank was still on the phone to hear the last sentence. He called Stokes. "Meet me outside in five minutes."

Stokes was already out looking at his Dodge. He looked up at Tobin. What's up?"

"Frank called. He obviously hasn't spoken with Vivian. If I disliked the situation last night, I seriously hate it now. They are not working from the same playbook. I don't think Frank knows that Vivian is in Greenville. We need to just get through the next 12 hours. He wants me over at the house early to make sure everything is good and call him if I find anything unusual."

Stokes laughed. "Unusual like his wife fucking Dexter Holder in the party house?"

Tobin almost chuckled. "That act would not be unusual, but to find them there, would. I hope she is long gone by the time the party comes together. I have written down the address and directions. You can follow Highway 11 all the way around to the turn off. You never even have to go into town. I haven't heard from Vivian yet. You good with all this?"

Stokes shook his head. "It doesn't matter if I'm good with it or not. I will have the girls there when Vivian says to have them there. But as soon as I drop Jillian off, I'm back here and in that Charger and headed out. I don't want to be anywhere around if the shit hits the fan between Frank and Vivian."

"Me neither. I will drop the guests off and be gone as well. I'll be leaving in about 30 minutes."

Vivian was awake at 6:30 am. She let Dexter sleep. Her phone had buzzed all night with threats from Frank. She looked at her watch and checked the map on her phone to confirm the location of the party. She had just been to this house with Frank and Jillian a few weeks ago. Frank had known then that he was going to pass off Jillian at that location. He knew that if she recognized the place, she would drop her guard. She texted Tobin at 8:30 am.

"I want my baby in my arms at the mountain party house at 2:00 pm. If you tell Frank anything about this arrangement, I will make sure you die a very slow and painful death."

Tobin received the message and believed every word. He didn't text Stokes, he called him.

"You have to be at the party location at 2:00 pm with all the girls. Vivian wants you to bring Jillian there too."

Stokes thought he would need to make a slight adjustment but he said he would have them there.

Vivian woke Dexter at 9:00 am. She handed him a one-hundred-dollar bill. "Dex, once you get dressed, be a sweet man and go get us some breakfast at that cute little bakery in the bookstore next door. I'm famished. Get me two of the largest pastries they have and whatever you want for yourself then hurry back. We may have time for some fun before we check out. Oh, and coffee. Lots of coffee."

Dexter got up as requested. Vivian had been surprisingly nice to him except for the little gun against his dick thing. He dressed and left to get breakfast.

Vivian was on the phone moments after the door closed. Stella St. John, the Nightshade attorney and the woman she had entrusted her son to, answered.

"Stella, how fast can you get to Greenville?

"Well good morning to you too, Viv. I can be there in a bit over four hours maybe longer if traffic is bad. Do you need me to leave now?"

"Soon, and I need you to bring Jessie with you. We need rescuing!"

"Have you been arrested?"

"Being arrested would actually be better. Frank has been conspiring to sell Jillian. I'm not going to let that happen but I need time to let him cool down and I need her safe. You will keep her safe until I come and get her, won't you?"

"Of course. Don't say anything else. I can be there by 3:00 pm at the latest. I will text when I get close. Jessie is up already and has finished his run. We will see you soon." Stella hung up. Stella hated talking on the phone to her clients, particularly these clients.

By the time Dexter returned, Vivian was dressed. He walked in and put the bag down on the desk in the room. He took his pastry out, then took Vivian her two and her coffee. "I guess there will be no playing around then."

Vivian looked over at him. "Dexter don't pout. It doesn't suit you and you flat wore me out last night. I couldn't manage another orgasm if I wanted to." Vivian thought to herself, false praise for this fool's manhood will put him right where I need him. She continued.

"I need to think this through. Tobin will already be on his way to the house. I want to surprise him and get there around noon. What time is check out?"

Holder looked at the hotel information. "It's noon. The house is about 30 minutes away."

Vivian smiled. "Then relax Dexter. We will leave here at 11:30 am and surprise Mr. Tobin."

Unbeknownst to the two in that room, three miles to the east the rest of the federal task force was getting organized in the hanger at the airport. They were interrupted when Claymore, still back in Atlanta at his control desk, alerted them.

"I hope you guys are ready. The detail on the two in the hotel just reported that Holder went out and returned with food. The car is still parked in the valet section of the garage. They paid for one night in cash and checkout time is noon." He paused to let that sink in.

"Mr. Tobin is on the move and headed back toward Greenville taking the scenic Route 11 along the foothills. That tells me he's not going into town. Last night, Dr. Morozov updated several of the addresses held by the holding companies. There are four in the direction he's headed. If he is there to coordinate a party, he may be headed to one of those sites. Dr. Morozov has requested a conference shortly."

Lily looked at Ludlow. "It looks to me like we could use some local knowledge. Is it OK to share this with Roseanne? I can have her here in 30 minutes.

Ludlow nodded. "Call her and have Wormer come as well. If we need one, we will need both."

As Lily stepped aside to call, Alex bounced into the area after she had a private conversation with Claymore following his briefing. "So, tell us about what we may be looking at. Birdman is making noises about a place called Caesar's Head State Park and every form of raptor known to man. Did you know he talks fast when he talks about birds? It's odd because he is so slow with everything else."

Everyone smiled and nodded. Phelps and Ludlow were looking at the new analysis that Dr. Morozov had sent them. They set up a video session with her and projected the image up on a sheet they hung on the wall of the hanger as a screen. Mary walked in fresh from briefing the AG.

Dr. Morozov came up on the screen. She was seated at her console with Rasputin sprawled across the carpet beneath.

"Good morning, all. You have been very busy since we last spoke."

Phelps took the lead. "It looks like you have been just as busy. There is a lot new in this report"

"Oh, it's not new, it's just been hiding in plain sight for someone with the right skills to find. My little machine and I have got our noses poked into lots of different rabbit holes. The Nightshade operation is definitely tied to all the properties you examined. There is no doubt in my mind that the rate they buy and sell makes lots of dirty money clean. The list I sent you for Greenville County and two counties in all directions are all owned by the same subsidiary that owned the locations in Atlanta. Any questions?"

Ludlow spoke first. "Did you find any connection with the location I sent you in Oconee County? We think that might be where Tobin has been staying."

"Just a moment. Let me adjust the search." There was a brief pause. "Oh, my goodness. It looks like a Christmas tree. One of the ornaments is that location Let me show you."

With two key strokes, a map appeared. Dr. Morozov continued.

"The red dots are those properties they currently own. They stretch all the way from Georgia to Charlotte and beyond. I have the cursor over the one you mentioned. Some of these are large multimillion-dollar homes but most are more modest even down to a couple of single-wide mobile homes. Now watch as I adjust the search engine to show you these properties plus the ones that they have owned and sold within the last two years."

Another 20 dots appeared on the screen. It was mindboggling. The view switched back to the doctor. Rasputin was now sitting with his chin resting on the desk. She stroked his head and smiled as she looked up.

Phelps asked the final question. "If you were to go to the larger more elegant properties on this map, which has the highest probability of hosting an exclusive private party without making too much of a commotion in the Greenville area?"

Dr. Morozov smiled broadly and added the tracker signals. They all looked at the flashing light of the tracker on Charles Tobin's BMW as it came to a halt over a red dot close to the border with North Carolina. "Phelps, I don't want to overstate the obvious but Rasputin and I believe it is that one."

Roseanne arrived and stood there fascinated looking at the map.

Lily greeted her. "Glad you could make it."

Roseanne smiled back. "Wormer is on his way. How can I help? This is really exciting. I didn't even know this type of stuff existed."

"Up until recently, it didn't. We think we know where they are going to be holding a party tonight." Lily pointed at the blinking light. "That is the tracker you help set last night on Mr. Tobin's car. We need some local knowledge on how to approach it."

Roseanne studied the map. "I've been up in that area several times with task force members. The photo shows you have two possible approaches from the rear. One is a fire road and the other is a power company easement. The last is the best this time of year, without the rain. It's a bit of a bumpy ride, but the best of the two. It gets you close, then it's just a walk through the woods to the rear of the house. Lots of trees between the house and both of the rear roads."

Lily stopped her. "They are probably rigged with sensors. Let me get Ludlow and Phelps over here." She motioned and they joined the two women looking at the photos. Lily nodded for Roseanne to continue.

"Looking at the aerial, someone has built this house for privacy. The drive is a quarter of a mile long and totally visible from the living room. You can see they've trimmed the trees to keep it that way with both sides of the drive having thicker cover. At the rear, it's heavily wooded. If you're not too obvious, you can use that power company road. That would give you command and control from the rear. Then just make sure to block the main entrance so nobody escapes."

Birdman had been looking over her shoulder. "What about the fire access road?"

Roseanne shook her head. "It's really rough. The easement is better maintained."

Birdman scanned the map. "Can you guide me to that location on the power company easement?"

Roseanne turned and stuck out her hand. "I'm Officer Roseanne Smith, and who are you?"

He blushed as usual. "You can call me Birdman. I fly drones for this bunch."

"Birdman, I can guide you and anybody else we need to that very spot. As long as there are not too many of us and we're careful, we won't be seen."

# CHAPTER 11

Ludlow and Phelps checked the tracker activity. In Athens the vehicles were still in place. Ludlow contacted the Marshals that were watching both locations. There was movement in the houses but no sign that they were pulling out. Ludlow figured that they would not leave until it was closer to the time of the party which was probably scheduled for the evening. It was Vivian and Holder that bothered him and Phelps the most. Check out time at the hotel was noon. They figured that they needed to get into position before Vivian showed up. Moving in too late would risk discovery and blow the entire effort. Ludlow consulted with the two local officers about a place to park the command vehicle closer to the party house. They made a suggestion and the arrangements and the entire rescue team deployed to a location behind a church a mile from the house. Once that was accomplished, Officer Smith, Deputy Wormer, Lily, Alex, and Birdman left with a team of Marshals to survey and secure an approach from the power company road at the rear of the property.

They arrived and as the Marshals set a secure perimeter, Lily and Alex put on their equipment. Officer Smith thought that in their gear they looked like they were from outer space. Both had fully integrated electronic assault helmets and were equipped with climbing gear and backpacks full of all sorts of little eavesdropping transmitters. They crossed over the rear property line through the woods. Roseanne lost sight of them immediately. They couldn't have been more than 20 yards from her, but they had blended in with the trees.

Birdman came up behind her. "It's amazing isn't it. One moment they're here and the next minute they're not. Let me show you some other interesting things."

They walked back to the Smithson vehicle where he had already set up the drone. It was two feet across with what seemed like an endless number of little fans that could rotate and move. He picked up his control console and the drone lifted silently. That would have been enough but two other smaller drones rose from the front of the vehicle at the same time.

"I can fly all three either together or independently. They are equipped with several small remote cameras with microphones they can install for us. But first we have to check and see how technical our opposition is." He spoke to Alex and Lily through his headset.

"The drones are launched. Stand by for sensor check. It will broadcast in five, four, three, two, one."

He turned the control console so Roseanne could see it.

"What are all those little blinking dots?"

Birdman smiled. "Those are sensors the property owners have installed to detect any intruders which is what Lily and Alex are about to become. They are active but have been shut off, probably because they are expecting friendly company at the house. This same map is showing on a heads-up display in the helmets the girls are wearing. They see and hear everything we do. Now with the push of a button, we lock onto their sensors and jam their signals. They appear to be working to those inside but they are completely useless." Roseanne stood there amazed.

A mile away in the temporary command center, the arrest team members were listening to all of this as they were going over the floor plans. The house had two floors above ground and one below. Each floor had four bedrooms. In addition to the bedrooms, the lower level had the garage, a walk-in wine cellar, a storeroom, and a central equipment room, probably for the alarm and utilities. The ground floor had the master and three other bedrooms, a huge kitchen and dining room and a large great room that looked out over the property. The top floor had four bedrooms, each with its own bath. Ludlow had positioned perimeter spotters hidden along the roads leading to the turn off for the property.

The house was a masterwork in stone, brick, wood, and copper. Alex had made her way to the left rear corner of the house and was climbing up using the decorative brick edging. The offset corner stones were perfect for giving her access to the roof. Lily was doing the same on the far rear corner but had to maneuver around a decorative copper downspout. Once on top, they both set an anchor so if they needed to rappel down when it came time to breech the door and gain entry, they could. Then they both went about setting listening devices on the upstairs windows.

Alex typed into her handset. "Top floor wired for sound. Returning." Then dropped down and fastened a device to a window on a downstairs hallway.

Lily stopped her descent at a balcony on the second floor. She swung onto it and placed a small dime-sized device that gathered not only sound but video as well. She then jumped silently to the next balcony over and did the same. Finally, she returned to the corner, dropped six feet and set a device high on the first floor window. She slipped to the ground, retrieved her rappel line so it wouldn't draw attention, and disappeared into the woods.

At the other corner, Alex concealed her rappel line and came back through the trees and joined the rest of the group. Alex took off her helmet and looked at Birdman.

"Are we broadcasting well enough?"

He confirmed they were working, but then added. "We might want to put up a directional aimed at the ground floor from the trees. That might pick up what's happening on the ground floor better. Lily, who had not removed her helmet yet, grabbed the stand and listening device, checked the charge on the battery, and disappeared into the woods. A moment later, sound appeared magically in their headsets.

Birdman spoke into his headset. "Guests arriving up the front drive. It looks like it is our suspects from the hotel. Nice Mercedes." He turned to

Officer Smith. "It's getting crowded down there. Lots more eyes that might look this way. Let's get back up the road farther."

"Will that controller work from up there?"

"It would work from town. And I have two more smaller drones we will use in this operation. The ones we have up now fly by themselves unless I override them. They give us all a bird's eye view." Roseanne just shook her head as they walked back up the road.

Holder held the door open as Vivian made her grand entrance into the party house. It was the only kind of entrance she ever made around the help. Her voice was velvet encased in razor blades.

"Charles, my daughter better walk through this door at the appropriate time, or tonight all the guests will find you filleted on the bar like cheap sushi."

Tobin tried to fake a grin. "Vivian they are already on their way here. I wanted to make sure we had enough time for you to get Jillian and be far away by the time the guests arrive."

Vivian smiled. "I may decide to stay. Dexter, be a sweetheart and fix me a drink. Double whiskey, the high proof one, neat." She turned to Charles. "What time does the food get here?"

"The food arrives at 4:00 pm. I will be happy to fix you your drink. I was about to set up the bar."

Vivian smiled. "Call them and tell them to deliver the food now and add something nice for lunch. Dexter, Charley will fix my drink."

Tobin's smile fooled no one. God this woman knew how to get under a man's skin. He poured her four fingers of Knob Creek and took it over and set it on the table next to her. She stopped and looked at him from two feet away. He paused, then picked up the drink and handed it to her.

The conversation inside the house was just casual chit-chat. Tobin was definitely being deferential to Vivian.

A spotter broke into the communication. "I have a delivery truck slowing down to make the turn into the target. Signage and South Carolina plates come back to High Country Catering."

Mary checked them out on her command module. "They seem legit."

Everyone agreed that they would just let the delivery go through. The people delivered the food and were back in the van and headed out in 30 minutes.

Mary who had been monitoring the conversation, laughed. "Vivian must be eating. No one but Charles is talking. Everyone listened more intently. "You got to hear this." Everyone could hear Charles for a three-mile radius in their headsets.

"Please, Vivian, I'm begging you. Just leave after she gets here."

Phelps looked at Mary. "Do we have any evidence that she or Frank or anyone else that high up in the organization ever supervises a working site?

Mary shook her head. "Nope. I'll see what type of legal status we have to detain her for questioning." She was on the satellite phone to the AG's office.

Phelps turned his attention to Ludlow. "It sounds like Vivian is here to pick someone up. It could be the 15-year-old daughter. She might be why Vivian is here. It doesn't sound like Tobin expected this."

Ludlow spoke into the command mic. "I need all entry teams to go to their locations and standby for multi-entry. Stay low, stay quiet, and stay ready."

All around the house, the proper people put on the proper gear and took up their positions.

Frank was going over his Vivian dilemma in Athens. He had to figure out where she was. His men were getting the women from Atlanta ready to head to Greenville for the party. That was the only thing that seemed to be going well.

He was startled by his phone ringing.

"Frank, it's Helena. I wanted to let you know things are quiet here. The crew we moved is already back out at work and I have increased external security. Nothing out of the ordinary has happened. I may have stirred things up for no reason."

"It's always better to respond than to sit there and wait for the knock on the door. What was it that made you think those cops weren't local?"

"It was their badges. One was a circle with a star in it. The other was dull brass like a regular police badge. I couldn't read what they said. They almost looked fake."

Frank stopped cold.

"Helena, I think they may have been federal. We need to have security take the electronic surveillance detectors and cover the entire building, inside and out."

"But they just came in, looked around, and left. How could they have done that? I was with them the whole time."

"It could have been a setup to make us clear the building so they could install listening devices. Just text me back if they find anything. Check the vehicles for the boxy tracking devices they use. You can't miss them. Search the entire property."

Frank hung up and called the house where the three carloads from Atlanta were staying. "Check the cars for trackers. If you find any, leave them and move the cars to a public parking lot. I will get you new vehicles. Call me back."

He thought about checking his own car but he had been nowhere near the Atlanta facility in months. He went out and checked for trackers just the same.

Hidden in the trees across from Frank, two Marshals watched this whole drama play out. They called Ludlow.

"Frank just got antsy about his car. We turned off the transmitter once we saw him come out of the house. It didn't look to us like he found it. Whatever that new thing is, it worked like a charm." They watched as Frank returned to the house brushing himself off.

Ludlow smiled. "I'll let the team at the other house know, but we turned all of them off once they were in for the night. Good job. Stay on Frank."

Once inside, Frank received a text from Helena that they found no transmitting devices. He convinced himself his worries were carryover from his crazy wife. The cops had never been able to keep up with Nightshade technology nor their flexibility in relocating. They couldn't keep track of one car let alone all these. There had been no follow-up on the news or the police band about the I-20 note thing. For Beth and Tiffany, fooling Dexter would be just one hand job away. But Jillian was smart. They would never get anything past her. Thinking of Jillian reminded him. The cops were the least of his worries with his goddamned wife out there somewhere making threats.

A mile away from the party house in Greenville, Stokes pulled the car over to the side of the road. He turned to Jillian who was up front next to him. "Jillian, I am going to take you in first. Just walk directly to your mother." He turned to Beth and Tiffany and spoke calmly.

"I suspect that Dexter's ass is in a bind from the note caper. I don't care shit about that. You're my responsibility now and my orders are to deliver you in one piece to work. You can't work if Dex does what I think he will. I will be locking this car while I take Jillian in. It's a two door. It will be tough to get out but for your own safety, stay here. I will come and get you and take you in. Stay close to me. When I tell you, walk straight to Tobin who will take you to your rooms. Don't answer that door unless it is Tobin or myself. Understood?"

Beth spoke. "Why are you being so nice?"

"Don't confuse nice with practical. My job is to deliver you to work not deliver you to be whacked around by a nut job that you already outsmarted. He's in trouble because of you."

Tiffany spoke. "He's horny and stupid."

"Listen to me. Those are both very dangerous things. Stay close to me."

Both girls nodded.

He started the Charger up, revved the engine to get his adrenaline pumping a bit faster and pulled back onto the road. Everyone on the team watched from their positions as the car traveled to the house.

When they arrived Jillian and Stokes got out. Jillian spotted her mother's car. As they walked toward the door she spoke quietly. "Stokes, why is my mom really here? She's never at these. Why come for me now?"

"I don't know. Let's hope she just misses you and wants to take you far away from here. If Holder is in the room don't even make eye contact with him."

They entered the house and Jillian walked through the living room straight to her mother and embraced her. Vivian held her tight and spoke softly.

"Thank God you're here. Let's go into the bedroom where we can talk privately. I have something to tell you."

They left the room. Stokes looked over at Tobin who nodded toward the stairwell that led downstairs. Stokes nodded back and left to get Tiffany and Beth. As they walked toward the front door, he spoke softly.

"If Dexter appears in front of us, stay behind me. If he somehow gets behind us, drop to the ground when I tell you. You're both tough as nails or you wouldn't have made it this far. We good?"

They whispered in unison. "We're good."

The trio got about 15 feet inside the door when Holder came at them from the downstairs stairwell they had just passed. Tiffany who was the last in, heard him first. Remembering Stokes' instructions, she dropped to her knees. As she dropped, she swiveled round and brought her fist up squarely into Dexter's crotch hard. He fell two steps back grabbing himself. Beth, who had dropped when she felt Tiffany turn leapt over her, pushed him backwards off his feet and jumped on him punching Dexter in the face several times before grabbing his hair and banging his head on the floor. Stokes pulled her off and kneeled down over Dexter with his knife. The only thing that stopped him was the barrel of Vivian's gun pressed against his temple.

"That's enough. You take care of the girls." She shifted the barrel to Dexter's forehead.

"Dexter, Dexter, Dexter. You know the rules. You do not beat up on the staff." She pulled the gun back, and kicked him hard, right where Tiffany had hit him. He lay there crippled and moaning.

Vivian looked at Tobin. "Well, that would have made a nasty little mess in the foyer. You and Stokes tie this idiot up and find a room downstairs with a drain in it that will make it easy for the cleaning crew. I'm tired of fucking with Holder. And before that clever little mouth of yours reacts to my poor choice of words you need to know I'm still not over that you didn't call me yourself when you saw Jillian being transported like the help."

There was no doubt what Vivian meant. Tobin got the message clearly. "There is a storage room in the basement with a drain in the floor. When Stokes gets back, we can put him there. I think we'll have to carry him. Your kick did some damage."

"And to the only useful part of the man. Pity. Such a waste."

Stokes arrived back after locking Beth and Tiffany in their room. Vivian turned her attention to him. "Mr. Stokes, I'm Vivian Bartram. I'm sorry we had to meet under these circumstances. Thank you for bringing them here safely. Please help Charles move Mr. Holder to a more secure location. After that, I think it will be a good idea for you to move your nice car to the back. Once I think things through perhaps you can take me for a ride in it."

Stokes nodded his head and helped Tobin gather Holder up and drag him down the stairs. Vivian put her small 9mm pistol back in its holster under her sweater and headed back to the bedroom to finish her conversation with her daughter.

# CHAPTER 12

Jillian was sitting on the bed staring out the window. Vivian walked in and sat down next to her and began.

"Sweetheart. It seems like ages."

Jillian got up and walked toward the window and continued to stare out. Everyone outside stayed motionless as they listened.

"It has been ages, Vivian. I've been cooped up in the Charleston house for days when I wasn't being hauled around the south in the middle of the night. I hope your little adventure was worth it."

That brought Vivian up short. Jillian had never used that tone with her or anyone. Vivian regained her composure and started over.

"Jillian, I'm sorry you felt abandoned. Please know I have loved you and your brother since the moment I saw you both. I have grown to love you both more as time has gone by. I realize that you haven't had the childhood other children have but we have a very different lifestyle that allows us to have nice things and go nice places."

Jillian turned and faced her. "Well, you certainly go nicer places than I do. I was locked in the bedroom of a run-down house in the middle of nowhere last night. But first things first, why did you give Jessie to Aunt Stella?"

"Sweetheart, Jessie is safe with Stella. It was just part of a larger plan to keep you both safe."

Jillian wasn't having any of it. There were no tears just a quiet measured tone.

"Safe? Was it safe for dad to have me carted all over the place with the other women in the middle of the night, switching cars? Am I being groomed to become one of them?"

Vivian looked away. "That wasn't my idea and I just learned of that."

"You being gone all the time allowed it. While we're talking about our 'different' lifestyle, by that do you mean when you forced Jessie and me to pretend to have sex with each other when we were what, seven? Not exactly the definition of 'motherly love' other mothers in this world might have. As for keeping us safe, you've rented us out, you've sold movies of us, you've made us dance naked in front of strangers who were disgustingly busy satisfying themselves. Were you thinking of our 'safety' then. I'd rather believe you were thinking about money no matter where you were or what you were doing. Don't tell me you were thinking of us."

Jillian paused, breathing hard, gathering her thoughts. Before she could go on, Vivian confronted her.

"I'm here now because your father, who engineered Jessie's departure has arranged yours without my knowledge. I am here now because those two girls were smart enough to leave a note on Holder's watch. I was sent to deal with him or I would have had no idea. You and I are leaving here before this whole party kicks off. We are leaving as soon as our ride gets here."

"And who will my chauffer be this time? Who will be locking me in a car or a bedroom for this trip?"

"Stella is on her way with your brother. We are going to get out of here and far away before your father finds out. He will calm down given enough time. You and I can hide until then."

"No."

"What?"

"I want him here. I want him to face me and explain how he could do this to his own children. Try to take me away, and you'll spend most of your time keeping me a prisoner. This mother and daughter shit has run its course with us. You two made me a whore before I could even say the word.

I won't play this game any longer."

"Now you listen to me. Your father is not a sane individual. He's dangerous enough when he's not mad. He becomes lethal when he's pissed. Their little scheme interrupted plans he had to trade you or sell you. If he finds us, he will kill me and do God knows what with you."

Jillian smiled. "Just so you know, the note was my idea. I told you. I'm done being your whore. Frank needs to hear that from me. If he gets mad and kills me, I don't care. At least I won't be what I am now. Call him. I dare you. Call him."

Vivian's plan was coming apart. "I can't do that to you. We have to get away from here."

Jillian was quick to counter. "Call him and we'll leave before he gets here."

Vivian stood and walked across the room and looked out the window. "I will give that some thought. You won't get what you want."

"At least I will get the opportunity to tell him I'm not his little slut daughter any longer."

"What did you three think that note you left would accomplish? Did you really think that anyone would come running to save you? Most people don't even know people like us exist."

Jillian broke into her lecture. "Or they don't want to admit that people like you and Dad exist."

"Sweetheart. Nobody paid attention to that note. We would know by now. No one is coming to your rescue but me."

Vivian put her hand on Jillian's shoulder. "Let me think about how to handle this."

Jillian just silently turned and looked out the window. Vivian left the room sobbing quietly. She had to get herself together before she got around the help.

Outside, 30 sets of ears belonging to that collective "nobody" heard and recorded the entire exchange.

Inside Vivian looked at Stokes as she walked into the living room. "Mr. Stokes, I would like you to stay for a bit. Then I want you to drive my daughter and me away from here. I will pay you extra."

Stokes smiled. "Mrs. Bartram, I'm a simple man. I stay in my lane. No offense but unless you point that gun at me and order me to do that, it's not going to happen. I will stay here until the others arrive to make sure the fool downstairs doesn't cause any more problems. Nothing more. I don't want to spend the rest of my life worrying about how far away Frank and his men are. As far as paying me, that won't be necessary. I've already been paid to deliver the three women I picked up in good condition. Once the others arrive, I will be leaving on my own just like always."

Vivian smiled at him. "I appreciate your honesty. It' refreshing. I will make other arrangements."

She walked over to Tobin. "What time are the others getting here?"

"They are supposed to be here at 6:45 pm."

"Unlock the girls, let them mingle. Jillian is lonely." Tobin nodded but had no intention of unlocking any doors.

The rescue team watched as Vivian stepped outside to call Stella.

"How far away are you?"

"We're about 20 minutes outside Greenville, but I don't know where I'm going."

"I'll contact you in 10 with a location to meet me."

Back in the living room she looked at Tobin. "Where is the nearest store, where I can get a pack of cigarettes? I need a break."

Tobin instantly become enthralled with the idea of Vivian not being there. He had plenty of cigarettes but he figured she just needed a break, as he did. He directed her to the nearest convenience store. She grabbed her purse and looked at Stokes. "I'll be right back. Keep my little girl safe."

Stokes nodded.

She walked back outside and texted Stella the location where she would meet them. She then returned to the house, walked into Jillian's room and tossed her phone on the bed. "Go ahead. Call your dad. I'm going for cigarettes."

From the drone they saw Vivian walk out to her car get in and drive away. The order was given to let her go. The tracker was still working and Ludlow and Phelps thought from the conversation that she would be retuning. After all, why would Vivian leave the daughter she had come for?

Ludlow gave the order. "Units six and nine, follow her. Everybody else get into final position in case we need to make entry. Alex, go high. I believe we heard the rest of the participants are arriving at 6:45 pm. I don't trust that, so we will use that as an outside limit. Everyone get comfortable, but no one goes till I give the order."

Everyone clicked their microphones in acknowledgement.

Lily and Alex moved slowly through the woods to get into position. Lily was concealed in the trees about 12 feet from the patio adjacent to one of the ground floor bedrooms. The sound transmitter indicated it was the same room where Jillian had the conversation with her mother.

Alex was on the roof tied into the rappel line. She was sure she heard voices just below her. Everyone was in place watching the feed from the drone should they have to make an emergency entry. Lily was surprised by Jillian stepping out onto the patio. Everyone saw it. Ludlow gave Lily two pings in her headset which signaled she was authorized to make contact. Lily took off her helmet remembering the name she had heard.

"Jillian, is that your name?"

Jillian turned toward the voice.

"I'm here to help but it's better if you don't look toward me."

Jillian understood immediately. "Are you here because of the note?"

"Yes, that was really clever. How many are watching you?"

"My mom and two others. There is a fourth, Holder, but he's tied up downstairs because he screwed up and allowed us to leave that note."

Lily continued. "Is your mom Vivian Bartram."

Jillian laughed. "She is the woman who raised me to be what I am."

Lily waited. "Sounds like there's more to that story."

"You have no idea. What do I do now?"

"How many can't just walk out of the house?"

"I'm surprised I could. The other door is locked. I can't leave nor can the two who left the note with me. We are locked in our rooms. There are more women coming for a sex party tonight."

Lily thought quickly. "Do you know where the other two are?"

Jillian turned around and looked up at the balcony to her left. "I think they are in the one on the right."

"What time is the party supposed to happen?

"I heard them talking about 6:30 or 7:00 pm. First there will be a bunch of armed men with the other working women. The clients will arrive after they get here. After that, the party won't take long and will be over by 9:00 pm. Then they will pack Beth and Tiffany up with the other women into a van and disappear. I don't know what will happen with me. My folks are fighting over that. I just want out."

Lily responded "That's why we're here Jillian, to get you all out."

"Just tell me what to do."

"Are you expected to participate in the party?"

"Who knows? I never have before at one like this, but this whole trip is different."

"After everyone arrives, start looking this way. I will flash a little red light and you just go lock yourself in the bathroom, get in the bathtub and stay there till I come and get you."

"Are you going to hurt my mom?"

"We are going to try not to hurt anyone."

"Then you need to know I just called my dad. He will be arriving with the others. Mom doesn't know that yet."

Everyone with a headset tuned into the conversation shuddered.

"It will be fine. Just go back inside and wait. Remember to look for my signal. It's really important you act like we aren't here."

Jillian turned to go back in. She stopped, turned back around and looked up at the treetops like she was looking at a bird. "Thank you."


It was confirmed that Frank had joined the Atlanta group and that they were on their way to Greenville.

Upon receiving Frank's change in plans, Ludlow consulted Phelps and Mary. "What do you think? Do we go in now, or do we wait?"

Phelps spoke first. "If Frank and Vivian show up and the party starts, we have the opportunity to not only save the girls but arrest two of the major players in Nightshade. From what we heard, there is a huge disagreement there. There are all sorts of possibilities there even if they won't testify against each other."

Mary had been listening quietly then she seemed to settle on a statement. "I'll call the AG. See what she suggests. "

Phelps looked at Ludlow. "What are the risks versus gains?"

Ludlow laughed. "Much better now before the security shows up. But what would we achieve? We already know Vivian is just being a mom here. Jillian walked out of the house. That is a lapse on someone's part if she is truly being trafficked. She could have kept right on walking. We have the two upstairs that might be enough to hold Stokes. All Tobin has done is plan a party, and if it is Holder secured downstairs, they have done our job for us. Let's see what the AG thinks. We will need an entry warrant unless we find out that the girls upstairs are being held against their will."

Mary heard him as she returned thought. " I have an idea. I need to talk to Birdman."

Upstairs, Beth and Tiffany had been going through the normal drill for a party, making sure there were plenty of towels and tissues located in strategic places. This was going to be a two on one for them. If they were lucky and their guy was older, it would be over quick and they could entertain him by pretending to please each other. It worked every time with the older guys.

Tiffany sat down on the bed, filing her nails looking out at the tree tops. She thought she saw something fly by the window. "What the hell was that?"

Beth turned around. "What?"

"Something mechanical just flew by the window."

"You mean like a flying saucer? What have you been smoking?" Beth walked over and twisted the knob to the patio door. She was shocked. It opened. "I guess they think we won't jump."

Tiffany got up. "Tobin is probably too freaked with Vivian to have checked properly. I wish I had bummed a cigarette from Stokes. I could really use a smoke." She followed Beth outside.

Both girls were looking at the trees when Birdman guided the small drone Kestrel to descend from just above them.

Tiffany shocked blurted out "See, I didn't imagine it. You think this is some new thing they have to keep track of us?"

Beth just stared at it. "Must be. I don't know where else it could come from."

A voice from just above them answered. "It's from us. Don't look up."

Tiffany started to look up but Beth stopped her. "Shit girl, listen to directions for once. Keep looking at those trees."

From above Alex calmly continued on the conversation.

"We got your note. My name is Alex. Our little flying friend is Kestrel. We are here to help."

Tiffany really wanted to look up but Beth kept a tight grip on her arm and answered.

"What do you need us to do?

"When does the party start?"

"It's supposed to start at 7:00 pm but our guy won't be up here until after 7:30 at the earliest."

"Why are you two together? Is it because of the note?"

Tiffany answered this time. "They didn't take that note seriously. We are a two for one tonight. Two girls one client. I think I heard there are eight other girls coming."

"How many are watching you now?"

Tiffany continued. "We don't know. Our driver delivered us and actually saved us from having the shit beat out of us by our original driver guy. I punched him in the balls so I'm going to need someone to kill that bastard because if he gets loose, he's definitely coming after my ass."

"We won't let that happen. If you wanted to leave, would they stop you?"

Beth answered. "Hell yes, they'd stop us. Right now, the door is locked. When they arrive, the security guys will be armed."

Alex thought then asked. "Are the security guys ever in the room with you?"

Both answered. "No, too spooky for the clients. But they will be in the hall close by in case the client gets too physical."

Alex thought again. "So, if you call them in, they come."

"Beth answered. "They're supposed to but we've never had to call them. We can take care of ourselves."

Behind them, they heard the key in the lock. The girls turned, hurried back in and saw it was Stokes with hamburgers. Beth spoke as he put the tray down. "This door is unlocked. What's up with that?" These girls were good.

Tiffany looked at him as they walked in and shut the balcony door. "Can I have a cigarette?"

Stokes laughed. "No. Your client specified no smoking. And brush your teeth and use the mouthwash after you eat. Your burgers have onions and they are only good the first time around. Eat now so you will be all nice for the client."

He walked to the balcony door, checked the lock and looked out at the treetops. "You'll break a leg if you jump. That is a great view."

Beth answered as she walked inside. "You have no idea."

Back at the command bus, Ludlow contacted the two marshals he had sent to follow Vivian. He needed to keep track of her. They reported that she was parked about a mile away behind a convenience store. She had gone in, bought cigarettes, and returned to her car. She was still just sitting there. Ludlow turned to Mary and Phelps.

"What do you think she is doing? She has had plenty of time to return to the house and get Jillian. That's why we left Jillian there. Frank is on his way and will be here right on time."

Phelps spoke first. "Maybe she is trying to figure out what to do. She has to know that Jillian has called Frank and he knows where they are. I think she is going to wait until closer to the party then take Jillian just before Frank gets there."

Mary looked pensive and interjected. "Maybe she has decided that it's too dangerous to go back if Frank is there."

The two men looked at her as she continued. They were having a hard time grasping the concept that a mother, even Vivian, would leave her daughter in such a predicament. Ludlow voiced their concern. "You think she would leave Jillian in that situation?"

Mary nodded. "She might think that Frank, with his men close at hand, is too much for her to handle. Maybe it would be a better plan to wait until she has a better opportunity to get Jillian when the odds are more in her favor. She can't count on Holder any longer if what Jillian said is true. He's likely not to make it out of that house alive. It doesn't sound like she would have any help from Stokes. Maybe he would want to curry favor with Frank and prevent them from leaving. As far as Tobin is concerned, who knows which side he would choose. My guess is he would stay out of it and hide till the smoke clears. Maybe she realizes that Jillian is safe because she is so valuable. I'm just thinking out loud here."

Ludlow thought. "We have the tracker on her car. We will monitor the situation and see what happens.

# CHAPTER 13

Vivian sat in her car behind the convenience store a mile from the party house. As tough as she was, Vivian couldn't make herself go back to the house. She loved her daughter but she knew Jillian was determined. Once Frank heard what she had to say there was no question he would head to the party and she had no idea where he was. If she went back, he would kill her, guests or no guests. He would have plenty of his security guys with him. He would be in control. At best he would shoot her right there. At worst, he would have them take her and kill her later when he could enjoy it.

She was sure he wouldn't hurt Jillian. She was too valuable to the organization. Vivian thought about turning herself in to the nearest FBI office, but she wasn't sure she trusted Stella to protect Jessie if she was gone. Stella had made millions off Nightshade. She would keep quiet and help her and the kids get safe as long as Vivian was still involved. But if she decided to cooperate with the feds, everything would change. She was weighing all of this when Stella and Jessie pulled up.

Vivian got out of the car and barely got to her feet before Jessie was in her arms. He had grown. Her little boy had turned into a man, and quite a man at that. Jessie was 6'1"and all muscle. And, his voice had changed.

"Mom, I've missed you so much.

"My you have grown. I've missed you, too. Have you been working out?"

"Yeah, Stella and I go to the gym when she's in town and I go by myself when she's not. She also bought me a membership in her gun club, and I've become interested in computers."

Vivian had to catch her breath. "Sweetheart, slow down and let me hug you some more." She looked at Stella and raised one eyebrow. Stella just smiled. "What is this car and did I see you behind the wheel?"

Jessie smiled broadly. "Stella bought it for me and I got my permit last week."

"But you just turned 15. How did that happen?"

Stella spoke. "We found a way. He drives me everywhere now and the car was purchased for cash from the money we have been setting aside for both of them."

Vivian finally let go of him and stepped back. Finally, the facade faded and she began to weep. She hadn't seen Jessie in over eight months and she hadn't realized until now how much she missed them both.

Jessie took her back in his arms and comforted her. "Where is Jill?"

Vivian hung on. "She's nearby. We are going to get her. Just not right yet."

Stella looked over Jessie's shoulder as he held Vivian and spoke.

"I don't know what you've gotten yourself into this time but it must be big. My phone has been blowing up with messages from Frank."

Vivian broke from Jessie. "Does he know you're here?"

"Of course not. I turned the tracking on both our phones off. Please tell me you did too."

"The moment Frank sent me to take care of Holder and his car, I knew something was up. Jillian just told me she wants out. She thinks she left a trail the cops could follow. She just confronted her father with the same speech."

Stella smiled. "If the cops had taken notice, I would have heard. Holder has become expendable I would imagine. Where is he now?"

"Up the road at the house where they are having an event tonight. He was tied up after he went after the girls that left the note. No doubt he has become very expendable. Frank won't waste a moment and Holder won't leave that property."

Stella stopped smiling. "Tell me you are not anywhere near a location where there is an event. You know how risky that can be. How far away is this house?"

"It's less than a mile back that way. I need you to go pick up Jillian before Frank gets here."

Stella was almost beside herself. "So, you and Frank are going to be at a party location. Vivian, you can't go back there and I can't be anywhere near there either."

Vivian looked frantic. "We need to go get Jillian now and get out of the area. I'm sure Frank is coming."

Stella was almost screaming. "Vivian, have you lost your mind? Say we go get Jillian and we get her out of there before Frank arrives, what then Vivian? What are we all supposed to do about Frank? Have you thought that far ahead? I am absolutely not going anywhere near that house, and if you're smart, you won't either."

Jessie had been standing listening to all of this. He stepped between them and spoke.

"I'll go get Jill. We both stayed at this house last summer. I know right where it is. Dad brought us here with Uncle Charles. We hiked all over this mountain. I'll go get Jillian. She'll come with me." He turned toward his mother. "You and Stella can head back to the beach in your car."

Stella shook her head. "The point is to get Jillian out not to get you both trapped with Frank."

Vivian looked shocked at both of them. "Absolutely not!"

Jessie kept making his point. "I know the house and the property around it. I'll come in from the back. There is a road back there. I can walk in. They won't even know I'm there. I will figure out how to get Jillian out."

Stella started to think about it. "Jessie what is your plan afterwards?"

"You guys go back to Stella's. Jillian and I will meet you there. They will all be busy thinking about the guests. Who else is there now?"

Vivian looked sheepish. "Charles Tobin and the driver, Stokes. The other driver, Holder, is tied up downstairs near the wine room. What will you do if you run into your dad?"

Jessie looked at his watch. "I don't think Frank will show before the party. If he does, I'll do what you taught me and think of something. If you and Jillian need to disappear, we can figure that out. Stella won't tell anyone where you are. I can still stay with her. That way if Dad comes, he won't know where Jill and you are. That will buy us some time to think."

Both women just stared at Jessie. Vivian hugged her son and walked over to her car. She spoke as she was getting in. "Jessie, I just realized how much I miss you both. Get your sister out of there. See you in Myrtle Beach. Come on Stella."

Stella looked at Jessie. "You sure about all of this?"

He walked over and kissed her on the cheek. "I'm sure. Stokes is the only one I'm really concerned about. I know their drill remember? I'll be fine."

Stella hugged him. All you're doing is picking up your sister." She kissed him again, got in and she and Vivian drove off.

Jessie got behind the wheel of his Bronco and looked at his watch. He would move the car to the fire road and walk in from there. He pulled out and headed east to the turn off.

On the far side of the store, two Marshals watched as much as they could from a distance without having a clear line of sight. They called Ludlow. "Target sat in her car. A second car approached and was there for about 10 minutes. Both vehicles have left."

Ludlow came on the line. "Did you see what happened?"

"Negative, not without being exposed. Do you want us to stop either one?"

Mary broke in. "According to the AG, we do not have legal grounds to stop or detain Vivian. She may have decided to leave things alone. We will monitor with the tracker. Do we know who was in the other car or even if she had contact with them?"

"Negative."

Ludlow concurred. "You can't arrest a mother for begging her daughter to leave a whorehouse." He spoke to his team. "You two get back to your primary positions. Vivian Bartram is now secondary. We should be able to find her by the tracker."

Jessie parked his car at the juncture of the fire road and the main road and began to hike through the woods. It was just over a mile approaching from the fire road. He was about 200 yards away from the property line when he saw the vehicles parked up ahead and the people around them. He wandered to himself about why Frank's men would be there. He ducked into the woods and approached slowly. He saw movement to his left. He crouched down and was able to see the outline of people kneeling down about every 20 yards. They all wore tactical gear. They were cops, and they were everywhere.

Inside the house, Tobin looked at Stokes. "She's taking an awfully long time getting her cigarettes. Do you think she's coming back?"

"How bad do you want her back? But somebody ought to go check on Jillian and make sure she's still around. The balcony door to Beth and Tiffany's room was unlocked. It's too high to jump but Jillian is on the ground floor."

Tobin's demeanor changed as a memory returned. "Shit, shit, shit.

Jillian has been here before last summer with her dad and brother. I'll go check on her. You go see that Holder is still secure."

Stokes walked down the steps and unlocked the storage room where they had stashed Holder. He was awake and in a great deal of pain. Stokes almost felt sorry for him. He looked pathetic. He walked over and made sure the flex cuffs were still secure.

Holder spoke. "You need to take these off me and let me go. You know Frank will have me killed. He may even have you do it then have you killed."

Stokes shook his head. "You fucked with my responsibility. If you had hurt either one of those girls, it would be my ass on the line, right along with yours. My guess is, after the party, Tobin will turn you loose, if Vivian doesn't come back and kill you herself. And, as far as my future, I drive people. I don't hurt them. I don't fuck or kill them. He turned and shut the door and went back upstairs.

Tobin was white as a sheet staring out the window.

Stokes noticed it immediately. "What is wrong now?"

Tobin turned around. "Jillian just told me that her father is coming with the security crew and the girls. That is not good. That is too many angry people under one roof."

Stokes took a moment to contemplate the new situation. "I don't think she's coming back. If Jillian talked to her dad, he already knows Vivian is here. That's not on you or me. It's pretty obvious that Holder has reached the end of his usefulness and will probably die and be buried in the woods. If we just stay calm, stick to the normal plan, have the party and move on then, I think we are good to go. You and I haven't done anything except our jobs. Hell, we've kept Jillian safe. Frank needs us for the next party. By 7:00 pm you and I both will be on our way to the next assignment. We just need to stay cool. Can you do that, Tobin? Can you just keep your shit together until we can get this party past us?"

Tobin looked away and then back. His eyes were watery with fear. "I will try. I just hope Frank is thinking clearly enough with all the aggravation that Vivian has caused." He busied himself finishing the job of setting up the bar and making sure the food was ready to be set out. They had about an hour until the party sequence would start.

In the woods, Jessie was moving silently behind the Marshals as they moved forward into their final positions. He steered clear of the vehicles he had seen as he approached. He knew at least three people were still there. He counted at least 20 armed police. Something had gone terribly wrong with the planning of this party. They were about to have way more attendees than anyone had planned for. There was no way he could risk getting closer, but he knew at some point they would be busy arresting the johns, the security thugs, and quite possibly his father. He would be patient and see if he could spot Jillian and perhaps get her away when all the confusion started. But right now, he just had to stay still.

Vivian and Stella were almost to the exit on the east side of Charlotte where they would then head south toward Myrtle Beach. They hadn't spoken since they started. Finally, Stella had to say something.

"Vivian, you need to slow down. You're going to get pulled over and that's the last thing we need right now. Do you want me to drive?"

Vivian jerked the car over to the shoulder, slammed on the brakes and hit the emergency flasher button. She got out of the car and motioned for Stella to change places with her. Once Stella was behind the wheel, all the rage and frustration that had been simmering just beneath the surface was expelled in one loud shriek that startled Stella.

"Stella, I want you to tell me the fucking truth. Do you know what

Frank's plans are for Jillian?"

Stella didn't even skip a beat. "I have no idea what Frank's plans are any more than you do. I swear, Vivian. I didn't know he was having her moved around and I don't know of any attempt to sell her or give her to anyone. I would have told you if I heard something."

Vivian turned in her seat and just stared directly at Stella. There was no mistaking the emotion behind her gaze. "All Frank achieved with all this middle-of-the-night nonsense was to give Jillian a quick and dirty lesson on what this fucking business really is. She's never been exposed to that without me being present. She said she is the one that left the note. I believe her. She won't go along willingly with anything Frank has planned for her. Have you noticed any changes in Jessie? Have they been communicating?"

Stella kept her eyes on the road. "Jessie has been fine. He's sort of blossomed. He has uncanny computer skills, and is a deadly shot. He's handled his growth spurt by spending time at the gym and helping me in the office. If he has spoken with Jillian, it hasn't been around me and I doubt that the two would conspire against you or me."

"Does he ever ask about me, Stella? Don't lie to me."

Stella had no intention of lying. "He has asked a couple of times where you were or if I had talked to you or Jillian. The honest truth is, I didn't know where you were so I just told him you were fine. It's not even been a year, Viv. You, better than me know how these kids are."

Vivian turned and looked straight ahead. "That's the problem Stella. I'm not sure I know my children at all. I should have never agreed to separating them. I've been lost since Jessie moved in with you and I think Jillian has, too. He has grown so much. I think it has affected Jillian more than we know. And, I haven't helped with my disappearances. She has been alone with no one but the help to talk to."

Stella had to ask the obvious question.

"Vivian, what are you going to do about Frank? I have no doubt Jessie will get Jillian safely out of that house and back to my place. What I worry about is what are you going to do after this party when Frank comes looking? You know he will and if he has promised Jillian to someone, the bosses will make sure that he honors that promise. How are you going to deal with that?"

Vivian didn't bat an eye. "Stella, the first chance I get, I'm going to kill the bastard and anyone else who tries to take Jillian or Jessie away from me. I know Frank better than anyone does, maybe even better than he knows himself. He's weak when he's angry and I will use that to make sure that my kids are safe or I will die trying to protect them. But what are you going to do Stella? Can I count on our friendship or do I have to worry that you will work with them against me to take my children away? You've come out really well in this whole deal with your little perversion for young men. Can I trust that your feelings for Jessie and Jillian will be enough to not offer me up to Nightshade?"

It was Stella's turn to pull to the side of the road. She didn't slam on the brakes and there was no outward theatrical drama. She turned and looked at Vivian.

"You, of all people, are not allowed to throw that word 'perversion' around with me. I haven't done anything with Jessie that you didn't expect and probably haven't already done. To answer your question, I would never put you or them in any danger. Jessie brings me more than just sexual pleasure, Vivian. I don't know how, but you and Frank have raised two pretty incredible kids. They are smart, talented, and resourceful. Furthermore, I will promise to work with you to give them an out even if we have to use the files we've been keeping. I've been stashing money away just like you. I've never kidded myself that Jessie would always be such a willing participant in this little game we hatched. I hope that answers that question once and for all. I work for Nightshade but I love you and the twins."

# CHAPTER 14

When Frank and his crew were about 40 minutes away from the house, Ludlow began checking everyone's position. The perimeter was set. Alex was in position on the roof and Lily on the opposite rear corner on the ground. The rear entry team had moved into position in the woods. The front entry team was staged to make rapid entry and block the driveway. Their warrants were in place based upon the statements made by Jillian, Beth and Tiffany as well as the entire dialogue they had recorded. Security was to be neutralized as much as possible without lethal means. Tasers were charged, the arrest van was ready and the rescue bus was standing by for survivors.

Ludlow looked at the situation map on the console in the command vehicle.

"I wish we knew how they sequenced this deal."

Phelps nodded. "It would be helpful. Go in too early and all we do is disrupt a dinner party. Go in too late and we risk the lives of the girls at a time security will be most vigilant."

Birdman overhead them. "Let's ask the two on top. They have experience with these types of parties. I will get Kestrel to knock on the door and Alex can find out."

The little drone descended from the roofline and checked what was going on in the room. The girls were all ready and just sitting on the bed talking. Birdman maneuvered the drone to tap gently on the glass.

Beth heard it first. "Our little friend is back. Let's see if Alex has more. I haven't heard security yet but I think only one of us should go. I'll stand by the door and signal if anyone is coming. You go talk to Alex."

Once Beth was in place, Tiffany stepped out onto the balcony.

"Alex are you there?"

"I'm here. Who am I talking to?"

"It's Tiffany. Beth is watching the door."

Alex made sure her mic was on.

"Tiffany, we need to know how these things work."

"Well, the men pay and we're supposed to do what they want."

Everyone listening choked off a laugh. Alex chuckled but continued.

"No, we need to know the sequence of events for the party, you know, when they eat, when they come to your room, what happens when it's over."

"Oh, duh. Sorry. The other girls should be here about 15 minutes before the party. They arrive with security and some servers. The servers are sort of security goons in training or dumb-ass girls like us who like a party. The food is mostly exotic snacks like mini-lobster rolls, caviar on blini, steak bites, that sort of stuff. Lots of fancy alcohol being passed around. Sometimes there are drugs, sometimes not depending on the crowd." She took a breath.

"The girls like us are normally taken directly to their rooms to get ready for whatever fucked up fantasy the clients want to live out. Once the women arrive and are in their rooms, the security on each floor unlock the doors. I guess they want the clients to think we are happily waiting for them. The clients usually get into the rooms about 30 minutes after they get here. They eat and then are brought up."

"So who usually brings them up, the well-dressed guy?" Alex pinched herself. Never ask a question with a possible answer in it.

"No, Tobin is long gone. He rides in on the bus they use to pick up the clients. We never see him again until the next party. Usually, it is the security guy assigned to the floor."

"You mean like the guy that was here before?"

Tiffany paused as she thought. "That is different this time and a bit odd. The drivers, like Stokes, the guy that brought us after that guy Holder fucked up, are usually gone as soon as they lock us up. It was odd that Stokes brought us the food, but he may be hanging around because of Jillian. Have you talked to her? Is she alright?"

"She's fine. What happens after?"

"They are only allowed an hour with us. Finished or not, all the johns are moved back to the party van and driven back to where they were picked up. We are given 30 minutes to take a shower and get our travel clothes on then we are loaded into the transportation and moved to the next place."

Alex had one more question. "Tiffany, do you know where you're headed next?"

"Alex, we're never headed anywhere. We are taken. We never know where. We're told when to eat and when to shit. Can't have a growl in your stomach when you're pleasing a millionaire. We don't make decisions. We still can't believe that Holder stopped to let us pee. We don't even get to choose that. I'm 23 years old, and I am often forced to travel in adult diapers. Sorry about the long answer but that's how we live."

Everyone surrounding the house was listening to Tiffany. No matter what their assignment or where they were positioned, they stopped dead in their tracks while she spoke. On the rear perimeter, Marshal Hal Story turned to Tim Collins. "You have any questions now?" Tim just shook his head and lowered the visor on his assault helmet.

Ludlow waited to let that last statement sink in. He keyed Alex's headset.

"Nice job, Alex. You take care of those two."

Alex keyed her mic twice, the signal for affirmative.

"Thanks Tiffany. Go back in. When the time comes, I'll be here."

Ludlow looked at his watch and up at the video of the front of the house. "Given the timeline, I would say it is just about time for the party bus to arrive. What is our location check on Vivian?"

Phelps looked at the tracker map. "It appears she is headed southeast toward the coast. We could still stop her."

Mary Close answered him. "Nothing she did gives us grounds to arrest her. Frank on the other hand is about to arrive with armed security and no doubt a couple car loads of trafficked women. We have the warrants now in place to arrest and detain anyone in the house when we make entry. We need to focus on that. Have you decided when that will be?"

Ludlow smiled. Mary was daunting when she wanted to be.

"From what Tiffany told us, once everyone is fed and in their assigned rooms, that might be the time to invite ourselves in. Everyone will go on my signal. I think I want to move Lily closer to Jillian. She is key to this case. I just need to amp up protection and recovery for the girls on the top floor. The house plans show four bedrooms on each floor. The rear entry team can cover the bottom floor, main entry team and Lily on the first. I'm short for help with Alex on the top."

Mary chimed in. "How about if Phelps and I make entry in the front and head straight upstairs?"

Ludlow thought. "I'll pull Collins in to support you. I've got two more Marshals and Birdman on the rear. I'll pull the Marshals up closer. I just don't think anyone is going to run that way. If they do the drone should see them and let us know."

Phelps nodded agreement as he looked up at the live feed. A fancy 12-passenger party van was pulling into the driveway. It went right around the small circle and pulled around to the main door. All watching could see Charles Tobin get on the bus. Ludlow looked up at the timeline that was posted to the left of the live feed and checked off the first point. Then he advised. "Next up Frank and the security detail should be arriving."

As soon as Tobin left, Stokes switched on the driveway sensors. Six screens came alive in the control room on the lower floor of the mansion. His job was to stay until instructed to turn those sensors off to allow the security and girls to drive up to the property. Once he saw that they were inside and he was relieved by the security man who would take over, he was free to leave. That is just what Lester Stokes planned to do. He had pulled his Charger out of the garage and parked it on the side of the driveway. He would drive out before the guests arrived.

Frank and the rest of his crew arrived right on time. They parked the vehicles around back near the garage and entered through the garage door. Frank led the way to the main floor as his security people placed each of the women in the bedrooms assigned and the servers got set. Stokes sat quietly watching the monitors until he was relieved. He walked out the rear door, got in his Dodge and quietly left the property down the main drive. He turned to head to U.S. 25. He thought Asheville sounded like a nice place to be and it was less than an hour north. He could see the rise of the mountains just ahead. Damn, they looked inviting right now. As he got near the state line, two unmarked police vehicles pulled him over. The Marshals took him into custody, tagged his Dodge for impoundment, and he was on his way to jail 20 minutes after he left his seat at the monitors.

Jessie had moved up as the assault team had moved up being careful to stay behind them. He had seen Stokes leave. He wondered why his dad even had these security people. They were looking right at the hidden cops and saw nothing. He formed a plan. He needed a garage controller just in case. He knew that these cops would get the signal and move into the house. That would be the time to get one then pull back and wait to find Jillian.

Back inside the house as the others got the food ready, Frank was pissed that the door to Jillian's room was locked. He had security unlock it and went in. Jillian was sitting on the edge of the bed. He walked over and gathered her in his arms. She faked a shudder and sob. Best to play Dad like her mother had taught her. He released her and walked over to the window. Jillian caught her breath. Two minutes earlier she had been standing there with the door cracked talking to Lily who was flat against the wall in the dark a foot from where Frank looked out.

"I can't believe these guys. They lock the door to the hallway and leave this one open. Some security hey?"

"Why was I locked in at all? Am I now just one of the others?"

Frank turned back toward her. "Baby, don't talk that way. You never have been nor will you ever be like them. You're special. Let's just get this party done then we will be out of here."

Jillian thought then asked. "Why don't we leave right now before everyone else gets here?"

Frank thought to himself how smart she had become. "I have a small bit of business with one of the people coming tonight that I need to deal with. But we will leave before the stuff in the bedrooms gets started. You wait here. I need to check everything then I'll be back and we will leave right after everyone eats." He turned and walked out of the room but did not lock it.

Jillian walked over to the patio door and opened it a crack. She knew Lily was there.

She said softly. "You heard that. What do I do?"

Lily spoke firmly but gently. "You asked your dad the right question. How much do you trust me?"

"What do you mean? You came to get us. I have to trust you."

Lily smiled to herself. "We will have to work on that trust thing. No, you don't but I'll take that as a yes for now. I want you to step out and come with me now. I think your mother was right and I think if you don't leave now, it will be harder and even more dangerous for you and the others. That person Frank spoke of has come for you. If it was someone you knew and trusted, he would have said the name. He didn't."

"They will have turned the sensors back on. They'll catch us."

"We've taken care of that. I know this is a big step, but it is the one you have been looking for since you left that note. We will take care of you, protect your friends, and work as hard as we can not to hurt your parents. But you have to decide now." In her headset, Lily heard the announcement from command that the party bus was coming up the driveway. "Please Jillian. Come with me now. Just step out, turn toward my voice and follow my instructions."

Jillian stepped outside turned toward Lily who immediately pulled her close to her and wrapped the two of them in a black anti-ballistic blanket and walked her slowly through the woods. Jessie had watched the whole thing and moved further back on the property to be closer to his sister. With all eyes focused on the house, he moved quietly and easily on the side undetected.

They reached the two vehicles parked on the road. Jillian's chest was heaving. Lily sat next to her on the tailgate and spoke in a calm voice as Roseanne Smith walked up.

"It's all going to be over soon, Jillian. Catch your breath. This is my friend Roseanne. Can we get you anything?"

Jillian regained some of her composure. "I'd like a soft drink."

Lily rubbed her back while Roseanne got the beverage. Lily continued.

"Are you hungry?"

Jillian started to cry. "Just don't leave me until Mom and Dad are cuffed."

Lily had to tell her. "Jillian, your mother isn't in the house. She left earlier and hasn't returned."

Jillian sobbed. "You're telling me that she left me, again? Lily, she left me and she knew that Frank was coming. She knows what Frank is like when he's angry. You and Vivian were right, Frank was going sell me off to someone. What kind of father does that shit, Lily? Why would he do that and what kind of mother would leave me in this situation?"

Lily put her arms around the sobbing teenager. "It's going to be OK, Jillian."

"How? How am I ever going to be, OK? I can't even ride a bike but I can give a hell of a blow job. Seriously, Lily. You really think I'm going to be, OK? And what about Jessie?"

"Let's get you safe and then we will find Jessie and make him safe too." Lily got up to go back to the assignment.

Jillian grabbed her. "Please don't leave me."

Lily spoke as she stood up. "Officer Smith is here and won't leave your side. I have to go help your friends. I will see you shortly."

Roseanne came over and sat next to Jillian and took her in her arms.

"It's OK, baby girl. I got you. Lily has to go help with the other girls but I won't let anything happen to you." Roseanne turned around because she thought she heard a noise behind her. She saw nothing but pulled Jillian in closer. "Let's go sit in the car and wait till all this is over. Then we will find Lily and the rest." They got in the car and Roseanne locked the doors.

# CHAPTER 15

Ludlow spoke to everyone as he was leaving the command bus to move closer to the house." We have about 20 minutes until entry. Survivor one is secured."

Birdman had planted the little drone, Quarterback, over the front doorway hoping that he could sneak it inside when the party arrived. It worked even better than he expected. Three security guards opened the front door, and left it open as they all posted near the front of the house. Quarterback was in and attached to the ceiling above the slowly turning fan. When the time came for the teams to move in, Birdman could trigger the device to make a high-pitched screeching sound louder and shriller than a smoke detector as a sensory diversion just before the teams tossed their concussion grenades in to startle the occupants. In the meantime, Quarterback was busy transmitting every instruction that Frank was barking to the security and servers. It took exactly 20 minutes for all of that to take place. The whole time, no one checked on Jillian. Her room was empty, but not for long.

Lily, with Collins as back up, made her way quietly toward the house. There was a guard posted at each back corner of the house. There were three in the front and six inside. That was a lot of security but Ludlow figured that was because Frank was there and might have overreacted to the Atlanta situation.

Tobin called security from the road and had them turn off the sensors so the bus with all the guests could arrive. It pulled up in front of the house and the passengers unloaded and went in. There was a surprise passenger that made Tobin change his mind about his exit strategy. After the last passenger went inside, he got back on the bus. The surprise passenger was more than he could stand. He didn't like being around Vivian and he didn't like being around Frank particularly with the latest unexpected arrival. He'd come back when all the shit had hit the fan. He'd hire a ride-share to the RV from the hotel. He hunched down in his seat. As the bus cleared the driveway, Charles looked back. He was glad to be missing the shitshow.

Frank met the guests as they came in. The video being broadcast by Quarterback gave them a good enough view to be able to identify each guest as they entered and were greeted. There was one guest in particular that stood out.

Frank spoke as she walked up. "Helena, you are exactly the right person to help with this little task. Since you'll be staying overnight, I've arranged the master bedroom for your stay. My daughter will be in the first bedroom on the right. I will leave a man here to drive you. I'll introduce you to Jillian later so you can get to know each other. You and she leave tomorrow. She may be a bit difficult at first, but she'll settle down. Foster will meet you and Jillian in Raleigh."

Helena smiled. "I'm honored to be given such an important role. I'm sure Jillian and I will come to an understanding. I have experience with headstrong young women." She stepped closer and touched Frank's arm. 'Will you be joining me later?"

Frank put his hand on her hand and smiled. "Not this trip, but soon. Let's get a drink and discuss the trip."

She made her frowny face with a fake pout, then walked with him over to the bar. She watched the clients stuffing their faces. She thought they looked disgusting.

Thirty minutes after arrival, security started leading the men to the various bedrooms where they would meet their dates for the next hour. Collins and Lily inched up, as she quietly used her taser to subdue the guard on their corner. Two of the assault team did the same to the guard on the other end. In two minutes, Lily was inside Jillian's room waiting and Collins had moved up toward the front entryway.

Upstairs, Alex swung down to the balcony from the roof and walked into Tiffany and Beth's room. They took one look at her and Beth spoke first. "Star Woman. Alex is Star Woman." Alex pulled off the helmet and smiled.

"Nope just Alex, your upstairs neighbor. I've got a plan."

Both Beth and Tiffany tried on the helmet as Alex told them her plan. They listened and then Tiffany came up with a slight variation with a much better outcome. "Alex, you wait in the bathroom. When I give the signal come out and help."

They heard talking and footsteps coming toward their room. Alex got in the bathroom just as the security guard opened the door for a gentleman in his sixties. He came in and smiled at the girls. Tiffany and Beth, dressed in matching college t-shirts, t-backs, and nothing else smiled back and helped him off with his jacket. They had him sit on the bed while Tiffany got behind him on her knees, letting his head fall back against her breasts, hidden partially by the V-neck shirt that he had requested. Beth undid his shirt and unbuckled his belt. She pulled off his loafers. Like so many good Carolina boys, there were no socks. The two helped him pull his pants off and Beth neatly folded them on the chair, then turned toward him and pulled her T-shirt off replacing it with the man's dress shirt. She left it open exposing her top.

Tiffany leaned back against the pillows, spreading her legs slightly, and motioned the man to join her. The older gent, stood up, pulled off his fancy boxers, and followed her directions. Beth got on the bed behind him as he got in position. Then Tiffany just spoke in a very breathy voice. "Come on, Mr. Man. I've got quite a surprise for you."

Alex stepped into the room with her flex cuffs. The distracted man had moved down on Tiffany and was just even with her navel. Starting at $12,000 worth of very provocative real estate, he was so distracted that he thought it was Beth messing with his hands as part of the fun. Even when

Alex tightened the flex cuffs, he thought it was an added bonus. It wasn't until Beth grabbed him by the hair and pulled his head away from Tiffany that he realized that it was his worst nightmare playing out.

Beth couldn't help herself. She spoke softly as she helped Alex safely gag the man's mouth. "Mr. Sicko, meet Star Woman. You're so fucked." Alex motioned for the girls to get in the bathroom. She had Tiffany call out for the guard to come in as they closed and locked the bathroom door as instructed.

The guard entered and saw the man disabled on the bed. He didn't get a chance to turn around before Alex hit him with the taser end of her Slick Stick, a collapsible baton with a taser on one end designed by Smithson for the British Police. He went down in a heap as Alex closed the door. She cuffed him, and after using a gag that allowed adequate air in and no sound out, she took his weapon. She would now wait for the concussion grenade.

Outside on his monitor Ludlow saw Frank heading toward the room where Jillian had been. It was time. He spoke into his microphone for all to hear. "Go, Go, Go!"

The front entry team advanced and subdued the front guards. They had grown used to these parties being a boring affair for them and had just been standing and smoking, looking everywhere except where they should. It wasn't much of a task. They were disarmed and cuffed. Birdman triggered the screecher on Quarterback just as the breach team tossed the concussion grenade, known as a slam-bang, in through the open door. It went off just as Frank opened the door to Jillian's room. The compression caused by the grenade threw him into the room face down. As the other officers burst in to deal with the bewildered security and guests Lily pounced on Frank and cuffed him. Ludlow walked up.

"Hello Frank, are we late to the party?"

The rear entry team had done much the same thing and taken care of the guard in the control room. The grenade along with the screech was just enough confusion. Jessie had followed the rear entry team in, ducked into the garage and taken a garage door opener.

Everywhere else, naked men were running out of their rooms and into the waiting arms of officers with flex cuffs. The frightened women huddled in the corners of the rooms, unsure of what was happening.

Collins, Phelps, and Mary had been the first three through the front door and they raced up to the second floor. The first guard dropped like a stone when Phelps hit him. Mary pointed her gun at the second, who was pulling his weapon out as Alex appeared behind him and with a tap from her Slick-Stick, the guard crumpled and the gun clattered to the floor. Mary stepped over to cuff him. Alex quickly disappeared into the first bedroom and speaking Spanish and English told the women inside to get dressed and wait there. They nodded. Phelps moved to the doorway in case anyone changed their mind or there was an unaccounted security man missing.

Collins moved to the next bedroom with Alex, which they found empty. After checking the bathroom, they moved to the third. Alex opened the door. Three young Asian girls were huddled in the corner while the two young men they had been entertaining were trying to pull on their pants.

Alex looked at them. "Take your time, gentlemen. For you, the party is over. But for us, it's just heating up." Collins stepped over and cuffed each one as they got their pants on. Alex went over and spoke softly to the girls. She finally settled on Vietnamese. They spoke English but hearing their own language helped calm them. It turned out they were sisters. The youngest was 13 and the oldest 17. Alex told them that Collins was there to help them and that she would be right back.

According to the plan, Alex would gather the women on the top floor in one room and she and Collins would stay with them while the johns and the security men were processed. She got Beth, Tiffany, and the Hispanic girls into the bedroom where they found the Asians. Lily, along with Mary and two Marshals, were with the women they had rescued on the lower floor in second bedroom. Most of them were from Honduras and very young.

All those arrested were being separated on the front lawn; the eight clients on one side and the stunned security men on the other side. Ludlow was trying to figure out how he was going to get all these people locked up. The AG had cleared the way for a federal holding facility in Spartanburg to receive the security men, and Greenville County Jail was ready for the johns.

Frank and Helena were cuffed and sitting on the couch on the first floor. Mary and Phelps were reading them their rights and they were ignoring what they said. Frank was straining at his double flex cuffs to the point that he was cutting into the skin.

Ludlow stepped in and smiled. "I'm Luke Ludlow, U.S. Marshals Service. You're both under arrest for human trafficking. I'm sure you know your rights. Oh, and Frank, stop working those cuffs. You look like a dog trying to chew its own leg off to get out of a trap. It's beneath you."

Ludlow heard his earpiece buzz and acknowledge and update. Thanks. Let's do the johns first." He turned to Frank.

"Just when I was worried about how to get all your guests transported to jail, your party van showed up. We're going to borrow it for a while. Just submit a receipt later and we will pay for our share of the ride."

The johns were put on the van, accompanied by the two local officers who had arrived with the vehicles from the back of the property. They would make sure the locals johns were booked and charged. The party van pulled away with the deputy in the van and Officer Smith following.

The vehicle to transport arrestees pulled down the driveway. The security men were loaded onto this one with three Marshals. Collins walked inside to the group standing in the living room and reported to Ludlow. "All loaded and ready to go."

Ludlow smiled. "These two will be going with us. They will get special treatment. The AG wants them processed separately. Phelps and Mary will be taking them."

As Phelps stood Frank up, put real cuffs on over the flex cuffs, Mary walked up. "We all good here?" Phelps nodded.

Spying Helena, she smiled. "Well, hello, again. I didn't expect to see you at this party."

Frank turned around and glared at Helena. She looked at him. "One of the cops from last night?"

Frank shook his head and glared at Helena. "Anyone else you led here?"

"As a matter of fact, there is." Alex was speaking as she and Collins walked up.

Looking at Helena. "You remember us, Ashley and Davey. You said you'd be happy to see us anytime? Well, we're happy to see you, aren't we Davey?"

Collins answered. "Yes, how was the champagne?"

Mary had Helena up and cuffed properly. "Let's go. The reunion is over and Frank, it wasn't Helena that led us here. It was you."

Frank blurted out as he was walked to the door.

"Put that bitch in another car. I don't want to ride with her."

Phelps answered him. "Oh Frank, you don't get to give the orders here. You both will ride where we put you."

Ludlow looked at him. "Separate them. We may want to have a little chat with Helena without Frank anywhere nearby."

The traffickers were all gone. The party goers had all been loaded and were on their way.

They pulled the survivor van forward to load those that had been rescued. Lily walked with Jillian to be sure she was checked in properly. One by one they were loaded on the bus as Lily and Alex checked them. While this was being done, a final sweep of the house was conducted to make sure it was empty. It was and the outside was locked and sealed with crime scene tape. Two Marshals would be left to secure the scene. They would be relieved every four hours. When the rest left, Birdman would reset the sensors to help secure the place for the good guys. As they were finishing up, the garage lights began blinking. That surprised everyone and several officers near the bus were dispatched to check it out while the others provided cover. Nothing was found and the house was resealed.

Lily and Alex had boarded the survivor vehicle just as it pulled out. The bus was several miles closer to Greenville when Lily glanced around and turned to Alex.

"Where is Jillian?"

Alex looked puzzled. "We checked her in. She was in the line to get back on the bus when we counted heads."

Lily looked back bewildered. "She's not here. Jillian is not here."

Alex was on her radio. "The blinking lights were a distraction. Jillian is not on the bus. Search the house and the area immediately. Repeat. Primary witness is missing."

Jillian and Jessie moved silently through the woods until they got to the car. Once inside he let it coast down to the gravel road with the headlights off. He didn't want to risk starting the engine or turning on the lights incase he had miscounted all the police.

Jillian looked over at him.

"You really scared me walking up behind me like that."

"Sorry, I couldn't risk being seen by the cops. Your timing was perfect. They were so busy with everyone else. I used the garage opener to buy a moment and I don't think they missed you until we were gone."

"They know I'm gone now. What do we do?"

"We head to Myrtle Beach on the back roads. We are meeting Mom and Stella there. Jill, I've never seen so many cops in one place. How did the cops find out about this party?"

Jillian thought a moment then answered.

"I left a note with Beth and Tiffany at a rest stop. I had a bad feeling about why I was traveling so much with the other girls. I think Dad was getting ready to sell me or trade me or whatever to someone. I didn't know about the party. I have no idea how they found out. I just walked out on the balcony when I first got here and they were there."

Jessie smiled. "Dad was getting ready to sell you? You mean like I got traded to Stella?"

"Worse, at least we know Stella. I think I was headed to a stranger."

Jessie thought for a moment.

"Why now, Jill? I mean I'm glad Frank didn't get the chance but how did you know to do it now?"

"I didn't know for sure. It's just not been the same since they separated us. We've always been able to rely on each other when things got too weird. Mom's been gone. I've been alone most of the time. I wasn't going to live like that."

Jessie smiled as he started the car and they turned east away from the units returning to the scene to search for Jillian. He put his hand on his sister's.

"Don't worry. We won't be separated again but we need to make a call."

Jessie dialed Stella's number. She answered. "Did you get Jillian?"

"Yes. But you need to pack and wait for a call from Frank. The party house was surrounded by cops. Everyone, including Frank and that foreign woman from Atlanta were taken into custody. We will head straight to your house. Stella, there must have been 30 of them hiding all around the house. They'd been there awhile, even while Mom was there. How did they know, Stella? How did they know?"

# CHAPTER 16

The revelation that the individual instrumental in starting this whole sequence of events was missing when the smoke cleared rippled through the justice system all the way to Washington. Team members had searched for Jillian Syms for two weeks without finding a trace. She was the cornerstone witness for the entire prosecution of Frank Bartram, Helena Reagan, Dexter Holder, and Lester Stokes. The nine foreign security thugs had kept silent but were all charged with trafficking. Of the survivors rescued during the operation, the two most promising were Elizabeth Ellers and Tiffany Holmes, Jillian's co-conspirators in leaving the note. The remainder were foreign, most without legal papers and too afraid to speak what little English they had learned. The case was turning out like many human trafficking cases. It was frustrating for everyone.

As with anything connected with government, the easiest efforts came first. Five of the guests at the party were charged by South Carolina prosecutors with soliciting for prostitution. They lawyered up, pled out, and received hefty fines, suspended jail sentences, and short probationary periods. The young studs that were caught partially naked in the room with the three under age Vietnamese girl's plea-bargained for hefty fines and 90 days in jail, followed by two years' probation in lieu of having to register as sex offenders. All of these defendants would likely have spilled the beans about the whole operation in exchange for lighter sentences, but they knew nothing. They had paid to go to a party where there would be good food and sex. Each of the clients had transferred the fee electronically to a different transaction account. In the end, it was doubtful that any of these men who paid for sex lost much relatively speaking, even in their social standing. The privileged in addition to feeling entitled are often easily forgiven. No one, even their family members, seemed to think about how parties like that happen. After all it's just sex you pay for.

The members of Frank's security group were prosecuted in federal court. Nine of them were charged with sex trafficking largely based upon the age of the young Asian women and the testimony, as sketchy as it was, from the Hispanic survivors. They were transferred to Atlanta to be held for trial. The three men in attendance at the party as service staff were found to be carrying false passports, had no legal documentation, and were immediately deported back to Bosnia. The serious focus quickly became Frank Bartram, Dexter Holder, Lester Stokes, and Helena Reagan. They were all being held in the Atlanta Federal holding facility pending trial.

The atmosphere in the conference room at the U.S. Attorney's office in Atlanta was pessimistic at best. Sylvia Stammer, a hard charging young Assistant U.S. Attorney out of DC who had begged the Attorney General for the opportunity was assigned the case. She looked at Phelps Wheeler and Mary Close as she spoke.

"I'm most optimistic about Holder. He is going to do a year in Georgia on the old absconding charge which will give us time to develop evidence on his case. Stokes started out talking like he was going to cooperate until the defense lawyer showed up. Since then, he has shut down. Neither Stokes nor Holder is likely to give us any information on the Nightshade Group. They are scared. We will need significant leverage to get anything out of them and I just don't see it here."

Phelps looked down at the charge summary as he spoke.

"How strong is the testimony from Tiffany Holmes and Beth Ellers? Is that enough to charge them with interstate trafficking? They seem to get stronger every time we talk to them."

"They are strong. Neither of them seems to give a crap about Holder and would like to see him go down but they softened their tone on Stokes. I've gotten caught in that before where the closer we get to the trial date, the softer witnesses become when we test them with defense questions. If we had the young girl, Jillian, it would be a different story. But, these two witnesses are adults and the case of being trafficked rests on them saying they were repeatedly not free to leave, held captive, and forced into prostitution."

Mary had been looking at their interim investigation report on Frank Bartram.

"Do we have any evidence at all that Frank ordered or traveled with any of these women to the Greenville location? We don't have clear visual or admissible audio evidence without Jillian to corroborate it. We knew he was riding in one of the vehicles from Athens, but I'm not seeing any evidence that directly connects him unless we get good testimony from the survivors. Is there anything specific from the women that were transported from Atlanta? Did he interact with them directly or did they hear him giving orders?"

Sylvia flipped through some pages in her own case file and shook her head.

"Without strong testimony from the survivors or the other defendants, it very well could be that he is the weakest of all. We know he is involved. Holmes and Ellers can testify that he has been involved at different points but not exactly how. They mention that both of the Bartrams were involved in their grooming, as was Charles Tobin. Have we got any further information on the whereabouts of Vivian or Charles?"

Phelps answered.

"We found Vivian's car. She traded it for a new one the moment she got back to South Carolina. The whole transaction was legitimate. I'm not sure she even knew she was being tracked. We have been monitoring houses that the intelligence analysis indicates have been used by the Bartrams, but nothing so far. As far as Charles Tobin, something must have spooked him. We found his BMW parked in the garage at the party site. Beth and Tiffany say that he normally leaves in his own vehicle when the clients arrive. We believe he never got off the party bus that night."

Sylvia interjected. "What does the bus driver say?"

Phelps continued. "He says he took Charles back to the Central Hotel and from there he disappeared. We think he used a ride share back to the house in Oconee County and left from there.

It was Mary's time to interject. "Speaking of that house, we found nothing there when the evidence team looked. The entire house had been wiped clean, and when I say clean, it was like a forensic cleaning. No trace of any human anywhere. There was an RV hook-up. They were so thorough, they even pumped out the waste dump."

Sylvia frowned. "Who has the resources to do that other than us?"

Both agents looked at her. "The Nightshade Group has those kinds of resources."

Sylvia continued. "I have the translations from the Honduran women that were amongst the survivors at the party. Their stories are frightening, but will make terrible testimony with their language barrier. They mostly refer to the security people and this woman from Atlanta, Helena Reagan. From your investigative reports, I didn't get the feeling she was anything other than a glorified employee. The prostitution survivors transported from Atlanta say she ran the Atlanta location and that there were others there that were taken to hotels as cleaners. The men were sent to various labor jobs like yard work and day labor. From watching the interview videos, she certainly comes off as more seasoned. She's not giving anything up about any of the illicit activities. Does Helena Reagan strike you as the kind of person that can run an operation like that?"

Mary spoke up. "Both Marshal Story and I had direct contact with her at the Buckhead location as did Alex Pellegrino and Marshal Collins. She struck me as someone who was totally capable. We have fed her details to our intelligence analyst for a thorough search which will include running her through Interpol. We have some preliminary results on voice analysis that indicates her native tongue is Czech. My opinion is that we will find that she is not who she says she is, and that she is totally capable of running the Buckhead operation and more."

Phelps shrugged. "I didn't lay eyes on her until the raid. I'm at a loss. Beth and Tiffany say they have never seen her before. By the way, interviews from the first five floors of that building all show that the leasing residents were completely in the dark and there was no crossover with the illegitimate operation on the upper floors. You will see that the building is listed as a possible forfeiture if we move forward with a good prosecution."

Sylvia seemed as exhausted as she was shocked.

"None of the legitimate people in that building had any idea what was going on above their heads? How does that happen? The people in my building know my business before I do."

Mary laughed. "You live in Washington D.C. Everybody knows everybody's business. It's also a mixed-use building. They're very popular with urban planners because you get retail, office, and residential all on the same footprint. The more functions, the less people question what's going on, unless it raises a problem. Half of those residents didn't live there fulltime and Helena and that security force made sure there were no problems.

Stammers closed the file. "What is our plan for trying to develop testimony from our survivors?"

Phelps spoke first.

"Lily Michaels and Alex Pellegrino are working with all of them. Smithson is providing additional security coverage. Lily is concentrating on Beth and Tiffany. Alex is doing some of that and working with the foreign survivors because of her language skills. It is going to take some time with the foreign nationals we still have. What was up with ICE deporting the trafficked workers recovered in Atlanta? Do you have any idea how or why they were deported so quickly before we could even process them?"

Stammers looked frustrated. "They were picked up and transported to a secure facility with plenty of translators and trained people. Two days later, ICE showed up with a bus and they were halfway to Honduras by the time we found out they were gone. When a person with a court order shows up, no civilian working at a supportive NGO is going to question that. The judge in question says he was working off a pleading produced by Stella St. John, the defense lawyer for all these people. She's good, well-versed, and experienced in this stuff. As for what may have influenced that Judge to sign the order, I am always either amused or mystified by what they do when hit with a private sector pleading from an experienced lawyer."

Mary asked the obvious question. "What do we know about Stella St. John?"

Sylvia looked at the ceiling as she answered. "Like I said, she is good. She also seems to be a step ahead of us all the time. During an operation it's easy to keep the investigation secret. It's different once you arrest someone. The booking and prosecution process is public. There are just too many moving parts and people who have to know. She was on the case before the trafficking suspects were even back in Atlanta. Make sure to keep your witnesses safe and let me know where they are."

Phelps and Mary got up. Phelps spoke for the two of them. "We will check with the people from Smithson on options for secure shelters. And we will concentrate our efforts on the rest of the foreign nationals before someone gets the bright idea to deport them. How strong would their statements be if that happened and they were deported?"

Sylvia laughed. "You know judges and you know juries. Without the person there to raise their hand and attest to their statements and answer questions about how they made those statements, admissibility is chancy at best. Even if they did, I just don't see enough with Frank unless they can place him in a car with the women, giving orders to have sex. Hell, you have him on tape yelling at his people to unlock the doors. I wish I could be more optimistic."

Mary smiled. "It's that age old deal. The good guys play by the rules and lose. The bad guys ignore the rules and win."

Sylvia stood to end the meeting.

"Do some work and let's get back together in three days unless something turns up that might aid our cause." It was obvious by her body language the two agents were being excused. They both took the hint, gathered their things, and left her office. They didn't even get out of the building before Phelps' tactical phone rang. It was the Attorney General.

"What do you think of Stammers?"

Phelps almost laughed out loud. "She's predictably pessimistic and young. We thought you'd send an old timer with more experience."

The Attorney General laughed. "I had my reasons for sending her. Did you mention, Morozov or her computer."

"Not directly but we did say we were taking a more thorough look at Reagan. She didn't seem to be curious."

"Good. The fewer people that know about SYBIL and Jeanine, the better. Stay on the case and keep reporting to me as well. I'm sorry that will cause you extra work but it is essential I know personally what is going on."

Phelps was curious "You don't think your prosecutor will keep you informed?"

"We will see, won't we. Be sure to take care of our survivors Ellers and Holmes. The reports I'm getting from our friends at Smithson say they are getting stronger by the day and responding well at the shelters. We need to keep them safe at all costs and they are not to be moved unless I approve it."

Phelps thought the time was right to finally apologize. "I'm sorry we lost Jillian Syms at the house. We still can't figure out how she got out of that area so quickly alone."

Gwen Evers chuckled. "She obviously had help and more moxie than anyone gave her credit for."

Phelps replied. "It's still on us. We failed her and we failed the mission and the result is that we are probably going to lose the case quickly on all of them but Holder. I'm sorry we got Frank and can't make it stick."

The Attorney General responded with kindness but firmly.

"We might not get them this time, but we are getting much closer and now we keep going. I will be meeting with Ludlow and Slade Smithson later about the next phase of this operation. Expect new orders for both you and Agent Close. Something has definitely shifted within Nightshade since those women left that note. They will either be busy trying to figure out how we found out about the party or they will be busy feeding on each other. Either way, that works in our favor.

Phelps smiled to himself. "How much of this does our prosecutor know?"

"Like I said, make sure to keep me in the loop directly. Did she ask you to keep her advised of where the witnesses are?"

"She did."

"She can have phone contact only. I will start making arrangements for alternate placement for Ellers and Holmes. We rescued survivors and made arrests that bring us closer to a final outcome. Stay safe, visit your family, and be prepared to work with Ludlow to find Jillian Syms."

Phelps hung on. "Some of our survivors were deported before we could talk to them adequately. That poses a problem."

"Taken care of." She hung up.

Phelps told Mary the extent of the conversation. She thought a moment.

"Sounds like the Attorney General was expecting a tough outcome for this case. It also sounds like she has no intention of stopping. That's different."

Phelps smiled. Ever since we were assigned to this task force, it has been different. We have the weekend off. I'm going home, you?"

"I'm going to stay here in Atlanta. I will keep going over the case. Give Charley and the girls my love."

# CHAPTER 17

The Attorney General suggested they move Beth and Tiffany to a shelter that provided extra security and additional services for medical or mental health support. She also arranged to have Lily and Alex move into the same shelter with them. Alex would leave periodically to check on the Vietnamese and Honduran survivors from the party to help support them, but the major witnesses were definitely Beth and Tiffany.

Beth was sitting on the couch in her room with her legs pulled up underneath her reading one of the dozens of books she had requested when Lily walked in.

"Good morning, Beth. How are you?"

Beth looked up from her book and smiled

"This place takes some getting used to."

"How do you mean?"

"For the last five years I've been locked up at night and most times during the day. I spent the majority of my time thinking about how to get on the other side of that locked door. Now, I just walk over and open it. It's more of an adjustment than I realized. I can't think of a time that I was ever in control of my own schedule. Last night, I woke up and couldn't sleep. I walked out into the kitchen and got myself a drink. You wouldn't think anything so simple could be something you have to get used to again. I settled in a chair and read my book for about 30 minutes and went to sleep right there in the chair. I was scared shitless when I woke up that I'd be caught outside my room. Then I realized I wasn't captive any longer. Weird right?"

Lily smiled. "We are creatures of habit. You've survived something that most women can't even imagine. It's going to take some getting used to. That's why Alex and I, and the shelter staff, are here to help you."

Beth laughed. "Lily, no offense, but you're mostly here to make sure we hold it together enough to testify. You don't even really know us. But, don't get me wrong. I appreciate the kindness. There hasn't been much of that in my life. Yesterday a woman came in and did our hair. While she was giving me a shampoo, I thought about how I couldn't remember the last time a stranger touched me with just plain old everyday kindness. Afterwards, when I returned here, I shut the door and bawled my eyes out. How silly is that?"

Lily looked down at the book in Beth's hand. "Even kindness takes time to get used to. Trust takes even longer so no offense taken. That is part of why we're here. What are you reading?"

Beth looked down and laughed.

"This is the third book I've started since I got here. I just can't seem to read enough. We weren't allowed reading material. I didn't realize how much I missed it. This one is about finding true happiness by the Dalai Lama. The counselor has taught us how to clear our minds and meditate. We have a group session everyday on how to stay in the moment. The Dalai Lama meditates a lot. I figured he would have some additional info that might help me."

Lily thought for a moment before she asked the next question.

"Beth, you seem so smart. How did you end up with the Bartrams?"

Beth took her time before she answered. She was getting more and more comfortable with the space Lily gave her to think.

"My mom died when I was nine. Dad remarried and Sheila hated me from the start. Then Dad died in a construction accident when I was 14. It took Sheila exactly six months to find another husband. Two weeks after he moved in, he got confused about which bed he was supposed to be in. I made a fuss and was on the street the next morning. I called my dad's brother and he and his wife came and picked me up. I lived with them as sort of a nanny to their kids. It was OK. They were real church people. I was back in school and one of the teachers helped me to read better. That summer, I was at church camp and the last night one of the deacons of the church molested me. Again, I raised a fuss but he was a deacon and I was just some kid. They didn't kick me out but they sent me to a church-based program for problem girls.

Lily broke in.

"How do you mean, sexually molested? Did he rape you?"

Beth laughed. "You are so sweet but so naive. He was an old hand at this young girl stuff. I was the last one up from the lake that evening after the campfire. The others had gone when he spun me around, forced me against the outside wall of the boat shed, yanked down my shorts and panties, and forced himself into me from behind. He pulled out just as he came so there would be no evidence. I reported him to my aunt and uncle but neither believed me. The cops were never called. I just became an embarrassment to them. They sent me to the church-based home for troubled teen girls. Almost all of us there had a similar history."

Lily frowned. "Church people."

"Yes. I stayed several months. They figured out that making me beg for forgiveness and mercy wasn't working so well as a therapy for being fucked from behind by a deacon. No matter how many bible verses I was forced to memorize, or multi-hour prayer sessions that were intended to cleanse my soul, I refused to change my story. I just seemed to get more unreasonable to them. I have to say, reading the bible did give me comfort and it was the first time in my life that I had others around me who were in the same screwed up situation. I think the counselors there really believed what they were saying. They all had good intentions and some of the girls there were really fucked up. Several had been abused many times by different men, some by family members. The counselors got that and at least they weren't unkind or abusive. I turned 16, and decided it wasn't a good fit anymore for them or me. I'm stubborn that way. I had no where to go even if I lied and said it had never happened. So, one night I left and hitchhiked to Augusta."

Lily held up her hand to have Beth pause so she could take notes. "No one reported you missing?"

Beth laughed. "When the troubled girl disappeared, the problem disappeared and they had no interest in looking for the problem."

"So, at 16 you're on your own with no family, no place to stay, and limited ways to make a living. How did you manage?"

Beth stopped and looked at her. "You're thinking I started hooking then, aren't you?"

Lily immediately shook her head. "I'm not thinking anything. It just seemed like a horrible situation. I don't know what I would have done."

Beth turned and looked out the window behind her as she spoke.

"I just thought it was my luck of the draw. On the road there were girls as young as 10 or 12 that had just been locked out of their houses. I can't believe I'm trusting you enough to tell you this. Let's change the subject, Lily. You've got a southern drawl. Where were you raised?"

Lily rarely shared her private details with the survivors she worked with. She had enjoyed her childhood, most of them had been robbed of theirs. But she decided to take a small risk. She really had no business asking for trust if she couldn't extend it.

"I was raised on the saltwater marshes of St. Helena Island in Beaufort County."

Beth turned around. "Low country on the water, huh? That explains your outdoorsy nature. When I saw you that night, you had a gun on your hip. Did your pappy teach you to shoot? I bet there was boating and fishing involved as well as fine little tea dances and debutante balls."

Lily sighed. "Now who's judging? As a matter of fact, as far as dances and debutante stuff there wasn't. Fishing, and shooting, there was. Both my parents are Gullah. Want to judge that?"

Beth turned all the way around. "Black Gullah?"

Lily laughed. "Oh yes. That Gullah. I speak the language and I was raised by their values. I was an abandoned infant. They set a place at their table and in their hearts for a little white girl. My mother, who prefers I call her Auntie, is still alive and we're very close. My father died six years ago while I was deployed in the Persian Gulf. He and his best friend, Billy, taught me to shoot, to fish, to live off the land for days, and to be self-reliant."

Beth sat down. " I'm going to use that to answer your last question. You asked how I managed. I became self-reliant and since you were so open with me, I lied about my age to a man and woman who ran a restaurant in Augusta and got a job as a waitress. They let me stay in a camper trailer they had parked out back of the restaurant. Because they provided my meals and a roof over my head, I worked almost 70 hours a week for minimum wage and I learned how to hide my tips. They were church goers, too. While they were praying each Sunday, I was scrubbing the entire restaurant top to bottom to make sure they passed the health department inspection. Oh, and when they came home, I was expected to have Sunday dinner ready for them. You have to love those church people. Were the people that helped you church folks?"

"They never missed church, but thought more about giving than taking. How did you get hooked up with the syndicate people that enslaved you?"

Beth looked surprised. "Lily, you are the first person to call it that. The answer to your question is that Charles Tobin needed some additional help at a party he was throwing after a golf tournament. He was buddies with the man I worked for. I think the woman was anxious to see the back of me.

Her husband, good churchgoer that he was, was getting a bit too friendly."

"Did he try anything with you?"

"I didn't give him the chance. I just always had the feeling that I was being watched. So, when Charles offered me a job and a place to stay with three other girls, I accepted."

"Did it start out that you were expected to provide sexual favors for men?"

Beth laughed. "Don't make it seem more dignified than it was, Lily. And it wasn't always men. Sometimes it was women and sometimes it was men and women But, at first it was just passing food and drinks. Then Charles suggested that I move to Atlanta. He got me job as a cocktail waitress and started buying me nice clothes, killer shoes, and asking me to hang out with his buddies. After about a year, most of the nice things stopped but he never came on to me. Then one night he asked me to be particularly friendly to a client of his. I woke up the next morning not remembering anything, naked, and discovering I was locked in the room. That was just about five years ago."

Lily looked at her notes. "How many others were in the same situation?"

Beth thought. "New girls always came and went. Some were foreign. I was never kept in the same location very long. I think they didn't want us to get to know too much about a place. The first two years, I'd say I worked with about 10 or 12 different women. Some I would see at different events just once. If you behaved yourself and didn't seem interested in running, you became a regular, like me and Tiffany. Tiffany didn't arrive until about three years ago and she was just real young. Not just in age either. There were two other girls along with me that decided to take her under our wing."

Lily looked up. "Who were the other two girls?"

Beth turned back to the window. "We only knew first names. One was named Lucy and the other Crystal. She was snatched from a student party in Charleston. Lucy had more of a history like mine, except she had been picked up at 12 and groomed for the business. The three of us sort of helped Tiffany learn how to protect herself with the clients."

"Protect herself?"

"Sorry, how to recognize when a client was getting too physical. That didn't happen to us much. We were used to servicing higher end clients at private parties. Most of the foreign girls were used at the service stations, lower end houses or trailers along the interstates where the model was more like a whore house. The motel in Charleston where Holder picked us up this last time was one of those. The higher end girls never turned tricks in these places. Don't get me wrong. We were forced to fuck a lot of rich guys in Charleston, Atlanta, and Charlotte but never in the service stations. We always worked in large elegant houses like the one you found us in."

Lily asked the obvious question.

"Where are Lucy and Crystal now?"

Beth took a deep breath. "Dead. They ran, returned, and were tortured and killed on video which Nightshade marketed as a snuff film."

Silence covered the room for 10 minutes as Lily and Beth both got their wind back. Lily finally spoked.

"You said they returned. Did they come back on their own?"

Beth nodded. "Twice, maybe three times. That always floored me. If I'd have had the balls to run, I would never have returned. I was too afraid of what they would do. I could never figure out why they came back, and they weren't the only ones. The foreign girls often came back because they had so few options. Dexter would beat the crap out of them and then they would start over in the service stations."

Lily was letting that settle in. "How do you know they were killed in a snuff film?"

Beth didn't turn around.

"The best tool to keep someone in line is fear. They made a big deal out of showing us that film. I guess it had the opposite effect on Tiffany and me. It pissed us off more than scared us. We were originally supposed to go with them. At the last minute, Tiffany chickened out. I didn't want to leave her there alone. I stayed. They made sure we saw the film several times. Dexter Holder was particularly fond of playing it loud on the nights we weren't working. I can't tell you how many times we both cried ourselves to sleep, locked in our separate rooms, listening to our two friends scream. After a while they quit. I personally think Stokes destroyed the tape one night. He never played it."

The room got quiet again for a good bit of time. Finally, Lily moved forward.

"It's obvious how you feel about Dexter Holder. You don't seem to dislike Lester Stokes as much. Why?"

"Stokes kept to himself. He never hit us or kept us up at night like Dexter did. Stokes wasn't interested in getting any sexual attention from us. That made him almost respectable in our eyes. Don't get me wrong, you didn't want to run from Stokes. His job was to move us safely and unharmed and he took that seriously. If it hadn't been for him, Holder would have beaten the hell out of us over the note thing. Instead, he protected us. He warned us that Holder might try something. He did and we were ready. Shit, I even got to beat the shit out of Holder before Vivian stopped it all. Vivian and Charles dealt with Holder while Stokes took us up to the room. We never saw Holder after that."

"What about Frank?"

"I saw Frank maybe once or twice a year. He paid absolutely no attention to us. He never spoke to us. We were like rental property to him. He didn't like it if we got bruised, hurt or sick. We weren't worth much in that condition. Don't get me wrong. Frank is a bad mother fucker. We think he is the one that killed Lucy and Crystal. None of us wanted to cross him. I hadn't seen Frank since Lucy and Crystal were killed until you guys brought him out in cuffs."

"You didn't see Frank at the parties on a regular basis?"

Beth shook her head.

"Nope. We were also very surprised to see Vivian at that house earlier. We almost never saw her anywhere. We just figured it was because we had Jillian with us. As fucked up as Vivian is, she loves those twins."

That stopped Lily dead in her writing.

"Is Jillian's brother her twin?"

Beth laughed. "How do you think all this shit with the note got started? The twins were adopted and raised by Frank and Vivian. They have been part of the organization and doing odd sexual things for select clients since they were little. Jillian was pissed when Jessie was sold, traded, or given to someone. They had never been separated before. They looked out for each other really well. We only got to know her recently. She never had any regular contact with us before that. We didn't trust her at first but she won us over. That little 15-year-old acts like a 30-year-old and her brother is as pretty to look at as she is and really, really smart. We had been talking about the note the last couple of times we traveled together. It was Jillian that came up with the plan. It was a good one, because here we are."

# CHAPTER 18

Usually, Alex started her day by going to the other shelter and checking on the rescued foreign women. They were still very afraid of being deported or hurt by their traffickers. In their countries, the police were often a large part of the problem. The shelter had been contacted by the Vietnamese government on behalf of the three Asian girls' parents and the AG had allowed a visit from their government. Alex had monitored the conversation and it was unusually supportive of the girls. Even with all of this, it was slow going with their caseworkers in establishing enough trust to have them fully participate in counseling or giving clear and consistent understandable witness accounts. Alex was also teamed with Lily to work with Beth and Tiffany at the new shelter. That's where she headed each day after working with the foreign women. Lily and Alex rotated talking with each of them.

The day after they were transferred to the new shelter, Alex arrived in the afternoon and after reviewing Lily's notes with Beth, went straight to Tiffany's room.

Alex could hear Tiffany crying through the door. She waited a moment then knocked.

There was a pause and Tiffany answered. "Come in."

Alex entered and went over and gathered Tiffany in her arms even though Tiffany was five inches taller than Alex.

"Tiffany, I'm so sorry to bother you. It's OK. You're safe here. Do you want me to come back later? We don't have to rush our conversations if you're having a bad day." Tiffany took a moment just because she was enjoying the hug. She let go of Alex and went over and sat on the bed.

"No, I'm good. It's just that I get these episodes when I realize what a shitty person I am. I've been that way all my life. I was horrible to my parents and the rest of my family. I always thought I knew best. When everyone was trying to help me, I turned away from them. Alex, I'm just a mess. I deserved all the hell the past few years have brought me. I've made poor choices all along the way, including the asshole boyfriend who promised me everything and sold me to Nightshade for $1,000 and a bag of coke. If I hadn't met Beth, I would have run my mouth and fucked up to the point that I ended up like Crystal and Lucy."

Alex sat down on the bed next to her. "Tiffany, you need to start understanding that, while you are responsible for some of the things you are saying about yourself, you didn't force yourself to have sex with whoever they brought to your room. You didn't lock yourself up or beat yourself up. They did that to you. I'm all for responsibility but it goes where it belongs. Tell me about these two girls."

Tiffany almost burst out in tears again. "Me and Beth were supposed to go with them and I chickened out. They got caught and were made an example. That could have been all four of us. Alex, I don't know what to do. I'm scared shitless to say anything about any of that. They will find me and kill me. Beth says we should help but they are too powerful and have too much money."

Alex got up and walked over to the chair and sat down facing her. "We have programs and people all over the country that will protect you. What are you feeling about your family?"

"My counselor told me they reported me missing as a runaway. They cared enough about me to do that. I was 17 when I left with my dumbass boyfriend. None of the cops in the low country were going to take that seriously. The age of consent is 16 in South Carolina and it was fairly common knowledge I left with Drew, the piece of shit that sold me. No one was going to spend much time looking for a girl that had the reputation I did. I fucked one of my distant cousins when I was 13. Sex was no big deal to me other than a way to get guys to do what I wanted and buy me what I wanted. How far is that from the classic definition of a whore? By the time the group got me I was already a very experienced piece of ass so it wasn't a giant leap for me to become a full-fledged regular earner for them. Most of the time we were in good enough places. A few times we were housed in some ramshackle joints they called service stations but we never had to fuck anybody in those flea flats."

"Tiffany, who made the decisions about where you stayed and where the parties were held?"

"I don't know. We were never told when until it was time for us to get ready. The transporters would pick us up and take us to the party location. The security thugs would take over from there. I don't know who was making the decisions. Tobin was the guy who found the clients. He was also the one that gave us specific instructions about what our clients wanted at each session. Sometimes, like when you rescued us, we had specific things we had to wear or things we had to do. Beth taught me how to get them satisfied early. It was a one and done thing. Once the clients climaxed, it was over. We knocked on the door and the goons took them away while we got cleaned up and ready to travel. Beth and me were teamed up for two on ones and two on twos together because we got good reviews. We even had to pretend to make love to each other for some of the crazy wackos that they sent into us. Men, women, boys with their dads, boys with their moms. It was pretty fucking sick, but we knew how to deal with it."

"Did you have other transporters?"

"Yeah, but over the last year we were mostly moved by Holder and Stokes."

Alex looked straight into her eyes.

"When we rescued you, you had a split lip. Was that a regular thing?"

"Only with Dexter Holder. I got that when he thought I had stolen his lighter. I had, but you know why. Dex was the only one who would risk hitting any of us. I seemed to bring out the mean in him. If it hadn't been for Stokes, that bastard would have killed us. Of course, Vivian had a hand in protecting us. Beth and me are good earners for them. We thought we had really put our necks on the chopping block when we left the note but Jillian pulled it off perfectly."

"Was Vivian a regular attendee at the parties?"

"Never. When I was first sold to them, Frank and Vivian gave me a test run. I never saw Frank again, and the first time I've seen Vivian since that night was when she had her gun pointed at Stokes' skull. I don't think she would have killed him and it was common knowledge that she fucked Holder on a regular basis. We kept waiting for Frank to put a stop to that but he never did. We were surprised when we saw him in custody after the party."

"Were you ever drugged?"

"Not by them. The shit heel Drew, the boyfriend, used to dose me sometimes and let his buddies screw me. But Nightshade had a policy that nobody wanted to pay top dollar to fuck a limp dishrag. None of the girls I met, foreign or otherwise, were junkies. Vivian, on the other hand, was rarely without a drink in her hand. I think I heard she did pills as well but I never heard what kind. That's what they call hearsay, isn't it?"

Alex laughed and nodded as she looked at Lily's notes.

"Beth has mentioned that Jillian had a twin. What do you know about that?"

"That was no secret. We even saw some movies that Jillian and Jessie made when they were young. Up until recently, they both lived with Frank and Vivian in the fancier houses. One time, at a party, I was put in a room to service a client. The closet was full of beautiful clothes that at first, I thought were Vivian's. But they were too small. They had to be Jillian's. They were all designer labels and all every expensive. I only saw Jessie three times before the other night when you rescued us."

"Did you just say you saw Jessie the night we rescued you?"

"Yeah. He was in the woods near where we lined up for the bus and I'm pretty sure I saw him in the woods just after the raid. You guys were busy and I was looking out the window to see what was going on. I thought he was with you guys?"

"Why would you think that?"

Tiffany thought and counted on her fingers. "Three maybe four months ago, Jessie was given to someone else. Up until that time, he and Jillian were inseparable. From the outside looking in it always looked to us working girls like they had an easy life. After we got to know Jillian, we found out that their lives weren't their own. Being outside for them meant lying around the pool naked. We made Jillian her first mayonnaise and tomato sandwich. Until she spent more time with us, she only had Jessie, and then she didn't have him. Things seemed to change after that. Jillian traveled with us more. She never worked the parties, but she was trucked around in the middle of the night just like we were. When the party was over and it came time to be driven to the next one, she stayed behind and was driven somewhere else. It was like Frank's system for babysitting her when he couldn't find Vivian. This time it was a bit different. If anyone could be left alone, it would have been Jillian and she wasn't. Hell, she spent a lot of time by herself, but it was always with at least one security guy somewhere in the house and she wasn't allowed to leave. It seemed odd that we were all held the night before that party at a service station. When it came time to leave, Stokes told her to get in the car with us. He wasn't happy about it and it was obvious old Tobin was beside himself over the deal. Jillian thought it was because we had left the note but Beth didn't think so. When I saw Vivian at the party house, I guess I just assumed that Jessie had arrived with her. After the tussle with Holder, we were whisked away to our rooms. But that whole deal was different from the get go."

"Why do you think things were different?"

"I don't know but I'd never seen Vivian or Frank at these parties and by the time this one kicked off, she wasn't there and Frank was. My guess is that if Vivian and Frank were there, it had something to do with Jillian. As for Jessie, like I said, I thought he was there with Vivian or you guys. But I'll tell you this about those two kids, both of them are way smarter and more adult than anyone thinks. Jillian came up with a whole better plan to leave the note. Beth and she wrote that note in the bathroom while I kept Dexter occupied. My role was to get his lighter and distract him. They did the smart stuff. I just got whacked in the mouth, and had to give Dexter a hand job. That gave us even more evidence."

Alex thought. "Did you think something was amiss when you were transferred in the middle of the night?"

"Alex, we never traveled anywhere in a straight line and we were always moved late in the day or after dark. It was no big deal to us and Jillian quizzed Tobin about it and that little creep couldn't keep a secret if he had to."

"Did Tobin run things?"

"Tobin took orders from higher up just like the rest of us, but he lived a much nicer life. The little freak never came on to any of us, so we figured he was gay. Turned out he had other weirder issues. He has naked pictures of his mother on his phone. That is way beyond weird even in the world we lived in. But he was not his usual self when he came back to the service station where we slept the night before the party. He was as jumpy as I have ever seen him."

Alex thought. "Could he have been afraid of Frank and Vivian?"

Tiffany laughed. "Alex, everybody was afraid of Vivian. We knew Frank was dangerous and we all felt he had something to do with Crystal and Lucy's murder."

'Why would you think that?"

"Frank just had a violent vide about him like he was about to explode at any moment. Crystal and Lucy were getting unmanageable. According to Holder, Frank hated anyone that was unmanageable. I guess it was just sort of a feeling. We knew he and Vivian were involved in the business at a high level we just never figured out how. The last time I saw Frank was just before Crystal and Lucy disappeared. Me and Beth had a command performance in a large house in Savannah. Frank and Vivian were there with some older guy. We performed together in front of all three while we were filmed. Something made us think that Jillian and Jessie were in the house somewhere, but we never saw them. It was odd. Once we both had faked about three orgasms, they stopped filming, shut the lights off, threw blankets around us and hustled us into a van. Stokes was driving that night. He pulled over after we got out of town headed back toward Charleston for us to get dressed without being tossed around. He even got out of the van and gave us some privacy. If that had been Dexter, he'd have been filming us."

"You seem to feel different about Stokes than you do Holder. Why is that?"

"Stokes never hit us or wanted sex from us. He never treated us badly. It was more like Stokes didn't care. He did love his car. I don't think he cared much for some of the others like Tobin or Holder. From what we saw of the interaction with Vivian, he took her seriously. Everyone took Vivian seriously. I guess we felt that if Stokes was driving, we could relax and just travel. He could be a bad ass, though. We were stopped on a dark road between Beaufort and Charleston one night after a party. Stokes was letting us pee. Three young dudes drove up and stopped, and I guess thought they were going to party with us. Stokes was friendly with them, they let their guard down, and he sent two of them to the hospital. The only reason he didn't fuck up the third guy was, he needed someone to drive them away. We knew Stokes well enough to know what would happen if you got on the wrong side of him. I think Holder got on his bad side and that's why he helped us. Holder was going to hurt me for sure, and Beth as well. Stokes' job was to keep us safe for the party and he did his job."

Alex decided to use a change of topic to see what that would produce in information.

"Why did Jillian sneak away the night of the raid? She told us she was ready to cooperate and talk with us."

Tiffany answered almost immediately.

"She felt safer with Jessie than she did with you guys. Have you asked Beth that question?"

"Not yet."

She'll probably tell you the same. For us, survival depends on finding safety. For us to feel safe, we have to trust. Jillian saw Jessie there and knew she could trust him more than she could trust you guys."

Alex didn't hesitate.

"Tiffany, you trust us, right?"

Tiffany laughed out loud and leaned back against the headboard.

"Since we were rescued, we have been in two places where the doors to our room aren't locked. We can go visit with the others and it does have a feel of being freer than we were before. But I know that I can't just walk out the front door. I know that there are armed men all around watching out for us. But a guard is still a guard. You do understand that right, Alex? As far as the trust question goes, I'm finding myself getting there with you and Lily. The one conversation we've had with the lawyer you're working with was a waste. How many times do we have to tell people that we've been locked up as sex slaves, only to have to live it all over again in a courtroom staring at the people who imprisoned us, while telling a room full of strangers what we went through. And that's not even getting to the judge. I can tell you whoever is on that big chair in the robe up there, he or she, won't be the first judge that's fucked us."

Alex looked down and sighed heavily.

"What do you think you and Beth need more than anything else?"

Tiffany looked at her in a kind way.

"Time. Alex. You and Lily, and all the other folks have been great to us. But we've learned to be very stingy with our trust. We watched two of our friends butchered. They were cut and burned as an example while they wouldn't tell them about anyone else who was thinking of running away. They said nothing right up until the end when Lucy had her throat cut and Crystal was nearly decapitated with a piano wire around her neck. Those two we could trust because in the face of all that pain, knowing what was about to happen to them, they kept our names to themselves. So, for right now, it is easier to trust the dead than it is to trust the system you work with. We've heard the 'justice must be swift' horseshit, but as someone who would have to testify, it takes time, Alex. You can't just go by the court calendar. Some days, I don't even think I know who I am that day let alone what I have been. And, I mean no offense by saying that."

Alex nodded. "No offense taken, Tiffany. Is there anything else I can get you?"

Tiffany began to weep slightly. "Yeah. Is there any way I can talk to my mom?"

Alex didn't hesitate.

"We'll make that happen."

Alex got up, walked over and hugged Tiffany again, and turned to leave.

Tiffany asked her a question as she opened the door.

"That night of the raid, you had a gun on your hip. If someone would have threatened us, would you have shot them?"

Alex turned around and faced her.

"Yes, and I would have shot to kill. And before you ask, no, it wouldn't have been the first time."

Alex walked to the room she shared with Lily at the shelter. Lily was standing in the room looking out the window. Alex spoke as she set her tablet down.

"I think that if Beth or Tiffany had any information that would be useful in the prosecution of Frank Bartram, they would tell us. I don't think they know anything at all about his involvement."

Lily turned around and looked at her seriously.

"I think they know enough to know that whatever they say, if Frank walks, they are in danger, and I think they know Frank is going to walk regardless of what they say."

Alex nodded. " I do, too. So, what do we do with this mess now? Phelps and Mary are getting heat from the prosecutor, and I think she knows that without Jillian's testimony, Frank is going to walk. Did you get a strange feeling about her? What's her name, Stammers?"

"I didn't like her or trust her. It stands out more when you have been working with a group of people that get it. I think Deputy U.S. Attorney Sylvia Stammers doesn't get it Alex."

Alex sat down. "Me either."

Lily continued. "Did Tiffany say anything at all about why Jillian snuck away."

Alex came around the desk and looked out the window.

"Actually, she summed it up quite nicely. She felt safer with her brother than she did with us."

Lily went back to her tablet on the table.

"So, what we know now that we didn't know before is that Jillian had help that night from her brother."

Alex added. "We also know he was smart and patient enough to wait until we were all busy to make his move. Someone that has just turned 15 and is that careful and clever, scares me to death. Both Beth and Tiffany talk about how smart and sophisticated they are beyond their years. But mostly we know that we missed it, Lily. We got so caught up in our mission that we didn't slow down and take it all in. We got too focused on getting Frank that we exposed our backside to a kid barely 15, who probably is going to be very good at hiding and protecting his sister."

Lily agreed but added, "We know that something changed in the situation that brought both Vivian and Frank Bartram to a party they never would have been at if Jillian didn't have some involvement. I think Helena wasn't just at the party. We need to go over the recordings from Quarterback and see if we can get any more information."

Alex pulled out her laptop and opened it. She pulled up the video and audio file from Quarterback. They both put their headsets on and connected to Alex's laptop. Alex played it through about four times before she caught the small phrase she was looking for. They both plainly heard Frank telling Helena that she would have time to get to know Jillian before she took her to Charlotte.

Lily spoke first.

"That's why Vivian was there. Helena was going to deliver Jillian to someone. Vivian had figured that Jillian was about to get sold or given away the same way Jessie was. She was right, and that has to be why Frank showed up."

Alex followed up. "The note must have triggered it. That is how Vivian got involved in the first place. That is how she found out Frank was going to sell their daughter."

# CHAPTER 19

All his friends knew that when Phelps Wheeler got mad, his face went to neutral. As they both stood with Sylvia Stammers, Mary Close watched him as his face gradually shifted into neutral. Sylvia was ranting. Neither agent was listening, both had quit the moment they heard she had agreed to setting Frank Bartram free without a fight. If she had resisted or mounted an objection, it would have given them at least another two weeks while the court considered the issue

"You two were supposed to bring me my case ready to go. Instead, you let the key witness slip away into the dark while you all ran around like amateurs with these Smithson people. I worked hard to get this case. God knows why the Attorney General assigned me. Maybe she really doesn't like me. I'm left with a bunch of foreign victims who can't speak English, two low level transporters who are so bad at their job that both have done time, and a woman no one really knows anything about. What a piece of shit you brought me."

Mary grimaced as Phelps said, "I can't believe the Attorney General would dislike you."

Sylvia exploded.

"What did you say detective? How dare you speak to me that way. I'm an Assistant U.S. Attorney."

Phelps had reached his limit. He paced his words and delivered them calmly.

"I said, I can't believe that someone, anyone, could develop even the mildest dislike for you, Counselor. And for the record, it's not 'detective'. I'm an FBI Special Agent in Charge of a multi-agency national task force. Mary is an FBI Special Agent assigned to that task force by your boss. We both have law degrees just like you. We also have more experience with these cases between us than you could compile in the rest of your career. The others involved in something you refer to as 'your' case are seasoned hand-picked members of the U.S. Marshals Service selected by the AG herself. While it is true that one of the key witnesses in this case disappeared, there are agents out there looking for that witness right now. There are two surviving women who are putting their lives on the line to help you make 'your' case. They are being watched over by 'those Smithson' people much better than we could. The only thing wrong here is that the moment that the defense finds a judge to challenge the status of the case, you roll over."

Mary was shocked at Phelps, but after she regained her composure, looked at Sylvia.

"Word to the wise for next time Ms. Stammers, if the AG gives you a next time. You can criticize us all you want. We more or less, mostly less in your case, have to listen to your bullshit. But don't ever, in my presence, criticize Smithson Evermore or their efforts. Without their technology, their experience with survivors, and the dedication of their people involved with this case, all of which I might add come to our government free of charge, we would be nowhere. Now on a more practical note, did you submit the paperwork for Beth and Tiffany to receive protective custody?"

Sylvia shocked by the quick change in demeanor looked at Mary defiantly. "I did not submit it. They have given me nothing that warrants the government protecting them. And, I've saved you the trouble, I called and told them myself."

At that, Mary lost what small bit of composure she had.

"Ms. Stammer, while you are in a federal facility, this one is operated by the Federal Bureau of Investigation. Please gather your belongings. I am going to have one of our agents escort you to the front door. I would do it, but you would never make it out of the elevator in one piece. I'm not kidding, Sylvia, get your shit and get out."

Sylvia. "Can you do that?"

"I'm doing it. You're on FBI real estate. Get out of our building and be advised that you will at one time or another in your pointless career, need FBI cooperation. I wouldn't hold your breath on that one. We tend to be a bit clannish and share who is worth our time and who it not." An agent showed up, Sylvia gathered her things and was escorted out of the building.

As Stammers was leaving, Phelps immediately updated Lily at the shelter. She and Alex ran down the hall to Beth's room. She wasn't there. They separated. Alex ran to Tiffany's room and Lily to the commons room and lobby. Neither one of the women was there. Just like Jillian, they had disappeared.

Then they both walked in through the front door. They looked puzzled. "What's up, guys?"

Lily and Alex explained what they had just been told.

Beth spoke first. "Yeah, she called. We tried to tell you that woman didn't give a shit about the case or us. How long before Frank is released?"

Lily answered. "Phelps is going to try to buy us 48 hours. We have made arrangements, if you two will agree, for you both to return with us to one of our new facilities in Tampa. We can keep you totally safe there until we find Jillian and can move forward with the case."

Beth laughed. "Is that instead of the promise of protective custody that the prosecutor was throwing around at our first meeting with her? We knew she had no intention of doing that from the get go. I guess we weren't enslaved long enough to meet her standards."

Alex stepped in. "That is why we are offering to make sure you are safe, regardless of what that particular prosecutor thinks."

Tiffany blurted out. " It's not just about Frank. This organization, this thing that held us, is huge with lots of bad people associated with it. Didn't that woman know what she was up against?"

Lily threw up her arms. "I really don't care what she knows or thinks at this point. We are offering you even better protection without any strings attached until we can work with Agents Close and Wheeler to carry the case forward."

Beth stood quietly with her arms crossed, then spoke. "No thanks."

The room became as still as a crypt while those two words bounced off the walls.

Alex looked down at the floor. "Beth, we are offering you better protection than protective custody. Why would you want to refuse that?"

"I've been a slave for the past five years. Before that, the only thing people worried about was how much work they could get out of me before they threw me out. Pardon me if the thought of being locked up again doesn't sound that wonderful. It's time I found a way to make it on my own. No offense, you all have been great. This place has been great. We've both gotten a lot stronger. But as long as Frank and whoever he works for think we are cooperating we have targets on our back. I'm tired of that. Holder will do his time and be slapping another girl around. Stokes will be back driving another set of women through the night within six months of his release. That bunch is too big for little old me. I'm done. I know Stokes will probably walk, but we wouldn't be here if he hadn't stepped up."

Tiffany listened to this then spoke almost as if she was carrying on Beth's conversation.

"All I could tell you about Frank Bartram is that he must have been a lousy lay because I can't remember him. Vivian, on the other hand was loads of fun but it was long ago and so much has happened, I can't remember that much. If I was asked if I told them no, I couldn't swear I did. We didn't know how they were involved and only suspected they were decision makers."

She paused to let that sink in, then continued. "My mother told me to come home last night and bring Beth with me. I was so bad, but they still love me. We love you and know how hard you both have worked for us, but I would feel safer with my family around me. Except for them, Beth is the only one I really trust, and just like her, I appreciate everything all of you have done for us but I'm calling for my family to come and get us."

Lily stood quietly. Alex hadn't given up yet.

"Aren't you concerned about the safety of your family?"

Tiffany laughed. "My two brothers were Marines. My cousins all served. They're good old southern boys raised on moonshine and fried fish. They hunt half of what they eat. Alex, they are family. Once they know what's up, they will do anything to keep us safe and allow us to get our feet back under us. That's what you guys would be doing. Supporting us until we could move on and make headway on our own."

Lily finally spoke. "Alex, Tiffany is right. "

Alex looked at them. "But you will stay here until your family comes and gets you, right?"

Beth walked over and gave Alex a huge hug. "You are so sweet. That is the least we can do for our Star Woman. We will stay here until Tiffany's family comes to get us."

Lily called Phelps and gave him the news. He actually supported their decision.

"I'll talk to Ludlow and see what we can work out. I want to supply them with survivor phones with direct connections to us. Do you think they will accept them?"

"I think we can convince them that it wouldn't be invasive. We will put location capability on them that is only activated when they turn it on and will only show up on our system. I'll let you know what they decide. So where does our operation go from here?"

Phelps answered. "The Attorney General, Slade, and Ludlow are on a conference call this afternoon. We will know more after that. All of our evidence and observations from this case have been fed into Dr. Morozov's system. I doubt we will stop our efforts on the Nightshade Group but this chapter will be over sooner rather than later."

Lily continued. "Speaking of Ludlow, how is he?"

"Off the grid with his smaller team. Even I don't know what they are up to."

Lily had one more question. "Did the Attorney General really hand pick Stammers? She didn't turn out to be such a good choice."

Phelps laughed. "No, she didn't. Mary threw her out of our building when she found out that she had called Beth and Tiffany on her own. The AG must see something in her that we missed."

Lily thought. "Perhaps Gwen Vespers had another reason to appoint Ms. Stammers. Without Jillian, we knew we were on shaky ground for Frank. Has anybody said sorry for losing Jillian?"

Phelps finished the conversation. "Well, whatever reason she had we at least have Holder. Stokes will walk. As far as Helena is concerned, several sets of people arrived from those agencies with three letters in them, the secret ones, and left with her. The only thing we now know is that her real name is not Helena Reagan. And, yes, I apologized to the AG. She accepted with her usual professionalism. I will keep you up to speed but I suspect that Slade Smithson has other cases he needs you and Alex involved with."

"Take care of yourself, Phelps. I'm sure we'll see each other soon. As soon as the girls are safely in the hands of family, we'll send you a final report. That conference call must be over because my boss is calling. Talk soon."

Lily switched over to the call from Slade. It was short.

"I need you to go home and visit your family. Enjoy the fishing and your mother's okra stew. Take all of your operational gear with you. I'm sending you some new equipment. See if you can find a place for Birdman to spend some time bird watching along the shore."

Lily paused. "Have I done something wrong? Why are you giving me time off?"

Slade laughed. "Who said anything about you being off? Consider this a strategic relocation of assets. We are just positioning for the next chapter in this adventure with the Nightshade Group."

"I thought they were closing down the operation."

Slade laughed. "Oh, the current operation as it played out is definitely closing down but you know what they say, when one operation closes, another opens. I need a place for Birdman to stay near you but not with you."

Lily thought. "I think Billy Ward would let him use the fishing cabin. It's got plenty of room and comes with its own boat. I'll call Aunt Lydia after I tell Alex, and leave right away."

Slade responded. "Alex will be headed to her next assignment. She won't be far from you. Text me when everyone is there. Lily, no one is to know you and Birdman are there. Can you get Billy to keep a secret?"

Lily laughed out loud. "Keeping a secret on St. Helena Island is a tough thing, you know that. But, if we can make the island telegraph believe that Birdman is there for the birds, that will work. There is no way my going home will not make a ripple. Is that OK?"

"That will have to suffice. Just limit the number of local government people. Billy will have to be in the loop but he is the only law enforcement in that area we trust right now. We have discovered that Holder is a former police officer from Charleston. That had been deleted by someone inside the federal records process. Keep this on a need-to-know basis and give Aunt Lydia my love." He hung up.

Lily called her mother and was on the road within the hour. When she pulled up to her mother's house, Lydia was standing like always on her porch with a cup of coffee in her hand. She was talking to Deputy Billy Ward as Lily walked up the steps and joined them. Lydia hugged Lily.

"I'll get you your iced tea. You can have a moment to talk with Billy." She turned to her husband's life-long friend. "You're coming for dinner, William. I don't want any backtalk. It's fried chicken, okra, red rice, and greens. All your favorites." She stepped inside.

Lily hugged Billy long and hard.

"You've put on a few pounds, Deputy, but you look good."

"Why is it that you and your mother always feel the need to point out my belly, first thing?"

Billy Ward released the hug. He had been a second father to her. He had attended her graduation from the Naval Academy and a year and a half later, helped bury her father. They had been quite a duo. Sam Michaels, Big Sam to most, stood almost 6'5" and was a legendary fisherman, carpenter, and hunter. Billy Ward was the white version of Sam. Through their young years, they were inseparable. Sam had talked Billy into becoming a Sheriff's Deputy when he returned from the Marines. It was Billy that witnessed the christening of a small white baby that Lydia and Sam adopted the minute they got permission to do so. It was Billy that picked Lily up in Norfolk and drove her home after she finished her obligation to the Navy. He loved Lily like she was his own.

"So, tell me about this fella that is going to be staying in our fish camp?"

Lily laughed. Her dad and Billy were known for getting right to the point.

"He is really smart. He has a PhD in aeronautical engineering from MIT. He also has a PhD from Cornell in Ornithology. Birds are his true passion. He has been with us for a little over a year now."

"I get the ornithology part with the nickname. But what does an engineer/ornithologist do for Smithson Evermore?"

"He flies birds he has built to help us see and hear better."

"Drones?"

"That's right. They are not your toy store variety either. He first built them to study his birds better. Now he helps us study other things."

Billy thought. "I have one more question. Does he fish?"

Lily laughed. "You'll have to ask him. We need to keep all of this between us."

Billy nodded. "I'm within a month of retiring. The Sheriff leaves me to patrol this island. I don't even go into the station unless I have a meeting, need supplies, or I need my truck worked on. You were really specific about not talking in the workplace. At some point, you or your boss are going to have to fill me in on that."

Lily sat down as her mother brought out her tea and the coffee pot so Billy could refill his travel mug. "I'm not sure yet why Birdman and I are here. We just had an operation go south at prosecution. If I had to guess, that operation may be over but there is a part of the investigation still going on."

Billy filled his cup as he spoke. "Sounds like someone thinks that the operation failed because of help from the inside. Any idea who thinks that?"

"The Attorney General of the United States would most likely be that person."

Billy whistled. "That's good enough for me. My lips are sealed. I best be getting back to patrolling. It's good to have you here, Lily. We miss you around here. Lydia, shall I come by at the usual time?"

Lydia smiled. "You should. Grace will be said at 6:30 pm sharp, and you miss grace, you don't eat. Be careful, you. It's harder for you to get out of the way with that belly you been growing."

Billy shook his head, got in his truck and laughed as he pulled out.

Lydia looked at Lily. "You tell that bird guy friend he's invited here for his meals as well. We have to make him feel welcome. Is there anything I serve that he might not eat? Nothing makes a person feel more like an outsider than to refuse food they don't eat."

Lily smiled as she hugged Lydia from behind. "I think he eats everything but chicken."

"I've heard of people that don't eat beef, or people that don't eat pork or lamb. I've heard of people who won't eat anything but vegetables. I can handle all of that but I've never heard of a person that doesn't eat chicken."

Lily laughed again. "I think Birdman loves anything that flies too much to eat them. But he understands that others love chicken.

Lydia harumphed and continued in Gullah. "I set a proper southern table and the table's not proper without chicken. I will make him some pork chops."

Lily got settled in her old room. She walked back out on the porch just as her phone rang. It was Ludlow. He spoke first.

"Are you all settled in?"

"Why, are you about to unsettle me?"

"Nope, just doing my job and checking our deployment."

"So where are you deployed?"

"Can't say but not too far away. Did the girls accept the phones?"

"They did and they have already called once to say they are safely with Tiffany's family. They're in . . ."

He cut her off. "Not over the phone, even ours. Did you get with Billy?"

"I did. We're expecting Birdman will show up here by dinner. Billy will then take him out to the fish camp."

"Collins will be with him and others will follow tomorrow. I'll be in touch when necessary. Take care of yourself."

Lily smiled. "You too, Luke, you take care."

# CHAPTER 20

It was hot and crowded in Myrtle Beach. Stella had left for Atlanta as soon as she and Vivian had returned to her house. She made calls to several people inside the justice system, then packed a bag and chartered a flight. The twins showed up two hours later. Because of the raid, Vivian had traded her car in the next morning. Other than Jessie's morning run, they had not ventured far, because the crowds offered ample coverage for whoever Nightshade might send to get close or worse. The twins were in Jessie's room talking.

Jillian sat next to Vivian on the bed and spoke to Jessie.

"She's out, Jessie. How much did she take last night?"

Jessie walked over to the bed and put his hand on his sister's shoulder.

"I have no idea if she took any. It may be just the booze. I think she's fine for now, but we need to find another place to stay. According to Stella, Frank could be released anytime now."

Jillian kept looking at her mother as she spoke. "You mean unless those women tell them what he's been up to.

"I don't think that will even be enough. There would have to be more evidence, direct evidence of the shit he has done. They don't have that, at least not from that party. Do you know who that woman was that they had in cuffs with Dad?"

Jillian thought back to the night of the party.

"I only saw her for a brief moment when they put them in the car to be taken away. I've never seen her before. Dad talked about a special guest that was coming that he had some business with. That could have been her."

Jessie got up and walked over to his desk where a sizeable computer sat with three screens and a small main frame humming away. He sat down and brought it to life. "Do you know her name?"

Jillian thought. "No, I never heard them talking. Dad came in and talked to me then shut the door. I stepped out to Lily just after that.

Jessie looked at the screen. "Stella had lots of success in hacking into the federal system. That is how she was always a step ahead. They'd file a report. She would see it before they did. They'd request a warrant; she would see it at the same time a judge did. She knew what they knew before they even knew it. But I can't find anything from this last party. It's being handled differently. If we could find the evidence, that is where the pictures would be and we could get a look at her."

Jillian rose and crossed the room. She stood behind her brother to look at the equipment and screens on the desk.

"Where did all this come from? I didn't know you knew about computers."

Jessie laughed.

"Stella got me interested in them and it turns out I'm sort of gifted in their function and how they can be used. I built this system from components I ordered off the Internet."

"Stella let you on the Internet?"

"As long as Stella gets the attention she needs, she pretty much lets me do what I want. Half of her system has links to what they call the dark web. She's pretty twisted but knowing what she likes helps me get her satisfied without too much direct involvement. I'm monitoring her now to keep up with Frank's case, but all I'm seeing is what happened at the house, and we know all of that. I know that once he is out, we need to move quickly and stay ahead of him. He will be after us."

Jillian kept looking at the computers. "I wouldn't even know how to turn that thing on. For all the private tutors, fashionable clothes, fancy food, and big houses, I'm not even sure I know how to use an oven or microwave.

Having everything provided for you can make you really stupid."

"It doesn't make you stupid, it makes you dependent. We both have a whole lot more to learn about normal life. We were never allowed to be kids. We are both really naive and have a lot of catching up to do."

Jillian bent down and kissed her brother on the head. "I know. And, we've become a liability to the people that made us that way. What will happen to Mom?"

Jessie reached up and put his hand on his sister's hand. "She is the largest liability Frank and the bosses have now. She's always been unpredictable but now it's obvious that Frank can't control her. I have a place we can go that they don't know about. It's a bit primitive, but is totally off the grid and defensible. It's about an hour south of here just on the other side of Georgetown. We need to get you and mom there. Stella doesn't know about it and can't know where it is."

Jillian crossed back over to her mother. "So, you don't think we can trust Stella. If we know we can't trust Mom, I'm doubtful about Stella. We really have no one else."

Jessie crossed the room and put his arms around Jillian.

"We have each other. That is the way it's always been."

Jillian almost whispered. "It's going to sound strange but the other women I traveled with in the end became my first friends. I learned to trust them because they would risk a beating to keep me safe. I thought that if I left the note, I could trust that help was on the way. It came. I trusted Lily. She got me out of there."

Jessie leaned in. "I got you out of there. If you'd have stayed, you would be in the same boat as Beth and Tiffany, still locked up. One thing I've learned from our freaky upbringing is playing by the rules always means you are more likely to lose. Winning, for us, means staying alive until we can be sure they have either lost interest in us or they no longer pose a threat."

Jillian got up, turned, and faced her brother.

"How are a couple of kids going to do that with a drugged-out mother and a father that wants us dead?"

"By thinking things through, and not being stupid." He walked her over to his closet and opened the door. Inside was a large safe. He punched the numbers on the keyboard and put his eye down to a small window. The lock clicked and he opened it. Jillian stood shocked as she looked at the array of weapons in the safe.

Jillian stepped back. "Where did these come from?"

Jessie laughed. "The Internet is a wonderful thing, particularly the dark side of it."

Jillian touched the wooden stock of a rifle.

"Do you even know how to use these?"

Jessie laughed. "I haven't spent all my time at the computer. Stella belongs to a shooting club. There is no end to the number of friendly men and women who want to teach her, and her 'nephew', how to be safe with each one of them, how to hunt, and how to shoot."

"So, you learned how to use them. Why?"

Jessie reached past her and closed the safe.

"Insurance. I don't plan on hunting anyone but I've learned that if you want to be safe, and the system can't keep you safe, then you learn how to do that for yourself. Sometimes that happens by doing some very dangerous things. These are just for insurance."

They heard Vivian wake up. They joined her as she was ordering lunch. She always seemed hungry.

During lunch Vivian was animated and conversive mostly about what she was going to have done to Frank when she found out which prison he was being sent to. Vivian turned her attention to Jillian.

"I was wondering, what was your plan when you walked out of that house into the arms of the police?"

Jillian spoke softly but looked squarely at her mother.

"I would have told them about being forced to dance naked in front of strangers. I would have told them that you forced Jessie and me to make movies pretending to have sex. I would have told them how the other women were treated."

Vivian took the news, thought for a moment, and then asked. "What do you think that would have gotten you?"

Jessie answered for her. "Away, Mom."

Vivian answered with the slightest bit of venom.

"Away from me. That's what you wanted."

Jillian almost shouted back. "No. You were never there. I wanted away from all of it. Particularly the fear that I never knew where I was, or when I would be ordered to entertain like the others. I was treated nicely, but I was a slave just like them. Moved at night. Locked in my room. Think about it. According to your story, I would have been whisked away after that party and given or sold to a stranger. You and I both know what would have happened then. We were together once. It was a weird kind of together, but at least you and Frank were there for protection. Then Frank left, Jessie left, and you left.

Jessie's phone rang and interrupted the conversation. "Hey, Stella. How's it going?"

"Better than expected. We called in a judicial favor and the prosecutor agreed that they had no verifiable proof that Frank was doing anything but attending a party. He will be out of the federal lock up this time tomorrow. I'm not sure where Vivian left off with Frank, but he will be free. He has already had me arrange to pick him up."

"Where is he headed?"

"He won't tell me, and I really don't want to know. It looks like Stokes is going to be released as well. The two women he was transporting with Jillian have decided not to testify against him."

"So, when can I expect you home?"

"I've chartered a flight for late afternoon tomorrow, after Frank is released."

Jessie rolled his eyes. "I'll see you at the private airside tomorrow. Just text me the time."

"That would be lovely. I have to go talk to Stokes. Bye for now."

Jessie hung up the phone. "It's time we got you two out of here. Frank is being released."

Vivian exploded. "How the fuck is he being released? They caught him at the party. I should have known Stella would rig the whole thing to get him out of there. She stands to lose as much as we do if he goes down. Did she say where he's going?"

"She said he wouldn't tell her."

Vivian began pacing. "Of course, he didn't. He knew Stella would tell me. He was at the Atlanta house. I think that's where he'll go. You need to take care of your sister. I need to go until I figure out what I'm going to do about Frank."

Jillian asked. "Wait, you're leaving me here? Where are you headed?"

Vivian spoke over her shoulder as she was walking into her room to start packing. "I think it's best if I don't tell you and Jessie has proved more than adequate in protecting you."

Jillian looked at her brother. "Some parents we have, Jessie. They won't tell each other where they're going, and now, they won't tell us. Quite the little family we've turned into."

Jessie stared after his mother. "Jillian, this has never been a family and they have never really been parents. That's OK. She is a creature of habit and will be easy to find. We need to be on our own now, anyway. I need to get you to my safe place. You can't stay here. Now, I'm sure Stella can't be trusted. We're on our own for the foreseeable future. Get your things together. We leave in an hour."

"What about Mom?"

"Eventually she will tell us where she is. When the time is right, we may have to keep her safe, as well. But if Frank finds her, or us, we will be dead. No question."

Jillian stood up. "You really think he would hurt you?"

"Jillian, he was about to send you off to God only knows who. I ended up with Stella because he was worried that I needed to be watched. He was right, except I'm the one that has been watching. He will eventually find out I was the one that helped you. If we are ever going to be free, we are going to have to help the people who rescued you figure out what to do about Frank and the people he works for. I've cloned my laptop to Stella's and I have some of her paper files. I haven't had enough time to figure out all of them yet."

"You've stolen files from her office? Aren't you afraid she'll find out."

"Stella is too busy cleaning up their messes to check the status of her own files. She has kept everything, probably as insurance. The records go back years. Some of the newer ones were encrypted but with a little research they were easily hacked. She even has old videos and paper records. There is one big one I need to get. I need time to figure it out. But first we get you safe. As soon as Vivian is gone, we go. I have everything we need already at the cabin."

He was interrupted when Vivian burst into the room with her bags.

"Jessie, please be a dear and put these in my new car. Mommy has to leave you both for a few days but I will be in touch. Stay with Aunt Stella, keep Jillian safe, and if anything changes, be sure to call me."

Jessie put her bags in the trunk of her car and she was gone. Just like that.

Jillian looked at Jessie when he came back inside. "Where do you think she's going?"

Jessie pulled out his phone. "I would bet she is headed for the Charleston house first."

"Why would she be headed there?"

Jessie laughed. "That's where she keeps the really big guns, she's so fond of, not to mention a stash of about a half million dollars. Are you ready to go?"

Jillian nodded. "All set. Are we taking Stella's car?"

"No, we'll take mine. You will be safe at the cabin. You need to stay there after I drop you off. I will see what else Stella knows and be back after I get a few more files and things we will need. Do you have any idea how to get ahold of the people who rescued you?"

"Lily gave me her card before I disappeared in the woods."

"Memorize the number then destroy the card. It's really important no one but us knows that we are in contact with them. I have a pre-paid phone for you. They call it a 'burner'. It's hard to trace, but for now only use it to call me."

Jillian's lip started to quiver. "What did I do, Jessie? I shouldn't have left that note."

Jessie walked over and took his sister into his arms. "You did exactly the right thing by leaving that note. Do you have any idea how to get in touch with Beth or Tiffany?"

"Tiffany's last name is Holmes. I think her people live near Ridgeland. That's all I know."

He hugged her even tighter. "That's all we need to find them. Now, let's get moving. I'm moving my computers and taking a couple of things from the closet. It's time we started securing our own future."

"You mean, you're taking some guns. I can't see you killing anyone. The computers I get, but you're just a kid. Do you think you would really shoot someone?"

Jessie began unplugging cords and packing them in a small roll around suitcase along with the console and two screens. He spoke as he packed.

"I found an unedited video in the records of two women being killed. I think Frank is the one doing the killing."

Jillian gasped. "That has to be Crystal and Lucy. Frank killed them?"

"There is no question in my mind it's Frank in the one version. There is one highly edited version that had all sorts of marketing stuff with it on the dark web. I believe Frank killed two women just to make a movie of their death, and then sold it to the sickos who get a thrill out of watching something like that. I don't think he would think twice about killing any of us. So, yes, if you were threatened, I don't think I would hesitate to pull the trigger."

Jillian began packing. "I'm not coming back here Jessie. I don't know where we'll end up, but it won't be here. If Frank did that and Stella had a copy of it, she knew. If she knew, then Mom knows. I won't be around that any longer."

Jessie looked at her as he finished packing his clothes.

"Neither of us will."

# CHAPTER 21

Mary Close had spent the weekend with friends in Atlanta and was about to return to Tampa when she received the call. Ninety minutes later Marshal Tim Collins picked her up and delivered her to the Smithson jet at the airport. He helped her with her bags, then drove away. She was shown her seat. Slade Smithson sat across from her with Attorney General, Gwen Vespers next to him. As they raised the stairs and closed the door hatch, Slade began.

"We felt that it would be best to have this little conversation in the air. You are going to be staying with Jeanine Morozov at her compound until the next phase of this operation is over. We will be feeding you information collected from a variety of different investigations being conducted simultaneously on several fronts. The rest of the team you have worked with will be sending you what they learn and you and Dr. Morozov will be compiling the evidence for a multi-pronged approach to shutting down the Nightshade Group in North America."

Mary looked across at the Attorney General. "Why me? Why not Phelps? He is senior with more field experience?"

Gwen Vespers smiled. "We are putting your partner's Rhodes Scholar brain and experience in Atlanta to work coordinating all federal assets and interrogations. You will still report to him. We are no longer just looking for trafficking offenders. We are looking for evidence on how they operate so cleanly in our country. You are particularly skilled in spotting small things in the intelligence. You picked up that Helena Reagan was more important than just running that operation in Buckhead. You speak Russian which will be very useful because we now know the Nightshade Group has strong connections there. You have seen all of these people in person. Jeanine has only seen pictures and heard voices. The equipment and communication system we confiscated in Atlanta is military grade. You are ex-military intelligence with a specialty in soviet technology. And, most importantly, you threw Sylvia Stammers out of the FBI building. That was brilliant."

Mary looked confused. "You knew Stammers was not the right choice?"

"I needed to confirm Ludlow's suspicions. We needed to see what she would do when confronted with Stella St. John and Judge Horton's order. She did what she was instructed to do. She made a call."

"To you?"

"No, not to me. She called the person who instructed her to call once she made sure the case disappeared."

"So, she is part of it."

The AG laughed. "And, you threw her out before she could finish what she had been instructed to do, which was to make sure both Frank Bartram and Helena Reagan, were both freed. Frank yes, Helena, no."

Slade broke in. "If I may. Ludlow had isolated information in his investigation that indicated the Nightshade Group had several lawyers within the Justice Department that were assisting not only in providing information to Nightshade, but facilitating the release of prisoners early, leaking the location of primary witnesses, and helping the group stay two steps ahead. They have also identified additional people of interest in Homeland Security and in the FBI itself, as well as members of the Federal bench."

Mary looked shocked. "Our own people have been helping these creeps enslave people." She paused a moment as she connected the dots. "That is why we were on Smithson communications for the last operation rather than our own network. What about the Marshal Service?"

The Attorney General responded.

"We have some people of interest identified there as well. That will be dealt with separately. And Ms. Stammers has already been removed from the playing field. She'll make just a mediocre jailhouse lawyer. Your main objective is coordinating the intelligence, checking the vetting process and making sure we don't take anyone into custody unless we have an ironclad case. You're a skilled attorney and a seasoned investigator. You are the right woman for the job. I hope you are not allergic to dogs."

Mary laughed. "You mean Rasputin? He's quite impressive and no, I love dogs and am looking forward to working with Dr. Morozov."

Slade laughed. "Mary, Rasputin is just the tip of the iceberg where that kennel is concerned."

Mary smiled." Am I allowed to know where we are heading, I mean geographically?"

The AG answered. "Not just yet. There are only a handful of people that know where Jeanine Morozov's compound is and even fewer who know what she and her staff do there. I hope you like your vegetables, because it is strictly vegetarian. She grows her own vegetables, has a personal chef that prepares all the meals for the people and the pets, and supervises the two-member kitchen staff. All have been vetted and cleared not just by us but by Interpol as well."

"How long can I expect to be living at the compound?"

The AG didn't falter. "As long as it takes to finally bring the Nightshade Group in this country down. One final note. It was Stammers who alerted a specific ICE agent to deport the foreign workers who were rescued in Atlanta. He is no longer an agent."

"And what about Helena Reagan?"

"She will not be seeing her home country ever again. She has terrorist ties you will soon learn about. You have been right about her all along."

The Smithson jet landed on the military side of McGhee Tyson Airport near Maryville, Tennessee. Mary was met by a tall man with bronze skin and a noble demeanor. He loaded her bags into the back of a Land Rover and they climbed in. Mary looked around the car.

"I was expecting Rasputin."

The man laughed. "We needed room for your luggage and he takes up a good bit of real estate when he is in the car. Besides, he is memorable and we don't need anyone paying that much attention to us. My name is Nathaniel. I work with Dr. Morozov. Please make yourself comfortable. We have a little over a half-hour ride."

Nathaniel headed east, and somewhere between the airport and Townsend, Tennessee he took a right turn onto a mountain road. About 3 miles in, he turned onto a private driveway that went another two miles climbing back and forth uphill past a series of cabins until they got to a gate near the top. Mary was impressed with the stone and brick fence that went in both directions. It came with a crown of razor wire slanted out on its crest. As they approached, the gate opened and they drove to the top of the driveway and into the last bay of a six-car garage.

Nathanial grabbed her bags and led the way into the house. She was greeted by Rasputin who was indeed one of the largest dogs Mary had ever been around. He was accompanied by Fritz, a Bernese Mountain dog, not much smaller than Rasputin, and Morton, a Belgian Malinois, who sat stoically off to the side while his two canine partners did the greeting with kisses and nuzzles. Mary laughed out loud.

"My goodness, everywhere I put my hand a dog's head magically appears underneath it."

From across the room a woman spoke.

"You must love dogs. They don't do that with everyone. I'm Jeanine Morozov. It's a pleasure to meet you in person, Agent Close."

Mary looked up and smiled. "They are magnificent and please, call me Mary, Dr. Morozov.

"If that is the case, then it will be Mary and Jeanine. Nathaniel, you have met. He and his family live here on the compound with me. His wife, Surette is in charge of the house and kitchen. You will see and meet other members of his family who help me in the lab, the kennels, and provide security. We can speak freely about our work. Everyone here has a top-secret clearance. Also don't be alarmed, most of them are armed. Before you ask, let me answer. Nathaniel and his entire family are First Nations people. We are standing on land owned by their tribe. They are gracious enough to let me live and work here. Let me show you around and then you can rest before dinner."

The two women walked down a long hall to a great room that looked out over the valley they had just driven through. They paused and enjoyed the view. Mary spoke.

"You have complete control of who comes up that road don't you?"

"Yes. You passed several points that were manned with armed guards and dogs. You would have never reached the gate if we didn't wish it and you are free to walk anywhere on this side of the wall."

Jeanine turned and walked to the far end of the room to what looked like a closet door. It turned out to be an elevator. Both women got in. Mary noticed that there were two floors above them, and a control pad on the top of the panel with button, a retina reader next to it, and a fingerprint pad. She commented.

"That is an interesting setup for a private elevator."

Dr. Morozov smiled, and activated the security panel, and pushed the button. The elevator started to descend. Mary was impressed. "How far down are we going?"

"Fifty feet into the base of the mountain. We do a great deal of work here for many international issues and we are completely off the grid. We raise all our own food and generate all of our own power. Our system is patterned after the secure doomsday compound for the U.S. leadership should we come under attack. Our little workplace operates off a more sophisticated system that I designed myself. And please don't worry. We are not going to turn you into a mole. Our living quarters are above ground and very comfortable. It is only the lab and the computers that are underground as well as our own little doomsday shelter should that day ever arrive."

Mary spoke as she walked. "This is impressive. When the Attorney General indicated that it was a secure facility, she wasn't kidding."

The elevator stopped and they exited into a central area where several electric transport carts were charging. They got into one and continued down a long tunnel. Dr. Morozov spoke as they drove.

"We are actually traveling under the road you drove in on. Our control room where we will work is another 400 yards. The rooms on either side are where the servers are located, spare parts are kept stored, and the central control console for the satellite communications system, air quality monitoring and life support systems are kept. The natural temperature down here is perfect for maintaining the equipment without added cooling. Above us is solid steel reinforced concrete and bedrock. Ah, we have arrived."

Jeanine opened the door to a room that looked like a futuristic war room. On one wall was a huge projected map that could be changed depending upon the geographic location and topic of interest. The remaining walls were giant computer screens reflecting what was on the consoles in the center of the room. One of those screens was obviously running an analytical program and keeping track of intermediate findings. Another was the map of the south with blinking lights. Several were in the low country of South Carolina. Mary looked at the map and smiled. "Those blinking lights are the team members, aren't they?" Morozov nodded.

Mary looked around in amazement.

"I have been to CIA headquarters, the joint Chiefs, and the National Security Agency world status briefing room. I have never seen anything like this."

Jeanine smiled. "That's not surprising. All these are different video and analytical interfaces with the system that I designed. Her name is SIBYL."

"After the Greek Goddess?"

"Goddess is too modest. Sibyl exists throughout many cultures. She is normally depicted as an aged female oracle. The Sibyl of old predicted events for the Gods just as the new SIBYL does for our efforts."

"When I was in military intelligence, we worked with several different analytical systems but this goes way beyond that."

"SIBYL takes all those little loose ends of information, in any format that they exist, from any source we designate and shows us patterns, relationships, and ideas. The probability that they are true intelligence and not just rumor or conjecture is calculated. I have set the probability standards very high. We have used her mostly for medical research, climate change, space exploration, and communication planning. One of our more significant projects currently is creating a realistic critical timeline for inundation from ice cap decomposition."

Mary looked around as Rasputin and Fritz entered the room. They immediately went over to their beds which were located near what had to be Jeanine's control station. She laughed. The doctor continued.

"You will see them everywhere. Not so for Morton. He and the rest of his kennel mates are used to patrol the property. And in case you think you are seeing double, there are 12 of them all trained and with a handler. But, let me show you something before I take you back upstairs."

Jeanine sat down at her screen typed in a few strokes and one of the large monitors started blinking. Within seconds, a picture of a woman Mary recognized as Helena Reagan popped up on the left of the screen. Next to it was a picture of a slightly older, harsher looking female.

"Let me introduce you to Svetlana Czerny on the right. SIBYL has crossed matched data from Interpol, our NCIC, and from Israeli intelligence. The probability that these are two pictures of the same woman is 99.8%. Helena really doesn't exist except in the Department of Homeland Security files. There she has been given a completely artificial identity. She has had her fingerprints altered, and as you can see, extensive plastic surgery and new identity papers. All of that happened in this country. That can't have happened without extensive help from inside that agency from several different people."

Mary studied the monitor. "And I'm guessing Svetlana has a more robust history."

Jeanine enlarged her picture as the one of the women known as Helena disappeared.

"You guess correctly. Svetlana Czerny is on every major terrorist watch list in the world including China and Russia. Human trafficking is just one of her many talents and assets to funding the world-wide business she is part of. I believe Nightshade is just the part of that located in the eastern U.S."

"And we were about to release her because we thought she was a nobody."

Jeanine finished the conversation as they headed back to the elevator.

"Other than finding out who she worked for here, she is no longer our concern. She has become an asset for several other organizations. Helena Reagan never really existed and now she no longer, at least in the records, exists."

The two large dogs entered the elevator with them, which left just enough room for the women. Once they ascended to the main floor, Mary was shown to her room and told dinner would be in an hour. She looked out over the valley. It looked beautiful, peaceful, like most of the others in the area. No one would ever know what lies under those pastures. Unless of course, they had a need to.

Helena Reagan AKA Svetlana Czerny had spent lot of time in various prisons all over the world. She had learned silence was the best policy. Over the years she had perfected the look in dealing with other inmates. They learned to keep their distance. Once you killed your first one, the rest came easy. She didn't need to worry about that yet. She had been totally alone since she had arrived at the federal holding facility. All they had done was fingerprint her and take her photograph. The female FBI agent she recognized from the Buckhead property was the one she had regular contact with but that had stopped abruptly when the others arrived. These new people made her nervous. They didn't wear suits and only talked with her through the bars of her cell. Svetlana was left alone most of the time. This was something new for her. She also had not heard from the Nightshade lawyer, Stella St. John. When she asked, she was told they were trying to reach her. Helena didn't think they were trying very hard. This was very different from the other times she had been arrested in this country. She had no doubt that Nightshade had enough people to find her and somehow free her. She knew too much to be left alone and she would deal with whoever they sent if they decided to eliminate her. Her colleagues in Europe would avenge that, if indeed the Nightshade people thought that was the best solution. She had taken a regional prostitution ring and turned it into a billion-dollar trafficking and money laundering monster then had taught them how to use their social and political contacts to infiltrate every arm of the system that was supposed to be hunting them.

But, as she sat in her cell, Svetlana had to admit that gaining her freedom was taking longer than it should given all those contacts and inside helpers Nightshade had invested in. She should have been on her way to Bosnia by now.

She heard voices and saw the door to the area where her cell was located open. Two women and two men entered the room. One of the women came over, unlocked her cell and approached. When she was within arm's reach, she asked Svetlana to extend her arms. She complied and was handcuffed. This had happened lots of times before. The other woman then guided her to her bunk where they sat her down. As soon as she sat, she felt the needle enter her thigh. As she began to lose consciousness, she felt a hood being pulled over her head and heard a gurney being guided into the cell. This had never happened before. This was something different.

# CHAPTER 22

Birdman and Marshal Tim Collins arrived at 6:15 pm for dinner at Lydia Michaels' house. Billy arrived soon after as instructed. When everyone was seated, Lydia rose, as did everyone else, and joined hands. Lydia Michaels had a voice tuned by angels. It was clear and strong

"Dear Lord who sent his own sweet Son to show us how to treat each other and care for anyone in need, please bless this food we are about to enjoy. Please watch over these folks as they risk their lives delivering the wicked for judgement. Please put extra care to those souls who have been damaged by the evil of enslavement. We thank you for the animals and plants that have sacrificed to keep us fed. Renew our faith, Lord, and please give my sweet Sam, who resides in heaven with you, my love. Thank you. Amen."

Lydia looked around the table at the new faces.

"I want to welcome all of you who have not been here before. You may call me Aunt Lydia which is what I make Lily call me. Everyone on this road and on this island calls me that and it is how I wished to be addressed. There is plenty of food. The rule here is that you can help yourself as Billy Ward's waistline will attest to. Which one of you is called Birdman?"

Birdman raised his hand. "That would be me, Aunt Lydia."

Lydia looked at Lily. "You're right he is smart. He learns quickly." She redirected her gaze at Birdman. "What is the name that your Momma gave you?"

"My real name is Henry Leonard."

Lydia nodded. "That is much better. I understand that you are highly educated."

"Yes ma'am. I have two doctorates."

"Well, two. Did you have trouble figuring out what you wanted to be?"

Birdman blushed. "No, Aunt Lydia. I wanted to be both an aeronautical engineer and an ornithologist."

Lydia nodded. "Then in this house, I hope this doesn't offend, you will be addressed as Doctor Leonard. Our people value education. And, by the way, I will not be offended if you do not eat my chicken."

Birdman looked confused. "Aunt Lydia, I love chicken and I'm sure yours will be the best I've had."

Lydia smiled and nodded at Marshal Collins. "And you, young man, please introduce yourself."

Tim Collins blushed. "Yes ma'am. I'm Marshal Tim Collins. Thank you for having me."

Lydia smiled and nodded. "You are welcome in my home anytime, Marshal Collins. I saw you make the sign of the cross as I finished the blessing. Are you Catholic?"

"Yes ma'am."

Lydia smiled. "Well, you're welcome here anyway and I hope, if your schedule allows it, you will accompany me to my church." She looked over at Billy. "Some men can only find the time to worship when it fits into their fishing schedule. Now please everyone, eat up. I'm sure you will have a busy day tomorrow. If you find the time, the coffee here is always fresh and always hot. Cups are in the cabinet above the coffee pot."

After dinner, Billy, Collins and Birdman gathered on the porch.

"Tonight, you guys can stay with me at my house." He looked at Birdman. " I'll run you out to the fish camp tomorrow morning." He turned to Collins. "What are you going to do about vehicles?"

Collins answered. "Other members of my team will be arriving tomorrow morning early with everything we need. I will be staying with them at a house Smithson has rented on Dataw Island."

Billy laughed. "Are you guys taking a golfing vacation?"

Collins laughed as well. "I hate golf but it is part of our cover story. We are here monitoring the activity of several persons of interest. Of course, when the time comes, we will be here to take any action deemed necessary."

Birdman spoke next. "I'll be the one staying at the fish camp. My mission needs some space and I want to observe the bird migration when I'm not working. If anyone asks, I'm an ornithologist studying sea birds."

Billy laughed. "Believe me, people will ask but we can make that work because I suspect it's true."

Birdman looked puzzled. "Why aren't we going there tonight?"

"At night, I give the road and the boardwalk to the gators."

"Gators? You do mean the reptiles, right?"

"Oh yes, I mean those kinds of gators. This is alligator mating season. And, of course, there is that migration you spoke of which, if I'm thinking right, is about over. There are just enough of them left to interest the restless young alligators."

Birdman was surprised. "You mean alligators eat birds?"

Billy laughed. "Birdman, I will have to teach you how to get along with them because they are all around the fish camp. That's why I want to approach it when the sun is up. An alligator will eat anything that it thinks it can get a good hold on. Anything."

The following day in Atlanta, Stokes couldn't believe he was being released. Stella St. John delivered the news.

"Mr. Stokes, without the necessary testimony they have no evidence that can be used to hold you. The prosecutor has dropped the charges, you will be a free man by this evening. But I would suggest you leave Georgia as quickly as possible. Disappear for awhile until things die down. They always do."

Stokes nodded his head. "So, Beth and Tiffany didn't testify?"

"Let's just say that the prosecutor didn't believe that what they had to say would have convinced a jury or a judge that they were there against their will."

He looked at St. John. "Bullshit. You and the company called in a favor. Maybe Tiffany would have cut me a break, but Beth is strong and she wasn't fond of any of us."

St. John laughed. "Stokes, are you telling me you want to stay in jail?"

"Listen, I've done one three-year stretch with the feds already. Fuck no, I don't want to stay in jail but it's probably safer than being out there once Frank gets out. What about him?"

Stella couldn't believe what she was hearing.

"What do you have to fear from Frank? You actually saved his daughter from Holder according to Beth and Tiffany. It wasn't your fault she disappeared during the raid."

"What do you mean she disappeared? She was there in her room when I left."

St. John was getting annoyed. "Look, Stokes, you did your job. You have nothing to fear from Frank. Just take this gift that's been given to you, keep your mouth shut, your phone on, and get off the grid. Go to one of those places you people hide the girls for awhile. Just lay low."

"What about my car? The cops took my car,"

Stella tried to hide her annoyance. She wasn't used to giving good news and having it questioned.

"They have your car at the impound lot. There will be an order to return the vehicle to you with your release papers."

That seemed to calm Stokes. "Can you give me a ride to the impound lot?"

Stella had endured this man long enough.

"I am not a taxi service. Call a cab or a ride share. Just disappear, Stokes, before they change their mind." She looked at her watch. "I've wasted enough time with you. Just keep your mouth shut and clear out. You open that mouth and Frank will be the least of your worries, do you understand?"

Now it was Stokes' turn to be annoyed. "Fuck you, Stella. Of course, I understand."

Three hours later, Stokes was released. He asked for a cab and it took him to the federal impound where he was given his car. He drove to the nearest fast-food joint and parked. He searched the car for a tracker. He found nothing. He opened up the glove box to check the papers and found a new phone and a note. It was from Vivian Bartram. "This is your new phone. All the pertinent numbers have been transferred. We will be in touch."

He went inside, ordered food, and sat at a table where he could see his car and think. He had to make a decision about where he was headed. Just as he got back in his car, the new phone rang.

"Mr. Stokes, this is Vivian Bartram. Thank you for taking such good care of my daughter. We need you to come to Charleston. We are suspending our normal operations for a bit, but I have another job for you. It will pay handsomely. By the way, I love your car."

Stokes was stunned. "Mrs. Bartram, I appreciate the offer but the lawyer just told me to get lost and stay low until things die down."

"This new task will be very low profile. I just need another set of eyes to help take care of my children. You have proven your loyalty by staying silent and caring for Jillian. How much would it take to completely restore that car of yours?"

She had Stokes with that. "Text me the address. But I won't kill anyone, Ms. Bartram. I'm just a driver."

Vivian thought how easy some men were.

"Lester, you can call me Vivian. Why don't we lease you another one of those powerful cars, a new one, while yours is being restored? All I need you to do is watch. I'll text you the address."

Two hours after Stokes was released, Stella St. John walked out of the federal holding facility with Frank Bartram. Once inside the car, Stella turned to Frank.

"I'm headed to the airport. Your men will meet you there with transportation."

Frank smiled. "Make sure no one is following us." Stella laughed.

"Even they wouldn't be so obvious to do that. We just handed them their asses."

Frank looked at her. "Stella, how successful would you be if we didn't have the people on our payroll on the inside? We both know that this could have turned out worse than it did. I need to find out how the feds fucking knew where I was and how that raid was planned. Someone within our organization fucked up enough that they got not only me but Helena as well. You know how serious that is?"

Stella nodded. "Of course, I do. I've already begun the proceedings and arrangements to get Helena out of the country. Deportation is the cheapest alternative and we have people inside those services that owe us favors. But your first concern was correct. The FBI doesn't like being beaten so easily. We probably need to just take a break from the business for a short time."

Frank just stared straight ahead. He thought about how stupid Stella could be sometimes.

"Stella, we can't afford to take a break. Have you got my new phone?"

"In the glovebox. Totally clean."

"Did you get the other thing I asked you for?"

"Next to the phone. It's from my private collection, also very clean."

Frank pulled out the 9mm Russian MP-443 Grach and two boxes of ammunition that went with it. He dropped the clip out to make sure it was loaded, reseated the clip and turned to Stella.

"Stella, do you know where Vivian and the kids are?"

Stella immediately felt the atmosphere in the car change. She chose her words very carefully to craft the lie that would buy Vivian time.

"I called Jessie to tell him you were being released. I think Jillian and Vivian were at my place with him. They are all safe and fine."

"Did you speak to Vivian yourself?"

"No, I was busy trying to finalize your release. But I know Jessie will give them the message. Do you want to fly back with me to spend some time with them? I'm sure you both can sort this whole misunderstanding out."

Frank thought about how he would sort Vivian out soon enough.

"No, I've got some business to attend to here first. Tell Vivian that I will meet her at the Atlanta house when she and Jillian are ready to come home."

They drove in silence. His security men from Charleston were waiting at the private airside parking area with two vehicles as Stella parked the rental. Frank got out without saying a word. He joined his men and both cars drove off. Stella watched them leave as she walked over to turn in the keys to her car and board the jet that had its engines already at a low whine. She thought to herself, "You're welcome, Frank. You're welcome for me getting you out of a case that could have resulted in you spending the rest of your life in a federal prison. You're welcome that I offered my own home to keep your children and your wife safe. You're fucking welcome for everything, Frank. My bill is in the mail."

As they drove, Frank turned and spoke to the man who had been waiting in backseat out of sight of Stella.

"Where are they taking Holder?"

"He'll be transported to the Jackson Reception Center for diagnostics and classification by tomorrow morning. That will take about 10 days by the time they render their results. The results will be minimum risk custody and he will be assigned to a transitional center."

Frank turned back around. "Holder cannot be released. It has to be done within the system."

The man in the back quietly responded. "It will. He will never leave the reception center alive."

The driver pulled out an envelope and gave it to Frank who handed it to the man in the backseat. They drove two more miles and pulled over to let the man out. He walked across the street and got into another car that was waiting for him.

The driver looked at Frank. "Where to next, Boss?"

"I think I need a bit of time in the sand. Myrtle Beach."

"You going to fly or are we driving?"

"Let's drive and keep it at the speed limit."

Dexter Holder was brought out of his cell. He thought he was being prepared for transfer to the correctional classification center when two guys in suits showed up with a court order to take him into custody for transport to another facility. Dexter had resigned himself to the fact that this time, he was doing time. Stella had instructed him to plead to the Georgia charges. He was actually looking forward to a rest with the Georgia Department of Corrections. He wasn't about to cooperate with anything that would risk Nightshade. He settled into the back seat to watch as the car moved through Atlanta.

But something in the back of Dexter's mind became unsettled once he started looking at the vehicle and people that were transporting him. These guys didn't look like they were from Georgia Corrections. Those guys wore uniforms and picked people up in transport vans. He was in cuffs, but no waist restraint or ankle chains. Then the thought occurred to Dexter that maybe the reach of the people he worked with was longer than he had anticipated. Atlanta is one of the most over-developed areas in the South, but still has plenty of places for a body to disappear. Nervously, he finally decided to ask.

"Who are you guys? Where are you taking me? I don't think you're with the Georgia Department of Corrections."

The man in the passenger seat turned around and smiled.

"Good afternoon, Mr. Holder. I'm Special Agent Phelps Wheeler of the Federal Bureau of Investigation. This is Marshal Hal Story. I'm arresting you on suspicion of kidnapping, interstate transport of a minor, and human trafficking for the purpose of prostitution as well as suspicion of engaging in activities that threaten the security of the United State of America." Phelps finished reading him his rights and turned back around.

Dexter was confused. "My lawyer just told he that I was cleared of those charges."

Phelps didn't bother to turn around.

"Mr. Holder, recently obtained evidence clearly supports the charges I just presented to you. These charges are new, based upon photographic and video evidence of you in the company of the three women who left a note indicating they were being trafficked for sex on Interstate 20. Further enhanced video from the rest stop security shows you approaching the women's restroom where the note was left. The girls, probably as instructed, kept their heads down. You didn't. The photo, supplied and attested to by a citizen witness, clearly shows you forcing three young women into a van from your vehicle. One of those women appears to be underage which supports information left in the note. Your DNA has been found at both sites. You are being taken to a private federal holding facility. Your lawyer seems to be in transit and unable to communicate. We will advise her that you have been taken back into custody."

Dexter sat quietly for a moment. "Wait, Tiffany and Beth must be behind this. My lawyer said they'd told you guys to stuff it and what's this threat to security of the U.S. shit? Where am I being taken?"

Phelps again, just stared straight ahead as he spoke.

"You are being taken to a facility secured and utilized for individuals suspected of terrorist activities. As I stated in your caution, you have the right to remain silent. I think for you at this moment, that is a very good idea."

"I don't know any fucking terrorists. You all are going to regret this shit."

The men in the front seat smiled and Phelps answered again. "We already are, Mr. Holder. But because of the threat to U.S. security, there are measures that permit us to go beyond the normal restraints. Would you prefer to travel gagged?"

# CHAPTER 23

Jessie watched the small jet land at Grand Stand Airport in North Myrtle Beach. He saw Stella walk down the jet's small stairway. Stella waved as she barked at the ground crew to bring her bags to the car. She hugged Jessie tightly but refrained from kissing him in public. Better to let people think he was her nephew rather than her lover.

Jessie started the conversation as they walked to her car. "How was the trip? Everything and everybody taken care of?"

Stella nodded as she got behind the wheel. "I've got a bit of work to do still with Helena Reagan. It seems the authorities have misplaced her. Stokes was released, Holder is on his way to a Georgia facility for a relatively short period of time and I walked your father out of the facility myself."

Jessie didn't want to seem too interested. "How was he?"

Stella laughed. "His usual grumpy self. You would think he could find one appreciative moment in his life. I dropped him with some of those men he travels with. I offered him a ride, but he said he still had unfinished business in Georgia. I think you'll be seeing him soon though."

Jessie faked a smile "I've no doubt."

"How's your mother doing?"

"She must be better she's gone."

That caused Stella to pull the car over and look at Jessie.

"Gone? Gone where, Jessie? She has to stay quiet for awhile until all of this blows over."

It was Jessie's turn to laugh. "Vivian, stay quiet? Are you serious? When have you ever known my mother to stay quiet unless she is totally passed out?"

"Jessie, this is serious. I'm not sure what mood your father was in, but he was definitely in a mood that I haven't seen before and I've known them both for 20 years. Where do you think she would go?"

Jessie had a pretty good idea but had no intention of sharing it with Stella.

"I've never been good at guessing what either of them is up to. I would never have thought that they would have farmed me out to you. I had no idea that Jillian was being moved with the other women. Did you?"

Stella pulled the car back out into traffic. "The fact that you live with me wasn't such a bad decision, was it? We have fun, don't we? I don't deny you anything, do I? No one but Frank had any idea what was going on with Jillian. How is she doing?"

It was time to start the lie. "She's gone with Vivian."

Stella shook her head. "Frank is not going to like that. He wanted Vivian and Jillian to meet him in Atlanta. Anyway, I've done all I can for the Bartram family for now. Let me make a quick stop at the liquor store and then we will go home, I'll unpack and you and I can play. I've missed you."

Jessie rolled his eyes again. "That sounds like a plan. How long has it been since you last saw Frank?"

"I saw him about two hours ago, why?"

"Just curious. I'm just having a hard time figuring out what is going on between Frank and Vivian. I'll wait in the car but hurry, I've missed you too."

While Stella was in buying liquor, Jessie was calculating the time of travel between Atlanta and Myrtle Beach. Jessie felt that the Atlanta thing was uncharacteristic for Frank He was almost positive Frank was headed to Stella's, and he didn't want to be in bed with Stella when Frank made his entrance. He figured that it was about a five-and-a-half-hour drive depending on which side of Atlanta Frank and the crew left from. It was now almost 6:00 pm and he guessed that with the business Frank had to tend to, that would add no more than an hour. Of course, that could have been bullshit, as well, and he could already be on the road. Jessie figured he had between an hour before, and an hour after, midnight as a window to exit, but all of that was speculation. He had to be gone before Frank arrived.

Stella returned with her bottle of Johnny Walker Black, and she turned toward her office rather than home. "I just want to drop off these files in the safe before we start our little party."

Jessie's mind began to race. He couldn't remember if he locked the safe after his last search. He instantly formed a plan. He reached over, pulled Stella's right knee toward him and pushed his hand up her skirt. "I want to go home now. Right now." He squeezed the inside of her thigh. "Right now." Stella almost lost control of the car but pulled over to the side. When it was clear, she turned back toward her house, and spread her legs as far as they would spread to give Jessie just enough access to keep the five minutes until they got home interesting.

Three hours later, Stella was asleep. He didn't fully understand adults and the sex thing. The physical stuff had been part of his life for as long as he could remember and he knew it well. He just didn't understand all the rest of what went with it. He had hoped the sex thing would put Stella to sleep this time, and it had. She was sound asleep.

Jessie was out from under the covers and dressed in five minutes. He gathered his keys, and was in his Bronco in another five. His first stop would be Stella's office to cover his tracks and get that big file. He used the key and the alarm code Stella had given him to water the plants when she was gone. It was a good thing his plan to divert Stella had worked, because he had forgotten to relock the safe. The big file was all the way in the back cabinet. It took both hands to pull it out of the drawer. It was marked Mid-Atlantic

Kidder. He remembered that name from his search of her electronic records he had downloaded. He didn't want to waste too much time here. Stella might wake up or worse Frank might show up. He took the file, closed the safe, and had just put the file in his car when he saw he had left the lights on. He turned and went back and remembered then to reset the alarm. He thought to himself what a shitty burglar he would make. He was half way to the back door when he heard their car doors slam out front. He retreated back into a side office and hid behind a desk.

The door opened and one of Frank's men turned on the lights. Frank came through the door next followed by a second man who had Stella by the arm. She was wrapped in the blanket they both had been under earlier. Two more men entered, and as they came through, Frank shut and locked the door.

"Turn off the alarm, Stella."

She had obviously been crying but she complied.

"I don't understand, Frank. Why are you doing this?"

Frank answered with absolutely no emotion in his voice. "Stella, you have had a good long run with us. You've enjoyed yourself and lived a great life. But it has been decided that we are to end our professional relationship. Sorry, Stella, I'm just a guy that follows orders. You know better than anyone that our professional and personal relationship has become a bit too intertwined. I need three things from you, then we will be done."

From his hiding place Jessie felt that Stella had to know what was about to happen. He pulled out his phone and started quietly filming. He was in the dark, they were in a well-lit room. He had been in enough films to know the lighting worked in his favor. It appeared Stella still didn't quite grasp what was happening.

"I'll answer your questions, Frank. Just ask, then go."

Jessie thought. "Nope, she doesn't have a clue."

Frank motioned for the two men behind her to grab her and force her over her desk. The blanket fell away and she was naked and held so she couldn't move. Frank took a position on the opposite side and leaned down to her.

"Now that I have your attention, where are Vivian and my kids?"

Stella sobbed. "Frank, I swear, I don't know. Jessie was there when I fell asleep. He says that Vivian left with Jillian but I don't know where they went."

Frank motioned to one of the men behind her who pulled out a knife and cut two slashes on her butt cheeks and one across the base of the spine. She screamed in pain.

Frank knelt down. "That's disappointing, because I don't believe you. Let's try the second question, where are the paper files for Mid-Atlantic Kidder?"

Jessie swallowed hard. He knew what that outcome was going to be.

"They are in the safe. The combination is under my desk pad. They are all the way in the back, the last file cabinet in the middle drawer. Please, Frank. You don't have to hurt me. I'll tell you what I know." She was crying almost screeching her pleading.

Frank motioned to one of his men. He found the combination, opened the safe, disappeared into it, then returned and shook his head. Frank motioned to the two men behind Stella. The one cut two more slashes on her back. Stella screamed in pain the entire time, but Frank held her head down on her desk to muffle her screams, almost choking her.

He bent down again, and wiped some of her tears away. "Stella, I didn't even believe the bosses when they told me they thought that file existed. Now, I'm concerned. Stella, if that file isn't in your possession, whose possession is it in? That is not my final question, by the way." He looked at his men. "Turn her over."

At this point Stella was no match for the four men. She was turned over and was now face up, spread eagle on her own desk. Frank bent down and almost whispered.

"Oh Stella, that last cut really hurt you. There's blood dripping on your carpet. But don't worry, there is just one last question. I hope you get this one right because it didn't work out so well for you when you've missed the last two. So here goes. I know Vivian was at the last party house. She was gone before I arrived, but Jillian was still there. I talked with her. Who helped my daughter out of that house Stella? Please don't tell me it was Vivian. She isn't capable of such a thing, particularly since the place was surrounded by federal cops. Who helped Jillian get out of that house?"

Stella just shook her head from side to side. "Please, Frank, I don't know."

That answer startled Jessie to his very core. She did know. She was covering for him.

Frank motioned to the man with the knife who sliced Stella's right nipple almost off. She screamed as Frank covered her mouth with his hand. He leaned down and whispered in her ear.

"I'm going to ask you one more time, Stella, how did Jillian get out of the house and back to Vivian? She just cried and shook her head from side to side. Frank just lowered his head and stopped the man with the knife before he could finish the job.

"Just stand her up between you." She was upright, supported by two men. He smiled at Stella. "That's all, Stella. We're done." Then he raised the Russian pistol, the one that was part of Stella's collection, and shot her once in the center of her forehead. He started walking toward the door.

"Get our cleaners here within the hour. I want this place spotless. Load her in the back of the van. I know just where I want to drop her. I want the paper files destroyed and see they wipe these computers. He was out the door as two of the men picked up Stella's body and moved toward the door. The other two stepped around the pool of blood, closed the safe and reset the alarm as they were on their way out.

Jessie had filmed the whole thing. He knew he had just a small window of time. He unplugged the computer console on Stella's desk and moved it toward the back door. He disabled the alarm, opened the door a crack to make sure Frank hadn't left one of his men to wait for the cleaning crew. He lifted the console set it down outside, went back in, reset the alarm, and closed the door. He loaded the console and drove south to the cabin where Jillian was waiting. On the way, he went over in his mind what he had just witnessed. Stella had covered for all of them. He couldn't believe Frank would do that to anyone let alone a person who had just gotten him out of jail. His mother had been right. Frank was capable of anything. As he drove, he considered one other thing. There had to be someone higher than Frank that had ordered Stella be killed. There was no doubt in his mind that the same person had ordered his sister and his mother to be killed. It wouldn't take Frank long to find Vivian. She didn't hide well. Thank God, Jillian was hidden where none of them knew to look, but look they would, and for all of them. They were just loose ends now. He tried to call his mother. There was no answer. Jessie felt sure his mother had gone to the Charleston house and that it was there, where Frank would look. He also knew that if Frank didn't find his mother there, he would leave Stella's body as a message for her. He tried again with the same result.

He pulled up to the cabin. It was dark. He could see that Jillian lying on the couch where she had tried to wait up for him. He pulled the Bronco around back. He got the console and the files and went in the back door.

Jillian stirred on the couch. She spoke as he poured himself a glass of water. "How is Stella?"

He looked down at his sister. "Stella is feeling no pain. Go back to sleep. We can talk in the morning. Right now, rest."

Once he was sure she was asleep, he opened the computer console and carefully removed the hard drive. He would make sure it was found with the body. He hoped his mother had been smart enough not to stay in Charleston because he didn't want to find two. Stella had covered for them. There was no question about Frank's intentions now. He was certain the next step was at the Charleston house. He left his sister a note that he would be back and explain everything.

Stokes knew his comfort zone and this neighborhood wasn't it. He was spending a very restless night in the Lexus sedan Vivian had given him to work in. He had met her at the address in the historic district of Charleston. She had also given him the keys to a Dodge Charger Hellcat to use while his car was in the shop. She had rented him a nice room in a nearby hotel where he had slept most of the afternoon. Just after dark he parked and watched where instructed. Now it was just after midnight. Stokes looked around him as he waited. Even though the car fit right in Stokes stood out like a sore thumb. He hunkered down and hoped that none of the people out late walking their dogs would notice him.

He had picked up girls here once after a New Year's Eve party. He wondered what all these fine neighbors would think if they knew what had gone on in that house that night. That led him to wonder what all these people thought of Vivian and Frank. Vivian could fit in anywhere, but what the fuck did these high-assed people make of Frank? Stokes guessed he scared the shit out of them as much he scared the shit out of everyone that was around him.

It was around 2:00 am when Stokes saw Frank and his crew arrive. He recognized their tactics as they approached the house. They looked ridiculous, like they had watched too many cop shows. It wasn't like Frank was arriving home. It was like he was invading his own house. Once the first group arrived, a van pulled around to the alley side of the house. By the pattern of the lights going on and off, Stokes figured they were searching for someone. Vivian had been right not to stay here. They were in there 15 minutes, then left. Stokes waited until he felt sure they were gone. He got out of the car and walked across the street to the rear door. He used the key Vivian had given him to go inside. He got as far as the dining room. He had no need to go further.

Back outside, he left the Lexus and walked the four blocks to where his new Charger was parked. He got in, pulled away and called Vivian. She answered on the second ring.

"Stokes, did they show up?"

"They did, and they left you a message."

"What does it say?"

"It's not that kind of message, Mrs. Bartram. Your husband and his men left the body of that lawyer woman who got me out of jail. She's all cut up, with a bullet hole in the middle of her forehead, naked tied to one of your dining room chairs. She's an awful sight."

Vivian began to tremble, but she made sure to check her voice. Now was no time to sound weak.

"You've done fine, Mr. Stokes. I'm texting you an address to one of my private places in Beaufort County. I want you to go there, get a room nearby, and wait until I call you. If you look in the glove compartment of your new car, you will find $15,000 in cash and a new phone. The money and the restoration of your car serve as payment. Keep the new one until your old one is ready. Destroy your old company phone as soon as we hang up. If he has killed Stella, he will kill anyone who was anywhere near the party house that night. Don't answer any calls from anyone with the company, not even Tobin. He will do whatever Frank tells him, and wouldn't think twice about leading you right to Frank. Stay safe. I have another small task for you later.

Stokes didn't need any prompting. He went back to the hotel, got his things and was headed south toward Beaufort County before daybreak.

Jessie got to the Charleston house around 3:00 am missing Stokes by minutes. There was no sign of anyone. He found Stella's body tied to a chair in the dining room. That was Frank's warning to Vivian. Frank had delivered his message. Now it was time for the twins to deliver theirs. He turned Stella and the chair around to face out toward the side yard. He hadn't realized how heavy a person was when they're dead. He placed the hard drive in Stella's lap. Jessie knew Frank was so obsessed with finding Vivian, it would never occur to him to think that the twins could act on their own. That would definitely work to their advantage. He was out of the house and arrived back at their little house in the woods within an hour.

Jillian opened the door with the note in her hand. "What's going on?"

There was no way to sugarcoat it. "Dad killed Stella last night. I'm sure he's coming for Mom and us soon. I have a plan but we need to wait until people are awake."

At 6:00 am, Lily's phone rang. It was Claymore.

"You just got a call to the number on your card. The caller number captured tracks to a burner phone. Voice identification on the message left is 99% accurate that the voice belongs to Jillian. I've forwarded the message to your new phone."

Lily played the voice message and immediately recognized Jillian's voice. There was a significant amount of stress. "Frank is on a killing spree. We have information."

Lily immediately dialed the number. Jillian answered on the second ring.

"We need your help. I'm sorry I disappeared, but I was afraid things had gotten out of hand. Frank is killing people."

Lily broke in. "Jillian, we can help. Where are you? We will come and get you." She waited. There was silence. She decided to try something different. "Is your brother there? Can I speak to him?"

There was a longer silence, then a young male voice came on.

"This is Jessie."

"How can we help, Jessie?"

" Give me a secure IP address, and I will send you a MP4 video clip that I took last night of Frank Bartram killing his long-time attorney, Stella St. John."

Lily didn't even hesitate. She gave him the address and continued.

"Are you two safe?"

"For now, yes. My mother, Vivian Bartram, is not. I will text you the address in Charleston where you can find St. John's body. Is this a secure number for you?"

"It is, but we need to come and get you now."

"No, we need to get more. There is something that was left with Stella's body. It should have something of interest on it. We will continue to be in touch, but I need to find my mom and get her someplace safe. Frank is going to kill all of us, and it looked like he enjoyed it too much. I have a copy of another video file of him killing two other people, Crystal Morse and Lucy Peters. I will send that, too. You have to get it right this time. What is your name?"

"My name is Lily Michaels."

"Ms. Michaels, thank you for helping my sister. You may be the only one we can trust. You are up against some influential people. Some of these people are ones you might trust under other circumstances. We have to get them all, Ms. Michaels."

"I understand, Jessie, are you sure you can keep your sister safe?"

"Yes Ma'am. I can keep both of us safe. Go get Stella's body. She didn't deserve being treated like that. She covered for us, but we won't have much time. Some very nasty people, some with badges, will be looking for us."

"Keep this number handy, Jessie. Good people with badges are here to help as well."

# CHAPTER 24

It was a beautiful sunny morning in Charleston. Lieutenant Liz Freemont, a seasoned homicide detective, was enjoying the fact that her caseload with Charleston Police Department had finally leveled off. She was good with that. It was starting to get too hot to be finding bodies anywhere in her jurisdiction. Most of her cases solved themselves and her team was experienced, but she was still happy to not have the 30-case backlog she normally operated with. Her desk phone rang. It was reception telling her that a U.S. Marshal wanted to speak to her. She told them to send him up. Marshals were normally not bad news for her. They rarely got involved in homicide cases unless they were hunting down a murderer.

Ludlow walked into her office. Liz thought to herself, "Not bad to look at. Not bad at all." She stood and extended her hand.

"Marshal, I'm Detective Liz Fremont. What can I do for the Marshals Service today?"

He smiled as he took a seat opposite her. "Detective, I'm Luke Ludlow. I'm here to report a murder."

Fremont was taken aback. "A murder? What murder?"

"I know it's a bit unusual, but we have it on good authority that a body has been dumped in your jurisdiction. The address has been on a watch list with us for sometime now. We are fairly certain the murder didn't happen here, but the body has been dumped at this address." Luke pointed to the address he had just laid on Fremont's desk.

"What kind of authority and how good?"

"We have a video of the killing."

"OK. Tell me the story."

"It's long and it involves the Nightshade Group."

Fremont was on her feet. "Let me get my team started that way and . . ."

Ludlow held up his hand. "Detective this is a need-to-know status. Our investigation is being managed under close security. It would be better if we did this quietly. We are 100% certain that the victim was not killed in your jurisdiction. I just want your cooperation to get a federal forensic team in that house without too much commotion."

Fremont sat back down. "Jesus, just when I was trying to relax. Why me?"

Ludlow cut her off again. "Because we've looked at your record. It's quite impressive and we feel we can trust you."

"Why would you think that you couldn't trust anyone here? Certainly, you don't think that the Nightshade Group has anyone in their pocket from this department?"

"We believe they have law enforcement help in almost every jurisdiction. You and I both know they operate here. I don't know if they have anyone on the inside of the Charleston Police Department, but we have witnesses out there that are vulnerable. I don't want to take that chance with just anyone."

Fremont laughed. "Well at least it's good to know I'm not just anyone. Sometimes I wonder around here. Your car or mine?"

Ludlow smiled. "I'll drive."

Fremont grabbed her hand-held radio, her purse and keys, and on the way out told one of her team she would be available on the communications channel reserved for the homicide team.

They arrived at the address south of Broad. It was located in a stretch of beautiful old homes. Fremont spotted something strange right off the bat.

"The silver Lexus doesn't have a resident parking sticker. It's been tagged once. She pulled her radio out of her purse. "D12 to central."

"Go ahead, D12."

"Please run the following tag check." She gave the dispatcher the make, model, and color and then the tag number.

"Central to D12."

"Go ahead, Central."

"Vehicle is a short-term lease from Palmetto Luxury Leases."

"Roger, Central. Send a hard copy to my email along with any information they have on who leased it."

"Central clear."

Ludlow and Fremont approached the front door and rang the bell. No answer. They went separate ways around the side of the house to the rear door. When Freemont came around the back corner, she had her weapon drawn. She looked at Ludlow. "There is a naked woman tied to a chair that has been turned toward the dining room window. She's not moving but someone wanted her found."

Ludlow drew his weapon and tried the back door. It was open. The two officers entered the first floor and, covering each other, cleared each room visually as they worked their way through the house. They again covered each other as they ascended to the second floor and checked all five bedrooms. They then came back downstairs and did the same procedure for the basement and wine cellar. Once that was done, they walked into the dining room and gloved up. Ludlow walked over, felt for a pulse, then shook his head at Fremont. He looked down and saw the hard drive, and made a mental note.

Fremont went into the kitchen and took the table cloth off the kitchen table, came back in and put it over the dead body. She looked at Ludlow.

"Who is she?"

"Her name is Stella St. John. She has a home and work address in North Myrtle Beach."

"You mean the lawyer, Stella St. John?"

"You know her?"

"I know of her. She has defended every whore, pimp, and john in the low country with a bank account large enough to afford her. What the hell is she doing in this house?"

"You know this house?"

Fremont nodded. "This is the old Hermitage house. For a long time, it belonged to one of the oldest families in South. I think most of them live south of here. I don't know who owns it now."

Ludlow looked at Stella as he responded. "This house is currently on the property list for a holding company with direct ties to the Nightshade Group. We believe it has been used for very high-end sex parties."

"Lord only knows what has gone on in many of these houses. They love their privacy almost as much as they love telling people about what they do in them. I could check around to see what the neighbors know but that would lift the lid you are trying to keep down."

Ludlow pulled out his command tablet, removed the cover that Liz had put over Stella, and took a picture of her. "Well, now I have to ask for that special level of cooperation we talked about?"

Detective Freemont thought. "You have my cooperation, but these neighbors will be curious about what is going on."

Ludlow dialed a number. "I have the cooperation we need. Send in the team as we planned. We will need one vehicle in the alley to remove the body without causing too much suspicion." When he finished, he turned to Fremont. "Let's talk in the living room. The team should arrive in about five minutes."

Fremont laughed as they took seats looking out on the street.

"Five minutes, huh? It sounds to me like you were pretty sure I was going to agree to all of this, but you really didn't need me to agree at all, did you?"

Ludlow smiled. "I wanted your cooperation for this and other things that are happening in your jurisdiction. I don't like coming in and walking all over local agencies. Just not my style."

"Well, aren't you a different type of fed. I'm usually the last to know if the state or federal people are nosing around in my patch. What else do you think I can help you with?"

"Have you ever heard of the Tide Times Motel?"

Fremont laughed out loud. "You did read my file, didn't you. I worked vice for three years. Every town has at least one ordinary old whore house or cooperating hotel or motel that looks the other way for all the sexual shenanigans people pay for. The Tide Times used to be a fairly nice motor inn. Now if there is a bottom tier for those kinds of places, that one is one tier lower. It's the exact opposite end of the spectrum from what you mentioned you thought was going on here. It's been quiet there for about a year. No calls for service, no problems at all. I can check to make sure, but I think I would have heard about it if there was a large operation going on there. Why do you suspect there?"

Ludlow's command tablet pinged. He looked up just as a truck pulled up in front. The logo on the side said Low Mountain Painting and Restoration Services. He pointed to it as he spoke to Freemont.

"Does that look like a good enough cover?"

Freemont smiled. "My, you are bankrolled well for the average investigation. That will do nicely. I take it the body will go out the back as draperies that need to be cleaned. No one will suspect a thing."

Ludlow opened the front door for the team. He answered her question as he returned to the living room. "The Tide Times is on the same property sheet as this house."

"You're shitting me. Why would the same company hold both?"

"There are also houses on James Island, condos in Mt. Pleasant, and a whole string of properties and houses between here and Savannah. Some of it is very desirable beachfront property, condos, etc. There are over a hundred just in the low country alone."

"Hiding in plain sight with all growth between here and Hilton Head. How did you find out all that?"

"We have someone that just looks for that kind of stuff all day long. Her name is SYBIL. But that's another story. Will you come with me for a look at the Tide Times? I need to see it for myself."

"Boy, you really know how to treat a girl. Sure, but if I get a call to a homicide that happened here in my city, I will need you to take me there."

"Agreed. That sounds fair. You've been really patient with me so far."

" My team would laugh you out of town for calling me patient, Ludlow. I'm anything but patient. But, if you're insistent on taking me to a low rent whorehouse, let's get to it before I change my mind."

Ludlow laughed as they got up. He said something to the team leader who went into the dining room and came back out with the hard drive sealed in an evidence bag. As he and Liz walked across the street to the car, they noticed two people were already gathered down the street pointing and looking at the house. Liz remarked as they pulled away. "Let's hope your team is good at maintaining your cover. It will be all over the evening news if they aren't."

They drove north to the Tide Times Motel. It looked almost deserted. Ludlow pulled around the block where they could get a good look at the rear of the place. There were five SUVs parked behind the motel. Liz started to call in vehicle checks, and Ludlow stopped her.

"We know who those belong to. No need to stir anything up at this address until it's time to clean it out."

Freemont put the radio down. "You know who those vehicles belong to?"

"Yes, they belong to another branch of the holding company we spoke of. The numbers will come back to vehicles owned by a Nightshade front company called Palms Transportation and they will all be on long-term fleet leases to another subsidiary called Solomon Security Limited."

"Did your girlfriend SYBIL tell you all this? She must have the most boring job on the planet if all she does is look up shit all day."

Ludlow laughed. "She is anything but boring." He looked closer at the fleet then pulled out his binoculars and studied the last SUV. "Interesting. Can you run this tag for me? It shouldn't stir up anything. I just need the name of the registered owner. I recognize it from something else."

Freemont called her dispatcher who ran the tag through their system then gave her the name of the owner. She said the name out loud as she wrote it down. "Dexter Holder. Now that name I know."

Ludlow looked at her. "You know Dexter Holder?"

"Yeah, he used to be a cop here. He was fired and his certification was pulled. Is he involved in any of this?"

Ludlow chose his words carefully. "We only recently learned about him being a former cop. Someone had deleted that part from his national record."

That totally surprised Freemont. "How do you even go about doing that?"

Ludlow shook his head. "From the inside. That is why we are limiting who knows what about this case."

He decided to fill Freemont in on a bit more and told her the story about Holder, the girls, and the note. He stopped short of telling her about the failed prosecution or the fact that they had Dexter in custody.

Freemont wasn't very surprised. "Dexter always had a problem with his ethics and he was piss-poor at judging women. His other problem was that he had a habit of not taking no for an answer. He smacked people, mostly women, around."

With that, Ludlow decided it was time to bring Liz fully into the investigation. "Have you ever heard of Crystal Morse or Lucy Peters?"

Freemont turned and looked at Ludlow. "We found their mutilated bodies floating in the mouth of Goose Creek where it joins the Cooper River. Later our techies found a snuff film that was making the rounds on the dark web. They were the stars. Those are still open and active cases. I didn't get much help there. They were known prostitutes, so nobody seemed to give a shit except me. My captain back then stopped me from working on the case after about three weeks. They sometimes worked out of the Tide Times. How big is this fucking thing Ludlow? You've got my undivided attention now."

Ludlow looked back at her. "What was the name of your captain back then?"

"Now you want me to grass on one of my colleagues. That is shitty, Ludlow. He was too stupid to be involved. He was one of the worst cops I've even encountered, but he moved on to another agency."

"If he was too stupid, and he no longer works for Charleston, then I'm not asking you to inform on your colleague. I'm was just asking his name, but now I want to know where he is now."

Freemont was troubled by this whole turn of the conversation. She turned and faced straight ahead. His name is Terry Mills. Last I heard he was an assistant chief deputy in Beaufort County. Great Ludlow, this was turning into such a nice relationship and now you've ruined it."

"Would this be the part about how patient you are? I didn't mean to upset you but you asked how big this is. So, you deserve to know. My team and I have been conducting an investigation at the direction of the Attorney General herself. We are teamed up with the FBI, the Smithson Evermore Project Recovery Group, and a high-level intelligence analyst. We are working on taking down the infrastructure of the Nightshade Group. That organization is responsible for the death of those two girls, Stella St. John, and God knows how many others. I need to task you in."

"Ludlow, I'm not even sure I want in. This is some heavy shit. This morning, I was celebrating having a backlog of only 30 cases. I've only ever heard rumors about the Smithson Group. They were all good, but human trafficking is dicey stuff to talk about in a town that is a major international family vacation destination."

"So, what are you going to do, Liz? I've shown you, my cards. What's it going to be?"

"Oh, so now we're playing I'll show you mine if you show me yours? Jesus Ludlow! You at least could offer a girl a drink if we're going down that road. I'll talk to my captain."

Ludlow put the car in gear. "No need. The Attorney General did that this morning before I ever walked in your office. I have a phone and a cool little tablet device for you. But you have to keep this a secret."

Liz looked exasperated but soon settled. "And what about the drink?"

"Later, I promise. First, I need to take you to meet the rest of the team. We have a hangar at the executive airport."

# CHAPTER 25

The videos Jessie sent were forwarded immediately to Dr. Morozov's operations center and a remote console at the new Charleston operations center. The St. John video was tough to watch and Dr. Morozov had to mute the sound to not upset the dogs who began to react at Stella's first cry. The other files Jessie sent were sent just to Dr. Morozov to be uploaded into SYBIL.

As that was happening, the other Marshals from the team pulled up to Lydia's house. Five minutes later Billy, Birdman, and Tim Collins arrived. Lily watched from the porch as Collins transferred some equipment to Billy's truck. Billy then left immediately with Birdman and one of the new Marshals for the fish camp. Collins had a new gear bag for Lily. He walked up to her on the porch.

"This is for you. We are headed to link up with Ludlow at a new command center they have set up near Charleston. We have a full team meeting in an hour to discuss the new information from the twins. We have increased the support for Alex. Birdman will be helping with that. How soon can you leave?"

Lily stepped off the porch. "Let's go. I figured that once we saw the video we would be ramping up. I haven't seen it. How bad is it?"

Collins just shook his head. "Bad enough it's not on our personal communications. Bad enough that federal and state warrants have been issued along with a BOLO for Frank Bartram and the men that were with him. And bad enough that we need to find Vivian Bartram before he does. I've not ever seen anything like it. Who buys that stuff? We really need to get the twins somewhere safe. What are our chances of that? You're the only one that has spoken to them."

Lily shook her head as she climbed into the car. "They didn't seem inclined to do that this morning. I have no idea where they are but they said they would send the video and the files and they did. What about the files?"

"Dr. Morozov has them as we speak. We'll find out at the briefing."

Lily stopped as she was belting in. "Sorry about the comment about your religion last night."

Tim laughed. "Don't be. Your mother is entitled to her opinion. It would be nice if everyone was as considerate and as honest as Aunt Lydia."

Lily smiled. " You're right about her. What you see is what you get and she never falters in giving." She looked straight ahead. "Has Alex got enough help?"

"Alex has Smithson people from their Atlanta office and a six-man strike team of U.S. Marshals less than five minutes from her. They are all rapid response trained and equipped. Birdman will give them aerial coverage. Speaking of that, we have a chopper standing by, as well as a small fixed wing prop six-seater should we need to move quickly. We need to figure out where Vivian is."

They arrived at the Beaufort Executive airport and climbed aboard the Smithson helicopter for the short flight to Charleston Executive Airport southwest of the city. Although Lily had been in helicopters many times, she had never flown over the coastal waters she was raised on. She smiled to herself and thought how smart Birdman was to consider this the best view. She hadn't realized until now how much she missed where she grew up.

In what seemed like the blink of an eye, the chopper landed on a portable pad at Charleston Exec, and as soon as the rotors stopped, they were pulled into the hangar where the command center had been established. There were at least 20 Marshals in full gear inside, not counting the ones that had been involved in the raid in Greenville. Frank was definitely a wanted man.

A large monitor was set up in the section of the hangar where the briefing would occur. One was already showing the familiar scene of Dr. Morozov's living room. A second had Phelps Wheeler seated in Atlanta at a desk. The original team was seated in the briefing area of this new command center. The rest of the Marshals were deployed to every corner both inside and outside of the hangar. This was going to be a private briefing.

An announcement was made that they were going to screen for listening devices. The electronic screening device emitted a tone once activated and would stop once it determined that there was no nearby or distant surveillance being conducted on their meeting. Everyone knew to turn off their phones and cover their ears partially until the tone quit.

Phelps was the first to speak.

"Good morning. A great deal has happened in the past 36 hours. As you can see, the Department of Justice has authorized a force magnification of manpower. We are still on a need-to-know basis but all personnel you see and will see during this briefing have been thoroughly cleared. As all of you are aware, evidence was received last night that clearly implicates Frank Bartram and four of his known associates in the murder of Stella St. John. There is an all-points out with the associated warrant for all five of them."

Phelps paused to let that sink in, then continued.

"In addition, we received five files that contain information that suggest a large conglomerate of legitimate and illegitimate businesses are linked through a series of ghost corporations set up over the years by Stella St. John. Dr. Morozov and my partner, Mary Phelps, will have more on that in a moment. Local and state authorities have been alerted to apprehend and alert us on all suspects. I am continuing my interrogation of o Dexter Holder in a secure location in Atlanta. He has been re-arrested for the trafficking of three of the women we rescued in Greenville. He is refusing to cooperate at this time. The evidence received last night pointed us here to Charleston. We will have more on the locations of interest in the city as we proceed. The car used in the I-20 activity has been located in Charleston."

There was a pause as Ludlow and Freemont made their way forward. Ludlow continued the briefing from the front.

"Good morning. This is Detective Liz Freemont of Charleston PD Homicide. She has been tasked to us for the duration of this phase of the operation. We went to the scene where Stella St. John's body was found. We recovered a hard drive from a computer we now know belonged to Stella St. John. It is at the FBI lab as we speak. We believe the circumstances under which it was found indicates it may have additional information concerning the case. We also found Dexter Holder's vehicle parked behind the Tide Times this morning. We have left it in place for the time being. On your command modules you will find a list of properties and businesses that are all related to a company called Mid-Atlantic Holding Corporation. SYBIL is analyzing that information as we speak. The people involved with those holdings should give us a list of subjects that will need further attention. Detective Freemont will be working with us on two additional murders that were videotaped here in Charleston."

While the group's attention had been focused on the front table, Dr. Morozov and Mary had joined the briefing via teleconference. Everyone's attention was now directed toward the other monitor. Dr. Morozov took over.

"Good morning. Analysis of the information from Greenville shows that the account numbers used by the eight johns in Greenville County were sophisticated one-time-use transactional accounts. The minute the money was received in the account, it forwarded the amount to another host account and automatically closed the transactional one. We have been able to identify five of the host accounts and they are all related to a group of companies that Stella St. John established several years ago. We will need more data but this appears to be a sophisticated international money laundering system. The illicit money is processed through a series of transactions involving several different companies. We are determining how many of them are real as we speak but we will need additional data before we can utilize any of this as hard evidence. I have forwarded a list of some of the companies that have already shown a strong relationship to activities you are focusing on." She turned to Mary.

"The testimony of the eight men who purchased sex in Greenville County indicates that they were all given the transactional account numbers by Charles Tobin. Based upon that evidence, we have issued an arrest warrant for Mr. Tobin at 09:00 am this morning. I just received notice that the hard drive Marshal Ludlow referred to will first have to be scanned for security purposes. We cannot attest to where the hard drive came from without further testimony. Since we have a strong reason to believe that it belonged to a practicing attorney, the Justice Department will have to appoint a special master to review the files first. All files from legitimate clients will be redacted. Then we must demonstrate that the hard drive belongs to a computer that may have been used in relationship to crimes currently under the umbrella of the investigative charge. I will update all of you as that develops. That is all I have for now."

Liz Freemont leaned over to Ludlow. "Did St. John have any legitimate clients?"

"I guess we'll find out."

Ludlow spoke to the group again.

Originally, we developed information concerning the murders of Lucy Peters and Crystal Morse from interviews with Beth Ellers and Tiffany Holmes. But one of the electronic files we received overnight along with the video of St. John's murder is a link that led us to the uncut version of the snuff film that documented the deaths of Peters and Morse. Both of these women have been identified as being part of the human trafficking network and prostitution operation that was run by Nightshade. Detective Freemont will be assisted by our personnel to look further into those murders,

As the operations leader, I have worked out our major objectives with assignments. Our first priority is to find and locate Jillian and Jessie Syms.

We have strong reason to believe they are somewhere within a 100-mile circumference of where we are sitting. The phone they used to contact us is the same instrument that was used to upload the murder video. The location on the phone is turned off, but the tower analysis performed indicates that the location they were in when they called, and when they sent it, is somewhere between Charleston and Myrtle Beach. Our next priority after the twins is to locate and arrest Frank Bartram for the murder of Stella St. John, and third, find his wife, Vivian, before he either kills her or she flees the country. Any questions?"

There were none. He concluded his briefing with an update on the protective surveillance being conducted on Beth Ellers and Tiffany Holmes. The briefing was adjourned. Liz was briefed on the operation of her command tablet and on security protocol for her involvement with the operation.

Ludlow caught up with her and led her over to Lily Michaels.

"Detective Freemont, this is Lily Michaels of Smithson Evermore. I thought you two should meet while you have the chance. Liz, Lily's main assignment now is to keep contact with the twins and either talk them into coming in or telling us where they are."

Lily smiled and stuck out her hand. "It's good to meet you, Detective. I look forward to working with you."

Liz answered. "Nice to meet you, Lily. I've heard about Smithson but this is the first time I've had the opportunity to work with your people. Please call me Liz.

Lily left with Collins as Ludlow led Liz to his car. They got in and once she was belted in, she looked down in amazement at the tablet she had just been given.

"Who has this shit?"

Ludlow laughed. "The military and now you. This particular version hasn't even been given to the military. The research and development arm of Smithson Evermore developed it. Try not to lose it. The bad guys would love access to one."

"Lose it. I may not want to give it back. If it is OK with you, I think I will advise my captain that I'd like to work out of this command center. That way I am close to the men you assigned me and it's less confusing for my guys. Once I get my car and my file, I'll head back here to get them and I will take them to go look at the spot where we recovered the bodies. The we can all go over the autopsy results with fresh eyes. Where are you headed?"

"I'm headed elsewhere to see if I can figure out where the twins are. I'm worried about them with Frank on the loose. I'll just be a click away on that piece of equipment in your lap."

"A click away, huh? That sounds good."

At a Nightshade owned hotel on the outskirts of Columbia, Frank answered his phone on the second ring. The voice on the other end still scared the hell out of him when he heard it.

"Apparently, you've taken care of Stella. I have been scanning the police monitor and you are all over it. They want you for Stella's murder. Why is that Frank? Who told you to kill, Stella? And, have you lost your touch in killing people quietly?"

Frank was stunned but still ignored the first question. "There is no way. There was no one around."

"Well, someone must have been because they can't get a warrant without proving to a judge that you were involved. You need to re-assess those goons you rely on so heavily. And the file, were you able to get the file?"

"No, but I have a good idea where the file is and it's safe."

"What the fuck does that mean Frank? How safe? That file could bring us all down. Where is the file?"

"I am certain that Vivian has the file. She and the twins had left Stella's house by the time I got there. I will get the file and destroy it. With it gone and Stella dead, it will be impossible to reconstruct anything that can be used as evidence."

"No, Frank, that still leaves you and Vivian. I'm not worried about the twins. They're not old enough to do any damage even if they knew anything. As long as you and Vivian stay loyal, we will not have to eliminate anyone else. What have you heard about Holder? He was much too close to Vivian for my liking, but I'm old-fashioned, I'd have killed the bastard the first time he slept with her."

Frank stayed steady and uncharacteristically didn't react. "We have made arrangements for Holder to never make it out of prison. I will make sure that Vivian stays in line and that the file is recovered and destroyed. What about Helena? I thought she would be out by now."

"Maybe she would be if you hadn't killed her attorney. They could keep her locked up forever and she'd still stay silent. She's old school Russian Mafia and will never talk. She's been detained by more brutal forces and never cracked. But our government doesn't have the resources to know who she really is. Our friends on the inside of Homeland are watching what they do with her. Even without Stella, that prosecutor will lower the charges and she will be deported back to Bosnia where we will give her a new identity and send her back. Tie up these other loose ends Frank."

"I will take care of Vivian, don't worry. When I find her, I will find the twins. What do we have planned for them?"

"I already have a buyer for Jillian. We will groom Jessie to work in the business. Do not get caught Frank. At your level of the operation, we will have to take drastic measures. You know what that means."

"I know how to stay away from the police. I'm not worried and you shouldn't be either."

The phone went dead. Frank hadn't shared his dramatic placement of Stella's body. It had to have been Vivian that guessed he had killed Stella and reported it when she found the body. She had to go and if the twins got in the way, they'd have to go too.

Frank had his men looking for Vivian and the twins. He had not received confirmation Holder was dead. He didn't feel particularly comfortable that he hadn't heard from Stokes. He hadn't said a thing about Nightshade to the cops while he was in custody and Frank knew he would keep his head down and wait for orders.

Beth Ellers and Tiffany Holmes had kept quiet but where were they? Their sources inside the federal agencies had not been able to locate them. He hoped that like many others, they would return to work. Like many of the women they had taken, they had nowhere else to go. He had men watching the main houses where they had worked. He had some of his men looking for them in the low country where he knew Tiffany had lived. He needed to find them, and bring them back. Stokes would have been helpful but he must have changed his phone. And, where the hell had Tobin gone? He should have been in Charlotte or Raleigh. But he hadn't been in either place. Frank figured he was driving around in his mobile palace.

Too many questions and not having the answers just drove Frank back into another rage. Fuck this hiding shit. He called his driver. His first priority was to find Vivian and that file. He suspected she had been at the office just before they got there with Stella and had taken the file. She was the only one other than Stella and himself that had a key. But why identify him as the murderer? That would just bring more heat on her unless she had decided to help the cops in exchange for some deal. But the more he thought about that the more he decided she wouldn't do that because of the twins. He had to find her. He had to get the file. Then Vivian had to go, permanently.

# CHAPTER 26

Totally annoyed by the constant ringing of her phone, Vivian finally answered the number that had been calling her.

"Mom, don't hang up. It's Jessie."

"Jessie, what is this number? I've been trying to call you at Stella's and a man answered and I hung up. Who was that and where are you and Jillian?"

"First, I need to tell you that Stella is dead, and whoever answered that phone, was either a cop or one of Dad's men."

"I know Stella is dead. A friend was watching the Charleston house and warned me early this morning."

Jessie continued. "Dad and his men tortured and then killed her in her office."

"How do you know this?"

"I was there. I saw the whole thing. Dad tortured her to find out where you were and who had helped Jillian out of the party house. He also wanted to know where a file was. He killed her when she wouldn't tell him."

"Jessie, my poor baby, are you all, right? Where are you?"

"Jesus, Vivian. I'm not your poor baby anymore. Will you please stop and think? Where we are is not as important as where you are. Frank is coming for you. He's probably coming to kill all of us. It sounded like he was ordered to do it. We need to get together and hide."

Vivian was totally sidetracked at the mention of the file. "What file was Frank looking for?"

"Mom, why can't you understand? We need to get out of this state, maybe the country. Frank and his men are looking for you. We know too much. Someone ordered Stella's murder. They have probably ordered our murders, as well. We need to figure out what to do."

"I understand, Jessie. What was the name on the file?"

"Kidder something."

Vivian froze. "Is Jillian with you?"

"Yes, we're in a safe place that no one knows about."

Vivian made sure to calm her voice. "Jessie, you need to come here. Together we will work something out. Do you remember the house in Beaufort on the water?"

"Yes, we can be there in a couple of hours."

"I will see you when you get here. In the meantime, I will figure something out by then. What phone is this?"

"It's a pre-paid. I bought it after I rescued Jillian."

"Who knows the number and that you have it?"

"Just you and Jillian."

"Leave now, and I will see you soon."

Jessie hung up the phone and looked at Jillian who shook her head then spoke.

"Do you trust her?"

"No, but I don't want her killed like Stella. She wants to meet us at the Beaufort house. When they were in her office nobody was looking for any other file other than that one." He crossed the room and took out the 9 mm Stella had given him.

Jillian stared at it in his hand. "Why are you taking that?"

"Only because we have to look out for ourselves now. Mom thinks she can make a deal with Dad to save herself. What she doesn't realize is that there is no way to make a deal with Frank right now. I've seen how he negotiates. I don't think she gets that we'll all be dead. The key to all of this is in that file. We need to call Lily. Let's figure out how to get that file to her."

Lily was being driven back to Beaufort County by Collins. In the brief conversation they had after the briefing, Ludlow had mentioned one name, Terry Mills, an administrative Captain with the Beaufort County Sheriff's office. Lily called Billy Ward.

"Hey, did you get Birdman all set up in at the fish camp?"

"He's an interesting guy for sure. We didn't talk that much; well, I didn't talk much. He just kept pointing out birds we saw along the way. He's all set up with his whirligigs and computers. It's good you sent the generators. He'd blow a fuse every fifteen minutes with that stuff."

"I need to ask you about someone in your department."

"Who?"

"Do you know Terry Mills?"

"Knew him. He left the SO about a year after he joined. I think he was from Charleston. He still has a place there and here. Never had much to do with him. I always thought he was one of those guys that got the job as a political favor. He didn't strike me as a great cop."

"Do you know where he lives here?"

"Yeah, he has a bigger house than he should near Hunting Island State Park. The gossip was that he had family money. What was he involved with?"

"I'll tell you later. Anyway, can we meet later today?"

"Of course. I'm about to retire. As long as I don't do something stupid, they don't give a damn where I am, as long as I'm doing my job. Will I be doing my job, Lily?"

"I think so."

"See you when I see you."

Lily had barely hung up the phone when it rang again. It was Jillian.

"Lily, we need to figure out how to get a file to you."

"First, tell me you're both safe."

"We are as safe as we can be. How can we get a file to you?"

"Just have Jessie send it to the same number."

"No, it's not that kind of a file. It's a real file, the old paper kind in a folder. It's huge."

Lily thought a moment. "What's in the file, Jillian?"

"A bunch of stuff we can't figure out about a bunch of companies, lists of people, stuff like that. It goes back a long way. We think there is information in it you can use. They were looking for it specifically when they killed Stella."

"Does this file have a name?"

"Mid-Atlantic Kidder."

Lily thought. "Are you willing to meet me in person?"

Lily could hear conversation between the twins in the background. You could tell they were driving somewhere. Jillian came back on the line.

"We're afraid that you will trick us and take us into custody before we can get to our mom and make sure she is safe."

"What we would really like to do is keep all of you safe. Do you think she would agree to that?"

Jillian was speaking to Jessie, and then Jessie came on the line.

"Lily, figure out a way for us to get you this file. Vivian is facing a long prison sentence if she comes to you and that has to be her decision. We will ask her, but she isn't the kind of person that will do well in jail. Call us back on this phone when you figure out how we can give you the file." He hung up.

Lily called Phelps. "The twins have a file marked Mid-Atlantic Kidder. They say it goes back a long way. It could be the evidence we need, but they don't trust me enough to meet with us directly."

Phelps answered without hesitating. "Who do they trust?"

" I have no idea about Jessie. He's fixated on trying to keep his mother alive. But I doubt either of them trust Vivian anymore than you or I would. Jillian might trust Beth and Tiffany."

Phelps answered immediately. "Then I think you should ask them how willing they are to get back into this."

Lily thought for a moment. "They might do it for Jillian."

Phelps continued. "I think I will check Vivian's maiden name and any alias she has ever used. There is just something in this whole deal that keeps pulling us back to the low country. Maybe you can give Beth and Tiffany a call. They have your survivor phones. See what they think."

Lily followed up quickly. "Phelps, I think they are close by, really close by. Billy says this guy Mills has a house nearby."

"You mean like Beaufort close by? I'll get the property check going. It shouldn't take too long. I just got a list of her aliases and maiden name. SYBIL is very quick."

Lily paused. "Where are you?"

"Not important right now. I'm where I can get lists in a matter of minutes."

"Can I get the list?"

Phelps laughed. "It's just showed up on our command modules under code name Mommy Dearest. Check with Alex on Beth and Tiffany and see if the surveillance has seen anything. If Frank is cleaning up, he won't leave them alone. He'll know he has to silence them."

Lily was half way through the list and she interrupted him. "Millsner is one of the aliases. That is awfully close to Mills. That's the name of the guy I just checked on."

Phelps laughed. "Terry Mills, the former police officer in both Charleston then with Beaufort SO. How do you get from Millsner to Mills?"

Lily continued. "Down here everyone screwed around with names after the War Between the States. Mills left the SO after a year. He's the type that wouldn't leave home. Maybe Vivian has history here too. I agree with you. Too much of this stuff is ending up down here."

"I'll start the check ASAP. Keep checking the command modules. It shouldn't take SYBIL too long to give us more on Vivian. Mary will make it a priority. I will alert them on this paper file. Once we have it, it's on a chopper on its way there. See you later."

Phelps called Ludlow.

"This thing has been limping along. We don't know where Frank is, we have only a minimal idea where these kids are, and the hair on the back of my neck is standing up. I think this is about to break loose quickly, and I want everyone mobile. Let's get a car for Lily. I want her and Alex to stay as close to Beth and Tiffany as possible. They may be the key to finding Jillian and Jessie."

Ludlow agreed. "I can understand the twins' motivation to get rid of that file. If Frank catches up with them, it won't matter where the file is. I'm having the car delivered to Lily. Where is she now?"

"She's headed to Lydia's house for a brief chat with her about this Mills guy. Lydia knows almost everyone in this county and where they came from. She might know something about Vivian Mills or Millsner or whatever."

"It will be there in 15 minutes. It's the one Collins was using. He can ride with me until we get another one down from the Charleston command center."

After Collins dropped her off, Lily found her mother sitting at the shady end of the porch where she always sat this time of day with a glass of iced tea. She was like clockwork. Coffee in the morning, iced tea in the afternoon. Lydia smiled as she saw her daughter arrive.

"I love having you here. It's such a pleasure to get a visit from you in the middle of the day. Can I get you some tea?"

Lily smiled. "I can get it."

"It's in the pitcher, and it's unsweetened just like you drink it."

Lily turned and smiled. "You are drinking unsweetened iced tea these days?"

"Don't make a big deal out of it. The doctor says I have to watch my sugar and that's what I'm doing. And yes, you can bring the pitcher. I've got a bit of time left before I start dinner. Will the team be here this evening?"

Lily returned with the pitcher and a glass, and poured them both a new glass.

"I don't know where we will be this evening. It seems like we are sitting on top of a powder keg trying to find a murderous father who is chasing his wife and two 15-year-old twins."

Lily got a text. "They are bringing me a car so I can be mobile, and I need to head down to Bluffton to meet Alex and two other survivors that might help us get these kids safe."

Lydia just shook her head. "I am constantly amazed at how close we live to real evil everyday, and how lucky most of us are, that we never have to confront it. You choose to. I'm so proud of you, Lily, for helping these survivors carry their burden but it hurts me that two children really are in such danger. I will just have a big pot of okra stew with shrimp on the back burner in case any of you need nourishment."

Lily smiled. "I am constantly amazed at you."

She got up and hugged Lydia. "I have another question and you may be the only one I know that can answer it. What do you know about the last name of Mills or Millsner? You know so much about the history here."

Lydia thought for a bit. "The name Mills is no problem. The old courthouse books tell us there have been families both black and white with that name in this area since it was first settled. Some of them were plantation owners and some of them were owned. The ones that did the owning were rice people, but later, during the reconstruction, turned to developing and breaking up some of the plantations between here and all the way to North Carolina on the coast. They are all over the low country. Always have been. Millsner sounds like someone was fussing around with the last name Millner. That name is also in the records. Not sure if they were connected but we had family, the Geechee branch down by Savannah, that took the name of their owners and were Millners. That's not much help, I know."

"That gives me a start. Thanks."

They sat there for 10 more minutes just enjoying each others company. Lily stood up as two team vehicles came into view. Ludlow was driving one and Collins was driving the other. Lily came down off the porch as they pulled up. Collins jumped out of his vehicle and into Ludlow's car as Lily walked up. He shouted instructions.

"Alex just called. Something is happening with Beth and Tiffany. They sent out a distress signal. We are headed there now. It may be that Frank's people have caught up with them. Follow us."

The location that Alex had texted was just south of Ridgeland on the Beaufort County side. Alex and her team were responding as well. Birdman had a drone following two black SUVs heading toward the location where Beth and Tiffany had signaled from. The nearest units were at least five minutes away, and it looked like the SUV's would arrive before any of the law enforcement units.

Ludlow and Collins sped up but they were in unfamiliar territory. They went past the turn their GPS indicated. Lily had seen it in time. As the two Marshals turned around the alert tone on their command units sent the four-tone signal that the situation was handled. As they got closer to the house, they could see a group of SUV's and pther vehicles with the Marshals cuffing men on the ground.

# CHAPTER 27

-Alex walked up as Lily approached. Alex had a smile on her face.

"It would appear that when Tiffany said that her family could provide adequate protection, she was correct. Follow me."

As they approached the house, they saw four men face down in the dirt at the bottom of the steps. Alex began her description.

"This is the house where Beth and Tiffany have been staying. Tiffany's family has been taking shifts watching and making sure that the girls are kept safe by moving them to different locations. They went into town yesterday to buy food. Apparently, some of the Nightshade security people were staking out the town. Fortunately, the family was watching the girls from a distance and saw that happening. They beefed up the normal four people watching with additional family members. These idiots didn't have a chance. The family got these four, and two more are in the back. These guys came roaring in thinking they were going to spray this place with automatic fire. They didn't get very far before the cousins had disabled their SUVs with homemade spike sticks. Then it was a matter of placing well-aimed shots and blowing out the rearview and side mirrors and the party was over before it started. All of them were on the ground like you see them flex cuffed and disarmed when we pulled in. Ludlow already has their weapons."

The Marshals took all six of them into custody. Ludlow joined Lily and Alex walking into the house where Beth and Tiffany were sitting with Tiffany's father and her uncle. Beth spoke first.

"Holy shit, Alex. When you said if we pushed the button someone would come, you weren't kidding. We didn't expect a whole army. Have you been watching us too?

Alex sucked at being cagey. "Sort of."

Beth continued. "Sort of, my ass. Look at this. Between Tiffany's family and all these uniforms there must be 30 people here."

Tiffany spoke for the first time. "There's not that many. Why are Frank's men here? I recognize one of them as someone who guarded us before and another used to be Frank's driver."

Lily stepped up.

"Frank Bartram is wanted for the murder of his lawyer, Stella St. John. Jillian and Jessie sent us video tape of the whole thing and a link to the snuff film of the other women you two spoke of. Frank is wanted for murder and every cop in the country is looking for him. The twins are trying to find their mother and running from their father at the same time. It may be that you two are considered a risk, as well. This intended attack would seem to suggest that."

The two women looked at each other. Tiffany spoke first. "What you're saying is that we, and my family will have to live like this for the rest of our lives."

Alex spoke.

"You have the same alternative that we offered you before. In addition, the Marshals Service and the Attorney General of the United States are willing to grant you full witness protection and relocation."

Tiffany began to cry. "I just got reunited with my family. Are you] telling me that I will have to give them up? On TV that type of protection means you can't ever see the people you love again as a condition. You have to move away, take on a new identity, and live a government supplied lie to stay safe. Is that what you're offering us?"

Ludlow stepped in.

"There may be an option for all of you if you're willing to trust us a bit more. Your family has done a great job of protecting you. We weren't really needed here except to take these fools into custody. This bunch will never bother you again. You are now part of a much bigger investigation than the one you were involved with before. We are very close to dismantling the entire operation that trafficked you both. I'm not sure we will even need your testimony. But we do you need your help with something else." He turned to Lily

Lily looked straight at both girls.

"We promised you we wouldn't be far if you called us. You did, and we were here. Jillian is out there with her brother running for their lives. They have a file they need to give us but don't trust us enough to meet us personally. I think that Jillian could convince Jessie to meet with you two and give you the file."

Beth interrupted. "And these guys would be there and prove we couldn't be trusted by taking them into custody."

Ludlow stepped back in.

"We promise that we won't take them or anyone else other than Frank and his buddies into custody if they even show up. His army is getting smaller. You set the rules. We need the twins to start trusting us to help them and if that means staying out of the way, we will do that. We will be close enough that if you need us, we can be there just like this time. But you have our word, we will not interfere."

Tiffany looked at Beth. "Tiff, we need to help Jillian if we can. If we ever want to be able to live our lives, we have to help these people get all of these fuckers. You and I both know Vivian is as bad as Frank and would give up the twins in a heartbeat. We have to help them get the evidence to take all of them down." She turned to Ludlow. "How big a risk is this file transfer thing?"

Ludlow thought before he answered. "I don't think Frank knows they have the file. I think they want to give it to us before they get anywhere near Frank or Vivian. It would be no riskier than what we just went through, and we would be just as close as you would let us get."

Tiffany made a motion for Beth and her father to join them in the other room. "Give us a minute."

They came back into the room. Tiffany spoke in a strong, clear, magnificent voice.

"Fuck Frank, and Vivian, and Tobin, Holder, and all the others. We want this to end. My dad insists that the cousins provide us cover if you will be there as backup. Get that guy with the little flying things to help. We will get the file then we will cooperate any way we can to get Jillian and Jessie safe, and the rest of these assholes behind bars."

Beth nodded. "Make the call to Jillian."


The twins were parked a block away from the Beaufort house. They had learned not to rush into any situation without seeing who and what might be there. Jillian's phone rang. It was Beth and Tiffany on the other end.

"Jillian, we want to help you get that information to Lily. The head Marshal has promised us they won't interfere and they won't try to capture you. Will you meet us and give us the file?"

Jillian looked at Jessie then answered.

"Are you sure they aren't going to grab us?"

Beth spoke. "They say no and I believe them although you guys should seriously consider letting them. What are you two going to do up against Frank and his little army?"

Jessie took the phone. "We will figure that out. If you promise it's just you guys, we will meet you and get rid of this thing."

Beth again. "Meet Tiffany and one of her cousins in 30 minutes in downtown Port Royal?"

"Where, it needs to be a public place?"

"Traveling Buoy Park at the end of Ninth. We will be in a white F-150. Just give us the file and leave. We can hug later after all of this is over."

Jillian almost sobbed. "Is it ever going to be over? We will be in a Ford Bronco."

Beth was strong. "You're goddamned right it's going to be over, and sooner rather than later."

Tiffany's family had the home field advantage. Just in case there were more of Frank's men, several of them left early to make sure it was safe around the park. When they reported it was clear, Tiffany and her cousin Hunter left, followed by two more truckloads of her family. All of it was recorded and watched from Birdman's drone flying high above them as they made their way from Richland to Port Royal. Beth rode with Alex and Lily just to make sure no one violated the agreement. Ludlow had agreed to keep everyone back far enough, that if they were needed, they could be called but to not interfere in any way with the twins.

As they drove toward the rendezvous, Beth talked with both Lily and Alex.

"These twins deserve a chance. The deserve the freedom everyone else takes for granted. The kind where you can make a decision, but still go back for help if necessary."

Lily asked. "Do you think they'll decide to let us help them at some point?"

Beth nodded her head. "Jillian told us that neither she nor Jessie were ever put in a position to do normal kid things, whether it was riding a bike or making a sandwich. She cried with us the night we shared our stupid note plan with her. Our plan would have failed and we would be dead by now. Her plan worked like a charm and here we are. If they are going to be free, they have to learn to trust and that is up to you guys right now. I think if this works, it will mean a great deal to them."

They waited at the outskirts of Port Royal according to plan. Tiffany and her cousin spotted the Bronco backed in on the far side of the parking. They pulled up next to them so Jillian could just hand the file over through the window to Tiffany. No one but the Marshals watching even noticed the shopping bag change hands. As soon as Tiffany pulled the bag in, Jessie pulled out and was gone.

After five-minutes, the white F-150 pulled up and Tiffany got out. She handed the shopping bag to Alex in the passenger seat. Beth got out and climbed into the backseat of the F-150. Tiffany got back in the truck and they left to meet with Ludlow, who would arrange for a coordinated plan with Tiffany's family to protect the girls fully.

Lily drove straight to the Beaufort airport where the Smithson helicopter was ready for takeoff. The file was in the air on its way to Dr. Morozov 15 minutes after the handoff had taken place.

After the handoff, the twins drove back to the house in Beaufort and parked away as they had before. They saw Vivian's new car in the driveway and another one across the street. Jillian spoke first.

"That red car wasn't here before. Do you remember Stokes, the driver that used to pick up and deliver girls?"

Jessie nodded. "The one that never talked much."

"That's the one. He had a car something like that. I think the red car may belong to him. He may have been the 'friend' mom mentioned."

"What would Vivian be doing with him? He works for the organization that is hunting her down."

"Stokes took care of me on that last trip. Holder was being an asshole and Stokes helped protect us from him. Stokes was different. He didn't argue with Vivian but he held his ground so she couldn't talk him into anything."

Jessie thought then spoke. "When I asked Stella how things had gone, she mentioned that Holder was headed to prison and Stokes was being released. What do you think?

Jillian shook her head. "I think we need to be really cautious with how we go in there."

"Let's go in the back by the pool house. We can see what is going on before we go in."

The two walked to the house and skirted through the side yard. They hid next to the pool house. True to form, Vivian was overconfident and standing next to the pool in her bathing suit with a drink in her hand. They had guessed right. It was Stokes who was standing across from her calmly listening. The twins couldn't hear what was being said but it was obvious there was a conversation going on and that most of it was Vivian. Then Jessie heard something from behind and pulled Jillian into the bushes next to the pool shed. They could just see the pool area and the living room. They were about to reposition when Jessie sensed movement coming from behind them and pulled Jillian back into their hiding place. Two of Frank's men ran past them with guns drawn. Before she knew what was happening, they grabbed Vivian just as Frank and two more of his men came through the front door. Frank didn't hesitate a second. As Stokes turned in surprise, Frank shot him in the face with no more care than swatting a fly. Stokes crumpled to his knees lifeless. Jessie had to put his hand over Jillian's mouth to keep her from crying out.

Frank was on his way to Vivian as another man walked into the living room from the back of the house. Frank turned to him and spoke.

"Hello, Terry. How have you been?"

The man looked at Stokes on the floor then at Frank as he shouted.

"Frank, what the hell are you doing? What have you done?"

Frank answered calmly and flatly. "Just this." He pulled the trigger. The bullet hit Terry Mills in the middle of his chest. He went down wheezing and Frank walked over and shot him a second time above the left eye. "You always needed to have things explained to you, didn't you, Terry?"

Frank turned his attention to Vivian. He walked over to her. "Where are the twins?"

For the first time in her life, Vivian was speechless.

"Frank, what the fuck? You just killed my brother for no reason."

" Viv. Where is the file and where are the twins?"

"They are on their way here."

Jessie had to tighten his grip on his sister's mouth. Two minutes later and they would have walked right into this.

Frank walked over to Vivian. "Where is the fucking file, Vivian?"

"Please don't hurt me or the children, Frank. They have the file. They have it with them."

He punched Vivian in the face knocking out two teeth and hit her a second time which knocked her out. "Tie her up and put her in the pool house. I'll wait for the twins then take care of all of this once and for all. You stay with me. The rest of you clear out. I'll meet you back at the Edisto house."

The men did as they were told. Vivian was now tied up one room away from where the twins were hiding. Frank's man made sure she was tied up and returned to the main house. He came back with a syringe and injected Vivian with something. The twins knew Frank was making sure Vivian stayed really quiet.

Once the man was back in the house with Frank, Jessie moved his hand from his sister's mouth. Jillian had regained her composure. "We've got to get Mom and get out of here."

Jessie stared at the house. We can't get to her without them seeing us. We need a distraction. Call 911. Tell them there are people who have been shot. Get someone with a badge headed this way."

"Are you saying we are going to turn ourselves in with Vivian?"

"Not just yet but we need a distraction. Make the call and tell them to come in with sirens and lights."

"I can call Lily."

"No time. She kept her promise. They are here and we need help now."

Jillian dialed 911. She gave her name as Vivian, the address, then said, "People have been shot." She hung up.

Frank's phone rang. He went back to the front of the house to answer. It was one of Frank's men who had just left. Frank got off the phone and turned to the other man. "We need to go now. Cops are on the way and will be here any second. Someone must have heard the shots. I'll kill her on the way out. Get back to the boat."

Frank hurried to the pool house. He burst through the door. Vivian wasn't there. He didn't have time to look. He headed straight through the seagrass to where they had beached the boat. His man already had it floating and the motor ready to go. Frank waded out and jumped in as it was pulling out. By the time the first units arrived they were out in the sound and headed across the bay back to Edisto where they had left their car. They were just about to the mouth of the inlet that led to the boat ramp when Frank walked up behind the man driving and shot him through the back of the head. "I told you to make sure Vivian was tied up and out." He slowed the boat, dumped the man's body overboard, and continued on to the boat ramp.

# CHAPTER 28

The first Beaufort officer arriving on the scene was Deputy Billy Ward. As the senior deputy, he took temporary command until everyone else arrived. Once it was determined there was no active shooter, he sealed the scene and waited for more help. While he waited, he dialed Lily.

"I'm not supposed to be calling anyone because our command and homicide people haven't arrived yet, but we just found Terry Mills, the guy you were asking about, and some other guy dead at Terry's house. This can't be a coincidence, so you guys need to make your presence official with the Sheriff. I'll call you as soon as I can."

Lily responded. "We will brief everyone and have Ludlow get in touch with the Sheriff. Is there any sign of the twins or their mother?"

"No. The scene is sealed. You know me. I play by the book, but I can tell you, Lily, this scene looks like they were taken by surprise and it just happened. We responded to a 911 call from inside the house. The dispatcher said it sounded like a young girl. They will have a record of that."

Lily hung up and sent out a message on the command modules to let everyone know what she had just learned.\, and then called Ludlow.

Ludlow answered as he drove. "I'm meeting the Sheriff at the scene. Collins is with me and if necessary, I'm leaving Collins there with the Sheriff as a liaison. I seem to remember that the ping from their phone put them north of Charleston. If they were here and managed to get away, that may be the direction they're going. You and Alex head back and wait for us at the Charleston command center. That puts you in a better position to move either direction. The team with Beth and Tiffany is in place. They seem to be on board if we need them and their dad was good to work with on keeping them both safe."

Lily laughed. "They're pissed, Ludlow. They have had a taste of what it's like to be out from under the control of those people. They are impressive. I think we will get more cooperation this time when and if we get to a trial stage. They still may be the key to the Nightshade investigation."

Ludlow thought for a moment. "I want to hear what is in that file that Frank wants so badly. Once I finish with the Sheriff, we will meet you there. Stay safe." Ludlow saw Collins pull in behind him

He got into Ludlow's car. "How much of this do you want to share with this Sheriff?"

"Just enough to get in the door and see the scene. I'm hoping that our intelligence guru will have something for us at the briefing. If this Mills guy turns out to be anything like Liz Freemont and Billy described him, I want a bit more information about how much the Sheriff trusted Mills before we trust him. Who do you think the other guy is?"

Collins thought. "It's either Charles Tobin or Lester Stokes. They are the only two I can think of that Vivian Bartram would contact. I'm just hoping that we're not going to find three additional bodies on the beach or in the bushes. I'll follow you."

As they parked and walked up to the scene, Ludlow spoke. "Let me take the lead. Once we're sure the twins and Vivian aren't here, we really don't need much more. If it is Stokes or Tobin, I can ask that we be linked to whatever they find. You stay with the vehicles and keep your eyes open. I don't want to leave you here if I don't have to."

Collins nodded. "Sounds like a plan. Billy Ward is an honest, no-bullshit cop. He won't cover for anyone. He can always update us."

The Sheriff came out to greet him and introduced himself and ushered Ludlow into the scene. Ludlow dealt with the question of his agency's interest by just saying they had just dealt with Stokes and he was still a person of interest. The Sheriff bought that story just fine. He was more concerned that his agency had a murder and the scene was already overrun with SLED investigators and crime scene techs.

It took five minutes to determine there were only two dead bodies. One was Mills and the other was an almost faceless Lester Stokes. Ludlow gave the Sheriff his contact information and then risked a very tactical question.

"You worked with Terry Mills. What was he like?"

"I appointed him as a favor for a family member. I created an administrative position with the understanding it would go away after a year. He seemed happy to have a job, and for a year I had him running an inventory of our equipment, checking for competitive bids, and covering some political events that I didn't particularly want to be seen at. We were both relieved when he got to the end of his year. He was ready to go, and I was done providing the resources to someone I really didn't need or trust. So. it's not just this Stokes guy your interested in."

Ludlow nodded. "Mills was a person of interest on the periphery of our case. Are you surprised he's dead?"

The Sheriff was careful. "Shocked describes it better and I'm not shocked by much anymore. I just wish if someone was going to kill him, they'd have done so in Charleston out of my jurisdiction. He was always up there. He dressed above his paygrade, lived in a house above his paygrade, and drove a car above his paygrade. That usually means he was partying above his paygrade. Like I said, neither one of us cried a lot when we parted company. I need to get back to this scene. You going to leave me with anyone else to stumble over or do you trust me enough to keep you in the loop?"

Ludlow laughed as he looked around. "Seems like you've got more than enough people here. I'm good with an update if you are."

"Thanks, Marshal. I appreciate the confidence." He looked around. "Man, nothing brings out the people you didn't even know you employed like a double homicide in the rich part of town. I see my deputy Billy Ward over there. He seems to have things under control. I'll miss him when he goes. I'll keep you posted. I promise."

As they were pulling away, Ludlow's phone beeped for him to call Birdman. He pushed the number and Birdman answered and spoke in slow measured tones. Ludlow put him on speaker.

"Two men left the back of the crime scene in a boat. They headed north toward Edisto. I was able to track it long enough to see the passenger shoot the one driving in the back of the head and dump his body overboard. He then kept on toward Edisto."

"Birdman, how did you know to be over that house?"

He replied sheepishly.

"I wasn't exactly over that house. It's not far from Hunting Island State Park and there are several species of shore birds there now and a couple of owls that I've been monitoring. It just happens that the house is near the park and I had programed the drone to pick up rapid movements. Sorry I didn't get more."

Ludlow laughed. "Sounds like you got more by luck than we did by effort. Send the film clip up to Claymore to fine tune it. See you soon."

An hour later the entire team, plus additional help from the FBI and the Marshals Service, were assembled in the command center at Charleston Executive Airport. Lily and Alex decided that something had happened other than the murder of Lester Stokes for this much manpower to be here. Phelps Wheeler was standing behind a podium somewhere. His image was broadcast on the huge screen that had been installed since their last visit to the site. He began the briefing.

"Most of you have already been alerted about the deaths in Beaufort. Lester Stokes is confirmed dead from a single gunshot wound just above the bridge of his nose. The second person deceased is Terry Mills, a former police officer. Mr. Mills' original surname was Millner. The house where the homicides took place is owned by Valerie Millner, AKA Vivian Bartram. Mr. Mills was her brother. Vivian's new Mercedes was in the driveway and the red Dodge across the street had been recently leased by her, most likely for Stokes. DNA evidence from blood spatter and two recovered teeth from the pool deck belong to Vivian."

There was a rustle in the room. Phelps continued.

"The analysis of the large hard copy file that was received this morning has begun. I will let Mary brief you on those details. However, the FBI lab has processed the film of the murders of Crystal Morse and Lucy Peters. Those results have been given to Detective Freemont. She will meet me in Atlanta to charge Dexter Holder as an accessory to murder. He has also been charged on several sections of the anti-terrorist codes as the result of a relationship we have uncovered with the woman we know as Helena Reagan. Her real name is Svetlana Czerny and we believe she is one of the three people in command of the Nightshade Group. We've had it wrong all along. She didn't work for Frank and Vivian. In reality, Frank worked for her. I'm going to turn the briefing over to my colleague Mary Close who is with Dr. Morozov preparing evidence and charging documents as we move through the file they received."

While they were waiting for the screen to shift, Ludlow motioned for Hal Story and Tim Collins to join him outside. Once they were outside so their conversation would not disturb the briefing, Ludlow spoke.

"Hal, you are going to take half our original team and stick with Lily. Birdman will be with you. Be ready to deploy as soon as this briefing is done. Your mission will be to find the twins and Vivian Bartram. We need them safe and her in custody. Collins, you are to take the rest of the team and stick with Alex who is assigned to Beth and Tiffany. Nothing is to happen to them or any member of their family. As far as both missions are concerned, if you encounter Frank Bartram, use the amount of force necessary to bring him into custody first, or eliminate him as a factor in this investigation. That file is going to lead us to lots of suspects. That will not be your concern. When this is done, a lot of people are going to jail."

Collins, ever curious, had to ask. "Boss, where are you going to be?"

Ludlow laughed. "Washington. Over the next 24 hours, I am tasked with arresting at least eight members of the Department of Justice, six members of the federal bench, and several within Homeland Security. That file has already produced enough evidence for those actions. I'm sure as Dr. Morozov produces more elaborate analysis, there will be more. Now, let's get back into the briefing. There is more you need to hear."

They returned to the group seated in front of the screen with Agent Mary Close conducting the briefing.

"The large paper file we received is still being analyzed by SYBIL. We have been able to construct a network of 60 shell companies, operating in states and offshore countries, that have lax laws related to corporate documentation regarding money flow and taxable income reporting. The transactions covered in the analysis we have already completed indicates that there are over 140 individuals that have been involved in the perpetuation and evolution of the Nightshade Group. Some of them are very well-known businessmen. Several are elected officials or high-ranking members in government. Some of them are also our colleagues."

"The oversight corporation at the top of this network is called Mid-Atlantic Kidder. Beneath it are more specialized operations. You have already had contact with Kidder Properties and Management, a company that provides management for Mid-Atlantic Properties in the south. They own over 350 sites across the southern states. A second company is one called Helping Hand Labor. That company provides illegal workers either smuggled or trafficked from foreign countries to hotels, meat processing plants, construction, and cleaning services. A third company is called Solomon Security Limited. Those individuals are mostly of foreign origin armed and well-equipped. We have taken 20 into custody thus far at both the party house in Greenville. Those in the recent attempt on the lives and welfare of two key witnesses, all work for that company. We expect there are at least that many still at large.

Finally, all the vehicles we have encountered are owned by Palms Transportation who utilizes not only land vehicles but boats and aircraft in trafficking people internationally and moving them between the locations we have identified. They have a legitimate vehicle leasing company called Palmetto Luxury leasing as a front that helps them launder money. We will keep you updated as the analysis continues."

The screen shifted to another more formal view. Attorney General Gwen Vespers was seated at her desk.

"We are very close to the end of a three-year effort to identify the tenacles of the Nightshade Group wherever they stretch. I'm sorry to say they have stretched not only into our government and agencies but several foreign governments, as well. It is vitally important that we take care of the witnesses we have already and keep them safe. It is now, even more important, that we apprehend Vivian Bartram alive and recover her children, Jillian and Jessie Syms. Some arrests will take place shortly in secret for those people who assist in keeping Nightshade informed. In 24 hours, they will all be in secure custody. That means Nightshade will be operating without inside assistance. The remaining arrests will be coordinated and carried out simultaneously once the total analysis of the file is complete and we have secured Vivian Bartram and her children. Please exercise the upmost caution for your own personal safety. Secrecy is still our best asset. These people have been allowed free rein for a very long time. They will not relinquish that readily. I will speak to you again, if time permits, as this investigation now moves into its final phase. Please be careful."

The briefing concluded and the original team gathered around Ludlow as the others moved to their individual commanders. His temperament and voice seemed to have changed.

"Team One will be airborne from this point on. Alex, you and Collins are headed south. Your mission is to protect Tiffany and Beth at all costs. The strike team that is already in place will be your ground resource. You will be staged with Smithson Rotary One that takes off from here in five minutes and will stand by at Beaufort Executive Airport. Make sure the girls and their families are updated and understand what we will expect once the final stage of this operation gets started." Alex nodded and left with Collins and two Marshals.

Ludlow turned to Lily and Hal Story. "Find those twins and their mother and secure them. Once you have the twins, I will give you the location they are to be relocated to. Obviously, Vivian will be headed elsewhere. If she needs medical stabilization, we will arrange that. As you heard in there, these people are at extreme risk and we have to assume that Frank is not the only one looking for them now. We cannot leave them to their own resources any longer. You will be staged here with Smithson Rotary 2 and a second U.S. Marshal helicopter and strike team. They will take custody of Vivian. You, Hal, and the rest of the team are not to leave the twins, no matter what. Birdman is on his way to support your mission. Lily, we need Vivian alive. This thing is coming to a head fast. The only thing we have going for us now is that they do not know we have the file. Our success in these early arrests will keep it that way."

Nobody could hear much of anything over the roar of the helicopter that was getting ready to transport Alex and her team. The remainder of the task force was posted as security around the entire section of the airport. Everyone was moving into place. Detective Freemont left on one of the jets for the undisclosed anti-terrorist black site where Dexter and Helena Regan were being held. All the moving parts were being placed where they were needed the most.

Once everyone was gone, it became eerily quiet.

# CHAPTER 29

Underground in Tennessee, Mary Close was watching the monitor as SYBIL moved through the digitized files from the Mid-Atlantic Kidder file the twins had provided. The doctor was busy typing in amendments to the program as she saw things develop on the large monitors. Mary had spent the morning preparing for her briefing and, when she wasn't doing that, she was preparing charging documents and warrant requests. All of these were being transmitted to the AG as she finished them.

Mary was petting the nearest canine when a call came through from Claymore.

"Mary, I can't seem to get Phelps which means he's in the air on his ops phone. We just received a notice from FBI Atlanta day desk that they received a call from a very excited lady named Marian Ackerman. She says it's vital she talk to you or Phelps."

Mary didn't hesitate. "Put her through, Claymore, thanks."

"Mrs. Ackerman, this is Mary Close. How can I help?"

"Hello, Agent Close, this is Marian Ackerman from Atlanta. You and that nice Agent Wheeler were here several weeks ago. I promised that I would let you know when and if these people showed up again. Well, the little fancy pants prissy one showed up and hour ago, and instead of parking on the street, he pulled around back. I thought you would like to know."

Mary smiled to herself. "Yes, Mrs. Ackerman. We are very interested to know that. Please don't confront them. Stay in your home. We are on our way. Call me back at the number I'm about to give you if he leaves."

Mrs. Ackerman wrote the number down. "Roger, I'll keep my eyes glued to that house and call you."

Mary hung up. She pulled out her command tablet and sent Claymore the contents of a message to transmit to Phelps with an alert signal so he would answer it. She hung up and called the FBI office in Atlanta and explained what she needed done, and that an arrest warrant had been secured. The command staff there assembled the regional FBI SWAT team and they were dispatched to the old Fourth Ward neighborhood as discreetly as possible. An FBI helicopter was sent as a support unit. Mary called Mrs. Ackerman back.

"Mrs. Ackerman, I want to make sure that you and Tess stay in your house for the next few minutes. Is that OK?"

"Of course, dear girl. Are you and Agent Phelps on your way?"

"No, but our colleagues should be there in just a few minutes. Do you mind staying on the line with me?"

"Of course not. We're in this together, aren't we. Finally, someone is doing something about those parties. I'm having a wonderful time. I have Tess upstairs watching in case he tries to run. She has a better view."

The SWAT team was set and waiting for the command from the team leader to make entry. The team had placed a listening device on a window downstairs to try to determine where the occupant, or occupants, were. A silver BMW was parked at the rear door just outside the garage. The command came to hold positions to better understand the situation and number of people on the inside. The audio feed had picked up bits of a conversation, so there was either more than one person or someone was talking on the phone. As they listened, it became clearer that Charles Tobin was in the house and was talking to someone. They were about to make entry when the team member stationed at the window held up a fist which meant stand by. The back door opened and an older woman in a full-length fur coat emerged being helped by Tobin. The woman made ample use of the railing as she crept her way down the four steps, one at a time. Tobin had her arm helping her. When they reached the bottom step, he walked ahead and opened the car door. Once she was seated on the inside, the team leader gave the go signal to take Tobin into custody as he walked around the back of the car.

Tobin never even looked up. The elderly woman in the car never became aware of what was happening until he was in cuffs, bent over the trunk of the sedan. She immediately reached inside her purse but was intercepted by a team member just as she was about to pull a small 32 caliber revolver out. She was gingerly, but carefully, placed in custody.

The team commander reported to Mary in summary form.

"Two subjects secure and in custody. Subject One, Charles Tobin, pursuant to your warrant. He is a white male, 42, and matches the description. Subject Two, Celeste Millner Foster, in custody for brandishing a weapon, resisting without violence and attempted impedance of a federal officer. She is a white female, and states she is 85, and Mr. Tobin's mother. Final note for report, Subject Two is wearing a full-length mink coat and silk pajamas."

Mary Close thought she had misheard the summary. "Command, repeat last notation."

The team leader finally laughed. "Mary, you heard me correctly. This little old lady is dressed for bed underneath all that fur."

Mary regained her composure and turned back to Mrs. Ackerman, who had waited patiently on the line. Tess had joined them on an upstairs phone. It was Tess, who had enjoyed the full view of the operation that spoke first.

"Agent Close, that was the most excitement I've had in a long time. Who knew that many people could be so quiet for that long and not be seen. I'm still not sure I saw all of them."

Mrs. Ackerman broke in. "Tess, you have all the luck. I only saw the ones in the front. Did we get our man, Agent Close?"

Mary laughed. "We did, thanks to you two. And, it appears we got a woman as well. Does the name Celeste Foster ring a bell with either of you?"

Mrs. Ackerman laughed out loud as did Tess. It was Tess who responded.

"Mrs. Foster used to live in that house. When she first moved in, she was Mrs. Dupont. It was later she became Mrs. Foster just before they moved out. She was well known in the neighborhood."

Mrs. Ackerman broke in. "Tess, you are being entirely too polite, which is your nature of course. That woman was a catwalk hussy if ever there was one. As I remember, you could put a drink in her and within minutes her clothes would be on the floor and she would be doing something unspeakable with whichever male was the closest. What in the world is she doing with Mr. Fancy Pants.?"

It was Tess that answered her question. "Didn't she have a son? I think Ronnie was his name."

Mrs. Ackerman laughed. "Oh yes. Little Ronald was quite the little prancing prince. My late husband called him the muskrat. He was always sneaking about. We were at a dinner party over there and he had hidden under the table trying to look up the women's dresses. I was the one that dug him out by his ear. Celeste didn't like that I laid hands on the little creep so she threw us out. We were only too happy to leave, but I did finish my martini before we got to the door. Another time we caught him on our second-floor balcony trying to peep into our bedroom window. My husband went outside and removed the ladder he had used to reach it, and we left him there and called the police. Nothing ever came of it, though. He was always roaming around the neighborhood in his underpants at all hours of the night. Is that the man we've been seeing over there?"

Mary was quick to reply. "I'm not sure right now. We have to get some additional information. One of we will be in touch to arrange take your formal statement."

"Of course, we will be happy to help." The call ended and Mary had Claymore pull out the stops to get Phelps on the phone. He finally answered.

"Hey, Mary. Sorry, we were in the air in a closed-door session to set a timeline on staging."

"Mrs. Ackerman and Tess called. We have Charles Tobin and his mother, Celeste Millner Foster in custody. It turns out Mrs. Foster was once Mrs. Dupont and Tobin lived there as a child. He was called Ronnie at that time."

Phelps broke in. "Ronald Dupont was the name he used in Greenville."

Mary continued. "Yes, it was. Hard to know which is his legal name, but it doesn't matter. We have him in the secure site you are headed to along with the woman he calls his mother, Celeste. He is so agitated that I have him on medical observation. He keeps going on about how we have treated his mother, and that he will have Stella St. John sue all of us. I don't think he knows that Stella is dead. I can head down there if you want."

Phelps thought then answered. "No, you stay there preparing the warrants and documenting the case. I'm headed to the secure site right now. The plane should touch down in about 30 minutes and it will take me another 30 to get there. I think it's time we brought some of these people up to speed on what is going on out there with their friend Frank."

Mary agreed, but added. "We are up to 160 individuals with enough hard evidence to justify the warrants. The Justice department has offered me help to get them prepared so that when the AG says move, we make all the arrests at one time."

She ended the conversation as Phelps sent a message to the Smithson team members on their command modules. It was short and direct. "Charles Tobin, AKA Ronald Dupont is in custody. Find Vivian Bartram and her children and secure as quickly as possible."

The twins had passed law enforcement racing to the scene at the Beaufort house and driven straight to their cabin near Georgetown. Jillian kept checking Vivian making sure she was still breathing.

"Jessie, I don't know what they gave her. I've never seen her this bad. We need to take her to a hospital."

"Check her pulse and her breathing on a regular basis. I don't think Frank was going to kill her with an injection before he got the file. I can't believe he shot Stokes and Uncle Terry like that. It was the same with Stella. He is one lethal son of a bitch. That's three times I've watched him murder someone in person. That is the last time. We will figure out what Mom wants to do with her life, but you and I are going to call Lily and get out of this mess."

After a time, Jillian sat on the couch next to her mother and noticed that Vivian seemed to be coming around. "She's waking up a bit. How are we going to tell her? Do you think that Lily and her friends would let Mom go if we agreed to come in?"

Jessie was quick to answer. "Nope. There's been too much killing and even if Vivian hasn't killed anyone, she is guilty of a lot. The cops want mom to tell them what she knows as badly as Frank wants her silent. She's in a bad place but she needs to make that decision. We will tell her what we want to do. I'm just not sure what she will do when she finds out we gave the file to Lily and her friends."

"Let's not tell her"

Jessie laughed. "Jillian, you'd lie to your own mother?"

"I know, shocker that anyone in this family would lie."

Vivian was continuing to come around. She blinked her eyes and looked over at Jessie then up at Jillian.

"What the hell did they give me? What time is it and where are we?"

Jessie answered. "We don't know. It was an injection of some kind. It's almost 8:00 pm."

"Where is Frank? How did I get here? I had a horrible dream that Frank shot Stokes and Terry. It was horrible."

Vivian was awake enough that she rolled her tongue over the front of her mouth. She bolted upright. "What happened to my mouth, where are my teeth?"

Jillian got up and walked across the room and sat in a chair next to Jessie.

"Your teeth are on the pool deck where they fell when Frank knocked them out. And it wasn't a dream. Frank shot Lester Stokes and killed Uncle Terry right in front of you, and us. He was on his way to kill you when we got you out of there."

Vivian blinked at them twice like it was taking her a bit to get the story straight.

"Your father has never raised a hand to me before."

Jessie had endured her act long enough.

"Vivian, let's get a few things clear. Frank Bartram is not our father any more than you are our real mother. I don't care what crazy fake document Stella engineered to make it look legal. Frank is a cold-blooded killer, who we watched shoot two people like he was swatting a mosquito. He would have killed you, and then us, if he been given the chance. We called the police as a distraction and were lucky enough to get you out. You told him we were on the way with the file. You would have sacrificed us in a heartbeat."

Vivian just stared at the two twins. "I could have handled Frank. I may not be your birth mother, but I love you just as if I was."

It was Jillian's turn. "I think your definition of 'motherly love' is very different from what the rest of the world uses. Most mothers don't screw their babies, and I mean that in the most literal way. Either way, you were going to give us up to Frank."

"No sweet babies, I was going to give Frank the file, and he would have been fine with that. He wouldn't have hurt any of us once he had the file. You don't know him like I do."

Jessie wasn't buying it still. "That's bullshit just like all the rest of the lies and crap you have fed us over the years. He is wanted for murder, and they have the video evidence to prove it."

Vivian stopped short, tried to stand up, but the drugs still had some impact, so she sat back down hard.

"What do you mean they have video evidence? Where did they get it?"

Jessie stood up and walked over to her. "From me."

"What, how? How would you even know who to give that video to? Don't be silly."

Jillian now stood up and walked over next to Jessie standing squarely in front of Vivian.

"Do you remember me telling you it was my idea to write the note and leave it at the rest stop?"

"Of course, I remember, but I didn't take you seriously. You're just a child for Christ's sake. You're not even old enough to drive. It was those other two girls"

"No, Vivian. It was me. That note led to a whole group of federal police officers surrounding that party, and that is how everyone got arrested. The house was completely surrounded the whole time you were there. Why they didn't arrest you when you left, I don't know."

Vivian just sat there blinking at them. Then somewhere, way back in the far reaches of her mind, it finally dawned on her what had happened. She looked down at the floor for a moment, looked back up at them, and said very quietly to no one in particular.

"They didn't have grounds to arrest me. I hadn't done anything."

She sighed heavily. "You also gave them the file, didn't you? They have the file that Frank has been ordered to get. If that is the case, then I only have one choice if you are going to live to see 16."

# CHAPTER 30

In Atlanta, Celeste Foster had been taken with Tobin to the secret holding facility, processed, and given a set of hospital scrubs which she had to be helped into. It wasn't quite clear if the woman had any idea what was happening to her. She was sitting in an interview room appearing to be totally lost and disoriented. A medical attendant was with her, and the FBI had called in a mental health advocate to sit with her as well. The background check had produced some very interesting information. Her record indicated she had been born Celeste Mason in Charleston, SC. She had been married at a young age to a John Millner with whom she had two children, Tim and Vivian. She divorced Mr. Millner and married Franklin Bartram who had a son, Frank Junior. Ten years later, she married a man name Thomas Dupont, a marriage that lasted approximately 10 months. Three months after Mr. Dupont dies in an automobile accident, she marries again to a man called Hollins Foster. The record indicates she is still married. SYBIL also finds two separate birth certificates for her. One indicates she is 62 and one indicates she is 82.

Phelps decides to interview Charles Tobin first and wait for the results of a preliminary mental health check on the person he calls "Mother," Celeste Foster. When Phelps enters the room, Tobin is in a chair facing the wall away from him.

"Mr. Tobin, my name is Phelps Wheeler. I'm going to need you to turn around and face me. I have a few questions."

"Fuck you. I know my rights. I want my lawyer."

"That is going to be difficult Mr. Tobin. You listed Stella St. John as your lawyer."

Tobin half turned. "So, when does she get here?"

"Never, Mr. Tobin. Frank Bartram killed her several nights ago."

Tobin wheeled around in his chair in a panic. "What are you talking about?"

Phelps played the audio documenting the murder but only got to the second set of screams before Tobin stood up, covered his ears, and began pacing, demanding he turn it off. Phelps did so, but continued.

"I am seriously going to need you to sit down. If you don't, I will have someone come in, put you in the chair, and shackle you to the table. I would much rather have a civilized conversation. You seem like a civilized man."

Tobin wheeled on him and slammed the chair up to the table and sat down.

"You people have my mother. She has nothing to do with anything. You have no grounds to hold her."

"We will have to talk about that. But first, look around you Mr. Tobin. Does this look like a regular police station?"

"I wouldn't know. I've never been in a police station. Check my record."

Phelps laughed. "We did. So, it is sad that the first one you end up in is a federal maximum confinement facility sanctioned for use with international terrorists.

Tobin laughed a very high-pitched nervous laugh. "I'm a party planner not a terrorist you moron. Your information is wrong."

Phelps smiled. " You're nothing but a well-dressed, well-spoken pimp, Mr. Tobin. And before you say much more, I should tell you we have a very extensive file on you and the people you work for."

It was Tobin's turn to smile. " I work for lots of people."

"You work for Frank and Vivian Bartram and arrange parties and payment in a variety of plush houses owned by a holding company called Mid-Atlantic Kidder.

At the mention of the company name, Tobin tenses. Phelps continues.

"You have worked with two transporters, Lester Stokes who was killed yesterday evening in Beaufort, and Dexter Holder, who is in custody down the hall on the same type of charges. You are a panderer for a very well-hidden international trafficking organization which is part of the Nightshade Group. Unfortunately, that group, because of its international association with an identified terrorist known to have supplied weapons and money to enemies of this country, and you are classed in that same category."

Tobin looked confused but it caused him to pause and think. He was about to speak when Phelps cut him off.

"Before you say something you regret, that person is a Czech woman who is also in custody. Her real name is Svetlana Czerny but you know her as Helena Reagan."

Tobin got up and started to pace. "I don't have anything to do with that woman. I've only ever met her once a couple of years ago. She has nothing to do with what I do."

Phelps decided to ratchet the conversation up a notch.

"Svetlana is the person who smuggles the foreign men and women into the country to work in the brothels and labor companies that Nightshade supplies with people. We have you on video tape in a bus that picked up your clients for the party in Greenville. She got on that bus with you. That bothered you so much you changed your plans and stayed on that bus, and took a ride share back to the house where you and Stokes had kept the girls the night before. Then you took your RV to Raleigh to visit your mother and lay low. I have a picture of it parked on its pad next to your mother's house. It's being searched as we speak."

Tobin became more agitated and stood up.

"Sit down, Mr. Tobin, I'm just getting started. I also need to tell you that Frank Bartram is on a killing spree that we believe was ordered by whoever is at the top of this organization. He has killed Stella St. John, and is the prime suspect in the killing of Lester Stokes and a man named Terry Mills. Do you know a man named Terry Mills, Mr. Tobin? It's really sad. He was killed in his own home in Beaufort where we believe his sister, Vivian Bartram, and her two children were."

Tobin was in a flat-out panic. He sat down, but began to cry. Phelps let him sob and mumble to himself for a couple of minutes than snapped his fingers to get his attention.

"Charles. If I were to let you out now, you wouldn't last a day. Frank is cleaning up loose ends. You are one of those. It is time you get your best deal while you still can."

Tobin let loose.

"There is no fucking way out of this. The organization is huge. We have people on our payroll all throughout your beloved justice system and this government. There is no where you could hide me or my mother that they wouldn't find us and kill us both. You are in way over your head, Agent Whoever You are. Way over your head."

Phelps turned to the mirror in the room and spoke. "Bring in the cart."

Another agent brought in a rolling cart with almost 200 files on it. They were all marked warrant to arrest. Tobin watched Phelps as he picked up the first five and read out the names of five federal judges.

Tobin hung his head. "Are you telling me that all of those are arrest warrants?"

"Oh, Charles, that is just the beginning. Every property that is actively under the current possession of Mid-Atlantic Kidder has a search warrant issued and ready to execute when we decide to move. A whole team of federal prosecutors have begun the seizure procedure for the federal government to take all of those properties, including the one you and your mother were arrested at. It's over Charles. It is time to minimize the damage to you and your mother."

Tobin just looked at him. Phelps didn't know whether it was disbelief or stupidity. Then Tobin seemed to get an idea.

"Well, Mr. G Man, if you have all the evidence, you certainly don't need anything from me. So I think I will just not say anything. You got me. I scouted around to find men willing to pay big money to have an hour with a woman or a man. whichever they preferred. Big fucking deal. I never moved women. I never hunted them down or hurt them or sold them outright. Do what you will with me. I'm not even sure I've committed a federal offense."

Phelps had him. "Oh, at the level you've been working, it's a federal offense. Thank you for admitting your role. To show my good faith, I am going to have them get your mother some clothes and we will have her taken to wherever you would like her delivered."

"You can't do that. They will torture and kill that poor woman just because of who she is. You can't do that. She is defenseless without me. You can't keep me here and let her go. It's the same thing as murdering her."

Phelps shrugged his shoulders. "Who do you work for Charles? Simple as that. It will take us about thirty 30 to get your mother dressed. That is about as much time as you have." Phelps turned to go.

"Wait. I can only give you one name. I know Frank was afraid of him. So am I. He would think nothing of killing my mother and making me watch."

Phelps stood there looking at him as he gathered up the files and put them in the basket. He turned to go and Tobin spoke.

"His name is Hollins Foster. He is my stepfather. Neither I nor my poor mother have had any contact with him in months. He has more contact with Frank and that horrible Slavic woman these days. That is all I can give you."

Phelps nodded. "Your mother is getting a mental health evaluation. If it turns out she needs those services we will see she is referred. That is the best I can do for right now."

Tobin looked up at him. "You will see. She doesn't even know who she is. She needs me."

Phelps stopped in the door. "Your compassion for her is touching. Too bad you didn't feel that way about the women you helped them enslave."

Phelps got in the hall and texted Mary Close the name. She and Dr. Morozov entered it into SYBIL The computer began generating information almost immediately. The screens lit up like a pinball machine.

Vivian sat at the table in the cabin and looked around.

"You've really set yourself up here, haven't you Jessie? How long do you think you can stay here before Frank finds you?" She didn't give him time to answer. She dialed the number. Frank answered.

"You have done enough. You need to get out of the country. The feds have the file. You know as well as I do the dominoes are going to start falling. Foster won't allow you to live once he finds out. You need to get out of this country Frank."

There was silence on the other end of the line, then. "Why are you calling me to tell me this?"

"Because unless you leave, our children are in danger. I want him chasing you not them. I don't care about myself anymore, but they need to have a chance."

"You really think that Foster will let them live?"

"I think you are about three steps behind, Frank. It's over. You must have missed the part where I said that the Feds have the file. When Hollins finds that out, he won't waste time on anything except killing you and then getting away."

Frank was silent. "How did they get the file, Vivian. Did you give it to them?"

"Stella gave it to them in exchange for immunity. They had her office bugged. There is a video of you and your boys killing her. Frank, you are wanted everywhere." Vivian could lie with the best of them but she also knew when to emphasize the truth.

"Stella had a great gig going. Why would she ruin that?"

"Frank, I long ago gave up trying to figure out why anybody we deal with does what they do. Why did you kill two girls just because they ran away? Why did you kill Stella? Why did you kill Stokes and Terry and most of all, why Frank did you hit me and knock my teeth out? You've never laid a hand on me before. Is hurting people turning into fun for you, Frank, or are you justifying all of this because you're just pissed off and want to remain free?

Vivian paused and laughed. "Neither of us have ever been free, Frank. We've been as enslaved as the people we managed. We just lived in better houses, dressed better, and were free to roam around as long as we produced the next party." She paused to collect her thoughts.

"I've had enough. You need to leave because I am turning myself into the Feds. I've had enough."

"You will die in prison without your booze, dope and sex."

"Maybe so, but I am going to try to get through that to be able to maybe someday visit my children. Besides, I bet there is plenty of all the of that in prison. You're the one who should be afraid of prison. You've made some bad enemies in just the last few days. I'm about to make some new ones in exchange for them protecting the twins. Between that file and what I have to say, I might just live long enough to earn their love back."

"They're not even your children, Vivian. Think for once."

Vivian sighed. "Frank, while I may have been maybe the worst mother on record, I don't have to continue that. I'm telling you one last time, you need to leave." Vivian hung up. She looked at the twins. "How far away are your friends?"

Jillian dialed the number.

Thirty minutes later there was a knock on the door of the cabin. Vivian answered it cautiously in case Frank had been able to trace the call and it was not who they expected.

"Hello, Mrs. Bartram. My name is Lily Michaels and this is Marshal Hal Story."

Vivian smiled. "My aren't you interesting, and Marshal Story, do come in. I'm assuming it's not just the two of you."

Lily stepped back and revealed several members of the team and the vehicles waiting.

Hal Story stepped up. "Can you please step out here Mrs. Bartram." It wasn't really a question.

Vivian turned around to be handcuffed, and Lily reached down and pulled her hands back in front.

"Vivian, if you turn into a problem we will deal with the cuffs. Right now, you are a mother trying to save her children. Just go with Marshal Story. I will stay with the twins, and I promise you I will not leave their side. Let's not have the last image they see of you be one of you being handcuffed."

Vivian looked Lily up and down. "You, dear girl, look like you could take on the world. I remember feeling that way once. Keep them safe and you will have my full cooperation. With whom in the American justice system will I be speaking to first?"

Lily smiled. "That will be the Attorney General of the United States, Mrs. Bartram."

"Oh my. We are going big, aren't we? Marshal Story, lead the way. I promise I'll behave myself. But if I were you, as soon as my daughter is out of sight, let's put the cuffs on anyway, just in case someone from Nightshade is watching." Hal escorted her to a waiting vehicle. When they reached the car, he searched her, cuffed her then helped her duck her head so she didn't bump it against the edge of the car roof. He walked to the far side of the car and slid in next to her. In five minutes, the Marshals' helicopter landed in the middle of the highway, and Vivian was on her way north escorted by two other armed helicopters.

Inside, Jillian was sitting on the couch. Lily looked around.

"Where is Jessie?"

Jillian just shook her head, stood up and walked over and hugged Lily.

"First, thank you for rescuing me the first time. I'm sorry I disappeared. I didn't know what I was really doing. And to answer your question, Jessie left after she made the call to my father and I made the call to you."

Lily looked confused. "Where is he, Jillian? You know he is in as much danger as you and Vivian are."

"I'm not sure where he is or what he's going to do. He is not the same person that left to live with Stella. He watched Stella be tortured and murdered. We both watched our father kill two people. I'm not sure where he is, Lily. But he is not here. I'm ready to go with you and cooperate. I was ready when I wrote that note. But wherever Jessie is right now, I will have to leave that up to you and him."

Lily guided Jillian to a separate vehicle and whisked her away to a waiting helicopter that lifted off from the same spot where five minutes earlier her mother had started her journey.

Jessie watched through his binoculars as his mother was loaded into a vehicle and whisked away from the cabin. From his vantage point, he saw the Marshal delay putting her in handcuffs. They obviously didn't know Vivian as well as he did. He waited and listened quietly. He heard the sound of helicopters. lots of helicopters. Still, he remained in the thicket, hidden from view. He watched as he saw the outline of several people move into positions around the cabin. He was impressed. If Frank found the cabin, they would be waiting for him. He had the phone his mother had used to call Frank. If Frank believed Vivian, he would warn the bosses. Jessie knew that the bosses would make sure Frank didn't go anywhere but into the ocean or down a deep hole. Jillian would be safe now. Jessie had the bulk of the funds his mother and Stella had stashed. It should give him enough to begin a new life. He walked almost a mile back through the swamp to where he had hidden the Bronco. He left the lights off and pulled onto the canal road in the dark until he got to the main road. He turned north. He had remembered a house in a small town between Greenville and Columbia. His mother owned it outright under an alias. He was sure Frank didn't know about it. It had not appeared on any of the lists that Stella had. That might be just the right place to rest, then disappear. If Frank did show up, he would do what he could to stop him. The small bit of freedom Stella had allowed him had affected him greatly. He didn't want to lose it again.

High above him, Birdman's Eagle II hovered following him. Birdman had been deployed to look at the property first to make sure the rescue team wasn't walking into a firefight. Oscar had told Birdman to keep flying and watching even after they left the cabin with Vivian and the twins. He had watched them all leave and had seen the follow-up surveillance team move into place just in case anyone from the Nightshade Group showed up afterwards.

# CHAPTER 31

Jillian was exhausted. They stopped to let her sleep at the Command Center in Charleston. Ludlow landed back in South Carolina and drove directly to Beaufort. He had called ahead to have Billy Ward and Lydia meet him at her house at 07:30 am. They were both sitting on her porch when he got out of the car.

"Thanks for agreeing to meet me so early."

Lydia handed him a cup of coffee. "It's not early around here."

He accepted the coffee with a smile. "I'm afraid I have a huge favor I need to ask."

Lydia smiled. "Marshal Ludlow, you can ask me any favor you want, and I will do what I can."

He looked at Billy as he spoke to Lydia.

"We need to keep Jillian Syms in safe place that we know we can protect from all sides. It won't be for very long, but it needs to be away from any location someone from the Nightshade syndicate would look for her. We have begun arresting those involved within the justice system, but until we progress with the debriefing of her mother, and get her father in custody, I'm afraid the government's regular locations could be compromised. It's just for a few days until we can get key people in custody. Then I think we can move her safely to one of the new Smithson shelters."

Billy interrupted him. "Hold on Marshall. I respect the hell out of you, but you are not stashing that girl here at Lydia's house. The last thing we need is for some of these people you spend your time chasing, finding Lydia. You shouldn't even be asking. I won't have it, you understand?"

Lydia started to laugh. She spoke once she finally caught her wind.

"Marshal, would you listen to this man? Somehow he thinks I gave

him permission to make decisions about what I will, and won't, agree to."
She laughed out loud again then turned to Billy.

"You listen up, Billy Ward. If that girl needs a safe place to stay to get
her feet back under her, and the Marshal and Lily think this is the place
for that to happen, then that will happen. I will never turn away anyone in
need, and if I have learned anything in my long and blessed life, it is how
to make decisions for myself." She turned back to Ludlow. "If you need her
to stay here, she is welcome, as are all of you that I know will be keeping
that child safe."

Ludlow just smiled. "I agree with everything you both said, but I
didn't get to finish."

He turned to Billy. "I think the perfect place to keep Jillian Syms safe
is your house, Billy."

Billy's mouth dropped open. "My house?"

Lydia broke in. "Billy Ward shut that yapper of yours and just nod
your head. I will be there to help you with that girl. You don't have any
idea what that little thing needs and my guess is that Marshal Ludlow is
suggesting that because no one can get within a mile of that thing you call
a house without someone noticing. You don't even have a proper kitchen
garden. Is that what you're thinking Marshal?"

"It is actually. It's very easy to protect from all sides. Even the water
approach is easy to cover. We would need to keep her there until it's safe."

Billy Ward looked back and forth between the two of them. "Do I
get a say in this?"

Lydia answered for him. "As long as it's yes, of course you do."

Billy hung his head and looked at Ludlow. "I have no idea how to
handle a girl."

Ludlow smiled. "I kind of disagree with that. Lily seemed to turn out well, and you had a lot to do with that. Your whole life has been spent protecting people. Half of your informants in this county are kids who respect you, and that is saying something for a cop. Jillian needs stability and a place that is safe to regroup. She needs to be around people who can care for her and let her start to recover."

Billy sipped his coffee and turned to Lydia. "I'm going to need a lot of help."

Lydia looked at him tenderly. "Billy Ward, you have never needed help being kind to people in your whole life. But I think you will need to take some time off. You can't be out looking for bad guys and worrying about that girl and me."

That got Billy's attention. "You mean you're going to move in there with me? Hell, yes then. I got plenty of vacation."

"Billy Ward you can just get those filthy thoughts about us playing house out of your head right now. You have plenty of room for all of us, and you're wasting time just hoping Marshal Ludlow here will beg you some more." She turned to Ludlow. "When does she get here? I'd like to get my things over there before she arrives so it will seem more stable."

Ludlow smiled. "She and Lily, along with a security team, will be here this afternoon. Some of them are standing by to move into position. She's sleeping now. She's exhausted.

"You tell those officers the coffee pot will always be on. It will take me a couple of hours to bring some things over from my place and get adequate groceries in that house. It will need my touch before it is ready for that poor child to feel safe."

It was settled. Jillian was moving to Billy's house where the feds could supervise her safety and Lydia could supervise them.

Jessie arrived just north of Greenwood about the same time Jillian arrived in the low country. He went to a convenience store and bought a gallon of milk, butter, a frozen package of something called tater bites, some peanut butter, grape jelly, hot dogs and a loaf of white bread, none of which he had ever been allowed to have. He also slipped a box of macaroni and cheese into his basket. He had heard Stella talk about this thing but he had never been allowed to eat anything like that. After gassing up, he drove to the house. Being cautious, he drove past the turn off and parked at a roadside park a mile and a half away. He locked the car and walked back to the house cautiously through the trees. He wanted to make sure that he would be there alone. Vivian had given him the punch code for the electronic lock. He walked all the way around the property keeping a safe distance. There was no one there and no evidence that anyone had been in the woods watching the place. Frank's men were pigs and Jessie had learned that they went nowhere without leaving a mess. Frank was always screaming at them about leaving their cigarette butts and trash. They did not fully understand the nature of DNA analysis like Frank did. Jessie found none of the normal piles that Frank's army might have left.

He approached the house cautiously and used the keypad on the back door to enter the garage. He reached up and took the garage door controller and slipped it in his pocket next to the small automatic pistol he carried now, just in case. He unlocked the door into the house with the code. He went in and searched each room. He satisfied himself that it was just as his mother said she had left it. He went to the master bedroom and opened the closet, slid the clothes back and found the safe. He opened it and found not just the money Vivian had mentioned, but several passports for herself, and one each for Jessie, and Jillian. He also found the code and controller Vivian had talked about that would activate an alarm system. If anyone came up the driveway, they would pass the one lone sensor that would immediately lock the house down so that only the person with the code, or the controller, could get in or out. Vivian had planned carefully for the eventuality that she would have to hide and then escape. Jessie was stunned. She had planned to have the twins with her. Their passports were in their correct names. He also found their birth certificates issued by the State of Kentucky that listed their birthdates and their mother's name as Anna Syms. Under father it listed unknown. One of the passports for Vivian was in the name of Anna Syms. He left everything he found inside the safe and closed it. He just needed time to think.

He walked the mile and a half back to his car, this time walking adjacent to the driveway to check if there was any evidence that someone had been watching from there. There was none. He noticed a car parked just down the road from where he had left the Bronco. He skirted through the woods to approach his car from the far side of the parking lot and found that there was a trail and a large stream located at the end of the path that led in. He didn't even see the man until he spoke.

"Enjoy your walk?"

Jessie hid the fact that he was totally startled.

"Yes, sir." The man was older, had a fishing pole with a line in the water and was standing next to a camp chair.

"It's beautiful out here first thing in the morning. You ever fish this stretch?"

"No sir. I've never really tried fishing."

The man smiled, turned around, and handed Jessie a pole that was leaning next to the chair.

"I always have two. I set one in case I get a nice channel cat cruising toward the lake down below. This other one is rigged for smallmouth bass. You're welcome to try your hand if you like."

Jessie walked over. "I'm not sure I know how to do it."

"You see me standing here, don't you? That's how you do it. Other than tying on a hook with bait or a lure likes on this one, that's all there is to it. The rest is up to the fish."

Jessie walked over and the man handed him the pole as he smiled. "Go ahead, give it a try. I normally have my grandson with me, but he's off up to Clemson to get him an engineering degree. I'm not sure you'll catch anything. Here watch me cast once then you try."

Jessie got the hang of it quickly and stood there quietly with the man for a long time. He had never met a stranger who was friendly with him for no other reason than just to be friendly. The man's bobber plunged beneath the surface and his rod bent. The man fought the fish to the shore, and it was a nice sized catfish. He showed Jessie how to avoid the dorsal fins taking the fish off the hook.

"You ever eaten a fresh caught catfish, son?"

"No, s ir. I'm not sure I've ever eaten anything fresh caught."

"Well let me clean this one up and you take the filets home and fry them up in some peanut oil with a bit of Cajun breading. I've got plenty in my freezer already."

"I'm not sure I would do it right."

"Son, you can't be sure of doing anything right until you try it once. Now take these filets home and give 'em to your ma. She'll show you how to do it, but remember, peanut oil and Cajun breading. Oh, you can maybe add a lemon squirt or hot sauce and some salt right after they come out of the oil." The man reached down and took a small plastic storage bag out of his cooler, put some ice in the bag and dropped the filets in. "Here you go. I hope to see you again sometime here. You have a good day."

Jessie accepted the fish. This was a completely new exchange for him. "Yes, sir. Thank you for the fish. I'll take them home right now."

Jessie walked back to his Bronco mulling over what had just happened. This was the first time since he had rescued his sister that he felt safe around another human being. He started the car and drove back to the convenience store. He bought a small bottle of oil and a small box of Cajun breading. He couldn't find a lemon but he did find some hot sauce. He returned to the house, used the controller to open the garage door, went inside, and then set the sensor so he would be alerted. He only had one direction to worry about and that was from behind the house but he could see that area well. He unpacked the food, and his computer.

He was starving. He read the directions for his tater bites and put them in the oven. He then took all the stuff out of the box for the macaroni and cheese, followed the directions and put it together. Finally, he read the directions on the box of breading, heated the oil, breaded the catfish and fried it just like the man had instructed. He took all the food to the living room where he could watch the back approach. He ate every bite, tasting things for the first time that most kids his age had tasted before. It was the first time in his entire life that he was totally alone. It was the first time he had fixed himself a meal. It was the first time he had met a total stranger who seemed to give more than he took. He thought to himself, once this is over, if I make it through, I'm going to buy myself a fishing pole.

# CHAPTER 32

The following morning after Vivian was taken into custody and Jillian was safely in Beaufort, Phelps Wheeler and Liz Freemont walked down the hall toward the interrogation room where Dexter Holder was waiting. Liz stopped in the hall before they went in.

"What's his demeanor been like since they told him I was coming?"

Phelps understood her question. "I don't think they have told him. He really doesn't understand the terrorist connection. I don't think he's faking that but he understands the murder part and is very afraid of that."

"How do you think he will respond to me?"

"How do you mean?"

Fremont was straightforward. "Being arrested by a woman he used to work with. There is no question his file reflects a problem with women, and while he never turned that toward me, I could feel the resentment even then."

Phelps thought a moment. "I think his history tells me he likes taking advantage of women who he thinks he can bully. He has no idea what to do with women who are strong. I also think that when men like Dexter don't know what to do with those strong women, they fear them."

Liz nodded her head as she opened the door and held it for Phelps. Dexter Holder was definitely not expecting to see Liz Freemont standing in front of him with a detective badge and a warrant.

"Freemont, what are you doing here?" Dexter looked totally confused.

Liz didn't smile. "Dexter Holder, I'm charging you with the murder of Lucile Peters and Crystal Daniella Morse." Liz then continued with the reading of his rights and asked him if he understood.

"Wait, this guy" pointing at Phelps, "said it was accessory to murder, not murder!"

Freemont kept a calm voice. "Mr. Holder, do you understand your rights as I have read them to you?"

Dexter sat down hard and nodded his head.

"You need to say it out loud, Mr. Holder for the recorder."

"All I did was hold the camera."

Phelps stepped in. "Dexter, are you waiving your right for an attorney to be present, yes or no, out loud for the recorder."

Dexter almost laughed. "What lawyer? The only lawyer I knew and trusted was Stella, and Frank took care of my options on that. But, he's not going to pin this all on me."

Freemont stepped in. "Dexter, we can get you a lawyer if you request one. Otherwise, you need to waive your rights or keep still until you talk to one."

Dexter smirked. "Wow, you guys are really crossing the i's and dotting the t's on this, aren't you? Yeah, I waive my rights, and I'll talk to you as long as I know that it will count for something later."

Freemont just shook her head at his reversed understanding of the common phrase. Phelps answered.

"Dexter, we are not offering you anything on this case, you have to understand that. There will be no deals, and don't expect any prosecutor assigned to this case to roll over like the last one. No one on the organization's payroll is going to come to your aid, not a prosecutor, not a judge, no one. Do you understand that we are not offering you anything?"

"I understand that if I give you any information about anyone else, I'm as good as a dead man. But what the fuck, I was supposed to be dead anyway."

The two police officers sat down across from him. Freemont continued.

"What do you mean you were a dead man?"

"The Bartrams are crazy. I knew as soon as I saw Vivian walking up with one of Frank's wetback idiots that she was probably there to kill me because of what happened out on the Interstate. That was my second fuckup, and you don't get three with these people. I was amazed when she took me to that house and screwed my brains out. There was this moment the next morning when she threatened to blow my dick through my asshole that I was sure I was a goner. That is when I realized that she had no idea Frank had me transporting Jillian along with Beth and Tiffany. We had ourselves a lovely time that night in Greenville then as soon as we got to that house on the hillside, I knew I was done. Shit, she kicked me in the balls so hard that the cops that arrested me had to actually carry me to their cruiser. I still ache from that. I knew I was never leaving that property alive. I'm probably not the first one that would be buried out there."

Phelps thought for a second. "Why do you think Frank had Jillian moved like that?"

Holder answered immediately. "Frank most likely had her on display to potential buyers, you know give them a glimpse then get them bidding."

Freemont looked disgusted but continued. "Dexter, I'm here for the murder charge. Tell me about Lucy and Crystal."

"Frank was fed up with them always hauling ass then coming back three weeks later. They were really good at taking advantage of Frank's security guards. Shit, every time they got away, he'd kill the stupid bastard that was supposed to be watching them. That's why Stokes and I were so careful in transporting them. I thought when Frank told me to bring them to the Charleston house from the place in Atlanta, that he was having another party. But it was set up in the basement to make a movie. He made Crystal handcuff Lucy to the bed and go down on her. Before I knew what was going on, Frank stepped into the frame from behind with a mask on and garrotes Crystal with a piano wire. He tightened it so hard he almost cut her head off. Blood is going everywhere and Lucy starts going crazy. Frank started carving her up like a roast chicken. He actually tried to cut her arm off. He got so amused, or pissed, Or whatever, at the racket she was making that he finally just choked her then stabbed her a couple of times, probably just for the camera. Then he cut her throat, too."

Freemont shook her head. "And you stood there filming all of this. Shit, Dexter."

"Hey, Frank is crazy. That wasn't the first time he'd done something like that. There were others. That was just the first one I was involved with. The others were mostly foreign girls with no one to come looking for them. God knows where they were disposed of."

"Who did the disposing?"

"That fucking cleaning crew of his. By the way, the two that dropped Lucy and Crystal in the creek that leads to the river, came back to that fleabag motel boasting about how they had done it and Frank had them killed. By the time he sent some people up to try to fix that cockup, you guys had found them."

Phelps had been listening to this. "Why do you think Jillian was with you that last trip?"

Holder just shook his head. "I have no idea but Vivian was convinced had found a buyer and was going to sell her to someone."

Freemont stood up. "Jesus Christ, Holder, we are talking about human beings and this one in particular is his daughter."

Holder pulled back. "Freemont, take it easy. Jillian was his adopted daughter along with that brother of hers. It's not like they weren't part of the business. There are films all over the dark web with them doing all sorts of shit to each other as kids. He didn't give a shit about either one of them. It was Vivian that actually protected them and cared for them. I think she really loved them like they were her own."

Phelps took a leap. "Do you know where the twins came from?"

Dexter blinked. "Kentucky. They were adopted."

Phelps stood up. "How did they come to be adopted?"

Holder nodded. "There was a girl named Anna Syms that was one of our early earners. She was a straight up whore, hooked on crystal meth, that Frank kept in a house up the side of a mountain in eastern Kentucky. She was one of three that worked that property. Lucy was another one. Frank and his partner back then had several trailers and mountain houses that serviced miners and farmers. Anna got pregnant and Frank got the bright idea to start growing his own stable of hookers, you know, like race horses. He took real good care of her. He got Vivian involved and she visited Anna on a regular basis. That's when Vivian and I started our sex thing was on one of those trips. I was young and stupid, but it didn't seem like Frank gave a shit that I was balling his old lady. Anyway, Anna up and dies in childbirth. The babies were fine and Vivian took them that night. After that it was just a matter of Stella St. John working her legal mumbo jumbo to make it all look legit."

Phelps and Freemont just sat there looking at him. Then Freemont continued.

"All this time you were working for the Charleston Police Department, weren't you?"

Holder got defensive. "Don't sound so self-righteous. You know how little we made. With the Bartrams there was big money, and I mean big money. All I had to do was just not work so hard on some cases. You need to go talk to good old Lieutenant Mills if you want to see a real dirty cop. He's the one that finally fixed the mess with Crystal and Lucy. He stopped you cold in your tracks, didn't he?"

Freemont started to stand up but Phelps put his hand on her arm as he spoke.

"You mention Terry Mills. What do you know about his involvement?"

"He was Vivian's brother, not as smart, but placed right. He made cases go away. He was in vice before he got a sweet deal into major crimes. Get it? Vice wasn't considered a major crime." He looked at Freemont. "You knew what a shitty cop he was. I was crap, and even I closed my cases."

Freemont stared at him. "Well, I guess it won't surprise you to know that Mills is dead. We're fairly sure Frank killed him at his beach house, along with Stokes."

For once, Holder summoned up some gumption. Maybe it was being locked up where he could sleep through the night. Maybe he had reached the saturation point of worrying when he was going to be murdered. Maybe it was hearing about Stokes. Whatever it was, Holder reached down deep into what was left of him as a man. He looked up at both of them.

"I hated watching those girls die. I hated rewatching it every time Frank felt it needed to be edited. I hated it when that Helena woman said she had a market for that type of film."

Freemont leaned in. "You played it to keep Beth and Tiffany in line. You made them listen to their two friends being tortured and murdered."

Holder shook his head back and forth. "If I didn't do it, the security people would. I thought hearing it would make them afraid to run. Frank was at that point with them. I know I slapped Tiffany around a bit, but it was no more than she was sometimes required to do with a customer. I had to make them fear me. You see what happened when I fucked up and let them leave the note? Vivian was sent to kill me. She was just playing with me until Frank arrived to finish me off. I would have never left that house alive. Frank would have killed me there just to make another snuff flick to scare the staff. I can't believe they haven't killed me in here. I don't think Vivian is a killer, but Frank would do anything she told him to. Don't be deceived by Vivian's charm. She is as deadly as Frank just in a different way. He's a psychopath but she, is something else entirely. No one wanted to get on the wrong side of her."

Freemont turned to Phelps. "I'm tired of listening to this man. I have enough to charge him with conspiracy to murder. You have enough to get a conviction on interstate trafficking. Can we please just lock him up until his hearing date?"

Phelps looked at Holder. "You mentioned that Helena suggested the snuff film. Did she make a lot of suggestions like that?"

"If there is a deadlier bitch on the planet than Vivian, it's Helena. She was becoming more active in decisions even above Frank and Vivian. She was the one that brought an endless number of foreigners in to work at whatever they told them to."

Phelps was ready. "Dexter, who is the person they were taking orders from?"

Holder smiled. "Like I said, I'm surprised they haven't had me killed in here already."

Phelps and Liz Freemont stepped out into the hall. He looked at the papers in his hand as Liz spoke.

"How did the system not alert your investigators that he was an ex-cop?"

Phelps just shook his head.

"Yesterday Ludlow arrested several people that had been paid to alter his record. We also found they had begun the same process on Terry Mills. It appeared that Stella St. John had used video provided from a party that showed the former employees of the Justice Department participating. There was also cash exchanged. It seems to be the pattern they used to build a whole network of people within the government at the federal, state, and local level to support their activities. Ludlow made enough arrests to shut that part of the operation down at least at the federal level."

Liz shook her head.

"So to discover he was a former cop, you would have had to find and ask the agency that had fired him. What a cluster. Without notation in the national system, Holder could have gotten another cop job."

Phelps shook his head. "It wouldn't have paid nearly what he was making with Nightshade."

Down the hall from Holder, Vivian Bartram was housed in a cell in the middle of a room, with a bed, a table, a toilet, a sink and a shower. She was under 24-hour direct surveillance. The lights were dimmed at night and she was given a sleep mask, but the lights were never completely off. She wore scrubs with snaps and was guarded by a team of close custody female Marshals. There were always two on duty. Her conversation with the Attorney General had been brief and to the point. All Vivian was offered was the ability to visit with her children if she cooperated. For the immediate future, she would not be housed with any other prisoners. The Attorney General's first priority was to get Vivian treated for her addiction. Strangely enough, her blood and toxic substance screens indicated she had nothing in her system.

Mary Close had been assigned to do Vivian's debriefing via tele-interviews from the compound in Tennessee. They started once it became apparent that Vivian wasn't under the influence of any drugs. Vivian sat in a chair at the table with a two-way tele-conference system opposite her on the far side of the bars. Mary sat in Dr. Morozov's command center. Mary would begin each conversation with a status report and the same question.

"Vivian, I'm happy to report that Jillian is doing really well in a secure location. Can you please help us find Jessie?"

Vivian would smile and provide the same answer. "Thank you. I appreciate you keeping me updated on Jillian. Jessie is safe, and you will be the first to know when he is ready to talk with you people."

Mary looked at her notes.

"Vivian, I'm curious. All of the information we have about you indicates that you have some sort of a drug addiction. We didn't find any illegal substances in your system. How long have you been clean?"

Vivian laughed. "Agent Close, I learned from my mother, a long time ago, that it is useful to appear to be something other than what you are. The company was always ready to supply me with any substance I wanted. You would be surprised at what people will say once they think you're wasted and unresponsive. It was really a matter of learning how to remain still and appear sleeping, which is really breath control. I do, however, have an addiction. I'm sure you will understand given what you have learned about me. I am addicted to sex. I can supply you with a whole list of therapists that have all come to the same conclusion."

Mary didn't flinch. "How long have you known there was something wrong there?"

"I think my first diagnosis was when I was 17 shortly after Frank came to live with us. My mother married his daddy and we got Frank in the deal, and what a deal it was."

"What happened to your real father, John Millner?

"That is quite simple. He got tired of my mother fucking everything, male or female, that she came in contact with. You don't suppose this sex addiction thing is hereditary, do you?"

Mary shook her head. "I honestly don't know. Was your mother always that way?"

Vivian thought for a moment. "The only thing that slowed my mother down in the sex department was aging, and I'm not sure that did. I was just glad not to have to witness it any longer. Our real father gave my brother Terry and me the house in Beaufort outright as long as my mother never set foot in it. We kept our end of the deal. When I would go on my little 'vacations' from Frank and the business, that is one of the places I would go. I think the first time he was ever anywhere near that house was when he killed Terry and poor Mr. Stokes. I do hope you find him soon. He has anger issues."

"Your charade about drug use just about got you killed. He injected you with Ketamine."

Vivian sighed heavily. "In my little fantasy world, I sometimes misjudge risks and I would have never have thought he would look for me there. I believe that someone had to tell him I might be there. Holder didn't know about that place, and I'm sure you have him somewhere or he is dead. Stokes only knew recently when I enlisted him to keep the twins safe. He wouldn't have said a word to Frank anyway, and Terry was always too afraid of Frank to divulge that house. He was always worried that Frank would kill him. His fear of Frank and the bosses is why he quit law enforcement, not that he was any good at it. As you well know, you do need a good bit of moral fiber to be a cop, but then, if it wasn't for some people in the justice system, having no morals whatsoever, the Nightshade Group never would have made a dime."

Mary nodded. "I would like to talk more about who those people are."

Vivian chuckled. "I'm sure you would, but as I said to the Attorney General, as soon as I am made aware Frank has been dealt with, and that my son is safe, you will know all I know. Believe me, it is more than enough to bring the entire Nightshade organization down."

Mary decided to try one more area of inquiry for this session.

"Vivian, tell me about Charles Tobin's involvement."

"Charles is a pimp, plain and simple. He has always been a pimp and a voyeur. I don't think he has ever made love to anything but his hand in his entire life, and even that is too freaky to think about even for me. He is not a killer or a kidnapper. He dealt with the customer supply side."

"Charles says he is your step-brother, that Celeste Foster is your mother and that Hollins Foster, her current husband, is the head person he took orders from."

Vivian thought for a moment. "So, you have Charles in custody, as well. Let me guess, you found him at one of the houses owned by the company. We share no blood at all. His poor daddy lasted just long enough for Celeste to get Charles as a new plaything out of the relationship, and then he was gone. Three months after Ronald Dupont died in an automobile accident, she became Celeste Foster although I think old Hollins had been in the picture for awhile. Charles sometimes uses his real name, Ronald Dupont Jr."

Mary decided to take a chance.

"Vivian, we have your mother here, as well. We took her into protective custody when we arrested Charles. She is being seen to by our psychiatric staff. She seems very disoriented."

Vivian seemed startled, but regained her composure. "Well, you almost have the entire family. Was she at least wearing her fur when you arrested her?"

"She was. Not much else, but she was wearing her fur."

"And you say she is being seen by your psychiatric staff. That is very interesting."

Mary was caught short. "Why is that interesting?"

"Agent Close, my mother may be many things, but 'disoriented' has never been one of them. Be careful there. Remember who taught me to appear as if I were something else. I need a bit of time to think this through. Once you find Frank, I will be more than happy to cooperate more fully.

Whatever you decide, I would suggest you be very careful around Celeste Master."

# CHAPTER 33

After her conversation with Vivian, Mary Close conferred with Jeanine Morozov. They added that information into the summary then contacted the Attorney General via secure tele-video. The AG listened to them then spoke; " I concur with all your conclusions, but I'm not going to execute all of the prepared arrest warrants until we have the last people at the top. I don't want to tip our hand and have them run. Any ideas?"

Jeanine leaned forward.

"There is no question that almost all the properties that we identified earlier have been used to launder money. Mary has all the details to document the different schemes that were used, Mid-Atlantic Kidder and the five non-real estate businesses that we have clearly identified relied on trafficked staffing. As far as the sex trafficking, Frank Bartram, Helena Reagan aka Svetlana Czerny, and Charles Tobin are the most frequently associated. Solomon Security is totally Frank's domain. Czerny ran Helping Hand Labor, Kidder Properties and with Frank's help, Palms Transportation. It was used to provide the vehicles to move everyone around. Stokes and Holder were on their payroll along with other drivers."

The Attorney General interrupted. "Someone has to be running all of this."

Morozov continued; "Tobin says it is a man called Hollins Foster who is most certainly involved at a higher level than Frank. But I wouldn't rule out Czerny. The data suggests that she may be equal to Foster."

Mary leaned in.

"I think I may have an idea of who is at the top of this organization, but I don't want to confuse our strategy until I have more information. I'm not convinced that Hollins Foster and Svetlana Czerny call all the shots. The good news is we have finished the list of suspected government and justice officials involved. We can prove either altered case records, disclosed investigative information, dismissed cases on shaky grounds, or outright stopped investigations. Ludlow has made preliminary arrests of the most involved."

The Attorney General listened then asked the question.

"Is Vivian willing to give us the information we need on these elusive ones we don't even know about?"

Mary thought. "I need to sit with her face-to-face and get Lily, and possibly Jillian, in the room to confirm. I think she, in the strange combination with Tobin, may have already led us in the right direction. I need your approval to travel to Atlanta where they are being held. I think we are close to having Vivian get Jessie to come in. Once that is done, she is key to getting Frank."

Gwen Vespers didn't mince words. "You go where you need to go and do what you need to do. We need to wrap this up. We are straining the limits of our ability to keep this a secret and we need to get Jessie to safety regardless. Now that Jillian is safe, he is my primary safety concern."

Mary called Phelps to arrange for Lily and Jillian to attend her next live interview with Vivian. She agreed with the Attorney General. It was hard to think about anyone other than Jessie with Frank loose. She hoped Vivian hadn't kept Jessie in the field to keep the pressure on to capture Frank.

Jessie had slept all night for the first time in a long time. He needed one more good nights sleep. He felt safe here, but he had learned that staying in one place was not a good idea with Frank looking for them and their mother. He believed Frank was unaware that Vivian had turned herself in or that Jillian had been rescued for real. That was the one advantage he had. Vivian had given him her phone for safe keeping. She said that it would be necessary later to deal with Frank if he didn't get arrested. He had a new burner. He decided to call Jillian on the phone Lily had given her.

He poured a bowl of a cereal he had never been allowed to have. Vivian had been very strict about what they ate. If it hadn't been for Stella, he wouldn't even know that these puffy things existed. After three bites he decided they didn't taste like anything but sugar and he made himself another box of mac and cheese. That tasted like something to him.

He took the small automatic pistol, set the alarm, and drove to the convenience store and bought a fishing kit. He knew it wasn't high quality but he was just getting started. He drove to the spot where he had fished with the man the day before. No one was there so he put the lure on that came with his fishing kit, attached a bobber, and threw the line as best he could out in to the flow. It was peaceful. He propped his rod up in a bush the way he had seen the man do it the day before and sat down on the ground. He pulled out his phone and called Jillian. He let it ring three times and hung up, which was the signal that he and Jillian had worked out. He set the phone down next to him and watched his bobber. He was startled by the familiar voice behind him.

"I see you went and bought yourself your own pole. Good for you. Had a bite yet?"

Jessie almost jumped out of his skin. The thought raced through his mind that seeking peace came with a risk. He forced a smile.

"Not yet. I just threw it out there."

"What are you fishing for?"

"That thing you caught yesterday. I fried it up like you said and liked it. I had it with macaroni and cheese for dinner last night."

The man smiled. "You know how to make good macaroni and cheese, do you?"

Jessie smiled "Well it was from a box. I'd never had it before so it probably wasn't the best."

The man smiled. "Boxed mac and cheese will do in a pinch but I'll give you my wife's recipe. It's a bit more work, but there is no orange powder involved. What you using for bait on that line?"

Jessie looked out where the bobber floated. "It's just the thing that came in the kit."

The man smiled and held up a small plastic tub. "I've got some worms in here that have been crawling around in corn dough. Let's get your hook baited with the right thing for you to catch your first catfish."

Jessie pulled the line in and handed the rig to the man. "My name is Jessie". He held out his hand to shake.

"My name is Ezra Miller, Jessie. I'm pleased to meet you. Are you new around here?"

Jessie didn't like questions but he figured this was what small talk was. "Yeah, my mom owns a house nearby. We're just here for a few days."

The man nodded. "Well let's get you set up with the proper bait and see what you pull in with that convenience store rig you bought."

Jessie's phone ringing broke the line of conversation. Ezra moved away and pulled the line in to give Jessie some privacy.

Jillian spoke first. "Hey are you OK?"

"I'm good for right now. How are you doing?" As Jillian began to speak, Jessie moved farther away from Ezra for privacy.

"You won't believe it. I can't tell you where I'm staying but I actually slept through the night last night. Lily's mom is staying with me and Lily. A friend of hers from when she was a girl is here too and of course lots of Marshals. They have been so amazing to me. Lily says I'm going to talk to Mom later today. Please tell me you're safe. I want you to come here and stop trying to fix things yourself."

Jessie thought for a moment. "Talk with Mom and Lily. I want to come in. I thought I could handle this, but I'm no match for Frank. I slept well last night too but I know I can't stay here much longer. I don't want to stay on the phone too long. Is Lily there?"

"She's standing nearby. She wanted to give me privacy to talk with you."

Jessie looked over at Ezra who had done the same. "Can you put her on then I'm going to have to hang up. I'm in the middle of something here."

Lily came on the line. "Good morning, Jessie. How can I help?"

"What?"

"How can I help? You wanted to talk to me."

Jessie almost broke out in tears and if Ezra hadn't been standing any closer he would have. He was sure Ezra couldn't hear what he was about to say.

"Lily, no one but you ever asked me that. I'm tired and have decided I can't stay away from Frank forever. I need you to help me figure out how to get to you safely. I'm certain my mom will help. I'm OK for now but can you talk to Vivian and see what she suggests. I want to help deliver him to you but I can't figure out how."

"This number looks like a new phone. Good idea, keep it with you. We will call you between two and three this afternoon. Find a place where you're sure Frank can't track you and don't turn on that phone Vivian gave you. We will be in touch."

Jessie hung up, turned, and saw that Ezra patiently waiting for him. "I'm sorry. I needed to talk to my sister."

Ezra smiled. "No problem at all. I wanted to wait until I had your attention to show you how to wrap this worm and dough ball on the hook.

You ready?"

Jessie nodded and 10 minutes later after Ezra insisted, he did it himself correctly. He cast his line into the water. Ezra rigged his own line for small mouth bass and cast it up near the reeds and an overhanging log. Then slowly pulled his bait back in using short tugs.

"I'm twitching that lure a bit to make enough noise and action to make a small mouth bass mad enough to come grab it. You don't have to do that. Catfish just need bait. They are very unemotional fish, but bass, they get pissed easily and they are not too smart about biting at whatever has made them mad. Let's see how we do. Take my pole, too. I'll get us some chairs."

As soon as Jessie had hung up, Alex, Tim Collins, five other Marshals from a rapid response SWAT team and Birdman were in a helicopter headed toward Greenwood. The new phone had pinged two towers. They would be in the vicinity in less than an hour. Jessie had said the magic words that he wanted to come in. They had figured out where he might be from a second questioning of Dexter Holder. Frank may never have been to the house in Greenwood but Dexter had spent several pleasant hours there.

Mary Close, Lily, and Jillian walked down the long hall toward the cell where Vivian was being kept. Her guards had allowed Vivian to get cleaned up and brought her fresh scrubs. She seemed almost elated, and even invited them to join her in the shower. She may have been in custody but she was still Vivian.

The trio walked into her area right on time. There were three chairs at the table across from the cell. Jillian and Vivian had already been told that there would be no physical contact of any kind. Vivian was her mother, but she was still Vivian, and Jillian agreed. Vivian had been warned that any difficulties she might present would be handled by no further visits and the loss of any potential to bargain for future visits.

They all sat down and for three minutes just looked at each other. Vivian spoke first.

"You know, sweetheart, I've never really just sat and looked at you. You are beautiful."

Jillian looked at Mary for approval to speak. Mary nodded.

" I see they have thought carefully about how to keep you safe, even from yourself."

Vivian laughed. "Sweet girl. I value myself too much to do myself any harm. Besides, I have an agreement with the Attorney General that I will be especially careful until she gets what she wants from me. Have they told you yet that I'm not really a drug user?"

Jillian didn't skip a beat. "I guess you just did that for our sake, right? It was important to burden your children with the concept that their mother was a raging alcoholic and drug user in addition to all the sex stuff."

Vivian smiled. "I hope someday we will be in a place that I can explain that to you and Jessie. You look well. Someone must be taking good care of you."

Lily spoke. "She is being looked after but to be honest, Mrs. Bartram, she is pretty good at taking care of herself. We are here about something more important than the games you like to engage in. Jessie needs your help."

Vivian stared at Lily. She didn't like it when another woman talked like she was the caregiver.

"As long as Jessie keeps his wits about him, he will be fine."

Jillian broke in. "He's not fine. I spoke to him this morning. He's scared and he wants to come in. You need to help us and them."

Vivian smirked. "My, my. How quickly the forces work to turn a daughter against her mother."

Mary spoke for the first time.

"Vivian, you don't want anything to happen to Jessie because you and Frank are playing games with each other. Right now, you are in a good bargaining position. Jessie ends up dead, it will be capital murder for you and no deal whatsoever. Do we understand each other?"

Vivian smiled. "Agent Close. You are much more exciting in person. I, too, want my son to be safe from Frank. I will be happy to help. I can't be the only one you have locked up. Who else is in custody? Don't lie to me. It is important that I be able to know who is still out there and who is not."

Mary thought for a moment then decided to risk it.

"We have Holder, Helena Reagan, Charles Tobin, and Celeste Foster in custody."

Vivian raised an eyebrow. "Does anyone outside of the people here know they are in custody, and have you begun arresting other people?"

Mary shook her head. "This whole investigation including this location has been guarded carefully. No one knows you are here and we are waiting to arrest anyone else until Jessie is safe."

"What about that little slut of a federal prosecutor, Stammers, that was handling Frank's case?"

Mary smiled. "She is not in a position to relay any details to Nightshade."

Vivian looked at Mary hard. "The kids said they had given you a file. Have you been able to look at that yet?"

Mary nodded her head. "We have not acted on any of the information. Jessie's safety and Frank's apprehension are our most important objectives. That is why we need your help. Frank is the only one with an arrest warrant for Stella's murder."

"What about the murder of my brother and Stokes? Has anyone in Beaufort charged Frank with that?"

"He hasn't been charged with that yet? The investigation is on-going."

Vivian sat back and thought. You could tell she was weighing everything and working toward a plan. Mary interrupted her. "If it helps you to decide, Vivian, we have a general idea of where Jessie is. We can get him to safety. We can then concentrate on Frank."

Vivian looked up. "What about the people you are so concerned about above Frank? I would think you would want to get them, as well."

Lily had been sitting quietly. She looked at Mary, and Mary nodded.

"Vivian. Please help us get Jessie safe then help us get Frank in custody. With your help we can find the others, but Jessie is out there now. We can't guarantee Frank doesn't already know where he is. Help us, please."

Vivian smiled. "Lily, someone raised you well." She looked over at Mary. "See all she had to do was ask nicely and say please. No profanity. No threats, just a nice ask. I left my phone with Jessie with instructions not to turn it on. If a call comes from that phone, Frank won't be able to resist. Once you have Jessie safe, and Frank either in custody or dead, I would prefer the latter, then I will sit down with you for as long as it takes for you to get the last one out there that is Nightshade."

Mary looked at her. "The last one? That makes me feel like we already have some of the leaders."

Vivian smiled at her. "You are a very intelligent woman for a cop. You have two of the three right here locked up already. If you can tell me who the first one is, I will give you the second. Please humor me. I need a little give-and-take to keep it interesting."

Jillian lost it. "What the hell is wrong with you? We need to get Jessie safe and you're sitting here trying to amuse yourself. What if she gets it wrong? What then, do you just not tell them?"

Mary interrupted. "We have Helena Reagan. Her real name is Svetlana Czerny and she has no hope of being deported anywhere. She is being held under the Patriot Act provision for supplying arms and opportunity to known terrorists. Even I don't know where she is being held. And we know about the insiders at Homeland Security."

Vivian looked shocked. "My, you do know how to play poker, don't you. That is correct. Things changed when she arrived on the scene. Frank didn't give orders to her as much as he received orders from her through someone else. He never caught on to that. Too big of an ego. Watch her closely. She will kill herself before she betrays others. She is a savage just like Frank. I will give you more after my son is safe."

Mary looked at her. "I guessed right. Who is the other one?"

Vivian smiled. "My mother, Celeste Foster. You were lucky. She rarely leaves her apartment. My guess is you swept her up when you got Charlie Tobin, wherever the little shit was stupid enough to get himself arrested. The one that is still out there is my latest step father Hollins Foster. You won't find him anywhere close to the operation. I would be willing to bet he won't even be in the country once he hears Frank has been arrested. But make no mistake, with Celeste locked up here, he will be long gone right after he discovers he can't reach her. Now, go get my son. I will give you the address."

She turned to Lily. "Get him safe, bring me my phone and within hours, Frank and what is left of his little army of aliens, will walk right into your custody."

Mary looked at her notes then looked at Vivian. "Are you telling me that Hollins Foster is the key person in the Nightshade Group?"

Vivian laughed. "No, Agent, he has always taken orders from Celeste. She is not what she appears to be. You said she was wearing hardly anything when you arrested her. Normally she prefers expensive pajamas, or nothing but a bra and panties under either her silk kimono or her fur coat. She is much younger than you would think. She just knows how to look and act old. My grandmother, Clarice, suffered from frontal lobe disorder and was paranoid and always taking her clothes off. Celeste learned how to appear crazy from her. Celeste is the one you've been looking for all along. She was just very good at making anyone who got close think she was a crazy, little old lady. Can I hug my daughter?"

Mary shook her head. "Maybe next time. We need to get Jessie."

They met Phelps in the hallway as Lily, Jillian, and Marshal Story left to get back to South Carolina. Phelps just shook his head at Mary.

"Do you believe her? We were about to transfer Celeste to a more appropriate facility."

Mary nodded. "If what Vivian has just told us is true, that would have been the same thing as releasing her."

"It still may be a problem. We need to factor this new information in and keep her under 24-hour close custody. Being able to spot a malingerer is one of the toughest jobs that forensic psychiatrists have. I would hate to think that the head of one of the worst criminal enterprises in history would be kept in less than maximum security. Could she really be that good at acting crazy?"

Mary shrugged. "Let's do a full background knowing what we know now. I can handle that. Are you going to be staging with Ludlow or are you going to South Carolina?"

Phelps thought. "I think I am going to stay right here and be ready with one of our teams. If what Vivian says is true, Hollins Foster may already be out of the country. But on the off chance that he won't leave unless he knows where Celeste is, I'm going to put out a BOLO for him at the airports and border and be ready to respond. I'll brief the AG.

# CHAPTER 34

Alex and the team approached the house in Greenwood from all sides at 25-yard intervals. Collins had taken the lead from the road and Alex was to post with Marshal Story from the rear of the house. Birdman had launched a larger drone above the site from a mile away at an abandoned car lot. The minute he looked at the monitor he pushed the feed to the team members and spoke into his microphone.

"I have two vehicles parked a half mile north of the house at a roadside park. I think one of them is Jessie's Bronco. Stand by until I get a better look."

On the ground, Jessie had just caught his second catfish. Ezra had helped him get the fish off the hook. Jessie sat down in one of Ezra's chairs and looked at his watch. Ezra saw him.

"If you got some place to be, I can help you filet these up and you can get going. You should eat them or freeze them. You shouldn't catch them and not eat them. Some people just throw them up on the bank to die. They think they are a trash fish. I hate to think they died just to rot or feed a fox or a neighborhood cat."

Jessie smiled. "Thanks. I'd love to stay and fish longer but I'm expecting a call in about fifteen minutes."

Ezra showed him how with the first fish, and Jessie picked it right up and did the second one. He had forgotten to bring anything to carry his catch home in, so Ezra gave him an extra bucket he had in his truck. He spoke as he put some ice from his cooler in on top of the fish.

"Will I see you out here tomorrow? The weather should hold."

Jessie smiled, "I don't know. I think my mom and I have plans. Thanks for teaching me how to fish. I really appreciate it."

Ezra smiled. "Everyone should know how to fish, Jessie. Remember it's not the catching that's important. It's the time spent doing that counts. You be well, and take care of yourself. You seem like a nice young man. You remind me of my grandson."

Jessie nodded and thanked him again. He turned and walked back to his Bronco and put his gear away and the bucket in the front seat. He decided to go up to the convenience store to buy his own bucket and ice and return Ezra's bucket to him.

Birdman via the drone saw the Bronco pull out and turn back in the direction of the driveway to the house. "Standby. Subject is mobile and headed towards the house." Ten seconds later, he came back on the air. "Subject is headed past the house towards my location. Repeat, subject is headed farther south."

Collins took a Marshal and headed back to follow Jessie. The remainder of the team stayed in place watching the house. Birdman came on the air again.

"Subject has just parked across the street from my location and is going inside a convenience store. It is definitely Jessie Syms. I'm launching Kestrel. I have an idea. Do I have backup headed this way?"

Collins responded. "Affirmative, we are there in three minutes."

"Tim, why don't you join me here alone? I think I can get Jessie to cross the street to check out the drone."

Collins responded. "I will meet you there."

Birdman added. "Don't look so scary when you walk up." Alex was mobile in 30 seconds headed toward them.

Jessie came out of the store and Birdman made sure that he flew the small drone, right past Jessie. It was like a magnet to a 15-year-old boy After checking traffic Jessie followed the drone and crossed the street. He was smiling from ear to ear and spoke as he walked up.

"Man, that is so cool. Can I see it?"

Birdman smiled. "Sure, I'm going to land it on the hood of my truck." Birdman carried the controller over as Collins walked with him. Collins was wearing his tactical pants but was down to his T-Shirt.

Birdman was filming the whole thing and transmitting it from Kestrel. Phelps and Mary were watching from Atlanta. Ludlow was watching from Washington D.C. Alex was watching as she was being driven to the parking lot, and most of all, Lily and Jillian were watching as they flew in the Smithson jet back to Beaufort. Lily asked the pilot to divert.

Jessie was completely absorbed with the small drone sitting on Birdman's truck. Given all he had seen, and all he had been through, he was still, underneath all the bravado, a 15-year-old kid. Jessie's phone rang. He looked up and smiled. "Sorry I've got to take this."

He walked 10 feet away and heard Jillian's voice.

"It's over, Jessie. You are safe. Do you have Mom's phone?"

"What? Yeah, it's in my truck."

"Jessie. I'm looking at you as I'm talking to you."

It was then that it dawned on Jessie. He turned back toward the people standing and realized that the drone was hovering just above him silently. He just stood there for a moment.

Alex walked over to him and stuck out her hand. "You must be Jessie. I'm Alex. Would you like me to take you to your sister now?"

Jessie crumpled into a heap right there on the pavement as Alex caught him. He was just sobbing. Alex spoke in a soft voice. "It's OK, Jessie but we have to get out of this lot. You ride with me. My friend Tim will drive your car and we will take care of it and bring it to you where your sister is safe. Jillian will tell you. Ask her."

Jessie gathered his wits and spoke into the phone. "Is it really over,

Jill?"

The Smithson jet landed 10 minutes after Jessie and his escorts arrived at the Greenwood Airport. As Jessie was getting out of the car he gave Collins his phone, pointed out Vivian's phone in the glovebox, gave them the door code, and told Collins about his guns and computers. Collins promised him he would take care of all of it. Them Tim spoke.

"Don't worry. I've got this for you. Have you ever ridden in a jet before?"

Jessie shook his head.

"It's a blast. Remember, Frank is our problem now. You go be with your sister and be safe. You're going to like where you're headed."

"Mister?"

Tim interrupted him. "It's Tim. My name is Tim Collins. I'm a U.S. Marshal."

Jessie smiled. "Tim, there is a nice older man named Ezra up the road. He helped me catch and clean the catfish in the bucket. Would you freeze the fish and return his bucket to him?"

Tim nodded. "I'll make sure he gets the bucket, and I promise that you'll see these fillets again."

Jessie turned and boarded the plane and fell into his sister's arms. It would not be a long ride to where they would be staying, but it would be one that both twins remembered for the rest of their lives. For the first time, they were flying toward freedom.

The jet landed at Beaufort Airport. They were transferred to Billy Ward's house. Aunt Lydia was waiting on the front porch. Billy met them at the car, hugged Jillian and shook Jessie's hand. As they walked toward the house Jessie noticed that everywhere he looked there seemed to be armed people hunkered down protecting them. He looked out beyond the house to the bayou beyond Billy's house and there were at least three boats keeping watch from the water side. He turned to Jillian.

"This doesn't seem too different from how we used to live. These guys look more professional, but we're still under guard."

Jillian looked at him. "There are two big differences. The first is all those people out there are not here to keep us in, but to keep Dad and his people out. Trust me, this feels way better."

Jessie looked like he didn't buy that explanation right off the bat. "And, what is the second difference?"

"You're about to meet her." She looked up at the dignified black woman standing on the porch waiting for them. "Aunt Lydia, this is my brother, Jessie. Jessie, this is Lily's mother. She insists on being called Aunt Lydia."

Jessie walked up on the porch and held out his hand. That lasted about two seconds before Lydia gathered him in her arms just as she had Jillian and hugged him. She whispered in his ear. "Welcome, Jessie. You are safe here." She held on to him until he stopped shaking and sobbing. "You must be hungry. Boys your age are always hungry. What's your favorite food?"

Jessie gathered himself together. "I am a bit hungry. I've become fond of catfish and the boxed mac and cheese stuff."

Lydia laughed. "Well, if you like catfish you've come to the right house for sure. I'll even get you started on some new things like shrimp, and crab fritters, and fried flounder. But you won't find any of that boxed mac and cheese here. I make the real thing. You go on inside. I'm sure these people will be bringing you your things as soon as they can. There are some things in your room for you to wear until then. You go get washed up and changed and I'll fix you a snack until dinner." She turned her attention to Alex. "Alex get your skinny little body up here and hug me. You look like you could do with some fattening up yourself." Alex stepped up on the porch and got her normal long prayerful hug from Lydia.

Lily walked up on the steps arm in arm with Billy who spoke first.

"You're welcome at my place as long as you like. I have to go back to work tomorrow so I can turn in my retirement papers. I have enough vacation that I can use until I get to that date. I've already talked to the Sheriff and he's good with the decision."

Lily looked at him tenderly. "So, you're really going to do it?"

"Oh yes. If I wasn't sure before, that scene up the road in that house where that Frank fella killed those two men was enough to convince me that I've seen all I need to. I hate it that those two kids in there had to watch that."

Lily half hugged him. "I'm just happy you're coming out of this intact. I'm looking forward to fishing with you and those two."

Lily leaned her head on Billy's shoulder as she looked at Lydia putting plates out for the twins.

"Phelps is getting ready to talk to Vivian Bartram tomorrow morning. He has already told her we have Jessie. They will work out a plan that will bring Frank in. Until then, I think this is about the best place these two could be. If this deal has taught us anything, it is the need for something designed for kids to make them feel safe."

In Atlanta, Vivian had just finished dinner in her cell when Mary Close and Phelps Wheeler came in and played the video of the twins acknowledging they were together and in safe hands. She sighed and turned away from them and gathered herself after a couple of heavy breaths that Mary took to be sobs. She gave her some time to collect herself. She wiped her eyes on her sleeve.

"What now? How do we work together to get Frank behind bars or dead."

Phelps quietly winced at the last reference. "We would prefer to have him in custody and have him cooperate with us."

Vivian laughed. "Frank isn't smart enough to see the benefit of that, and even if he was, he has little he could add that I can't provide you. He doesn't want the file, Foster does. Frank's usefulness to the bosses was intimidating people and hurting them both physically and emotionally. You can't run a human trafficking ring without those two elements. As you have most likely figured out, Helena is the foreign connection. She met Celeste and Hollins Foster several years ago. She was supplying girls from the Balkan states to several prostitution rings on the east coast. With her contacts, and the Foster family's access to influence and money, it was a match made for trafficking humans, drugs, rare animals, you name it. The business expanded rapidly beyond belief. If Hollins finds out you have Celeste, he will run but not before he takes care of Frank."

Mary looked at her. "You think he will have Frank killed?"

Vivian looked down at her hands as she sat down at her table.

"I think you will be very lucky if Frank isn't already dead. If you want him alive you better hurry." Phelps continued.

"What do you suggest we do?"

Vivian chuckled. "My preference would be wait until someone finds his body but if I know Hollings Foster, you won't. That would be a very uncomfortable lack of closure for me, and more importantly the safety of my children. I think if we can lure Frank into thinking he can have the file, he will think he can barter with Foster and you might get both. But to do that, I will need to call him on the phone that I gave Jessie. If we can make him think that I'm still free and have the file, he won't be able to help himself."

"How and where would you do that?"

Vivian thought. "Frank is only comfortable in two places, the Atlanta house and the Charleston house. He will pick one of those and he will insist on picking. What has happened at those locations since he killed Stella?"

Mary answered. "We sealed both and have had them under passive surveillance. We got lucky. The Atlanta house is where we arrested Tobin and Celeste. Is she really your mother?"

"I know, with all the lies and misinformation, it's hard to determine what to believe but yes. She is really my mother. I haven't had any direct contact with her in years."

"Does Frank have contact with her?"

"Frank gets all his orders through Hollins I doubt he would suspect Celeste. That is why I think that if I call him and tell him I have the file and will meet him, he might have Hollins Foster with him."

Phelps shook his head. "That is too much of a risk for you."

Vivian smiled. "Agent Phelps, I'm touched that you care. You won't get Frank without risk."

Phelps shook his head again. "That would still mean you had to be there. I'm not sure there is anyone we have that could impersonate you to get Frank close enough. Vivian you are key to our case. I can't let anything happen to you. Being in the room with either of them is out of the question."

Vivian laughed out loud. "I have no fear of being there. I will give you enough before we do this to bring the organization down. This is all a long shot anyway. Frank may very well be dead already. All I will need is my phone. If he is alive, and I call, he will come because he will want one more crack at me. He won't want to do it from a distance. He will want to look at the file and me."

Phelps thought. "How about if we meet halfway. Do you really think you could you get him to show up with Foster?"

Vivian thought. "I can get Frank to do almost anything particularly if he still believes that the organization is intact. Remember, he thinks I am a worthless drug addict. That is how Stella and I were able to create the file you have in the first place. That file was supposed to be our insurance. It was an accident that they found out about it at all. I should have known one of us would pay the price. Stella died to give me and the twins enough head start to get away. We both underestimated the bosses."

He laid the phone on the table and let Vivian look at it. She smiled and spoke as she looked at it.

"You are a gutsy one, aren't you. What a rare quality."

"I haven't agreed to anything. I want to take a closer look at each location. That will take some time. How sure are you he will pick one of those two?"

"Frank is a creature of habit, but you will have to move quickly and get there before he or his crew show up. They will case the place totally."

Phelps nodded. "We better get started. I will need some time to get things moving. I won't risk your life and you are going to have to do this our way. How do you feel about sitting down with Mary tonight and providing information on the file. I will get busy putting the plan together for Frank's capture and be ready to make the call tomorrow. Seriously, Vivian. It has to be done safely."

"Why Agent Phelps, are you suggesting we pull an all-nighter?" Phelps nodded as he picked up her phone and put it back in his pocket.

Vivian stayed up most of the night with Mary and a stenographer. She identified seven documents within the file that were critical to the identification of key people who had helped them grow the business. She swore to affidavits on video and signed statements. At 06:00 am she pushed back from the table and told them she needed sleep. They had been at it over 18 hours straight. At 11:00 am she woke up and gave them two more hours of critical information, mostly about the Russian link through Czerny and the potential places Foster might go to hide. She then looked at Phelps.

"Time is running out for us to get Frank in, and I'm done talking until that part is over. Afterwards, we can continue. I want to see him either in cuffs or dead. It's time I make the call."

Phelps nodded and pushed the phone to her.

She confirmed that it was her phone, made sure the locator capability was turned off and made the call. Frank answered in three rings."

He snarled into the phone "I thought you turned yourself in? Where are you and where are the twins?"

"All in good time Frank. I have the file. If you want it come and meet me."

"Why should I believe you? I thought you were tired of running and wanted to go all Mommy to the brats."

"I do, but the twins won't be with me. They are somewhere safe. I want them to stay that way. You will have me and you will have the file and that is all you and Foster really want anyway, isn't it?"

Frank took his time answering. "I will check with him and see what he thinks."

"Oh Frank, for God's sake, grow a set of balls and make the decision. Aren't you man enough to get both me and the file and take us both to Foster? Think how much better that would be."

"Foster wants the twins."

"Ah, I see. Well, he's not going to get all he wants. You will have me, you will have the file, but the twins are not up for negotiation. Do you want to keep on doing business or do you want to continue to argue with me? I really don't give a fuck, Frank. Make a decision."

"I will call you right back. You had better not be fucking with me." He hung up.

Vivian looked up. "Well, it's a start anyway. Foster will agree to the plan. If he is in the country, you might even get both of them."

Phelps answered. "We will have the file so he can check it."

Vivian laughed out loud. "None of them have ever actually seen it. My guess is one of their "cleaning" staff spoke enough English to see a big file and wrote down the name. But you know more about what's in that file than they do."

Phelps looked shocked. "They are killing people over a rumor?"

"Stella changed the code to her office doors and the safe. I'm not sure how Jessie got it, but I can tell you that file hasn't been seen by anyone in tin control of the organization. Yes, they are killing over something they are not even sure exists. Please don't underestimate Frank or Foster, Agent Wheeler. I would really like to see my children even if it is with bars between us."

Two hours later, Vivian received a text. "Atlanta House tomorrow. 5:00 pm."

# CHAPTER 35

The following day, Mary and Phelps prepared Vivian for her role in the process. She was fitted with a new lightweight protective armor under her sweater. She understood that nothing could guarantee her safety. Frank had a penchant for shooting people in the head and he certainly wouldn't think twice about doing it to her. They agreed she would not be in the same room with whoever showed up.

Mary asked first. "I think our plan is well-suited for taking Frank into custody. As you say, he's predictable. If he shows up, does Foster have anything particularly against you.

Vivian laughed. "Hollins Foster considers me a drunk, a drug addict, and a slut. I worked hard on that image so he wouldn't fear me. If anything, he feels indifference but that doesn't mean he won't kill me. I know the plan."

Phelps reminded her. "I want them to get a glimpse of you. You are not to be in the same room with either one of them. They are to see you at a distance and hear your voice. That's it. Don't ad lib on this Vivian. I don't want you getting hit in a crossfire."

Vivian was startled. "Agent Wheeler, you almost sound like you care."

Mary and Phelps knocked on Mrs. Ackerman's rear door at 3:00 pm after Birdman confirmed that two cars had left Columbia and were headed toward Atlanta on Interstate 20. The number Vivian had called was in one of those cars. They relieved the FBI agents that had been there watching and saw Frank's men come and go. They updated her and Tess on the situation and they both agreed to relocate for the remainder of the evening to a safe location that had been arranged.

By 3:30 pm everyone was in place. Vivian arrived at 4:00 pm in a driverless car that was being piloted by an FBI agent. She used her key and went inside, placed the file on the dining room table, and took a seat at the far end of it near the kitchen and basement door. The entire house was wired for sound. Birdman was tracking not only Frank's progress but any movement around the house. There were agents on the top floor and in the basement and wine cellar. At 5:10 pm Vivian received a text from Frank's phone. He was running 20 minutes late. He wasn't, but she acknowledged the text and waited. On the drone feed, the team watched as three of Frank's men approached the house on foot and took up positions in the rear of the house. They had walked right past members of the SWAT team. At 5:40 pm two black SUVs pulled into the driveway and went directly to the back and parked. Two of Frank's men got out of the vehicles with their weapons drawn. Frank got out behind them. He passed them as he approached the back door. As soon as Frank's hand hit the door knob, his head exploded into a red mist; the shot having been fired by one of his own men who was behind him. Inside, a federal agent grabbed Vivian and pulled her down the basement staircase to the wine cellar to a safer position. Phelps had everyone standby. They hadn't expected that, but there was no more helping Frank, and he felt one of the others might be Foster.

Three more men approached the house from the second car. Vivian watching on the screen held by one of the SWAT team, and confirmed it was Hollings Foster in the lead. He called out for her as he entered the house. She was instructed to answer. "The file is in the dining room, Frank."

"It's not Frank, Vivian. It's Hollins. Frank is no longer a problem. He walked across the room, sat down, and started to thumb through the file as he spoke to Vivian. She appeared at the top of the stairs in the doorway but no further. He didn't even look up. He just kept flipping pages in the file.

"What was it, Vivian? Why would you and Stella prepare such a thing? You were being paid well, lived a rich and I'll use the word 'colorful' life. Why would you want to bite the hands that fed you so well all these years? And then Stella. Why in the world would she help you prepare such a voluminous and dangerous set of documents to hurt our friends in high places?"

He waited a few moments for her to reply. "Vivian, you are as quiet as I've ever seen you. What is it? Frank's sudden but expected death? I don't think so. Frank was not a nice person and could be such a bore. I'm sorry we have to be so thorough. I will leave the twins. They don't know anything anyway that anyone will pay attention to. But you are a different story. I'm sorry Viv, you are lovely and fun, but you have to go."

He nodded at the man standing across from him who started in Vivian's direction. She turned as instructed by the agent and headed back down the stairs. Hollins continued. "Vivian, don't make us chase you around this house. You've nowhere to run." Foster's man got to the top of the stairs and no further.

The agent with her covered her with his body as Viv closed her eyes and waited, not even sure she would hear the shot that killed her. There was just the sound of breaking glass as the man at the top of the stairs in the doorway fell forward down the stairs, narrowly missing them at the bottom. The shot had caught Vivian's would be assassin in the temple. She saw the room fill with other federal agents. When the other men with Foster figured out what had happened, they fled toward the back toward the cars where they were quickly arrested. Foster was on the floor and cuffed in seconds.

Phelps and Mary had Vivian between them as they led her out of the house and into a waiting car and sped away with her. Other agents moved in to secure the scene and begin the evidence collection. The house would be sealed and no one in the old neighborhood would ever know what had happened.

Vivian was returned to the detention center, but was taken to a more comfortable room with some privacy. She was met by a counselor who sat with her most of the night and let her vent and talk about what she had just been through. She wept, she screamed, she paced, then as expected, collapsed onto her bed. The counselor had ordered a mild sedative so she would sleep, and sleep she did for almost a day. She awoke over twenty-four hours after she had walked into that house in the Old 4th Ward, and discovered that she wasn't in a cell at all. It was an apartment. The doors were locked and there were still two women with her, but she was no longer kept in a cage with no privacy.

The counselor came in with Mary Close and Phelps Wheeler. Phelps directed her attention to the screen that hung on the wall. He looked at Vivian.

"Want to have a private chat with your kids?" He used the remote and nodded at the two custody personnel to leave with him and Mary. "The counselor will stay for this conversation for you as much as for the kids. They can hear and see you."

Vivian smiled at him. "Thank you both for keeping them safe. I will be ready to sit down and give you all you need tomorrow. I never realized that all that time I was talking about Frank being killed, that I would ever witness it. It was bad enough seeing him kill Terry and Stokes, but hearing it and seeing the aftermath was just as horrible. I swear I didn't think that would happen. Why did you just shoot him?"

Mary spoke as they were leaving. "We didn't. That was one of his own men. It would appear that you were right. Hollins had no intention of leaving Frank alive. It also appears that Frank's own men were tired of him killing them off and were only too happy when the boss gave them permission. You're having a delayed reaction to seeing death. You never should get used to it. I will be back tomorrow to further our conversation. Enjoy your kids and get some rest."

Vivian Bartram was true to her word. She went through the entire file with Mary Close, Phelps Wheeler and by video link, Dr. Jeanine Morozov. Vivian was able to verify dates and descriptions. Vivian knew most of the key individuals and was able to identify them and the activities they had engaged in to help protect and perpetuate the Nightshade operation.

The arrests had begun of current and former individuals working for the U.S. Government. Five members of Congress, two U.S. Senators, and 11 former prosecutors were in the first group. There were also several federal and state judges that were taken into custody. It was unprecedented.

The FBI focused on the larger picture of human trafficking and made over 230 arrests. Many were charged with heavy enough crimes that plea bargains were not an option. Everyone else was busy testifying against the others to reduce their sentences. The few cases that went to trial ended in convictions based on the file and backed up by testimony from Vivian Bartram, Beth Ellers, and Tiffany Holmes.

Nationally, over 200 survivors, trafficked for labor were rescued. Some returned to their home countries voluntarily and some were assisted by new programs to help them gain enough time to declare their legal status and remain in the United States. Eighty young women were rescued from the various service stations and holding operations that had been trafficked for sex. They received coordinated assistance led by the Attorney General herself and her close support staff.

Several days after Frank's death and Foster's arrest, Marian Ackerman watched from her chair as she saw three dark SUVs pull up in front of her house. She called Tess to open the door. When Tess opened the door, the woman spoke first.

"You must be Tess. My name is Gwen Vespers. and this is Howard Forbes, the Director of the FBI. I think you know agents Close and Wheeler.

We would like to see Mrs. Marian Ackerman please."

Tess opened the door wider. "Please come in and welcome. She looked at the Attorney General. "I've followed your career and seen you on the television. I'm not at all sure how I should address you. Is it Madame Attorney General or just General? I never thought I would ever get to meet you."

The Attorney General smiled. "How about you just call me by my name. The title has always been awkward in conversation."

"I will take you to Mrs. Ackerman. She is receiving guests in the main room."

The Attorney General smiled. "I'm not used to people recognizing me, Tess. Lead the way, please."

Mrs. Ackerman rose when she saw them enter extended her hand.

"Madame Attorney General, it is an unexpected pleasure to have you in my home." She turned to Howard Forbes. "Director Forbes, I've seen you on CNN. You are welcome as well. I'm sorry, I can't believe that I have the two of you here. I may have to sit down."

Tess moved quickly, but Gwen Vespers was closer and gently took Marian's arm and helped her into her chair. "We won't keep you long. We wanted to give you a small token of our thanks for everything you did to help bring down one of the largest human trafficking networks in the country. It's just a framed certificate, signed by the two of us, thanking you both for your help." She handed one to Mrs. Ackerman who looked down at it. She turned to Tess as Mary gave her one as well.

Marian looked at it "Human trafficking. I'm not sure I understand totally what that is."

Tess answered before anyone could. "It's modern-day slavery, Mrs. Ackerman. I can explain it to you later. Thank you both so much. This will hang right next to the picture of my late husband and my favorite former

President. You didn't need to take time out of your busy schedules to come and do this personally. What a gift. And, you gave me one, as well."

Marian Ackerman spoke. "Of course, you got one, Tess. You are way more important around here than you think."

Phelps stepped forward and spoke to the Attorney General. "We need to get going if you are going to stay on schedule."

The Attorney General turned and moved toward the door then stopped and turned back toward the two women now standing together. "This is going to be the most important thing I do all day, ladies. Thank you so much for watching and then speaking up. I would love to return one day to just sit, have a good southern biscuit that Agent Phelps has been raving about, and a good glass of southern sweet tea."

Marian Ackerman used Tess's arm to stand. This house will always be welcoming to any of you."

Eight weeks later somewhere off Sheep Island, the line on Jessie's rod bent double. He set the hook just like Billy had taught him to do. Billy smiled from the back of his skiff.

"Keep enough tension on the line and just let him tire himself out. That looks like a keeper and redfish make great eating particularly in Lydia's kitchen"

Jessie pulled the fish in close and Billy lifted it out of the water in the net. Jessie smiled.

"This is one beautiful fish. Do we have to eat him?"

Billy looked perplexed. "Now you're going all Lily on me and putting them back." Jessie pointed at the boat that was approaching as it came off plane and settled into the water. Jillian was at the helm with Lily standing right beside her and Alex standing on the bow. They pulled up next to the guys.

Alex spoke. "I'm being picked up after dinner to fly home so we're going to head back in. We have a cooler full of sea trout, a few snappers, and a couple of redfish. Should make a nice dinner. How did you two do?"

Billy held up the redfish. Jessie took it from him, removed the hook and rocked the fish in the water gently to revive it. With a flick of its tail it was gone. He turned to Billy. "We have enough for dinner, right?" Billy smiled at him. We always have enough for dinner in this part of the world. Let's get our lines in and we will follow the girls. You take the helm."

After they docked and secured the boat at Billy's house, the twins carried the cooler up to the kitchen while Alex went ahead to change and pack. Lily walked into the bedroom she shared with Alex after she had checked in with Lydia.

"I bet you'll be glad to see Claymore."

Alex smiled. "He's been there since we recovered Jessie and dealt with Frank and Foster, but Slade has given us two weeks off, and I think we are going to spend some of it house-hunting. I will be glad to see him. I've spent too much time away from him. I'm actually thinking of asking for a reassignment. I think I'd like to work in the new shelter with the survivors. They have plenty of new people in the pipeline and they always have you."

Lily looked out across the grass flats behind Lydia's house.

"Actually, I'm thinking of doing something different, as well. I'm not sure what yet. I feel like I need to spend more time with Lydia. Besides, it won't be the same without you in the field."

Alex stopped packing and hugged her long-time partner.

"Did you hear that Collins has been accepted to come work for Smithson. He turned out a lot different than what he was when we first met."

"He'll be good at it. Not as good as us, but good enough."

They heard Lydia's voice from the hallway.

"Dinner will be ready at 6:00 with grace said at 6:05. Alex, I'm not even going to hear of you leaving before you eat, and we have some guests arriving soon. I'm sure one of them will be your ride home. Everyone get cleaned up for dinner."

At 5:45 pm Billy watched as two vehicles pulled up to his house. Mary Close and Phelps Wheeler got out of the first one. Ludlow, Collins and Vivian Bartram got out of the second. They all walked to the front porch. Billy looked at Phelps. "I hope you warned Lydia about the extra guests. She don't like surprises like that and I'm not sure my table is big enough."

Phelps laughed. "We did. We've learned."

Billy looked at Vivian who was walking in with Mary. "Who's the pretty lady?"

Phelps followed the two women with his eyes as he answered. "I'm not sure what her new name is going to be but her old name is Vivian Bartram."

"That must mean they are going to give all of them protection."

"Justice has agreed to give all three of them new identities and resettle them. Vivian explained enough of the accounting system to recover millions of dollars and the federal government has worked out an amended sentence for her in exchange for the substantial assistance she provided. We just got word this morning that two individuals were arrested getting on a plane in Paris headed to Venezuela. They are 99% sure that they are the last two in the Nightshade organization. The Attorney General felt it was time for Vivian to have a conversation with her kids in person."

Billy looked up at the porch. "Those kids deserve a new life. If I wasn't so old, I'd take them. Lydia seems to have stopped aging not that she ever did. She is so alive around them. It's fun to watch.

Phelps smiled. "She remembers how much she loved the time she spent raising Lily. She did an amazing job there. Both of you did."

"I've got to say, I'll miss those kids."

Phelps patted Billy on the back. "Hold on to that thought."

Lydia found enough room for everyone at the table with room to spare. They all joined hands as Lydia looked around the circle at each of them and paused at Vivian."

She didn't bow her head this time but looked directly at Vivian as she spoke.

"Let us pray. Lord God, the greatest gift you gave us was the ability to look ahead with hope and that is what we are about here tonight. Hope can't grow without forgiveness which is another gift you taught us through the many prophets and teachers including your son. Believing is not about talking, it's about doing good for others. Forgiving is not about forgetting things ever happened but taking the lessons learned from the mistakes and moving forward toward hope. That is at this table tonight. Bless this food and the people who helped gather us together. Keep them safe and warm and let the leftover love we have here tonight stretch out across these waters I have lived on all my life, and comfort those less fortunate and those in need. Amen."

Mary had to slip her arm around Vivian to help her ease down into her chair. She was quietly sobbing. Lydia moved around to Vivian, took her by her elbows and helped her stand and encircled her in her arms and whispered another soft amen into Vivian's ear. Then she spoke softly so no one else could hear. "These babies are gifts. It doesn't matter what else happened in the end you would have sacrificed yourself for them and the others. You be strong, baby. You just be strong from here on out. I will take care of them until they can care for us all. You do what you need to do.

When that's done, they will be ready and will love you just as much as you truly love them."

After dinner, Vivian, Jessie, and Jillian walked out toward the dock. Vivian spoke to them both with tears in her eyes.

"I have one more task that I have promised the government that I will do. Once that is done, I have agreed to a plan that will mean I cannot have any personal contact with either of you for five years. When you turn 21, you will have the option of making the decision about where you go from here and how much contact you want with me. I will be able to write you letters that will be passed to you. If you choose you can write me back. All of this will be coordinated through the Marshals. We all need space to become normal. There is little chance that we are in any further danger. Anyone that might have been a threat for you are either dead or in custody with no hope of release. There is just no reason to reignite the case by doing either of you harm."

Jessie spoke. "What about you? Are you in danger?"

Vivian smiled. "I really don't think so but that is what the time is for. It's not a bad thing. I need some time to grow up a bit. I didn't have much of a childhood either. My treatment for my addiction is going well. I will have all the help I need and maybe be able to give some help along the way to others that have been touched by this stuff. I just want you to know that I love you as much as your real mother would have loved you."

Jillian teared up. "Will you tell us who our real mother was?"

Vivian settled her voice. "When you turn 18, the court will release the official records of your birth. Your mother had lost her way enough that Frank took advantage of her. She died having you. Now give me a hug. I have to leave with the Marshals. I won't see you again for awhile so let's not waste time blubbering with each other. Be as strong as you have been the past few months. Just know I love you both very much and I am sorry for all we put you through. All of it. All of it."

She hugged them both and then they walked back up toward the cars where Ludlow, Collins and Alex waited. The twins kept walking toward the steps where Lydia and Lily were waiting for them. She never looked back and the twins didn't turn around until she was in the car and headed out.

# CHAPTER 36

Celeste Foster had been moved every three weeks to a different secure mental health assessment facility. It was part of the process to determine if she was really mentally incapacitated to the point that she was unable to participate in her own defense. There was no longer any doubt that she had been a major player in Nightshade. The files proved that. The problem was they had to proceed carefully with someone who exhibited such behavior. She was never without an advocate and never un-observed. She had not faltered nor made a mistake. She remained convincing in her act as a disoriented old woman. Research had indicated that she was actually 64 years old. There was no clinical evidence of dementia, Alzheimer's disease, or frontal lobe disorder. Still, she was consistent in the behavioral markers. If she were acting, she was extremely good at it. The system was running out of time. They would have to make a decision soon. It was not that she was ever going to be released but how she was going to be housed.

It was Gwen Vespers that came up with the idea and posed it to Phelps and Mary. They discussed it and paid a visit to Vivian who was housed in a federal minimum-security facility where she had been sentenced.

She smiled when she saw the agents walk up.

"I didn't expect to see you two when they said I had visitors. I expected to see my protective handlers. What brings you here?"

Mary started the conversation.

"First, how are you doing Vivian?"

Vivian smiled. "Let's save some time. I'm doing well. I'm adjusting and sort of catching up on normalcy Now, that's done, what is it you want?"

Mary laughed. "You are making progress. We are not making as much progress with your mother.

Vivian continued her thought. "And you need me to help you break her act. That won't be easy and I guess I don't have much choice."

Phelps interrupted. "You do have a choice. We are standing by our commitment and agreement. You don't have to do this."

Vivian thought for a moment. "I got a letter from Jessie. I haven't heard from Jillian yet but it's early days. I think if you don't put Celeste where she belongs for the rest of her life, she will figure out a way to get out. If she is successful then my children are at risk of never having a chance at freedom. What do you have in mind?"

Phelps continued. "What if you went to see her?"

Vivian laughed. "She doesn't give a shit about me. It was probably her that ordered Frank to kill Stella and everyone else. Hollins likes money but I was shocked he was so close by when Frank was killed. I don't think I'd have any effect on her at all."

Mary continued. "What if you went there with Tobin?"

That stopped Vivian in her thoughts. She looked up. "She might not be able to hold it together if she saw us together. There is just some sort of unholy connection there. He has always been her baby even though he was adopted. She always seemed to gravitate toward him more than her own children."

Phelps explained the plan. "The people doing her assessment are just looking for small signs that she is pretending. She is under constant video surveillance looking for any reaction that they can use. We thought if both of you visited and you gave the appearance of being free and Tobin obviously wasn't, it might produce a reaction."

Vivian thought then spoke. "Do you still have her fur coat she was arrested in?"

Mary smiled "I like where this is going."

"Does she have any idea that I'm in custody?"

Mary shook her head. "There is no way she would know that."

Vivian nodded her head. "If she thinks I made a deal and am totally free, with the money, and Tobin is in jail, that might produce a reaction. Nothing will piss her off more than seeing me in that coat. If you agree to it, I'll even put on the silk pajamas she loved so much. I won't go naked like she used to around Charles, but I will do the sleepwear. That is a diabolical plan. Which one of you came up with that?"

They both spoke at the same time. "Neither one of us."

It took a week to arrange the meeting. Celeste was being held just outside of Baltimore. Charles Tobin was being held in a maximum-security facility in Kansas. He would be flown in. Phelps, Mary and Vivian flew together to Baltimore. When they arrived, Mary laid out the plan.

"We want you to go in first and tell her how well the twins are doing and that you are fine. You are free to tell her that Foster is in custody and that Frank is dead. We will see what reaction that draws. Then one of the custodial matrons will tell her she has another visitor. You remain in the room and they will bring in Tobin. He has actually lost weight in prison and we have dressed him in one size larger to accentuate that. I have your clothes here. We will leave so you can change. We're ready to go when you are."

Vivian had no emotional reaction. "Let's do this. I can't stand being here and even this is too good for her. I'll need a minute after I change to fix my makeup. Are we good with that?"

They nodded.

Vivian then smiled. "And the other thing, were you able to get that?"

They nodded again handed it to her and stepped outside. When the door opened, Vivian was standing there looking radiant as only a woman with her beauty could look. The fur coat fit her perfectly and set off the color of her hair and complexion. On her left wrist was the watch Tobin had worn that had led to his identification. They led her down the hall and then went into the observation room with the doctors after checking that Tobin was with two custody officers waiting in another room. He was agitated, shackled and his wrists were cuffed to his waist chain.

Vivian entered the room. She didn't walk in. It was more of a prance.

"Hello Mother. It was nice of them to let me visit. I hope you're doing well."

The old woman looked up, blinked twice in recognition and then went back to her mumbling and nodding and rocking. The three doctors observing began taking notes. Vivian continued.

"I see they have bought your little act. How marvelous for you. Hollins isn't enjoying the same accommodations. I'm not sure anyone will ever find Svetlana they have her so well tucked away. Poor Frank, well he's dead but you knew that would happen. You probably ordered it knowing you."

The old woman rocked a bit faster but still maintained her composure. She did look at the fur coat and mumble softly. "I had a fur coat like that. Is that my fur coat?"

Vivian laughed. "Yes, it is as a matter of fact. It was one of those little things they were more than happy to give me after I helped them find Frank and Hollins. You all shouldn't have killed my best friend, Stella. That was a mistake, Mommy."

Still the old woman sat there mumbling and shaking her head and rocking back and forth. She was obviously agitated but maintaining her character well.

Vivian kept smiling. Celeste wasn't giving up easily. "Oh, and I've come with another visitor for you." Vivian looked at the matron who opened the door as Charles Tobin shuffled in shackled and chained.

Celeste looked up and for the first time since her arrest, her eyes cleared. The doctors wrote furiously in the observation room. Charles Tobin stood there staring at Vivian before he started to shake.

"Vivian, that's Mommy's coat. What are you doing with Mommy's coat? You look just like a younger Mommy." Charles turned and looked at his mother. "She looks just like you used to Mommy."

Vivian had her cue just as she had planned it. She turned and faced Charles.

She spoke as she opened the coat to reveal she had nothing on underneath. Perhaps it was because he had been locked up in solitary but Charles' involuntary reaction to Vivian standing naked in his mother's fur coat was all it took. "Mommy she looks amazing."

As if to add a punctuation mark to the whole affair, Vivian pulled back the left sleeve of the coat as she closed it to reveal the watch Charles had coveted in more prosperous times. "Oh, I had this sized down since I didn't think they would let you keep it."

That was all it took. Celeste was up out of the chair moving like lightening toward Vivian screaming as she went. "You fucking bitch. Give my boy back his watch. You fucking bitch. I'll kill you just like I had Frank kill that twat lawyer you were so fond of. I knew we should have killed you first!"

The doctors stopped writing and just stared. The matrons were moving as quickly as they could but it was Vivian that reached out with one hand and caught the older woman by the throat.

"It is a shame they won't let me kill you Mother, but they just won't. You've done enough of that for both of us."

The matrons got to Celeste and managed to get her secured. Vivian quietly closed the coat completely and turned toward Charles and spoke as she looked down. "Charles, it seems you've had a bit of an accident down there. Good luck wherever they have decided to keep you."

Phelps and Mary met Vivian as she was going back into the room to change. She took off the watch and handed it to Mary. "Sorry, I adlibbed a bit but it seemed to work. It will just take me a moment to change. Did you get enough to see the real Celeste?"

Phelps just nodded his head. Mary spoke. "Remind me never to get on your bad side."

Vivian laughed. "If you haven't already gotten on my bad side, it is doubtful you will. Don't worry. I wouldn't have choked her to death. It didn't even cross my mind. If I had, I'd never hear from let alone see my daughter and son again."

Based upon the video taped session of Celeste Foster breaking character, she was indicted by a federal grand jury on 167 counts of human trafficking and 205 counts of conspiracy to launder money and several counts of murder. With the path clear for prosecution, her assets were seized which tripled the amount available to the victims' compensation fund. She was sentenced to life in prison without parole which she served in a maximum-security facility designed for aging prisoners. She offered some information about the European contacts which led to further arrests by Interpol that afforded her a special confinement condition. There was no one left at the top of the Nightshade Group for her talk about. They were all dead or in custody.

The two FBI agents walked out of Celeste's final sentencing hearing. Phelps spoke first.

"I've decided to leave the FBI."

Mary looked surprised. "I was the one that was going to say that first. So am I."

Phelps smiled. "What are you going to do?"

"I've accepted a legal position with an advocacy group representing survivors of human trafficking. I'm sick of watching them get dumped back to the country they ran from. Gwen Vespers has announced she will be leaving the Justice Department to head it up. I don't want to waste that opportunity. What about you?"

"I've actually accepted a job with Jeanine Morozov's operation. The whole family is moving to the mountains. My girls love the Smokies and it's time for me to start being home every night. This was a big win for the good guys. I'm not sure they will ever throw so many resources at a single problem again. It's a good one to close out on.

# CHAPTER 37

A week after the case was officially closed, Luke Ludlow arrived at Billy's house. After they were all seated in the living room, he began by speaking to the twins.

"We were wondering what the two of you would think if we were to suggest that you remain here with Lydia and Lily for a while? You will move back to Lydia's house. You'll have more room, and we will arrange for you to finish your education either privately or, if you wish, in the public school system. You have the freedom to try each system for a bit if that helps. Lily will be here most of the time, and you will have a visit from a Smithson caseworker at least weekly. If you decide you want to handle things differently, then you can go over that with everyone and we will make adjustments."

Jessie was the first to speak. "Will I get my car back?"

Ludlow laughed. "You won't get that exact one back, but you will get one just like it. You will have to get a regular license just like any other person."

Jillian spoke next. "Will we be staying with Aunt Lydia full-time?"

Lily smiled. "It was her idea to suggest you live here with her under the conditions that you both follow her rules, and if you want to leave, you work that out with us and the Marshals. You are no longer prisoners, Jillian. You have choices."

"I want to stay here with your Mom. Is that OK with you? Can we share her?"

Lily laughed out loud. "I don't get a say in what she wants. But to answer your question, I'll be happy to share her with you both. She will explain her rules to you but they are easy to follow."

Lydia nodded. "My rule is I know you're safe. When it's appropriate, you can stay out but have to be home by a certain time or call. I will not tolerate any bad behavior, which means drinking, drugs, or any of the other stuff young people get into trouble for. You probably already know more about sex than I do, so as long as you understand how to say no as well, we will be good on that scale. And, under no circumstances, let Billy Ward be a role model for anything you do. He is fully retired and I guess he will be hanging around here a bunch more. He had a wild life as a young man. He turned out alright, but that is only thanks to God's grace and forgiveness."

Billy, who had been sitting quietly, suddenly found his voice.

"Wait a minute. When did I become the bad guy?"

Lydia didn't miss a beat. "Billy Ward, don't you sass me. Get in the kitchen and help me finish up these dishes, and let these kids talk about the rest of the stuff they need to discuss with the Marshal and Lily."

Ludlow smiled. "For a few months there will be two Marshals assigned to remain nearby and you will get a visit from the Smithson counselor, as mentioned. We will keep you posted on the safety of your mom. You can receive letters from her and will be allowed to write her back if you want. Lily can answer any questions you have." He turned to Lily. "I'll see you soon."

Jessie went in to the kitchen to help clean up the dishes with Billy and Lydia. He sensed that Jillian needed some girl time with Lily.

Lily sat down next to Jillian on the couch. "Jillian, if you have questions, you know you can ask me anything."

"I've never had a girlfriend before. The closest I came was Beth and Tiffany. I know how to act around adults. I have no clue how to act around other girls or boys my age. I'm scarred to death I will make a fool of myself."

Lily took her hand. "Listen, you can go slow. I will be here to help and you can talk it over with your counselor. You have always had Jessie.

He's your age."

Jillian shook her head. "With what he has been through, I'm not sure who he really is now. Don't get me wrong, but sometimes he seems as old as Billy. He was with Stella for months. I'm not sure what he went through or how trusting he will be. He's going to need as much help as I am, just maybe not the same."

Lily looked deep into Jillian's eyes. "You are going to get all support and help you both need, I promise."

Jillian smiled. "I'm sorry to be such a baby. I know you will have to go just like Alex soon. Other people need your help more than us. I will miss you."

Lily hugged her. "Don't spend a lot of time missing me just yet. I'm here for a while and as long as you need me. We will work something out."

In the kitchen, Jessie was drying dishes as Lydia cleaned them and Billy was putting them away. Lydia didn't even look up when she spoke to Jessie.

"What's on your mind, Jessie? I have a sixth sense about when people have a question. Go ahead and ask."

Jessie seemed uncomfortable but spoke anyway.

"In that prayer you say before dinner, you mention forgiveness. I'm not sure I believe in God, but do you think that is true? Do you think I can be forgiven for what I have done?"

Lydia never stopped washing dishes. "Jessie, stick your hand in this water. Tell me what you feel."

"It feels warm."

"You're right, it feels warm. But to me it feels just right for doing dishes. If it was hotter, I would cool it off. It was too cold; I would warm it up until for me it felt just right. My belief in God is like that. It makes me feel just right. But I only feel it when I'm giving, not taking. I was taught that by my people. Our beliefs go back centuries to Africa. We didn't come here of our own free will. Some other people's version of 'just right' was to have free labor, consider us animals, make us into things rather than people. We still survived by pulling together, sharing what little we had, and even though many families were ripped apart, we believed that if we did right by each other, we would survive. Here we are two centuries later, still working on getting it just right. We're all a work in progress, Jessie. Even me."

Jessie thought a moment as he took his hand out of the water. "You mean like slavery. Like Jillian and I were. Your people survived. I think I could use some lessons in that regard. Maybe I could learn to believe in God the way you do."

Lydia smiled. "Sweetheart, you can start by believing in yourself and your ability to believe in the act of helping others. I think that is the act of believing in God. That is what feels just right to me. In our little meeting house, most true believers spend their time praying for guidance to understand how to help others instead of asking anything for themselves. To me, that's where miracles come from. I will say this, if you don't believe in God or something as powerful, that energy gets directed at false and evil promises like money or greed, power and envy. You have to make your own decisions."

Billy had been putting away dishes and kept quiet. Lydia couldn't help herself.

"So, Billy, what is it you believe in?"

Billy turned and looked at both of them.

"I think it's pretty damn amazing that these two kids, after all they've been through, ended up here with you. I think it's even more amazing that Jessie here, who has been through what he's been through and seen what he's seen, still asks these questions. Finally, I believe that I saw young Jessie here catch a beautiful redfish and instead of flipping him in the cooler, decided to return him to his life in the ocean. I'm not sure how that is going to work when we go duck hunting and quail hunting this fall, but it will be interesting, I'm sure. Most of all, I believe in you and your faith, Lydia. That's the sum of it."

A slight look of shock flashed across Lydia's face as she struggled with tears. Then she turned to Billy.

"Billy Ward you are a sweet man but don't you go swearing in front of these twins. They've had enough of that already."

Billy shrugged his shoulders. "I always seem to be the bad guy."

Lydia turned to him and smiled as she touched his face. "Sweet man, you need a bit of work but never, ever, in my eyes, are you a bad guy. Now let's start getting these twins ready to move back to my house."

Jessie reached over kissed Lydia on the cheek. "Thank you. I want to talk about this more with you and thank you for the fish. Were those the ones I caught?"

Lydia smiled and looked at him. "Those were your catfish from upstate. Collins brought them frozen so I could fix them just for you. He said to tell you they were from a man called Ezra."

Two days later, the twins had relocated to Lydia's house, and Billy was back in his. Lily was working with the Marshals, and the counselor to help the Jillian and Jesse settle into their transition.

Three months later, Slade Smithson called and asked to stop by the following day. The next afternoon he stepped onto the porch as Lydia and Lily walked out to meet him. Lydia spoke.

"Welcome, Mr. Smithson. It's good to see you. Are you here to take my sweet Lily away from me?"

Slade smiled "No one could do that and you know it. When are you going to start calling me by my first name? I'm actually here because she asked me to come. I'm afraid she may be giving me some news that I have dreaded, but expected. I hope I'm not intruding."

"Slade Smithson, you are never intruding in this house. Where are you staying?"

"Actually, I've got some legal business to tend to here in the low country and I'm staying with one of my lawyers. We're working on some new opportunities here in South Carolina and I thought I'd check in on the twins."

Lydia smiled "Slade, I'm blessed again. These twins have been sent to me to recharge my life. They are doing so well. Jillian decided she wanted to try public high school. She tested high and they placed her in the 11th grade. She decided after a semester that she needed to slow it down a bit so we have her in a private school. She's doing better there and adjusting to the smaller class size. She even has a little circle of friends. Jessie is the one that has made huge progress. He tested even higher and got into an honors program that specializes in computers. Do you know that Dr. Leonard comes down here to visit him once a month?"

"Dr. Leonard? Birdman. I didn't know he visits."

"Dr. Leonard and that nice Tim Collins, who I think works for you now, have both visited. Because of Dr. Leonard, Jessie is absolutely obsessed with drones, not so much with the birds. He and Billy managed to fill a whole freezer with ducks and quail last season. The closest to the Audubon Society that Dr. Leonard can get him is Ducks Unlimited. At least he is getting an understanding of conservation. He's also become quite the fisherman. Will you join us for dinner?"

Slade smiled. "Not tonight, but I would love a raincheck for tomorrow. There will be five additional people with me if that is, OK?"

"It's supposed to be beautiful tomorrow evening. I think we will set up outside under the oak. Will that do?"

"Okra stew?"

Lydia hugged him again. "Yes, sweet man. Okra stew and all you can eat of it. See you tomorrow. Dinner will be ready at 6:30 pm and grace will be said at 6:35 pm. I'll leave you and Lily to talk."

Slade nodded and turned to Lily. "I feel you asked me here to tell me you're leaving. I want to talk with you further about that tomorrow when we have more time but I still need to take care of some arrangements. I just wanted to confirm about the dinner. Our discussion will need more time."

That made Lily wonder what was going on but she hugged her boss.

"I'll be ready to have the talk tomorrow."

The following night was as beautiful as Aunt Lydia had predicted. Lily and the twins took on the responsibility of helping Billy set up the tables outside and Jillian and Lily decorated and set the table. At 6:20 pm two cars pulled up. Slade, Alex, and Claymore Jenkins got out of the first one. Alex and Slade helped Claymore get into his chair as Tim Collins, Beth Ellers, and Tiffany Holmes got out of the second. The twins were off the porch in an instant. Jillian ran to Beth and Tiffany, and they all grasped each other for a long hug. Jessie reached out his hand to Tim. "You kept your word. I got my car and my license two weeks ago."

"That's no surprise where you're concerned. Birdman has been keeping me posted. He says you're doing well and that you've already designed your first drone."

"It's nothing like he makes. It's primitive but it flies. He's helping me build one from a kit so I understand it better."

Lily was all over Alex and Claymore. "Have you two set a date?"

For once, Claymore spoke first. "Three months. We want you to be the Maid of Honor."

Lily hugged Alex, who couldn't contain herself any longer. "We've bought a house. It's perfect for us. We can't wait for you to see it."

Lydia cleared her throat and got everyone's attention. "Will you all please find your seats under the oak. We will be saying grace as soon as we bring the food out."

The fried chicken, catfish, red rice, collard greens, okra and tomatoes, and field peas were heaped on the table. Lydia spoke. "We have a special volunteer to say our blessing this evening. Jessie would you please do us the honor?"

They all bowed their heads and joined hands as Jessie started to speak.

"God, You and I are sort of new friends so excuse me if I don't get all of this right. I don't even know if I fully believe or understand what You are, but I just know I have a lot to be thankful for, and a lot of it was brought about by a power that must be close to what everyone thinks You are. I want to give thanks is all, just thanks. I want to thank my sister and her friends who left the note. I want to thank strangers on the highway that found that note and did something about it. I'm thankful for the people around this table, and many that aren't, that haven't stopped trying to help all of us, including my mom, wherever she is, have hope. If You are responsible for helping us with handing out forgiveness and blessings, I'm asking that for all of us around this table. Help us to remember to pay attention. Help us to remember to listen more carefully, and help Jill and me to be as considerate as all of these people here. Thank you for the fish and birds and vegetables that gave up their lives for this meal. Help us to nourish each other and honor their sacrifice. Sorry, this is going on so long. It's my first time praying. Amen"

Jillian almost collapsed into her brother's arms sobbing. "I need to write Mom, Jessie."

He hugged her. "Write her tonight. I'll help if you need me, but first, let's eat. I'm starving."

Jillian laughed. "She may not be your real mother, but you sure do have her eating habits."

After dinner, Lily and Slade walked out toward the dock. She spoke first.

"Slade, it's funny. It seems like most of the serious and important conversations I've had, have been at this dock. So, I'll just get right to it. I am going to resign from Smithson. I don't even know what I'm going to do but I know my place is here now with Lydia, Billy, and the twins for however long they stay. I hate breaking the team up, but I know it's what I have to do now, just as sure as I knew when it was time to sign on with you. I'm sorry."

Slade put his arm around her. "I have an alternative if you want to hear it."

She hugged him. "You can't change my mind. I know this is where I need to be."

Slade continued gently. "I do too, that is why I would like you to stay and help me set up a survivor shelter designed for children and young adults that will be located right here in Beaufort County. I just closed on a twelve-bedroom house with enough land to do whatever we decide we need to help younger survivors stabilize. Will you give that some thought?"

Lily whacked him on the arm.

"How do you do that? How do you leap ahead and come up with the perfect solution all the time? It's maddening, but I love that you do, and yes, count me in."

"Good, because Beth and Tiffany have decided that they want to add their expertise, as well. The are both using their victim's compensation money for education. Beth is becoming a nurse and Tiffany is studying to become a counselor. They will be splitting their time between the new facility here and another one I'm setting up in Greenville. The federal government gave us the house on the hill where the party was held. It will be operated by a private provider until we can get our own people in there. That detective Roseanne Smith from Greenville Police Department you told us about is heading up that effort. And, before you ask, Alex will be doing the same at our new location in Tampa."

They walked back to the group who were all busy listening to Billy talk about Lily throwing every fish she caught back for the thousandth time.

Lily gathered the twins and brought them back to Slade. They both sat down with the twins. Slade spoke.

"I have established a trust for both of you to support you now through when you either graduate from college or pick a career. I normally do that for abandoned children but I have altered that plan to start helping younger survivors like yourselves get established. You can remain here or I will be happy to resettle you in our new shelter in Beaufort. It's your decision. If it helps, Lily will be in charge of that shelter. We're designing it for young people just like you."

Jessie spoke first.

"Thank you. I'm saying that a lot tonight, I guess. If Aunt Lydia agrees, can we stay here?"

"Yes, that is an option. You would still have your coordination through the Marshals with your mother, and still have the ability to write and eventually reunite with her. She has asked me to handle the sale of her house here. It was not confiscated in the assets because she and her brother owned it as part of their father's gift, and the only illegal sctivities that occurred there were the murders of Mr. Stokes and Mr. Mills. She doesn't want to go back there so my lawyers will handle the sale. The proceeds will be held for her to give her a new start in a few years."

Jillian teared up. "She's locked up somewhere, isn't she? She's in a prison."

Smithson put his arm around Jillian. "She is spending some time in a minimum-security unit demonstrating her ability to make better decisions. Your mother played a large, very positive part in making whatever right could come out of this happen. She is continuing to help us understand how all that worked to better help people who survive it. She is doing well in her treatment for her addiction and helping other residents at the facility to deal with anger issues. She shows a great deal of promise. I intend to do everything I can to make sure she continues to help survivors. She is doing her part in the role she has chosen. I hope, as you said at the table, you write to her Jillian."

Later that evening after everyone had gone, Lydia was turning out the lights and found Jillian at the table in the dining room trying to write her letter in the dark. Lydia turned the light back on.

"I didn't mean to disturb you sweetheart. Just turn out the light when you leave."

"Wait, Aunt Lydia. I don't know how to start this letter. I don't know what to say to my Mother. Hey, I'm having a great time and feel loved while you're sitting in a jail cell doesn't sound that great."

Lydia sat down with her. "I can only tell you how I have started every letter I have ever written to Lily, even when she was overseas. I always start every letter with the truth. I start by telling her there isn't a day that I don't think about her. Jillian, most people suffer from people not even thinking about them. That is the best thing you can say to someone you love. Besides, I think you know how to write notes just fine. It was your courage that left that note on the highway. Seems to me you got enough courage to write the woman you love who no matter what she has done. Your mother put herself in harm's way to make sure you two could be free of worry. It's time to heal, baby girl. It's time to forgive and get on with it. You've got this. Don't forget to turn out that light." Lydia got up and left Jillian sitting there.

Jillian looked down at the paper. She picked up the pen and wrote the first sentences.

"Dear Mom. There isn't a day that I don't think about you often. I miss you. I hope to see you as soon as I can." Five pages later after she had told Vivian about all the new things that were happening in her life, she finished her letter.

"P.S. I just turned 16 last week."

The End

# About the Author

Vance Arnett is the author of two other books with the Smithson Evermore Series. The books are based on the experience he gained during a 38-year career as an applied anthropologist in the American justice system. He worked at the local, state, and federal level as both a researcher, program developer, planner, and program director starting first with the Kentucky State Police and finishing with the Office of the State Attorney in Pinellas County Florida. He helped develop programs for the mentally ill, domestic violence survivors, first time and habitual offenders and spent the last 9 years working on the programs to deal with both juvenile and adult violent street gangs. He began writing upon his retirement in 2013. After living most of his life in Florida, post pandemic, he and his amazing wife moved to Greenville, South Carolina for cooler weather, steeper hikes, and the incredibly friendly people of Greenville and the Palmetto state.

# Afterward

During the final editing and design phase of Traffick Deadlock, my amazing wife and life companion Jane Arnett died of breast cancer. To say we are all heartbroken is an understatement beyond comprehension. I'm finding a good many things beyond comprehension as I work my way through my grief and mourning. The people who have also been on the team for this reckless project to raise funds for the survivors of human trafficking, Jen Ripple, Shawn Scalise and Meaghan Scalise continue to be steadfast in their dedication to this effort and were unbelievably supportive at Jane's death. They continue to lift me up, help me to see things differently, and fill what is the rest of my life with hope powered by the memories of an unforgettable soulmate. The book was dedicated while she was alive. My life and work will continue to be dedicated to her mission and memory as I live out my days. She made me promise to keep writing. I will keep that promise.

Vance Arnett
July 2025
Greenville, South Carolina

www.ingramcontent.com/pod-product-compliance
Lightning Source LLC
Chambersburg PA
CBHW030347120726
47901CB00007B/1941